THE IRON ROADS

THE IRON ROADS

by

FORBES BRAMBLE

ST. MARTIN'S PRESS
NEW YORK

Copyright © 1981 by Forbes Bramble.
For information, write: St. Martin's press,
175 Fifth Avenue, New York, N.Y. 10010
Manufactured in the United States of America

Library of Congress Cataloging in Publication Data

Bramble, Forbes, 1939-
    The iron roads.

    I. Title.
PR6052.R26817 1981   823'.914   81-8725
ISBN 0-312-43638-6   AACR2

PART ONE

The Railway King

One

'Mr Kelleway, Mr Kelleway!'

Henry, who had just stepped from his carriage, was annoyed at having his name called out in front of the crowd, and annoyed by the man's accent. The crowd looked and smelled rustic and he did not want to attract their attention. He understood city crowds with their banter and quick wit, but these people stood gazing like cows. He could not judge if they were stoic or truculent. Now heads turned to stare at him, and they whispered among themselves, a thick, clotted noise of country accents that he could not understand. He glanced quickly in the direction of the voice. It was Braxton all right. Damn the man, it was typical of his lack of tact. What could you expect from an Engineer! He felt even more annoyance when he saw the man was coming over to him.

Mr Braxton affected the loose clothes of his profession, with stretched waistcoat pockets and a stove pipe hat. Copying Brunel, Henry thought, and probably just as vain. They all did except old George Stephenson, who preserved his own brand of arrogance.

A large gold chain drooped from Braxton's waistcoat, but did not appear to be attached to a watch. Perhaps the chain was not gold after all. There was a greenish sheen to the elbows and knees of his suit that was either wear or dirt. Another affectation of his trade. Henry was fastidious about his clothes and the sight of Braxton's made him want to dust himself down. Henry could see no glamour in Braxton's attire. It seemed juvenile and untidy. He had no wish to be delayed by the man and identified with him, but with the bovine eyes of the crowd upon him, he could not be rude.

'Good day, Mr Braxton. Are you going in?' He judged, correctly, that Braxton would not find haste offensive. Henry moved towards the Town Hall steps. Yellow dust clouded his sparkling boots.

'Of course, Mr Kelleway, we must. Are you in good form, sir? I hear they intend to set up quite a battery of artillery, these local interests. The proprietors here are a shrewd lot.' Braxton lowered his voice to a confidential whisper that led him to stick his whiskery face close to Henry. The man had side-whiskers that grew so far down each cheek that they could have been tied

7

together under his chin. They started off black enough but became bright ginger lower down and round the edges. Henry would have shaved off the ginger hairs. Braxton had been drinking too, and Henry turned his face away slightly with an unencouraging grunt.

'They're expensive to buy,' Braxton continued, not at all put out, 'and know the value of obstruction. We have one or two Sibthorpes here, of the local variety – more stupid and more obstinate. I don't know about you, Mr Kelleway, but I can't gauge the mood of this crowd. It seems to me they're divided. I am told, taking a little refreshment, that the directors are divided, but will settle for the best deal. They have brought in all they can to protect this local thread of theirs. It isn't much of a railway, from Royston to Hitchin!' Braxton chuckled, keeping an eye on Henry to see if he was impressed.

'It's no thread, Mr Braxton. If they extend it to Cambridge as they intend, and as a double line, it will be a damnable nuisance. They have a good agreement with the Great Northern.' Henry was short with the man in the hope that he would go away. His hand was on his hat ready to raise it, but Braxton detained him further by taking his arm.

'I meant as a railway, Mr Kelleway. It is a pathetic little thing. No engineering, no cuts, no tunnelling. They hurl themselves over a wet ditch or two, that's all. In an engineering way, it's nothing at all.'

Braxton constantly tried to impress and persistently missed the point. He had no grasp of strategy and no subtlety. However, Henry thought, these things must be a drawback in his occupation.

'We must go in,' he said firmly, walking on.

'In any case we have a good agreement with the Great Northern too,' the man continued, 'Mr Hudson did very well out of that.'

'I don't think things will go so well with this plan, Mr Braxton. The Great Northern will not allow us to cross their line. It has never been done. It will set a precedent of the greatest importance. We aren't here to demolish the Royston and Hitchin railway, sir, that is just a small matter to the side of things. We must make sure it stays there. Now, Mr Braxton, I must get to my seat.'

They had walked up the steps of the Town Hall into the small lobby. The building was inadequate for the crowd as no local issue had provoked such heady passions in fifty years. Two constables at the door asked who they were, and let them in with a polite salute. They were weathered, red-faced countrymen, not at ease with this kind of work.

8

Behind them, Henry could hear boos and cheers from the crowd as other men arrived. They had done the same to him, although they could not know which side he represented or who he was. He judged they were in for an illogical and uneasy time.

Those who had arrived first for the meeting had come in glossy carriages with braided coachmen, and with sprawling carelessness had taken up all the space in the market place. Men in shining black hats had swept into the building with the arrogance of feudal barons. They were the directors and proprietors. In lesser style, coaches of men dressed like Mr Braxton in serge, and favouring stove-pipe hats, had arrived clutching rolls of drawings. The barons had been greeted with a buzz of curiosity. They were men of influence and money. The men in stove-pipe hats were mere underlings, employees and universally detested. They received the boos. Hitchin was becoming tired of being trampled upon by the railways.

By 1847, the Great Northern had already chewed its way through the heavy clays of Hertfordshire, spewing out yellow muck that destroyed meadows and streets, stifling wildflowers and hedgerows. The clay set as hard as concrete in summer. Idle boys, throwing lumps of it at brick walls, could not burst it, and gave up to wallow in the river.

In the winter and spring it turned into yellow and grey treachery, so soft that men sank in to their thighs and cows died. Seeds of dandelion and ash, plantain and clover tried to establish themselves in the barren marl but, when their tender roots were no thicker than white hairs, it shrank and crushed them.

The line crashed into Hitchin at a tangent then broke out towards the north and Doncaster, a furrow made by the devil's plough-share, deep in the ground here, on an embankment there, blasted through rock and hills. Houses had been overwhelmed, woods and streams obliterated. Fields were sadly discontinuous. Venerable hedges had been grubbed out.

The surveyors and engineers were hated because they had come as stealthily as spies with ranging rods and theodolites, planning this Grim's Dyke. They had posed as country gentlemen, then when this had failed had explained that they were only mapping. At first they had seemed a great curiosity and as they were liberal with money and no man went without a drink, they were well liked. When it was fully understood what they were doing, feelings were mixed. Some landowners proved difficult with dogs and guns and watchmen. Then the navvies appeared to protect the surveyors, as they said, viewing the prospect of battle with open glee. Other owners were roundly bought off and sang the praises of the railway. Those who would not succumb had been skirted and their

9

land isolated so that they were left to stare at the works of Mammon without enjoying the rewards. Now a second line was proposed, and a third. Hitchin was flattered, or angry, or amazed, or proud.

Mr Hudson had come to town with Mr George Stephenson. A royal visit could not have provoked more excitement. Hudson was the man who could dazzle the Commons, could outlast Peel, could turn an ailing line into profits in a year. Hudson was a wizard.

Henry pushed his way through the crowded lobby, acknowledging greetings with a perfunctory nod. Braxton, to his annoyance, still followed him, weaving in his wake.

'Good-bye, Mr Braxton,' said Henry, stopping squarely in front of him, 'I must leave you here.'

'Good-bye then, Mr Kelleway.' Braxton sounded put out. 'May I wish you luck.'

Damn his impudence, thought Henry, luck has so little to do with this sort of business. It needed careful management and skilful judgement of human weakness. He entered the hall and suddenly saw Sibthorpe. Braxton had said there would be one or two local Sibthorpes, but here was the genuine original. Sibthorpe's opposition to all railways was legendary and unfettered by the shackles of reason. He opposed every Railway Bill as a matter of course, as an inroad on private property, and boasted in the House that he had never assented to one. Henry feared that such reasoning could be strong today. His eyes swept over the seated rows of Royston and Hitchin directors. They reminded him too much of a circuit court jury. They would ponder for four hours upon unchallengeable facts and then return seeking direction on an irrelevancy.

Hudson was already in his place. Tables had been laid out to form three sides of a square, the rest of the hall being filled with wooden benches. The place was already packed.

Hudson sat in the centre of the top table, very calm, reading through papers as though his surroundings did not exist. He was signing documents with a pen, working. He was large and corpulent, reminding Henry of Humpty-Dumpty. His clothes hung from him as though he cared little for the physical trappings. Henry knew this was a pretence. In his evening wear the man was most particular with a taste for vanity and extravagance. Hudson's face was weathered and lined, in contrast to the city pallor of those around him. He spent his time on lines as much as he did in offices or in Parliament. His head was almost bald except for flattened streaks of grey hair that he spread forward with pomade to cover as much as possible of his tanned pate. There was the vanity.

It was a hard face, Henry thought. That of a man you would not like to owe money to. Yet Henry did. If heavy calls were made upon the stock he had been so glad to receive, he would have trouble meeting them. He had been bought by the man, and was committed. He had been flattered, too. Now he was wary and resentful.

Beside Hudson sat his allies, Sir John Lowther and George Stephenson. Henry's seat was vacant beside Lowther. They put flattering faith in Henry's abilities. It was a formidable array for the little Royston and Hitchin Railway. They were glad that they had the Great Northern to protect them.

Hudson looked up at Henry, but did not rise from his brooding position.

'Good morning Mr Kelleway.' His voice was strong and his accent robustly Yorkshire. 'We shall have a set-to here, I'm sure. They've brought Sibthorpe the performing bear to enliven proceedings. More seriously, they have Hildyard as their barrister. Do you know the man?' Henry had shaken hands with Lowther and Stephenson.

'I know him.'

'Is he any good? They're fussing round him like royalty.' Henry looked at Hudson, sensing jealousy, but Hudson's face was blank. It was clear that Hudson would never fuss round a mere lawyer.

'Yes he's good,' Henry replied. 'He's a top man in his business.'

'Aye, I've met him before.'

Henry was annoyed that Hudson should openly test him out, probe his objectivity. He seemed perpetually to do it, taking no man on trust.

'Mind you,' Hudson continued, 'I can't keep track of you lawyers. Every branch, every twig of a line has one. It's a good line of business. I have respect for it. That right, George?'

Hudson's face remained bland through this patronising utterance. George Stephenson smiled and nodded broadly, taking delight in the pursuit of any man who was not a true railway man.

At sixty-six, Stephenson's eyes remained clear and lively as a youth's. His complexion was burned as dark as a farm labourer's. He never raised his voice in dispute but was always adamant in his opinions, expressing them in a Northumbrian dialect that sometimes needed interpretation. He dressed in an old-fashioned style that contrasted with Hudson, his coat black and neatly cut with square tail pockets. From his watch ribbon hung a large bunch of seals by which he could be identified anywhere. He had the air and manner of a prophet. Only Wellington commanded more universal respect and *he* was not a self-made man.

'Aye. It seems that to be properly constituted there has to be a lawyer. A handful of right honourables, a brace or two of ex-Members, a thin brace of parish priests, a money-bags and a lawyer.' His smile did not quite blunt the edge of his observations. Henry had mixed feelings about Stephenson. His admiration of him was unstinting, but he resented the paternal arrogance of the man. There was also a remoteness about Stephenson which was not contempt for his fellows, but rather that he had concluded that other men had nothing to contribute to his life.

'There was a time,' Stephenson continued, 'when we were compelled to have two or three to make up the quorum, but '45 put paid to all that. We shall have a rough ride here, Mr Kelleway. These small line people are all the same. They have been on a railway twice in their lives and think they understand it. When the talk is of gradients and gauges, fish-plates and flanges, they will start to nod. When we get to boilers and tubes, steam blasts and, cylinders, they will look positively intelligent. That is the dangerous time for by then they're all experts and are prepared to give an opinion on anything. That's when the promoters put it to the vote. I've seen all that. They are committed to their line here, by ignorance and romance. We shall have to pay them well. Money is the perfect antidote to romance.'

Hudson snorted. 'Money is the perfect antidote to almost anything in these country districts. There is nothing more rapacious than a country gentleman. I would sooner deal with a Liverpool coal-owner any day. Aye, and preserve us from titled gentlemen!'

Henry produced his flat leather case and opened it on the table. Hudson caught Stephenson's eye, and they exchanged a dry look.

'Mr Kelleway wants to get to business,' Stephenson observed.

'Very proper,' said Hudson. 'The east coast route is the biggest enterprise ever attempted. I will have it. Stephenson here,' he said to Henry, 'has half sold himself to the devil by dabbling in the west as well. I tell him he's going the wrong way, but he won't listen!' Stephenson smiled and said nothing. They had been friends for too long to argue. Each would hold his own course.

'Be assured, Kelleway, that I won't be held up here by the Royston and Hitchin line. You understand that. I have to complete my east coast route before Glyn gets through on the west. The London and North Western stretches from London through Crewe to Liverpool, with a junction at Rugby. My Midland line ends at Rugby, as you know, Kelleway, and I shall have to make my own way to London, for Glyn won't let me use his track. Why should he? If the situation were reversed, I would feel the same. If I don't get an agreement here with the Great Northern to use their track, then I shall be squeezed completely. I must get in to King's Cross, this end is crucial. The northern end is falling my way and I shall get from Rugby to Edinburgh. I shall shortly have control of the Great North of England and the pieces will fall into place.'

Henry understood the broad strokes of Hudson's plan, but he could not keep up with the detail. Hudson controlled the Midland Railway, the Eastern Counties and a number of lines north of York. In assembling this network Hudson had neglected to establish a route into London for his Midland Railway. Now he would have to share the Great Northern track, when it was completed, from Hitchin to King's Cross, or make a long detour over his Eastern Counties track to end up in shabby Shoreditch. What he really wanted was a junction at Hitchin, close to London, between the Midland and the ailing Eastern Counties. To do it, he would have to cross the Great Northern track.

Hudson's recall was perfect and his ability to produce statistics and figures was his most powerful weapon. He could beat a meeting down with them. His grasp of strategy was masterful. His grasp of finance left sceptics speechless and even bitter opponents drowned in their own doubts.

The hall was full. The constables at the door were involved in a heated exchange with some late arrivals who managed to push their way in. Hildyard was staring pointedly at Hudson.

'It seems I should begin,' Hudson said.

'Aye,' said Stephenson, 'I can't stand this sort of crush. The meeting were best over.' Hudson rose slowly to his feet, then stood looking calmly around the hall until there was silence. The sheer bulk of the man added to his presence.

'Right honourable gentlemen, gentlemen, directors and proprietors of the Great Northern, of the Midland and of the Royston and Hitchin Railways, the purpose of this meeting has been well advertised to you. In fact it has been well advertised around the county and some distance beyond as I can see.'

There was some good-natured murmuring at this. Sibthorpe, at whom it was principally directed, inclined his head and accepted it as a compliment that he had been singled out. Hildyard sifted through his papers as he always did in moments of annoyance or feigned boredom.

'It is the proposal of the Midland Railway to extend the Midland south to Hitchin and from here use the track of the Great Northern Railway to gain access to the terminus at King's Cross. We have promoted our Bill for the extension of the Midland, and our negotiations with the Great Northern are well advanced. It is the proposal of the gentlemen of the Royston and Hitchin to construct a railway between these towns, and to extend from Royston to Cambridge and of the Eastern Counties to construct a branch from Hertford to Hitchin. In short, Hitchin has become something of a junction. We fear there will be unnecessary complications in the establishment of routes unless arrangements can be made to the benefit of all.'

Hudson continued fluently. He moved away from the problems that faced them and elaborated, instead, upon the value of Midland stock, on the yield, on the unlikely event of any profit being made by a small line in competition with big lines unless they came to a sensible agreement.

'Hear hear!' called Braxton, true to form and on cue. It was one of his additional jobs to be cheer-leader.

Hudson gave a report on the stock of engines held by the Midland and the eighty-eight locomotives at present running daily. He reported on the progress of installation of the electric telegraph, on the opening of new branch lines and colliery lines. He spoke lovingly of the permanent girder bridge at Burton which had replaced the swing bridge and had effected the saving of two signalmen; he spoke with pride as he assured his audience, of the new engine-house and repair shops at Derby.

It had given him great pleasure, he said, to lay before the proprietors of the Midland such a satisfactory report. During the half-year, two million passengers had been conveyed along the Midland line without a single injury. On saying this they made no boast; but it certainly gave them cause for congratulation that their line had been free from those accidents which were so distressing to the Directors and so shocking to the feelings of the proprietors of any company.

He appeared oblivious of the growing anger displayed by the directors of the Great Northern. He went on to assure everyone that what had been done with the Midland was an indication of what could be done anywhere. A link with the Midland, it seemed to Henry, was being advertised as the perfect way of bringing them nearer to both God and Mammon.

Henry had been watchful throughout. Hildyard was suspiciously relaxed, as though allowing Hudson to run his course until short of steam. The analogy was accurate, for Hudson in full flow had the same fuelled-up, pressurised quality as one of his engines. The speech was no novelty to Henry or any of Hudson's supporters who had heard it all before. Hudson believed passionately that the way to influence events in business was to point out the glowing financial advantages of his own railways at every available occasion, declare a solid dividend at half-year, and let avarice take its course.

The investing public had no interest in the grand plan of things or in the technical aspects of advance. If a couple of men were made redundant here and another there, they would vote through a small fortune to achieve it. If the accounts were lacklustre and he was pressed, he invariably introduced staff savings as proof of devoted endeavours by the proprietors. He held to the cynical view that the proprietors should look after the pennies and allow him to look after the number of noughts. 'Never stretch their imaginations,' he had said to Henry, 'they are all little men. Dismissing a man or two has real significance to them. They have no understanding of money.'

Henry disliked Hudson, calling him 'the linen-draper of York', but covertly in the Temple, where he felt it necessary to be derogatory about his close connection with the man. It was stupid of him because it only called attention to what his friends and enemies knew – that he was so expertly trussed up in Hudson's financial bonds as to be compromised. The huge retainers he had been paid had been swiftly invested in Hudson's lines, and now he was reeling under the calls being made on those shares. He averted his mind from these unpleasant facts.

Henry admired Stephenson as much as he disliked 'the linen-draper' but knew that Stephenson cared for him as little as a puff of smoke. Henry was an outsider, among railway men. Most of them had come up through hard circumstances, Henry had been appointed.

Stephenson sat with his head tilted back, staring at the ceiling. He had risen from the rural poverty of a small country colliery, and remained a countryman at heart, loving all creatures and plants, observant of every detail of nature. He was also a single-minded and robust realist. He had in turn been cow-herd, horse driver, coal picker, fireman, engine man, brakesman and self-taught inventor. His first locomotive had been made in the pit workshops of West Moor with the pit blacksmith as leading mechanic. It had worked and from then there was no holding him. There was nothing he could not turn his hands to. As scholars talk of the complete Renascence man, Henry thought, Stephenson was the complete engineer. What a petty trade the law must seem in comparison, with its narrow confines, like some old blinkered horse nodding down a furrow while the world and its wonders roar past.

Hudson had finished. He sat down, taking some care to tuck up the tails of his coat so that he could drop the last few inches into his seat. Hildyard was immediately on his feet. He waited patiently while Hudson's supporters gave him their customary ovation. They were notorious for it and were mainly Yorkshiremen, dubbed the 'Flying Squad'. Quite a number of the Royston and Hitchin directors thought well enough of a link with the Midland to join in. Hudson smiled at them benevolently, nodding his head in approval. He ignored Hildyard. Henry felt nervous. There was going to be more to this than salesmanship. He could see the fool Braxton standing up and still thrashing his hands together. The Great Northern directors remained stony-faced. Henry smelled trouble. He had become attuned to atmosphere and put trust in it.

'Mr Hudson has outlined, even extolled the virtues of his own great line, the Midland Railway,' began Hildyard. Henry had a sudden vision of the quiet, shallow flight of rooks before lightning. Hildyard was too calm. 'I must agree with the honourable gentleman about the size of the venture and the vigour with which it has been prosecuted, but at the same time I cannot detract from the scale and speed of the construction of the Great Northern. The Midland Railway is a fine undertaking. I pay it the compliments of the Great Northern, as one fine undertaking to another.' He paused for the appropriate applause to these sentiments, which followed as though at his command.

'However, between size and success, lies money. Great undertakings take greatly from those who subscribe to them. They do not always give back in like manner. As we have had a sort of prospectus from Mr Hudson, M.P., on behalf of the Midland Railway, I am obliged to raise matters which I am sure can readily be answered, but which have not figured in anything that the honourable gentleman has said.

'In February of this year, Mr Edward Ellice, the Member for Northampton and a gentleman well known to Mr Hudson, attempted to move a Bill which would refer all Railway Bills to five paid Commissioners who would examine railway schemes and report on them before they were submitted to Parliament. Mr Ellice was particularly concerned with Bills promoted by Mr Hudson, being of the opinion that the accounts of the companies over which Mr Hudson presided or had a controlling interest were in such a state of confusion that it was impossible to estimate the amount of capital involved, or to calculate the engagement of these companies. I have here the Company Report of the Midland Railway which bears out what Mr Hudson has just said. It is a nicely balanced account but suffers from want of detail.' Mr Hildyard held aloft the Report. Henry wondered if he should intervene, but a calm stare from Stephenson gave him the party line. Hudson merely looked distant.

'On the same day,' continued Hildyard, 'Mr Hudson presented the Company Reports of the York and North Midland,' Hildyard brought the Report down on the table with a dramatic slap. 'The York and Newcastle.' Slap. 'The Newcastle and Berwick.' Slap. 'The Reports of which all suffer from such want of detail. Indeed I notice that the proprietors of those lines themselves pressed for that detail, Mr Ellice noted that it was rumoured that the liabilities of the Midland were now no less than thirty million pounds. Now I know that Mr Hudson has replied that the liabilities of the Midland amount to no more than fourteen million pounds. But this is a different picture from that we have just had painted!'

Hildyard sat down to uproar. Men jumped to their feet and shouted at Hildyard, at Hudson. A chant of 'Question, question, question!' broke out from the Great Northern directors, who pounded the table with their fists to emphasize the justice of their demands.

Hudson seemed to sit further back in his seat and recline as though he were an emperor at the arena, called to give judgement. It was a disarming ploy. Hudson had expected this sort of thing and only felt contempt for Hildyard that it had been so crudely done. He supposed that Hildyard had been appealing to his rustic audience on the Royston and Hitchin, more than the directors of the Great Northern who were beating away with such gleeful determination.

Henry tried to catch Hudson's eye. He felt he should act, and that he was being too eager to please, to show his worth. He wondered if he should take the initiative and object to Hildyard's comments, but knew that he was afraid to do so without permission. That was the measure of his financial involvement. He despised himself.

Hudson saw him and gave a shake of his head. Henry nodded, thinking more about himself than Hildyard. He had become a lackey, his independence of action and thought eroded. His standing in the legal profession was high, too high to be treated like this by the linen-draper. He would have to get himself out of it, it was too much for his pride.

George Stephenson stared at the ceiling, head tilted right back. He had no interest, his pose said, in farmyard commotions. He was in fact thinking that they were all like hens scattered by a fox. They are all so intent on escape that they fail to watch their pursuer and are eaten. It was all a far cry from those places where railways are made – the engineering works, the sites. Yet these creatures held the purse strings that controlled the making. His contempt for them was profound. The twelve percenters. 'Show me a line that yields twelve percent! That's the line for my money!' These financial lemmings with their slogans.

His mind drifted away from the thumping and shouting. It was all vacant and meaningless. He thought contentedly of his greenhouses at Tapton House. As a boy he had grown the traditional things of mine workers: cabbages, potatoes, giant leeks, nurtured with special brews. Now his ten greenhouses were a wonder, kept tropic by hot water pipes and hot beds. He grew pineapples and melons to compete with the Duke of Devonshire's. Melon houses, vineries and pineries.

Melons were his greatest success. He had made wire baskets so that each fruit could be suspended from above, taking the strain from the stem which would otherwise buckle and restrict the flow of nourishment. A wonderfully simple precaution, and yet no one had thought of it before. There was another pleasure. Straight cucumbers, of which everyone made so much fun. It had taken time. Now he grew them in glass tubes he had had blown, as straight as a length of track. They had perfect symmetry in section, perfect distribution of cellular matter. They could be turned and ripened evenly, bettering nature.

It was fundamental to his thinking, that man help nature to improve herself if he is a sympathetic tutor.

Hudson finally rose to his feet. It was like a whale breaching, and brought an immediate hush. The silence distracted Stephenson from his musing and he lowered his head.

Henry caught a glimpse of Stephenson's far-distant eyes and wondered as often why the man lent his name to these adventures. To please Hudson or to please his own vanity? He was wealthy, famous, had refused all titles except a Belgian knighthood. In spite of all this, did he need to be in demand? Was he so insecure? Was this what kept him alive? Stephenson sensed Henry's gaze and their eyes met, darted away. There was an instant of naked communication, of curiosity, the one about the other, then fleeing cowardice.

'Mr Ellice of Northampton,' Hudson declared, 'doubtless had his own good reasons for asking such questions.' His voice had an aggressive, hectoring tone. 'His opinion on the accounts of my company are not worth a dead cinder. Rather less. I am sorry, Mr Hildyard, that you have seen fit to drag out such a matter again, like a dead mouse that some cat is proud of. Each time it is older and less attractive. I had not thought to expect it from the Great Northern.'

'Do you gentlemen, like Mr Ellice, think that we are all very young gentlemen; that indeed we have never seen a railway? If directors have been freely placed to manage the affairs of a

18

company, then it should not be thought that they are entirely ignorant of the first principles of commerce!'

His supporters cheered and banged their table. They shouted hear, hear! and looked smug and excited. Games, thought Stephenson. They enjoy this verbal puffing. Hudson barged remorselessly through their acclaim.

'In the case of the Midland Railway, we enjoy the full support and confidence of our shareholders, who are in my opinion, and I daresay in their own, better placed to judge the situation as they have more to risk than their breath. As a result they have been rewarded with a good deal more than hot air!'

More cheers, more thumping of the table top. How they enjoy battle by proxy, thought Henry. He was embarrassed by this kind of oratory. Hudson never used the rapier when the bludgeon would do.

'There seems to be an element of heavy breathing about Mr Hildyard's statement, which I do not like,' Hudson concluded, 'I would answer any question if I knew what the question was.'

'But you have not answered the point!' shouted a Great Northern director, leaping to his feet. He was very thin, with a thin face and a fiery, blue-veined nose. His voice crackled with anger. A man with a short temper and a bad liver. 'What are the liabilities of the Midland, sir?' There was more confused din. The 'Flying Squad' from York were standing now, and thrusting handfuls of the company reports in the direction of the Great Northern table, then throwing them up in the air. The directors of that company responded by shaking their heads in extravagant dumb-play, while beating the table with their hands to a rhythmic chant of 'Question, question, question!' It reminded Henry of the House of Commons.

'If they could be let at each other,' said Stephenson, leaning over so that he could be heard, 'they wouldn't be so brave.'

An over-dressed man rose from the Royston and Hitchin table. He was urged to his feet by others. Henry judged him to be a local landowner. He had that heavy-in-the-saddle look; clearly a man who demolished his hedgerows rather than taking them.

'Mr Hudson!' the man called in a useful bellow, 'Why have you not invited the Eastern Counties Railway?'

'Why should I, sir?'

'Because, sir, I found the damned vermin on my land, and put them off!' It was a voice to turn hounds. 'They were surveying, sir, without my permission. Be assured that I know them and shall ventilate their hides if I catch them at it again!' There was laughter and cheers.

'That's Woolmer, a local mogul,' murmured Lowther. 'One of

Sibthorpe's friends and soul-mates. He has money, but is thought a bit of a clown and fool.' Henry was anxious at this revelation. He knew nothing about Woolmer, had not been told.

'There's no secret in it,' Hudson said. 'The Eastern Counties are surveying their branch from Hertford to Hitchin.'

'Then why was I not informed?'

'I have no idea, sir. I have no idea who you are, but you will be approached, sir, if you leave your name. See to it, Mr Braxton.' Hudson stared at the engineer who vigorously nodded his head. 'No doubt compensation terms can be agreed. Mr Braxton will attend upon you directly after the meeting.'

'Hold hard, Mr Hudson,' commanded Woolmer in a truculent and confident tone. 'My land is nowhere in the path of the Hertford Hitchin branch. The Great Northern runs through it at Wymondley. I think that these surveyors are up to something else.'

'I have no idea why the Eastern Counties should want your land, sir.' Hudson was dismissive. 'Perhaps my engineers can help you. There is more to finding a route than meets the eye. Perhaps the Great Northern can help you. They have an agreement with the Eastern Counties. I hope that this is not an attempt to get greater compensation, for if we do not want your land, we certainly shall not buy it.' Hudson sat down.

Woolmer's arms were flailing up and down as though beating about him with a crop. He clearly felt he had stumbled upon a truth only to lose it again.

'Hold hard!' he commanded again, but with less certainty as he tried to clarify what he wanted to say.

'Sit down, sir!' shouted the Midland directors. Woolmer would not be deflected.

'I *will* have an answer to my question Mr Hudson. As you control both the Midland and the Eastern Counties, it seems to me that these vermin could be acting for either.' He ignored the increased volume of shouting. 'The Midland is to use the Great Northern's track to get in to London, and will join it – by Hitchin. The Eastern Counties has a track to London and is to stop – by Hitchin. If the Great Northern could be crossed where it passes through my land, then the Midland could link with the Eastern Counties, sir, and avoid the Great Northern altogether. I do not believe, Mr Hudson, that a man of your experience has ignored that possibility!'

The chanting of the Midland supporters had failed to drown the man out. It was suddenly very clear to Henry that the man had stumbled on the truth as fools do. He, Henry Kelleway, knew nothing about it, he had not been told. It was how Hudson worked, feeding fragments of his plans here and there, but keeping the whole picture to himself. It left him free to shuffle the pieces, change routes, transfer dividends and profits. It compromised everyone who worked for him. The meeting was a diversionary tactic to keep attention focussed on the tiny Royston and Hitchin. He looked at Hudson, suddenly angry. The man was impassive again and staring with feigned indifference at the heavens. Henry was alarmed to see Hildyard rise to his feet and go over to the Royston and Hitchin directors where he talked in the ear of the thin-faced man. The man began to tug at Woolmer's sleeve, to get him down, but Woolmer was too impassioned to pay any attention. Angrily he snatched his arm away. Henry felt panic. They were trying to contain the man and use him later. He found himself darting glances at Hudson, seeking a clue as to what was expected of him, but Hudson ignored everyone. Henry was afraid to make a mistake, but more afraid of what might develop if he did not interrupt. He jumped to his feet. The gesture was wholly ineffectual and Henry was painfully aware of the contrast he made with Hudson who rose from his chair like Leviathan. Stephenson, never taking his eyes from his private contemplation of the ceiling, suddenly spoke.

'Knock over the water, man! Make a fool of yourself, it's better than have a scandal.'

Henry made a sweeping gesture with his arm, but the carafe merely rolled on its side, soaking his papers and making Lowther sit back abruptly. Henry grabbed at his papers and the carafe obligingly tipped on to the floor and shattered. Fragments of glass scattered over the polished wood. With a wry smile, Henry held aloft a dripping document, allowing the water to fall on the floor. He did it well and it bought him silence. Hudson was looking at him with interest. He was impressed.

'Gentlemen, I have made a mess of my papers, and we look like doing the same with this meeting. Mr Woolmer!'

Woolmer was surprised that Henry had learned his name, and discomfited that it should be called out. Henry repeated himself.

'Mr Woolmer! You have suffered some inconvenience, for which I am sure the directors and owners of the Eastern Counties are very sorry. It is a matter that can readily be cleared up. The Eastern Counties extension from Royston to Hitchin is only at Bill stage, gentlemen, and no definite route has been decided upon. Surveyors must look this way and that. They do not fix upon a path like a Roman, then drive it straight over the nearest hill and through the nearest river. They seek a route with the best gradients and few bridges and embankments. I understand Mr Woolmer's anger, but the surveyors have a job to do, and do it under perilous conditions. Even under fire!'

He noted that there were smiles and a few chuckles, but that Hildyard had returned to his seat, and was writing a note which he then passed to the Great Northern directors. Henry found that he was sweating. He cursed Hudson for putting him in this indefensible position.

'As to Mr Woolmer's particular fears, I know nothing about them. The Great Northern has taken certain unusual but very stringent precautions to protect their own interests, and I am sure the directors are alert to anything that would conflict with their interests. Indeed, they have insisted that Midland trains shall be timed to connect with those of the Great Northern at this Hitchin junction. This is a very strict clause, and one that has cost the Midland dearly. But Mr Hudson is not to be deflected by such considerations, and is concerned only to make an agreement. I will remind Mr Woolmer, however, that Mr Hudson is not to be wildly accused of making forays of one sort or another into different territory. This meeting is not a pillory and gentlemen should restrain themselves. The Midland protests most strongly, Mr Hildyard, and asks the Great Northern to put its influence to stopping this. The public at large has some notion of the railways as stock brokers armed with cutlasses and with eye-patches. Mr Woolmer seems to view us in this light. If it were not for the foresight and drive of men like Mr Stephenson and Mr Hudson, we would not have the railways that we have today. Much of what they have done has been at their personal risk. It is a very small attitude indeed to pluck at fragments of this vast enterprise, and examine them with a glass to see if some fault can be found.'

He sat down to great applause from the Midland table. Neither Hudson nor Stephenson joined in, but Henry assumed it was because he had invited acclaim for them. Men on the other two tables clapped politely, a few with enthusiasm, and even rising to their feet.

It was not the sort of unanimous enthusiasm which Hudson expected. His face was grim and angry.

'My name is Sibthorpe!' announced that gentleman to a storm of applause and cheers. 'I have never made any bones about my attitude to these iron roads. I believe, sir, that every line is seekin' to have its own terminus in London. If it do, then London will be cut into slices like a birthday cake. We shall have trains running down the Strand! We shall have another Great Fire, with sparks flying into houses. They will set fire to the ladies! No, sir, I shall oppose this extension of the Eastern Counties to Hitchin. I can do no less, I have opposed everything else. I opposed these good gentlemen of the Great Northern. A coach and horses doesn't lay claim to *own* the ground beneath it! And it don't make sparks!'

This light relief was treated with good humour, and Sibthorpe acknowledged the cheers and jeers by waving his hat. Henry sat down, pointedly.

Hudson leaned over to Stephenson.

'This meeting is a waste of time. I will settle this with Hildyard afterwards. Mr Kelleway, you must deal with Woolmer, and any more like him.'

'Aye,' said Stephenson, 'but you must play the game. They expect an occasion and will want an hour or two.'

They left the Town Hall at four. Henry felt exhausted, and Lowther and Hudson seemed grim. Things had not gone their way, and Henry knew they were disposed to blame him for it. The injustice of it ate at him. They treated him like a tuppenny pettifogger, and now he was to dance attendance on Hudson while the latter sought out Hildyard.

Brand Street, outside the Town Hall, was still crowded with country people, who sat in the June sun on cart shafts or boxes, or in the dust. They had passed the time drinking, and some were asleep. It was Hudson and Stephenson they wanted to see, and when the two men appeared on the steps, they struggled to their feet like a weary army that has been bivouacked.

They cheered the two men, and pressed close to look at them. Dust drifted over their clothes. The crowd was incurious about what had been going on. There were no shouted questions.

'I've agreed to meet Hildyard and two directors at the Sun Inn,' Hudson told Henry. 'It will be brief. We've wasted too much time on this place already.' He set off at a heavy walk, the crowd falling back so that he made a portly royal progress along Cock Street and through the Market Square. He was cheered all the way, and although he affected not to enjoy it, he raised his hat from time to time. Lowther paced beside him.

Henry was surprised to find that George Stephenson laid a hand on his arm. The elderly man gave a small shake of his head. Henry fell back with Stephenson.

'Let him go before, Kelleway.' They walked on in silence, Stephenson lifting his hat occasionally as he was recognised, but not bothering to look one way or the other. He seemed to be weighing something up, his eyes following the dusty toes of his boots.

'That didna' gang too well,' said Stephenson to the road.

'I did what I could ... ' Henry began, rather more hotly than he had intended. Stephenson held out his left hand, a small gesture commanding peace.

'You did all ye could, lad. It is an awkward situation.'

They continued to walk for half a minute, Stephenson very slowly, so that Hudson and Lowther were ahead and out of earshot.

'I never get involved in the promotion of lines, Mr Kelleway, I hope that you are well versed in the ways o' my good friend Mr Hudson.'

Henry looked at Stephenson sharply. The lively eyes were meaningful, then questioning, then blank.

'This clay dusts up badly,' said Stephenson abruptly. 'It's treacherous material, prone to drying and shrinking.' Henry nodded. He was trying to grasp what Stephenson meant. The arrogant old autocrat was sparse in his concern for others. Henry had believed that Stephenson disliked him, yet there was a clear warning in what he had said and particularly in his manner. He would have liked to have asked more, but knew he would get nowhere.

The Sun Inn had an uncared-for, bleached-out look. The half-timbering was pale as birch bark and knots stood out as though it were driftwood. The colour-washed plaster had once been an ochrous yellow, but had faded to tinged grey. No stage-coaches stopped here.

The courtyard was ill-kept, and horse-droppings and spilled bran lay about, unswept. Very much a country inn, well patronised by flies. Two local coaches stood in the shade, the drivers smoking clay pipes and talking idly, the horses shaking their heads at the flies. The horses snorted, harness rattled and jingled. An old familiar sound, thought Henry, as they walked to the saloon door, I wonder if horses will disappear. At least from the main roads and turnpikes. He wondered what Stephenson would have said about that.

Hudson and Lowther had gone in and were being shown to a private room by the landlord. The man had put on a spotless white apron for the occasion, but it was old and frayed at the edges. He had not changed his shirt, which was dirty and stained under the arms. Henry and Stephenson followed, their boots clumping on bare boards.

Hildyard had preceded them and stood by the window, waiting, in a proprietorial stance. Hudson took one glance at him, muttered 'good day' and seated himself at the ancient table. He was not to be treated like that. The three men followed suit, leaving the Great Northern directors standing.

Hildyard, mastering his annoyance, gestured towards the table. The Great Northern men sat.

'I could do wi' some refreshment,' said Stephenson.

'What can I get you, gentlemen?' asked the landlord, anxious to please. He was short and rotund, but moved nimbly. One sleeve kept unrolling, and he spent the whole time with the other hand upon it, rolling it up and straightening it.

'That depends on your ale, man,' said Stephenson. 'If it's no good, bring us wine. Bring us both anyway.' The landlord left, closing the door.

Hildyard looked smug. He knew that Hudson would not have agreed to this meeting unless he was worried. Henry laid his papers out on the table, carefully. Hildyard was doing the same, as though they were both marshalling their troops. It helped to fill the silence.

'If this is the best that Hitchin can offer, then Hitchin needs every railway that will come here,' said Hudson. Hildyard smiled briefly, no more than a muscular twitch.

'It's good to see you again, Mr Hudson. I don't like public meetings. They encourage antics. I think we have enough expensive men cooped up here to come to the nub of things, don't you?'

The speaker was a well-dressed man on Hildyard's right. Edmund Denison, Member for Doncaster and Chairman of the Great Northern. They were the first words he had spoken. He had remained silent in the Town Hall.

'It's good to see *you*, Mr Denison. I would like to think we can talk sense.'

'That we can.' His glance turned to Stephenson. He smiled. 'Mr Stephenson, I'm honoured again. I haven't seen you these four months.'

'I keep myself busy at Tapton. I've had a look at your line, sir. Up and down by horse. It's a fine piece of work.'

'I would be honoured to show it to you. You'll attend for the opening?'

'I will, sir.'

Hudson was tapping on the table with his thick fingers. He was jealous of Stephenson, possessive. Henry, watching Hildyard, knew that Hildyard had not missed it. It was strange for the two barristers to be confronting each other in this way. They knew each other well, had opposed each other in court, but there was something uneasy about the intimacy of their surroundings. Henry liked the remoteness of the courtroom. It was uncommercial and blessed with the authority of the state. Here he was a soldier out of uniform, a man without the confidence of a civilian.

The others talked, waiting for the landlord to return. It was about costs per mile, new engines, new stations, gauges, passenger returns. Denison was formidable. Like Hudson he was a Yorkshireman, but his game was quite different. In every way he was as singleminded and hard in business, but he chose to appear urbane, friendly and casual. It could be disarming.

The landlord brought a tray with glasses and tankards. It had once been Sheffield plate, but the copper shone through from hurried scouring.

'We ought to come to the point,' said Denison, sipping claret.

'We ought,' agreed Hudson.

'My directors are very opposed to the proposed extension of the Eastern Counties from Royston to Hitchin. We shall fight it tooth and nail in the House.' Denison smiled again. 'That's no more than you would expect.'

'I don't see why we should expect it,' said Hudson loudly, with a return of his hectoring tone. 'It will do you no harm, and will bring more traffic to the Great Northern by the Hitchin junction.' Hildyard grimaced, a twinge of indigestion at the raw nature of Hudson's words. He extracted a paper and laid it on the table as though it were gold leaf and might disintegrate.

'We have this agreement with the Royston and Hitchin,' he said, affecting a mincing style of speech. 'Your company's proposed line directly affects them, and so directly affects us. There is no nicety about it. We have an agreement. Mr Kelleway must know ... '

'The Royston and Hitchin can never survive on its own,' interrupted Hudson bluntly. 'No branch that size can pay.'

Henry was annoyed that he had not been allowed the scrap that Hildyard had tried to toss his way.

'In order to defeat us in the House,' he said warmly, 'you will require more support than you enjoy at present. It is much more logical to those who hold stock, to unite two great lines like the Eastern Counties and the Great Northern and share the increased volume of traffic. You surely don't suggest that you will throw that away for the sake of acquiring an insignificant branch that can never pay.'

Denison sat back in his seat. Hildyard made play of consulting him with a look and a raised legal eyebrow. It was all well acted. Denison nodded.

'We are not, I think, talking only about the Royston and Hitchin,' continued Hildyard. 'We have intelligence that the Midland intend to promote an extension of their line to this Eastern Counties junction with our Great Northern track, and *cross* it, avoiding us altogether, so that the Midland can use the Eastern Counties route to London, instead of sharing ours. That would be a matter of direct competition. I can see no element of co-operation there, no matter how I look at it.' He paused and looked at Henry again. 'Perhaps there is some answer ... ' Before Henry could feel gratitude to the man for this professional ball-tossing, Hudson crashed in angrily, the weight of his body buffeting the table as he lunged forward. There was no pretence at urbanity.

'I have no idea where you get your news, sir, but you must stir for it with a stick!'

'Do you deny it then?' asked Denison, mildly.

'That is not a proper question,' Henry interrupted, treating Denison like a bad child. 'It is not correct at all. The future plans of any company are in all cases a matter for that company until they become public knowledge.'

'Even in so far as they affect another company, Mr Kelleway?' asked Denison, still mild.

'Yes. Particularly in so far as they affect another company. There is no question of confirming or denying anything. My learned friend will, I'm sure,' said Henry, trying to toss the ball back to Hildyard and sap the situation of unprofessional passions, 'agree that these are words for gossip or speculation. They are not relevant to this sort of serious discussion, although the journals may love them. My learned friend's company is no less jealous of its own plans than any other. It is as silent as the sphinx until it sees fit. Surely our company is not expected to alert its rivals by releasing its plans? Even under this questioning?' He tried to sound light and good-humoured. Denison raised his eyebrows at Hildyard in a theatrical mime of surprise that was hardly necessary in the small room. He waved a hand at him, consigning to him the task of bandying words.

Hildyard selected another piece of paper. It was of a coarse yellow texture and Henry could see printing upon one side of it.

'I am sure I have the utmost confidence in my learned friend,' began Hildyard smoothly. His entire manner was that of the Court. 'I regret that on this occasion I have the misfortune to differ with him. I am pleased that we have adjourned to a less public place.' Hildyard took a reluctant sip from his glass of wine.

'When agreements have been entered into, and it seems that the future plans of one party are in breach of the spirit of that agreement, then it becomes a matter for both parties. Forgive me.' Hildyard coughed into his hand. He pushed the glass of wine an inch from him. It was clearly rejected.

He was right that the matter would have to be dealt with. Henry was desperately trying to think of a way out of the situation. He had not been briefed and was furious with Hudson and with

Lowther. Had Stephenson known? He would ponder on that.

Henry was in no doubt that Hudson was trying to do what the lawyer said. Under cover of extending the Midland to Hitchin and promoting an extension of the Eastern Counties to the same town, he was trying to buy a way through to link them and use the Eastern Counties track into its London terminus at Farringdon. The agreement to use the Great Northern track was a nonsense, to lull them into not opposing his plans. The Royston and Hitchin lay right in Hudson's way and must be exterminated. Henry visualised it briefly as a naked earthworm wriggling on the Hertfordshire clay, waiting for Hudson's heel.

Hudson was staring at Hildyard, obviously very angry, and shaking his head slightly, implying idiocy at the least. It was beneath him to reply. Henry looked at the others. Lowther was white and nervous. He kept glancing quickly at Henry, then away again. So Lowther was in the know as well. Stephenson, on the contrary, was calm and very attentive, his bright eyes missing nothing. He appeared concerned.

I am being paid three hundred pounds a day, thought Henry. Of that I owe half to Hudson for his calls on my shares in his companies. There is the house to maintain and enough to keep Jane clothed and quiet and unsuspecting. To keep her socially busy. Then there is Kate. I can't afford righteous anger.

Hildyard was holding out the piece of coarse paper.

'I am sure that no such crossing and junction has yet been promoted, or my learned friend Mr Kelleway would know of it,' he said. Henry tried to read Hildyard's face for irony or sarcasm, but Hildyard was addressing himself to Hudson. 'Yet I have here the pull, or impression, of an advertisement to that effect which is due to appear in the journals in two days' time. It seems that this impression has been privately circulated by some person, possibly from the printers, for personal gain.' He put the paper down on the table. Hudson glanced at it, Lowther did not bother. Stephenson picked it up and read it, passing it to Henry. It was as Hildyard said.

'We cannot believe this advertisement was placed without the knowledge of the Midland Railway, even though it comes from the Eastern Counties. Its purpose is to promote the Eastern Counties branch from Hertford to Hitchin, and also to obtain powers to *cross* the Great Northern track to effect a junction with the Midland.'

His hand again strayed towards his glass of wine, but he thought better of it. All he wanted was a dramatic pause.

'We see this scheme as promoted with the sole object of frustrating an agreement that has already been made for the use

28

by the Midland of the Great Northern line to London, and we see the proposed extension of the Eastern Counties from Hertford to Hitchin as promoted with the sole object of frustrating the most legitimate application made by the Royston and Hitchin Railway, which would lie in the way of this ambition. We shall lend that company our support, as we have an arrangement with them. These arrangements are being interfered with in ways that are not being made plain. We regret that we have to assure you of our resolute opposition in the House of Lords.'

Hildyard smiled. Rapid as a lizard flicking its tongue. A punctuation that he had finished. There was an unpleasant silence; a blow had been struck and it was the hesitation before revenge. Henry saw that Lowther was likely to be imprudent. His nervousness would lead to bluster. Hudson was inhaling air for some mighty rebuff. Stephenson seemed to have removed his spirit from the proceedings, leaving his husk in limp occupation of his chair.

'I respect the fact that my learned friend must protect the interests of the Company he represents,' floundered Henry, only too aware how flat his words sounded. 'It is what I would expect. It is however normal to have any route surveyed before a line is promoted. I can't see there is anything unusual in that ...'

Hudson broke in, his voice full of ill-mannered irritation. He bombarded them with facts and dates about the operations of the Eastern Counties and the Bills they had promoted. He protested the legitimacy of the Eastern Counties proposed branch. He declared its antecedents were as good as any other. He threatened and breathed on them, dwelling on the effect of lack of co-operation. He evaded any point central to the issue. As a diversionary skirmish it was well delivered. He made it plain he felt he was doing Henry's work in bothering to reply.

'But,' said Hildyard, sticking to the point like a burr to a blanket, 'it is usual to declare an interest if negotiating an agreement with a party and at the same time negotiating a similar one with another.'

Denison smiled and nodded, without humour. Hudson struggled to his feet, glaring at Henry.

'We have not come here to be taught how to conduct business. We think we are capable of doing that ourselves. If this is the only point we can come to, then I think we have spent enough time on it. You seem to have decided your position, so there's an end of it. Good day.'

Hildyard caught Henry's eye. He raised his eyebrows, pulled a face. Mock sympathy for Henry for having such a client. Henry looked at him woodenly, gathering his papers. Whatever he might feel he was not going to give Hildyard the satisfaction of sharing it.

Hudson walked ahead, kicking up the dust of Sun Street, Lowther hurrying to keep up. Henry made no such attempt, hoping by delay to emphasize his own anger. He would not be humbled like this. Hudson looked round for Stephenson, seeking support. There was nothing bland about his face. He was hot and sweating. All the irritation, Henry thought, of an unhorsed Prince of the Blood glaring round for his squires and grooms. And with as much humility and charm.

Stephenson lagged behind, to avoid Hudson. He would not afford him the sympathy of proximity. Henry was uneasy at the rift between the men.

'That was only a skirmish,' Stephenson said to Henry's surprise. 'A few feathers ruffled, but none torn out. But their posturing is serious enough. They will take up their positions like cockerels and seem to be all show. That's where mistakes can be made, because they will fight to the death to defend them.'

The rustic, wiseacre remarks were an affectation but his concern seemed to Henry to be real enough. It was the second time the man had gone out of his way to warn him. His pointed distancing of himself from Hudson seemed a deliberate touch of frost on a long and friendly relationship between the two men.

'Thank you, Mr Stephenson, I will be careful,' said Henry with his best effort at humility to the old tyrant. 'This junction is very important.'

'It is crucial, sir. Not any less, taking a view of all Mr Hudson's operations. You hold shares, I understand, in a number of lines, but you don't have the mind for railways like Hudson. It is a picture of continual change, like a battle, and he is the general, moving here, feinting there, deploying and decoying. You should keep a closer eye on it. Men and money.' Stephenson speeded up and walked ahead of Henry. Two paces. Two hundred miles.

Henry was upset. He had been lax and his failure was a lack of any geographic grasp of what men like Hudson or Denison were trying to do when they chose routes or towns. Stephenson was right to describe it as a tactical war. There was obviously something amiss as far as Stephenson was concerned, but loyalty prevented him from being explicit.

They crossed the Market Square by the east side, weaving between carriages and people. Men who recognised Hudson fell back to allow his royal progress. Hudson turned into the churchyard of St Mary's, which was deserted. He stopped and turned. He had chosen this place so he could not be overheard, Henry thought sourly, it could not be because it was consecrated ground. He was standing on a grave while the others had consciously looked about them and avoided the grassed forecourts of tombstones.

'I can't waste more time in this place, so I'll be brief. I have to go north immediately and must rely on things being put right here. Mr Kelleway, we did not do well out of that. You must call in Braxton and the others and brief them. The money will be made available for purchasing this route. You will find a way with these landowners. When we have secured our line we will be in a strong position.'

The statement was made with such blunt command that Henry's anger overflowed.

'I hope you don't blame me for this. We could have done better in there, sir, if I had had the facts put before me. I knew nothing about this advertisement and this scheme to cross the Great Northern track. As your adviser I have a right to be kept informed if I am to do my job. Hildyard was able to take advantage of it. Why was I not informed?'

Hudson gave Henry a bovine stare.

'Well, sir, do you expect me to feed you personally with every scrap and scraping from the pot? These matters of detail are what I leave to others and what I pay them for. Braxton could have advised you if you had enquired of him.'

'But it is central to the thing. Could you not have advised me, Mr Hudson?'

'I have not the time for everything, Mr Kelleway. You are a lawyer, and I feel entitled to expect you to fight with what you have to hand. You must learn to expect the unexpected. That is how it is in business.'

'I expect to be briefed.'

The other two men were concerned. Lowther was tramping at a tussock of grass with one foot, Stephenson moved forward as though he might have to intervene.

'We won't quarrel, Mr Kelleway. There's no future in it. You are an eminent man in your profession. I have paid you ten thousand a month to ride in Hyde Park so that you should not act for the opposition. That is a measure of my respect, I think.'

The brutal insult stunned Henry to temporary silence. He wondered if the man comprehended what he was saying, if he genuinely weighed everything in terms of money and held all men in such contempt. His one desire was to walk away, but he could not, for Hudson had him tied financially. Henry did not think for a moment that that was one detail Hudson had overlooked. Henry held his peace, feeling sure that Hudson would not hesitate to make his humiliation worse. It would take skill and care to disentangle himself from the man, and remain intact.

31

'I think Mr Kelleway's career speaks for itself, George,' Stephenson was saying, trying to make amends.

Henry arrived home in Gower Street both tired and depressed. The long uncomfortable journey had afforded him an opportunity for solitary contemplation that had degenerated into self-pity. He had come to hate coaches. The railways, which he was now accustomed to use, were always diverting and there was companionship. The coach was a solitary sort of cell, crude and jerky. It had outlived its usefulness.

He had contemplated his personal situation, staring at the fields of yellowing corn and sunk into a black mood. Corn, in its abundance, growing, and sudden mortality under the scythes of the reapers seemed so much like mankind. A blade more or less made no difference, indeed whole acres could be flattened by natural causes with no disastrous effect on the harvest.

He was trying to find some way out of his dependence upon Hudson. He found no solution, only gloom.

There was no doubt that Hudson's lines showed profits, and showed them with remarkable speed. Henry had a vision of Hudson touching the very track, and it turning to gold along its glistening length; the bolts, nails, fish-plates, everything. A locomotive caught in full flight during the magical transformation. Golden wheels, rods, boiler, even the fireman's shovel.

Henry had heard a great deal about Hudson's methods and read what the journals had to say. Even if the bulk of it was malicious or just part of the hurly-burly of competitive business, there had been a worrying minority of informed critics who had in earlier years drawn Henry aside. There was no way of proving anything, they had said, from the way the accounts were presented, because Hudson kept everything very close to his chest, and of course Hudson was successful and there could be no doubt that some of his lines were very profitable indeed. They were reasonably sure, however, that Hudson issued new stock in one company to pay a comfortable dividend on an ailing line. His principle was that happy shareholders ask no questions of the accounts.

The men who had called him aside no longer did so. They raised their hats to him, smiled, but were tight-lipped. Henry had risen with Hudson. He commanded enormous fees, had grasped the man's Promethean fire, and was now predictably bound. It seemed they were only waiting for his punishment.

In the Temple this had two directly contrary effects. His old friends became distressingly wary. They remained unimpressed when Henry discussed his relationship with Hudson with fluent candour. They treated it as an act of penance that might or might not be just an act.

New friends forced themselves upon him, importunate lovers determined to woo from him some lover's secrets that they could realise in gold coin. These speculators from his own profession fawned on him and sustained the image he tried to destoy, that he was some particular intimate of Hudson. They were from every position. Judges vaguing on the Bench with their quill pens were as likely to be working out dividends as noting carefully argued points of law. Solicitor's Clerks blatantly concluded their business by requesting, 'on behalf of the gentlemen at the office' if he had any particular news, as they called it. Some of them were men of probity to whom the business itch was an excitement and a diversion from law dust. It was, however, too easy for his detractors to accuse him of a lack of fastidiousness. The more cunning profited by both investing and detracting. Henry was close to a position on the Bench. The Law, he thought, is akin to the ancient Roman Empire, cluttered with pillars behind which lurk assassins.

The manservant in livery opened the door before he could reach out for the bell pull. Jane came down the stairs to greet him in the hall. It annoyed him unreasonably that she should be so attentive when part of him that was unfaithful rejected her. He suspected she was aware of it, but with Jane he could never be sure. She made a point of herself taking his hat. She was elegantly dressed, and he imagined that she had done so specifically for his return although he had only been away for the day. There was no doubt that she was beautiful and that in entering the house he was entering a setting which in every way appeared appropriate to his position, if not his current financial position. To the unwaveringly curious eyes of his neighbours, they presented trappings without blemish.

'How was it in Hitchin?' Jane was solicitous, but could not conceal a genuine note of anxiety in her voice. She knew Hudson, had met all the principals in Henry's business. Her opinion of Hudson in particular was very poor. It annoyed Henry that she took a deeply censorious attitude to his whole dealings in railway work, as though it were some lesser branch of work. She was defensive about it among their friends.

'It was not a great success. It's a long journey and it was hot.'

Henry helped himself to a glass of brandy. He would change from his travelling clothes later. Jane, who had expected a kiss on the cheek, was upset. Henry usually observed that formality at least. There was obviously more to it, and yet she knew that the more she questioned him, the more general his replies would become. It made her angry that he should simply sit and drink brandy and she determined to have some response from him.

'Henry, it obviously went badly. Tell me at least if Hudson is to get his line?'

'What line?' asked Henry obstructively. He had to be at court tomorrow, he thought, he must try to get some work done before going to bed. It was a simple enough dispute over compensation, but he was aware that the pressure was on him from Hudson, not just to succeed, but to excel.

In the afternoon, provided it all went smoothly, there was Kate. But he must see Braxton and fix things up with the man to go knocking on doors in Hitchin – it was no more than that. They had to buy agreements. Braxton, he thought, is where the corruption bubbles out of the mountain of Hudson's respectability.

Jane sat at the small writing-table in her room, reading what she had penned. It was an expedient she had never tried before, but it seemed appropriate because of Henry's attitude. She would not be able to express her suspicions to Henry in spoken words without accusatory bitterness, and she knew from experience he would react to that like a child, with denials and anger. Almost with tears. She would not allow herself to be put in the position of a mother so that he could escape to a lover. It was the feeling of being steered into this position that made her sure he had a woman somewhere. It was a matter of experience, she thought. It made the hurt no less. At their age, should they not have mellowed?

She examined herself candidly. She was still a passionate and responsive woman. Henry found her sexually satisfying, or seemed to, as far as she could tell. His needs seemed to increase with stress, rather than with domestic relaxation. Needs and love were capable of being the same; capable of being a disguise for resentment and unrecognised hate. Things had gone so well for a long time. Henry had prospered and risen in eminence, grown in stature as their two children had grown. He doted on their daughter, took pride in their son. It was the thought of Elizabeth finding them quarrelling, she supposed, that as much as anything made her avoid any further confrontation. Frederick was out with some party of his friends and would no doubt quarrel with Henry when he returned. The pride was not reciprocated, Frederick, just twenty, taking a censorious view of his father's dealings with the railways that his age afforded.

She looked at her note.

'I wish you would tell me more than you do. I wish I knew more about Hudson. I wish I knew more about *you.*' It seemed ridiculous and inadequate when she looked at it, but she suppressed the thought. Some action was better than nothing. She took the note through the dressing-room to his bedroom, folded it twice and stood it on his pillow. She returned to her own room feeling ridiculously nervous, like a housebreaker, and undressed by herself and went to bed. She listened in the dark, hearing carriages, voices, the whistle of an engine.

Frederick returned. Servants passed up and down the stairs. Frederick went to bed. It was like being a rabbit in cover at night, she thought. I hear the smallest sounds because I am afraid.

Henry came upstairs late. He did not seem to pause. If he had read her note, she could not guess. She had expected him to come to her door, to be angry, to make excuses, to demand to know what it was about. She had expected something, but there was nothing.

Two

Passing down from the rim of the Weald into its misty blue bowl was at first like passing magically beneath the sea. From the summit of downland, with its big trees and spongy topping of leaf-mould, it was possible to see for miles from horseback, over to stranded copses and church spires on square towers. Each seemed an island, the mist a place for silent barges bearing warrior kings to their burial or weeping maidens whose hearts were not able to contain the woes of the world.

Edward Kelleway enjoyed the fanciful scene it evoked. He indulged in it, defying the thought that it more suited a boy of fourteen than a man of twenty-five.

The track he followed now through the big trees had been worn into the chalky earth and showed white through the mulch of beech and oak. It had become scoured through successive winters so that it formed a smooth rounded rift as it plunged downwards.

The soil improved. Grass and weeds clung to it where it had been carried down the slopes by erosion. The beech trees and saplings so overgrew the road that they interlocked overhead, forming a continuous green tunnel through which only occasional shafts of sun struck the floor that now sparkled with crushed flints. In this welcome light, insects danced as though contained in an invisible column. As the horse moved through them, they parted and re-formed, each taking its appointed place in the dance as before. Edward had to lean forward over the horse's neck, so low was this canopy. On a sunless, dripping day, it would have seemed oppressive as a cave. Birds lived above this layer, preferring the tree tops.

As the land flattened out and the wealden hills formed an amphitheatre behind Edward, the trees gave way abruptly to fields of corn, and the track to a country road between two hedges. The ageless scouring of the chalky hills and their carpets of leaf had produced a rich soil. The wheat was sturdy in the stalk, heavy-headed but still green. In some fields where deposits of flints made hot barren patches, poppies grew like a crop. The mist that had seemed so dense from above was no more than a slight haze. The tired horse, glad to be on level ground and off the difficult slopes, seemed to stretch itself forward in the sun. Its gait was clumsy with fatigue.

Edward passed farm workers slashing the hedgerows. They hacked and bent the saplings, laying them downwards against nature, weaving their branches to secure them. They watched Edward ride by with critical eyes, noting the condition of his horse, and replied indistinctly when he wished them good day. They used his passing as an excuse to pause and sharpen steel, spitting on their blades and caressing them with a whetstone, so that they trilled.

Edward had made this journey before and knew how to keep to his way, coming out on to a broader road, unmetalled but of old English width of thirty feet between two hedges: a drove road that allowed alternate strips to be used when one became impassable. He had already seen the village, sited on a slight rise, with the church behind on a higher mound. He felt apprehensive at meeting his uncle John. He was always unpredictable, capable of great warmth and friendliness at one moment which could so easily change to cold withdrawal. It was his cousins Charlie and Nell he had come to see. And Louise, his aunt. She bemused him. She was the perfect older woman, he told himself in more analytical moments. If she were not his aunt, he would throw himself at her. He might anyway, he thought, excited at the idea, for the sheer game of it. If it was a game. With Louise it was never possible to draw lines, never possible to know what she really meant. In any case she would not keep it secret and would flaunt it in front of Charlie and Nell and Uncle John. It would be another of her games that might not be a game.

The village was a compact but messy place, off any stage route but busy enough about its own activities. A cluster of houses, three shops, an inn and some farms faced one another across a trampled and cattle-fouled pond and green. The church, on its higher eminence, was out of proportion. It was a village that had not fulfilled the ambitions that had been planned for it five hundred years before.

Beyond the church, on the same high ground, stood several larger houses close to the rectory, and obviously seeking to share its respectability. Houses for gentlemen of reasonable means and without land; for the corn chandler, the doctor. They were built largely of brick, unlike the half-tiled or weather-boarded buildings below, and were surrounded by walls of knapped flint, dense and black.

Edward passed through the open gate of one of these houses, tried to spur his horse to a smart gallop, but succeeded only in a brief trot. He dismounted before the house on the gravel drive, noting that it seemed much as before. It was slightly run down. A tile had slipped here and there on the roof and the wood of the windows showed grey through the paint. The kitchen garden was half-heartedly used, grass covering the ridges of former cultivation. Uncle John could not or would not afford a gardener, insisting on carrying out some meagre cultivation himself. The glass-houses had broken panes and the inside of the glass was rimed with green algae. Stained glass. A cathedral to neglect.

'Edward Thomas! Bring the horse round, I'll look after her. Have you ridden without resting the animal? It's no way to treat a horse.'

John Kelleway appeared with the ill-disguised promptness of a man who has been waiting, although he could not have known, within the nearest hour, when Edward would arrive. He shook hands formally gathering up the reins in a proprietorial way that immediately annoyed Edward. It implied that the horse was no more than on loan to its owner. He clapped Edward on the back in a cordial enough manner, but as always there was some constraint that made the greeting uneasy. Edward looked round quickly for his cousins or his aunt. John interpreted immediately. Another uneasy knack.

'Louise is inside. She is not ready, she says, and it is something to do with her hair or some other rearrangement.' He said nothing about Charlie and Nell. The two men looked at each other as people will who try to read the passage of events from the veneer of appearances. Edward was neither fair nor dark and had the grey eyes of his father. He wore moustaches that were fine and silky, contrasting with his wiry hair. John was a greying fifty-four. His eyes were evasive, darting. It was difficult to note their colour.

Edward dressed well, too fashionably perhaps, too modish for the best circles. His uncle, in contrast, hardly seemed to care about garments at all, wearing his shirt open at the neck and an old pair of trousers and boots.

'Well, where are they?' asked Edward eventually, as much to avoid his uncle's continuing appraisal, as provoke an answer.

'What are clothes?' said John, not answering. 'They are not so important. Yet young people find them so. In the animal kingdom, plumage or coat is important because it shows the condition of the animal. Whether it is ill, or in its prime. I suppose it is the same with clothes.' John then seemed to sink into a momentary abstraction, as though his mind had gone completely blank. The horse, perhaps sensing something animal and frightening, shook its head, eyes all white.

'Edward!' called a man's voice, and Edward looked up to see Charlie and Nell leaning from an upper window on the staircase landing. They seemed content to remain there. Nell smiled and gave a small parody of a wave.

'Don't you come down to greet relations?' demanded Edward, realising they were teasing him, but hurt nonetheless. 'Is this civil?'

'It depends if we like the relations,' replied Charlie and disappeared from the window. Nell remained there for a few moments longer than her brother, smiling at Edward. Edward thought she looked wonderfully beautiful. Her skin was naturally dark, of that colour and smoothness that is called olive-skinned although it is more like vellum. Her long black hair was curled and lustrous. When she smiled she showed her mother's broad mouth, full of humour. She held her face there, reluctant to take it from the warmth of the sun, her eyes slightly closed against the glare, her head tilted slightly upwards.

It was such a typical gesture that Edward found himself smiling back at her, sharing her sensual pleasure. There was a languor about her to which he was attuned. John grunted in displeasure at this time game. There was too much of her mother in the girl, he was thinking. The sensuality embarrassed him.

'Come down, Nell!' he commanded, more roughly than he intended. It was as though he were shouting at an errant eight-year-old. But Nell responded by smiling at the face of the sun and holding up her own. John made for the front door, suddenly angry, found that he still clutched the reins of the horse and hesitated to throw them over a briar by the front step. Edward followed, painfully aware of these erratic moods and tensions that crackled like summer lightning. His uncle's swift stride and general muscular strength belied the uncared-for look of the house. He was a very fit man, and made Edward feel defensive about his own vigour. Yet there was too much concentrated power in his movements for it to be sustained. It must be followed by collapse.

A servant girl hovered in the hall, uncertain what was expected of her.

'Tell Robert to take care of the horse,' he said to her, and she bobbed and disappeared downstairs. Cooking smells made Edward's mouth water. His legs and seat hurt from the long ride. Perhaps he should have rested up the horse, but he had never considered it.

Charlie came down the stairs into the hall and clapped him on the back. He also was dark of complexion, strongly built and with a rapid way of moving and talking which gave his manner a quixotic quality. He then took Edward by the shoulders and turned him round as though he was so much mutton for sale, looking at his clothes and general condition. He would have proceeded to prod him like a beast if Edward had not backed away.

'Putting on weight, I see,' said Charlie, 'and dressing fit to kill. Things must be well with you.'

'Things seem well enough with you. And you don't look noticeably slimmer yourself!'

'Ah, but my brain has improved wonderfully. It has had total peace and relaxation from strain. This village is not so much dead, as still waiting for the first breath of life.' He looked slyly at his father as he spoke.

'There is plenty of honest activity in this village,' John declared, 'Don't you bait me, Charlie, because honest activity is not to your taste. I know your taste, sir, in idle pleasure, and I don't approve.'

'Edward, it's good to see you!' interrupted Nell, walking down the last flight of stairs. She gave her father an admonishing scowl that she pretended was in fun, but to everyone looked real enough. 'It *is* quiet here, and it's good of you to come to visit us.' She kissed him on each cheek, and he returned the greeting.

'Mother will be down in a few minutes,' she explained, 'she didn't expect you so soon. Why don't we walk in the garden until luncheon, and you can tell us all your news?'

'Why don't we give the poor fellow something to drink?' said Charlie. 'That poor fellow there, and this poor fellow here!'

'If you will excuse me,' said John Kelleway stiffly, 'I will see to your saddlebags.'

'No,' protested Edward, 'I must deal with that.'

'You will leave it to me, Edward. You take your drink, sir, and your walk in the garden. I have other things to attend to, and will have your horse looked after too.'

Edward would have protested again, but Nell caught his eye and gave a slight shake of her head.

'Thank you then, uncle. It is very kind of you.'

John gave them a strange half bow, as though he knew no other way to take his leave. It was an awkward gesture, almost that of a servant. It expressed distance, disapproval.

The garden at the rear of the house was extensive and had originally been well laid out within flint-and-brick walls. It backed on to the graveyard and ran surprisingly close to the church.

The same neglect was evident here. The gravel paths had been cleaned in patches without particular method, scraped bald. Elsewhere they were matted with weed. Some fruit trees in the orchard had been pruned back hard and were stumpy and full of vigour, others were extended and spent. The lawn had been maintained in an agricultural manner by scythe and those shrubs that could support themselves without attention had grown woody

40

in their hearts, collecting leaves and the nests of successive years.

'None of us are gardeners,' said Nell quickly, seeing Edward's glance. 'Father won't employ one. He says we can't afford it and in any case it is a vanity and nature's good enough for him. Mother and I scratch about a bit at the paths and beds, and Charlie prunes the trees and digs the vegetable garden, when he's here, but father would rather let it grow into a wilderness. He says he prefers it.'

'It would be more melancholic,' added Charlie, 'and to his taste.'

The two men had drunk large glasses of brandy. The quality was not good and Edward felt it burn in his empty belly. Things seemed in all respects a little bit worse than on his visit the previous year. There had been no mending, he assumed, between John and Louise.

'How is he?' he asked, trying to sound lightly conversational. The high broach spire of the oversized church threw a blunt mid-day shadow across part of the lawn, like a giant sundial. They walked through it in silence before Nell replied. The grass was still wet.

'It's all more difficult than that. You will see for yourself. Why don't we talk about London. I really do want to go back there.'

'It's a question we have to answer, though,' said Charlie. 'We can't just let Edward flounder.' He was watching Nell, encouraging her to take the lead in any explanation.

'I don't want to talk about it,' she said, dropping back and then stopping. It was a very childlike gesture. Despite the maturity of her appearance, Edward knew what was behind the façade.

'It's only fair to Edward,' reasoned Charlie. 'We are not the most normal family to come and visit.' Nell was stubbornly silent. 'Have you brought your evening clothes?'

'Yes. Highly compressed in my bags.'

'Good, we will get them ironed up this afternoon. We are going out this evening.'

'You don't give me much chance to rest!'

'Nonsense, you've only been riding for four hours. You need more stamina. It is a dance – I can't call it a ball – given by one of our local gentry. Nothing grand, but the best we can offer round here. It should amuse you and you can ogle our local beauties, who are droll, being of the giggling, blushing variety and extremely healthy. My word, above all, they are *healthy*! Brought up on butter and eggs and cheese!'

Charlie was grinning at Nell as he spoke. 'I have also located a pair of reasonable horses, which round here means that they are actually shod, and are not used for ploughing. Lighter work possibly, but not ploughing. So tomorrow we can take ourselves off on these sons of the Arab and jolt up your constitution.'

'No you won't, Charlie,' Nell was compelled to interrupt, 'Tomorrow, Edward will be mine.' Charlie grinned at her. 'We shall take a picnic and he will tell me about Aunt Caroline, and about Henry, Jane, William, Maria, and everyone. Then he shall tell me about what I should be wearing, and what novelties there are in the Coliseum or at Cremorne and Vauxhall. Then I shall run away from this dreary place. It's all right for Charlie, he spends half his time in London. I am a prisoner. My life is considered feverish if the Sunday sermon is controversial!'

'Join us,' said Edward warmly, holding out his hand. Nell took it and tucked her arm in his. As they had always been as children, he thought.

They walked on again, through the vegetable garden with its unpainted, broken frames and neglected forcing-beds. The greater signs of decay seemed to decide Nell.

'Things are bad,' she confided, 'not just what you see here, and round the house; that could be tidied up readily enough. Charlie is right, Edward. You ought to know, and before lunch. Things are if anything rather worse than last year. Louise is certainly no happier with father and no happier here although she has found some distractions.'

Edward was not clear, although he could guess, as to what the remark referred. He would wait for Nell to come to it.

'She can't want to return to Virginia? I know that she did at one time.'

'No, not Virginia. To London. She won't talk of Virginia at all now, except in obscure ways, which upset father. If we go to London, she says, she will come with us. That makes me twice a prisoner. How can I possibly go if father is immediately deserted? It's not fair. But on the other hand, as things are between them, she can't stay either. That's what things have got to. Do you wish you hadn't come to visit us, Edward? It is an unnecessary thing to become involved in.'

'Don't be silly. By that token, any difficulties should be avoided. I don't intend to avoid Louise or John.'

They walked through one of the glasshouses. Seedlings had sown themselves and grew thin and under-nourished against the glass. Edward pondered the situation as they walked in single file down the board walk. Charlie and Nell and he had been brought up together by his mother Caroline. The three had been one family for four formative years and the closeness between them remained a potent thing.

In this time, John Kelleway had been in Virginia, looking for Louise, who had deserted him there, as far as the children had been able to discover, because he ill-treated her. What had happened in those four years was never revealed. John and Louise had returned to England apparently reconciled and happy. And they had returned married, an omission in their previous relationship that John had seen fit to correct quietly in America. There were other quiet things about John. The marriage lacked passion, in the loving sense, but they were hardly newly-weds in a conventional way, and the children, all-knowing, at first ascribed it to that.

Louise had seemed larger than life to the children, a strange flamboyant godmother of pantomime proportions, beautiful and extravagant. School friends of that brief, interesting period were brought to inspect her and admire. They were impressed but doubtful that she could really be a mother. 'She's your aunt really,' they said, 'She must surely be your aunt.'

She was too wondrous a creature. Quiet John, in place of passion seemed determined to impose a proprietorial love that was a discipline; perhaps to himself. Louise, it seemed, was to show gratitude in order that John should feel deliverance from remorse. Charlie and Nell discussed these things knowingly when they met on Sundays at Caroline's house in Highgate. At these meetings the contrast between Louise and Caroline was striking and perhaps too obvious. The visits became infrequent. Charlie and Nell had continued to live in London for about another year, and the wrench of separating from Edward was to that extent modified. However the children were clear that it was John who had made them leave London and he was not forgiven.

Charlie and Nell had described to him how rapidly they had gone. It was as though John had erected a dam to his emotions. The longer it held, the greater their weight. The jobs he had taken were humdrum and came to nothing. His quietness became suspicion. He would come home in the afternoon, find that Louise was out, and wait for her, stalking up and down. His anger was unreasoning, his accusations violent. Charlie and Nell listened at the drawing-room door, terrified at the disintegration of these two people who had been put in front of them as parents. Abruptly they had left London for the Kentish Weald.

Edward was recalled to the present by Nell.

'Watch your head,' she said, 'the doorway.'

They passed from the barren glasshouse with its dried-out seed trays by a short lobby separating one house from another and passed instantly into a different world. The temperature was high and the air humid and pungent with the smell of rot. It was a smell both brackish and sweet, the smell of leaf-mould and ferns and decaying wood. Fronds and thick leaves obscured the light. Long, questing roots hung down over the walk from above and were clammy, almost animal. The glass dripped on them, and on the leaves of the plants, making fat splashes.

'Good God,' Edward demanded, 'what's this? This wasn't here before.'

'The tropical house,' said Charlie in the declamatory manner of a professional guide. 'Here you may see specimens of plants from many countries of the world, collected by John Kelleway Esquire. The house was designed by his brother William Kelleway, and the hot-beds are heated by steam which is conveyed by pipes buried in the soil before the windows and by hypocausts of Welsh slate beneath the forcing beds themselves. The boiler was stoked today by Charles Kelleway.'

'Dare I ask?'

'You may, sir,' said Charlie.

'What is it for?'

'For meditation.'

'For who to meditate?' Charlie laughed, as it was obvious from his cousin's face that Edward thought it might be he. Nell had turned to Edward as well, and the two regarded Edward with stagey raised eyebrows. They looked very much brother and sister.

'You mean that uncle comes here?' asked Edward, sensing they were teasing him. Charlie and Nell nodded in concert. 'But it's soaking wet!'

'He sits under an umbrella,' said Charlie. 'It is his private rain forest.' They were looking at Edward, trying to judge how he was taking this information. They were practised at hiding their embarrassment and had both adopted faces of unnatural gravity. It made Edward want to laugh.

'Well,' he said, 'I suppose he has an interest in tropical species.' It was a vacant remark; he had no idea what to make of it.

'He comes here to escape from Louise,' said Nell. 'His interest in botany is rather second to his interest in the whole effect. Charlie says he meditates; I say he broods. He can indulge himself in self-pity, revert to his days in Burma. I suppose he is slightly mad.'

'Other men build tropical houses. I don't see that it makes him mad to enjoy one. It's very heady and exotic.' Edward was unwilling to see John Kelleway as anything more than melancholy. 'When you get accustomed to the drips, it's an amazing place really. I can see the fascination of all the forms of roots and leaves.' Charlie and Nell said nothing, their silence contradicting this easy, reasoned explanation. All three were now quite wet about the head, and Nell's dress of yellow silk was dark and clinging at her neck and shoulders. They moved on to a clearing in the vegetation, where the glasshouse took a leap upwards to accommodate palms. A clerestory light ran around a square area, and was roofed with a glass lantern. The atmosphere here was much less humid. The floor was paved with York stone and a garden table and seat had been positioned in the shade of one of the trees. The impression of translation to some tropic part was real enough. The palms rustled in the upsurge of warm air venting from the windows, and nodded slightly. A sighing of soft wind could be traced, prosaically, to the gap round a door to the garden. Yet sitting at the wood slat table on the white painted seat, looking into the green tunnel of the board walk, it seemed as though it were a mere clearing; that the jungle was pressing in. Sunlight flickered through the palm leaves and made intricate, ever moving patterns on the floor.

'All it lacks is some monkeys and a parrot or two,' said Charlie, voicing Edward's own thoughts. 'I thought of bringing some birds from London. Indeed, I must! And release them in here. Scarlet macaws.'

'They'll fly out of the windows,' said Nell.

'I'll put mesh up then,' declared Charlie. They still enjoy their bickering and nonsense, thought Edward. In that respect they are very young. Something in them has never flowered and grown as it should. They act out a childhood that they were denied, and I suppose that I am an essential part of it. Otherwise, what am I doing here? He wondered whether he encouraged it or whether the reality of his maturity would inhibit them.

They had fallen into a reverie. Nell, seated on the bench, was really very beautiful. Edward wondered what would become of her in London. She would be able to make a good marriage, provided the man was not too scrupulous about her parents.

'I think it is the permanence of the plants that father needs,' said Charlie, who had obviously been pursuing his own thoughts.

'It has only been here a year,' replied Edward, lost.

'Yes, but you can't pick them up and move them about. A plant is rooted and sunk in the ground. Louise continually has the furniture on the move. You will see when we have lunch soon. She is always re-arranging the rooms. It makes father furious. He says it is destroying his identity, laying claim to everything for herself, denying the simple right of personal choice.'

'That's being emotional, isn't it?'

'Father is emotional about things like that,' said Nell. 'He gets very angry when his things are moved. He says he cannot feel secure.' She stood up, deliberately ending this critical train. 'But I wanted to talk about London, not about us. Let's go outside, this place makes us gloomy.'

They left the glasshouse. It seemed fresh outside.

'We will go back to the house,' Nell continued, 'lunch must be ready, and I shall have to attend to my hair. Your fine clothes are spotted with water,' she said slyly to Edward. 'Tell us how you make your money.'

'A little bit here, a little bit there, as they say.'

'Don't be evasive. We know it's from the railways.'

'Yes. From our iron roads.'

'But what do you know about railways, Edward Kelleway?' Nell teased.

'I know quite a good deal about them. I know the ones not to touch, which is very important, and I like them. You've never been on a train, have you, Nell?'

'No, I have not, and I'm sure I would be too terrified.'

'Nonsense. A lot of rubbish is talked about the railways. They are very safe. I would sooner travel at sixty miles an hour in a train than at sixteen in a curricle. Fast coaches are much more danger-ous, more flimsy. I shall take you on a train one day. Will you promise me you will come if I ask you?'

'I won't promise, Edward, but I'll try.'

'Father does not approve of railways,' said Charlie, 'but he is thinking of other risks as well. He says that investment is a euphemism, and it is only gambling. He is bound to tackle you.'

'When I get advice from Uncle Henry? And Uncle Henry gets his from Hudson and Stephenson? There's nothing more rock-sure than that! This isn't 1845. Two years have passed since the "mania".'

'You don't have to convince me!' Charlie seemed to have made up his mind with difficulty, for he turned to Edward, very earnest. 'You see, I have been dabbling in it myself.'

'In investment?' Edward was surprised.

'Yes,' Charlie was defensive.

'You have nothing to invest,' stated Nell baldly, 'so how do you manage?'

'You can still pick up a lot of shares for a few pounds,' said Charlie.

'But that's the worst sort of line, Charlie. That's the sort that melts like snow when it gets before a hot parliamentary committee. Then you find the directors have allotted themselves ninety percent of the shares and it's gone on promotion expenses. Why didn't you ask me for advice?'

Charlie kicked about in the gravel path with his boots.

'I was keeping quiet about it, in case father found out. He wouldn't understand and it would only upset him.'

Charlie at that moment seemed like a small boy who has broken something and hidden the pieces. His handsomeness counted against him, because no man of his age had any right in Edward's opinion to look so charming and gauche. His face was bland, without life's marks. It was unfair of him, Edward knew, because it was as much Charlie's complexion and skin type as cherubic preservation that enhanced that blandness.

'You must let me look at these lines of yours,' he said. 'What are they?' They had stopped walking now, and Nell, infected by Edward's anxiety, had taken Charlie's arm as though to restrain him from any other foolishness, and was looking him in the face. Like mother to child, Edward thought unkindly. Charlie had discovered a dandelion in the path, and hacked at it with his heel. Edward wondered if Charlie would refuse to answer, but anxiety overcame reluctance.

'The Dorchester and Weymouth, and British and Irish Union. Isle of Jersey Railway and Pier. Some others, with canal companies. I can't remember all the details.' Charlie laughed. It was a nervous snort. 'I'm a director of two lines, one of them an atmospheric. I don't believe there's any future in atmospheric railways, do you? They seem to have failed.'

'They *have* failed.'

'But they might still improve them. The idea isn't dead.'

Edward was not disposed to argue, so held his tongue. From what he knew, atmospheric railways were as successful as a square wheel. Charlie was angered by the silence.

'Devil take it, Edward, I don't need criticism, I need advice. Another time? Not here in the garden.' He kicked a snail down the path. It smacked against the edging tiles, oozing bubbles. Nell cried out.

'Charlie! Look at it!'

Charlie shrugged, caught Edward's disapproving eye, and, moving over quickly, crushed it.

'Don't be so tender-hearted,' he said to Nell, 'it's only a snail. Good Lord! You'd think I was a murderer.'

They returned to the house without further conversation. Edward had already had a surfeit of surprises.

The dining-room had been rearranged. He saw that immediately, because the long case clock with its lazy tick was against the left-hand wall, and the sideboard at the far end of the table. They looked in to see what progress was being made. Edward was relieved to see that meats and silver dishes had already been set out. Wine was on the table. Louise must have been watching them enter the house, for she appeared on the stairs as they were speculating.

'Edward, it's so good to see you! So elegant, I see, and so hungry.' She embraced him warmly, and Edward was immediately aware of her in a physical way. She was perfumed and dressed for him, quite obviously. Edward was uneasy about this deliberate attention, knowing John would be resentful, watching everything. Her embrace had been too warm for the convention of an aunt, a soft pressing of her body to him, oblivious of age or kinship. It was how Louise felt and therefore behaved. 'You arrived early. Destroying your horse, I hear!' Edward was sure that John must be hovering nearby. He wished she would talk with less open admiration in her voice.

'Hardly destroying it. The poor jade had to be nursed.'

'I don't believe you, Edward.' Again the tone was too warm and contained no reproof.

Louise was dressed rather out of fashion. Edward judged the style to be ten years behind the vogue, but that, in the country, was nothing. Her day dress was of excellent fine wool trimmed with satin in pearl grey. The neck was rather more 'V'-shaped than it should currently be. She wore a choker of jet that was no more black or glossy than her hair.

Louise stood back from Edward, much as Charlie had done. It seemed to be a characteristic, this eager examination of the outward man. Edward was embarrassed by it, but he could take no offence for her eyes were admiring, not critical, and avid for detail. He felt he had to stand in a pose.

'There. I am statuary. A fashion plate. Do I pass?'

'I hardly have a chance to see anyone who is properly dressed. You have to forgive our rustic ways.'

'Rustic ways are not so quaint they need forgiveness,' said John, curtly interrupting. He had entered the hall from the back of the house, and whatever he felt about the scene, he showed nothing on his face. 'City ways are more artificial to my mind.'

Louise pulled a wry face at Edward, careful that it should not be seen.

'Edward must be hungry. We should dine.' Her tone was matter-of-fact.

'Indeed we shall. I have been waiting for them to come back from their walk. Everything is ready.' John was equally unemotional, his tone flat. It made Edward's heart sink.

The food was good, but the wine sparingly poured. Because of their uneven numbers, Edward found himself on one side of the

48

table, facing Charlie and Nell, while John and Louise sat at each end. He felt very exposed.

Louise had questioned him unceasingly about London, about friends and relations, about amusements, events, fashion, the theatre. Edward had had to plead to be allowed to eat or he should not have the strength to answer. These topics did not please John, who had more than once tried to ask direct questions about Edward's occupation.

'How is Caroline?' Louise asked. 'The house in Highgate must be very empty when you are away. I have often thought that I should visit her. It has been years. We should all visit her. I liked that house.'

'She is very well and quite her independent self.' Edward tried to avoid the obvious reminder, seeing John frown.

'Charlie and Nell would like to see it again, I'm sure. Can you remember it, Nell? You left it when you were very young. You should remember the raspberries. You gorged yourselves on them every year. Caroline told me. I remember, when I first saw you, I arrived unexpectedly. We crawled up that long hill in a carriage – the horse had to stop to drink, half-way up – and when I arrived you were called in from the garden. You were both wounded with juice. Scarlet!'

'I was also there,' said John. Louise ignored his words.

'It would be lovely if we could go back. Country life can be very dull. Nell sees no society except our mud-caked squires and the vicar. We need a railway here. Could you not arrange a branch line, perhaps on the far side of the church, to whisk us all out of here?'

Edward smiled, non-committally. He knew John had seen his opening, for he clashed his knife and fork down on his plate.

'In the countryside there was peace before the coming of the railways. If they ever attempt to run a line through here, I shall fight it.'

Edward had heard so many men say the same thing that the phrase was a common place. He had not, however, heard other men say it with quite the same intensity of emotion.

'The railways have brought many benefits to the country-people,' Edward said reasonably. 'They have allowed produce to find easy routes to market, to achieve better prices and to eliminate the stranglehold of carriers and local merchants and millers. Cattle arrive in prime condition, milk is available in cities that has been poured from the pail only hours before.'

'Railways introduce to simple people all the lusts of the towns. The landowners reap all the benefits. I have never seen such cupidity.'

49

Edward thought it prudent to say nothing. John's tone was not reasonable. It smacked of the pulpit. He was cast in the role of the sinner.

'You play with these things,' John accused, 'and you make a great deal of money out of them, it seems. I cannot see, sir, that it is a moral way to make your living. Half these lines that are floated are mere frauds. There is no intention to build anything. The money of ordinary, simple people is scooped up and the lines disintegrate. Directors have a magical quality of invisibility.'

'I know you feel strongly about it,' said Edward, making one last attempt to be pacific, 'but it is far from true that it is the poor and simple people that get scooped up, as you put it, in these things. Those that speculate are quite as unscrupulous as those that skin them. You can't feel much sympathy for the ticket porter who is down for ten thousand shares on an income of a few shillings a week, or for the man with a writ against him who subscribes for the same. They have no intention of paying. In any case, all that is becoming a thing of the past.'

'I feel sympathy for any creature who has temptations of this scale put in his way. I have travelled, sir, as you know, and seen temptations and I think I know them for what they are.' Edward glanced at Louise. She was white and still. We are in the eye of the hurricane, he thought. No matter in what direction we move, we are in trouble.

'Here, in this little corner of Kent,' John continued, 'we do not have these temptations, do we, Louise?' He paused, looking at her steadily. 'We do not have these London things, and in our northern climate we do not have equatorial passions. We are the better for it. Instead we have peace. Peace of mind.'

'And that is why I am not allowed to go to London, and am kept here a prisoner,' said Louise suddenly. Her voice was as scornful as John's had been pointed and sanctimonious. She looked angry. It was the first time since Edward's arrival that she had addressed her husband directly.

'These temptations that you talk about must surely be irresistible to you if you dare not expose yourself to them. What sort of strength is it that's never tested? The devil won't come and sit on your shoulder in your greenhouse!'

'You get plenty of water, though,' said Charlie foolishly, starting to laugh.

'How do you know what devils sit on my shoulder in the greenhouse!' John shouted. He jumped to his feet in anguish. The remark was so incomprehensible to Edward that he stared openly. Charlie and Nell froze.

'My temptations are behind me but my guilt remains with me.

50

Can you say that of yourself, Louise? Your guilt is behind you, but your temptations – I don't know where your temptations are.'

'That's true. You don't!'

'Don't answer me like that!' John was suddenly plaintive. Edward found the scene deeply embarrassing. He accidentally caught Nell's eye, but she avoided him, blushing. Her hands gripped her knife and fork as a prisoner grips his iron bars.

'If you want to be drawn to London, like a fragment to a magnet, I can't stop you. I thought we had a sort of peace here, but there is no peace on earth, apparently. You have made my life impossible with your shifting and changing. Nothing is mine. If I lay down a book, you close it. If I hang my stick in the hall, you move it. I don't exist in this house. I sometimes wonder if I exist for you at all. You are washing away the ground beneath me and you will bring me down, roof, walls and chimneys.' He walked quickly to the door. 'Talk about the things you want to,' he ended, dismissively, 'but I won't listen.'

He walked out, diminished in stature, seeming shrunken into himself, unable to cope, escaping rather than fighting. Edward suddenly identified it as a characteristic, realising he had been slow. He glanced at Louise in the silence that followed the bang of the door.

Her skin was noticeably dark in the severe midday light, her hair shiny as split coal. She did not seem dismayed, as Edward expected, at John's behaviour. Rather, there was the trace of some other emotion. It could be triumph, he thought. There was the merest hint of a smile in her lips, a blemish that suggested cruelty. Medusa, he thought, or La Gioconda which he had never seen but which he imagined to be very like Louise. Beautiful and vulpine. But Medusa had started as a Gorgon and had been transfigured by the artists of centuries into a beautiful form. Louise's hair had a strong snake-like quality.

'Well, Edward?' She was looking at him quizzically. He had been staring at her. 'I'm sorry you've been exposed to this.'

'He's not always like that,' added Charlie fatuously.

'I think I upset him,' said Edward. 'He doesn't like me coming here. He doesn't like the way I dress. I seem to be a carrier of the disease of disquiet. I think I should leave.'

'No.' Louise, Charlie and Nell had all spoken together.

Three

The two huge mansions that stood on each side of Albert Gate were popularly dubbed 'Scylla and Charybdis', because of their lowering aspect and to the danger of negotiating the narrow way between them. They were of a simplified Classical style, which meant that their proportions and ornament were debased. Essentially flat-faced, with cornices and pediments as mere lines of stucco, the pair had been built by Sir William Cubitt as a speculative development. 'Scylla' was pointed out to visitors as they rode round Hyde Park as the largest private house in London, and, it was added, if the company considered themselves to belong to society, the most vulgar. A popular palace, built only five years before, raw, suburban, clinging to the edge of London. Beyond, there was nothing until the village of Kensington. It seemed blessedly appropriate that Hudson should live in such a seven-storey pile. It was as new as the man himself, and without style. Yet these same critics were happy to attend Mr Hudson's numerous entertainments. That, they said, was business. They said that Almack's Venetian Oligarchy went all to smash when Albert Gate issued invitations. The Railway Despot was not given to the social caprices of the Lady Patronesses of that tyrannical institution. Almack's refused to admit the Duke of Wellington at the height of his glory, because he arrived later than the appointed hour. Outside Albert Gate, ducal carriages vied for parking places beside the Park railings. Peers, judges, barristers, bankers, bishops, ministers and generals all seemed to find that the value of their stock might be enhanced by social intercourse with the Midas of the age.

The view from the building was splendid, for anyone who had eyes to see. The impression was entirely rural. Only the numbers of riders and carriages taking the air betrayed the presence of the city.

At night the Park receded to become a black and unknown hinterland. The houses and the Carriage Road became unified with the city by rows of gas-lights. Ancient plane trees nodded and swayed, the seed clusters of last season weighing down the petioles of the leaves and making a multitude of shadows. It was not yet dark, but that quivering moment of dusk that hesitates between day and night as though it has a choice.

The house was alight from steps to eaves with the yellow glow of gas mantels. The bare pile was relieved at ground level by a stucco porch of undistinguished proportions in front of which carriages were stopping in a continuous succession. Flunkeys were busy, anxious to hurry guests without seeming to do so, anxious to calm the more impatient guests who were peering from their carriage windows and scowling at the delay. Carriages approaching from the wrong direction were directed to join the queue, and their occupants were affronted, but only with the flunkeys. Music could already be heard from the drawing room on the first floor. A ball at Albert Gate could compete with Carlton Terrace. If the conversation within the ducal carriages was uncomplimentary in the streets of Mayfair, it ceased abruptly at Albert Gate, and became fawning compliments within. Gold conquers all.

Within, Hudson had had the building decorated and furnished to his taste. He was a man accustomed to new bricks and mortar. It seemed in all respects suitable to him. He had no time for the discomforts and inconveniences of ancient piles with ancient families camping in them in conditions of bone-cracking damp. He would have no ancient kitchens and primitive drainage. He was fond of saying that every one of his stations had better appointments than the so-called stately homes and that he would sooner spend a night in a station any day and had frequently done so.

It was an expression of his intention to live in his own way in his own age, and not to bend to the pressures that would set him up in the style of a latter-day duke. It was an aspect of Hudson that Henry admired, although he could easily tire of hearing about it.

There was no emphasis on antiquity in the furnishings or fittings. Everything was of the best quality and of modern style. The carpets were English, the silk curtains, chairs, cabinets, glass, silver were all of English manufacture. Hudson took a special pride in light fittings. Great glass globes predominated, singly or piled in multiple pyramids like cannon balls in a battery. The furniture was sparse so that the house always appeared as if it had been cleared for the occasion. The huge main staircase was angular, a straight flight of white marble with one sharp right-angle bend. Nothing was curvilinear or swept, as though Hudson had deliberately chosen to reject the natural curves dictated by the railways which had paid for it all, to reject their rapid motion for the clumsy pace of humans. There was a predominance of square columns and pilasters.

Henry and Jane were hemmed in by the crush that surrounded Hudson.

He was dressed as befitted a king in a royal blue tail coat with white trousers and pale blue silk waistcoat. He was the centre of all conversation, the sun of this system around which other planetary movements rotated with Keplerian precision.

Henry had been trying to edge away. He had heard so much of this conversation before. It had turned upon the Midland line, Hudson's favourite and greatest, and the man was glorying in facts and figures. Ostensibly the conversation was at the elevated level of ideals and the great future of the nation, but all the time these noble stock-holders edged in like whippets to seize some fact as though it were a chunk of meat. They probed and intruded and thought themselves clever but Hudson gave nothing away that they could not have read in the *Railway Times*.

Henry allowed himself to be displaced by them, knowing that Hudson kept an omnipresent eye on his subordinates. He had no illusions that he was a colleague, although Hudson used that definition freely. Hudson had no colleagues except George Stephenson. Stephenson had turned up for the ball, making one of his rare appearances, and stood near Hudson, saying little except when asked a direct question. He looked worn and old, Henry thought. He had greeted Henry with warmth, but whether there was pleasure in it, or relief at finding someone he knew who would ask no damned-fool questions, Henry was not sure. Stephenson was dressed as always in a black coat that seemed a decade out of fashion, and sported the bunch of seals on his watch ribbon. When Henry eased away, Stephenson followed suit, answering some technical question on power-to-weight ratio to a small man with a beard who, from his blank look, had evidently not asked the question.

'It is a law of nature,' Hudson was saying like a prophet warming to his theme, 'that when a railway crosses a farm it must cut up the fields, and it appears to be a law of nature that it cuts the fields from the farmhouse at precisely that point at which it is most important it should not be cut off!' There was laughter. Henry could see that it discomfited some of the landowners that surrounded Hudson. Hudson appeared oblivious but Henry knew he was perfectly aware.

'We have had one experience with a landed gentleman – who is not amongst us tonight – who objected so forcibly to a line passing five miles from his house that the Board was compelled to vote him compensation of £100,000 in order to cure his eyesight. The gentleman then invested funds in the line, hoping no doubt to stand with both hands outstretched and have them filled by the directors. Meanwhile, we had surveyed the route again as it seemed an expensive way of achieving a straight line between two points and we found a new route that avoided the gentleman altogether. When this worthy fellow, now a stockholder, heard the matter put to the Board, his objections to us avoiding him were most forceful and he suggested that compensation should now be paid because he lacked the amenity of a railway!'

Hudson looked solemnly round as though he had made a profound point with his parable.

Henry steered Jane clear of the immediate throng. Her arm felt cool in his hand. It was a memory of sensations of the past that had become abstract and no longer part of her. A woman's arm, soft and cool. A woman's flesh. He felt a pang of hatred for himself and his fickle emotions which led him to make a distinction between a woman and a wife. For a fleeting moment he had been able to encapsulate the two and realise that the whole was greater than its parts, but then it all fell away again.

'Mr Kelleway, permit me to say your wife is looking charming this evening. Can I coom wi' you?' Stephenson twinkled at Jane. He always had an eye for the ladies, Henry knew. The contrast between his compliment and the broad Northumbrian request, which was almost plaintive, was immediately touching.

'We should be delighted, Mr Stephenson,' said Jane.

'Can she take my arm, Kelleway? I'm an old man and they won't think it amiss!' Henry inclined his head. Stephenson was so much the puritan gentleman that the idea of anyone taking it amiss was laughable. He was puzzled, however, by Stephenson's renewed cordiality.

'Mr Hudson needs no support from me, Mrs Kelleway. To tell you the truth, I need to sit down.'

They moved outward to a row of seats against the wall. At the far end of the room on a dais covered with baize the string orchestra was playing. They could be heard only at the edges of the crush. The dancing would open shortly, if Hudson could disengage himself. Stephenson nodded towards the musicians, who sat on spindly chairs.

'I prefer a brass band myself. It would make itself heard better, too. I find I spend a great deal o' time escaping at these dances, Mrs Kelleway, for men coom here wi' the sole intention o' cornering you and quizzing you about dividends and half-yearly statements and capital appreciation and its twin, capital depreciation. I know nothing about bits of paper, I say, except they have plans on them.' They sat down. Jane had not wanted to come but could not refuse. Both Elizabeth and Frederick had driven with them in the carriage, although she had lost sight of them now. She could not have borne the waiting alone in the house for Henry to come home with the uncertainty of his behaviour when he did

55

return. Here, she could at least stay in contact with his mood, and she found there was still warmth. When he attended events alone he seemed always to return impatient and intolerant. She could not understand why, or what the stresses were.

Stephenson seemed very inclined to talk and Henry, knowing the man, was sure he was working round to something in his own good time.

'These affairs must be very boring for the ladies,' Stephenson observed. 'The talk is all the same and all business. It is only thinly disguised as a social occasion.'

Jane smiled a social smile, in return. 'It allows the wives to find out in some degree what their husbands are doing.'

'Do you take an interest in railways, Mrs Kelleway?'

'I try to. I cannot grasp the technical matters but I like to know what lines are projected from where to where. I can see a day when roads will be a thing of the past. At least, main roads.'

'Aye, the stage coach will disappear, and the carrier's wain and the farmer's wagon and the private carriage. It may seem strange from a man dedicated to steam engines, but I always regret the killing of a stage line. I think horses are amongst God's most beautiful creatures. But you watch steam power, Mrs Kelleway. These steam carriages are becoming efficient on the roads. As the roads improve, so do their chances. People forget that the select committee of the Commons reported in favour of steam vehicles in '31. We have done our best to stop them, of course. They will have to fight their own battles.'

Stephenson continued chatting to Jane. He was a great talker. Henry was watching the groups of people.

Mrs Hudson was surrounded by her own satellites. Her accent was as broad as her husband's and she was the object of much malice from those who considered themselves to belong to society.

They dare not assail Hudson, Henry thought, so they ridicule his wife over the scandal-water and bone china of Mayfair houses that are paid for out of the railways. Stories of her gaucheries were legion, few of them were true. It was clever chat to retail the latest invention about her efforts at some French phrase. Her blind spot was to the enemies that surrounded her; the ingratiating young men who wrote slight columns for the journals were the wits who made up the tales.

Wylie and Brancker, powerful Midland men from Liverpool, attracted their own gathering. The attitude of the men was tense. Wylie and Brancker had opposed Hudson in the past and would do so again. They were seen too often in each other's company for Henry's liking. It smacked of conspiracy. They were in disagree-

56

ment with John Ellis, a Leicester man due for the House of Commons, they said, and a strong supporter of Hudson. Heads were shaken, Wylie who was short and stout, was expounding, his large hands waving clumsily. John Ellis, small and dapper with a thin alert face, was listening carefully. Henry caught a general sense of unease. Stephenson's unusual friendliness, the tensions between directors, the oblique manoeuvres at Hitchin, all added up to a disquieting whole. At meetings the tensions broke out in angry wrangles on the floor, and accusations of misuse of money. He remembered Stephenson's obscure remark in Hitchin. 'This clay dusts up badly, it's treacherous material,' Stephenson's hints.

'Things didn't go too well in Hitchin, did they, Mr Kelleway?' said Stephenson unexpectedly to Henry as though he had access to his thoughts. Henry started and was momentarily confused. Jane was watching him with interest. He had lost track of their conversation and she must have been quizzing Stephenson.

'No. There is a lot to sort out there. It was not one of my most brilliant days.' Stephenson's craggy face was pensive, his eyes strayed to Mrs Hudson, avoiding Henry.

'I was saying to your wife that I don't think I shall attend any more meetings. I have enough to look after, what with the collieries and lime-works and my melons. I am a great gardener, Mrs Kelleway. Did your husband tell you that? No, I doubt he didn't.' His attention was back to Jane. Henry was irritated by his habit of tossing in a hint then changing the subject. 'Do you know,' Stephenson went on, stooping toward Jane with enthusiasm, 'I took first prize in all England for grapes at Rotherham. They were such grapes! Not only plump and juicy, but the symmetry! You see, a bunch o' grapes can grow all to one side and they must be encouraged by turning to spread themselves. Aye, some folk may think me mad! The secret is that there's no symmetry in nature without man helps it along. The sun comes and goes, east to west, ripens things one side. Everything has a best side. An apple or a peach is ripe on just one face. But I can improve on that!'

Stephenson stopped, embarrassed by his own intensity and glancing covertly at Jane to find if she had found anything ridiculous in it. On the contrary, Jane understood, and encouraged him.

'I find it all very interesting. My gardening is restricted to the simplest flowers.'

'Flowers are suitable for a lady, but a man likes to get to grips with vegetables. There are some men who perfect blooms and the Dutch do it, but it's not a manly art to my bigoted way of thinking.

It gives me as much pleasure now to perfect a vegetable as it used to getting a new steam valve just right.'

Henry, totally indifferent to any aspect of horticulture, felt that the conversation had become slightly ludicrous. Around them, the groups of men were tending to disperse and go back to their wives. There was much wealth in evidence, an emphasis on clothes and jewels. Perhaps it was all rather vulgar, but it suited Hudson's house, which was after all an immature building, lacking the patina of age. He felt this talk of apples and vegetables was tactlessly out of place. Stephenson had moved on to leeks and cucumbers and his voice carried to those who passed.

'Any way,' he concluded, 'I don't like coming to London any more. The place is full of new engineers, young lads wi' down on their faces who don't know me, and I don't know them. I'm too old in this business. I suppose they know their job, but even the job's not the same. We had to invent things as we went along. Now it's improvements, very essential, but not the same. Take that Braxton fellow the other day. I have never seen him before, I know nothing about him and I didn't take to him. I have never felt like that about a plant, or an animal!' He got stiffly to his feet. Mr and Mrs Hudson had advanced together, to the centre of the floor, seeming to shake off a few adhering followers. The string orchestra seized its moment and dashed in bravely. Dancing had begun.

Henry knew that he should take the floor. It was expected of him as one of Hudson's known intimates. The knowledge was mother of his recusancy. Jane was looking at him expectantly, with, it seemed to him, some pleasure. He damned Hudson, blaming him for creating the situation. He could not catch Jane's eye and he cursed himself for being so vulnerable.

Jane saw too easily that Henry was going to ignore her, not just on this occasion but possibly through the evening. She wanted desperately to go home, and to be alone with her emotions. She was not sure that she felt sorrow, although it might manifest itself as tears. There was an admixture of rage and contempt that Henry could hurt her so casually.

George Stephenson bowed to her, a slight tilt, stiff with age. His eyes were kindly. His heels were together and he proffered one arm. To Jane it seemed protective, like the wing of a bird.

'Mrs Kelleway, I should be delighted to take a turn around the floor. Will you accompany me?' The arm was extended. Jane took it like a life-line. She was furious to see Henry nod and smile as though he were her husband and cared.

When Braxton, who had waited for Stephenson's departure, spoke, Henry jumped slightly. His thoughts were far away; he was thinking of his Kate and of other women there had been and concluded that he had a need to hurt, or at least that it was inescapably part of his life. The look he gave Braxton was one of pure annoyance. The man had blundered into his private sanctum again.

'Good evening.'

'Good evening.' Henry was only just civil. Braxton was not put off.

'This is a very fine affair. Very lavish.'

'Yes, I suppose it is.' Henry had not really taken it in. He had been to many of Hudson's receptions, and this was by no means the most extravagant. It in no way rivalled Hudson's previous Christmas banquet in York where he had dined five hundred in the Guildhall, entering in a regal procession to fanfares of trumpets. A banquet where roast peacock had been served, as he remembered, with the feathers put back. They had looked extremely ruffled and their eyes had been replaced with holly berries.

'There are some fine pieces of silver.'

'They are certainly large.'

'Some of them are very expensive. The big one over there, the candelabrum, cost seven hundred pounds.'

Henry wondered why he should be plagued like this. Braxton's taste was not even of passing interest to him. The cost of the vulgar objects seemed absurd. He watched Stephenson dancing with Jane. They were talking. If he had danced, he might have avoided Braxton.

'I really came over to talk to you about Hitchin,' Braxton was saying. He leaned his whiskery face close to Henry in a conspiratorial manner. Henry moved away, rudely.

'What about Hitchin? Surely we can talk about it aloud?'

'Certainly.' Braxton flushed. He looked very hot and uncomfortable. His coat was of heavy material, unsuitable for the mild evening, and he must have been suffering. Henry got satisfaction from it. 'I have had the pleasure of a few words with Mr Hudson. He wants something done, and he asked me to convey it to you as soon as I saw you.'

'I see.' This piece of rudeness from Hudson was to be punishment for the Hitchin meeting. 'What has Mr Hudson suggested? I shall speak to him later on, and he can tell me ...'

'I feel I ought to deliver my message, Mr Kelleway. Mr Hudson was most concerned.'

Henry knew he would have to listen. He was Hudson's slave and was afraid of his financial position. He was surprised that he could be so lucid when his temper urged him to turn his back on Braxton and walk away. There was no point in precipitating things, because he would certainly be the loser. Hudson could call on him for upwards of a hundred thousand pounds and he had no means of paying. It would be perfectly legitimate to make such a call. He had seen so many bankrupts, had listened to their stories and heard their cries. They were left limp, bone-broken and mindless. He must avoid that at all costs.

'Very well.' Henry affected to gaze at the dancers. The string orchestra waltzed on and on. Henry did not like Strauss.

'Mr Hudson asks you to go to Hitchin with as much speed as possible, letting everything else take second place. I am to accompany you and we are to secure a route for this link between the Midland and Eastern Counties and survey it. We are to deal with Woolmer and his like, and do it quickly.'

'Woolmer won't be dealt with. Not unless he has a change of heart.'

'Then he must have that change of heart.'

Henry looked at Braxton coolly, intending to wither the man with a look and mentally damning his impertinence. He was surprised that Braxton stared back at him with hesitant rudeness, as though practising. It was a change since the Hitchin encounter and must mean that Braxton had somehow ingratiated himself with Hudson, and felt himself secure. Henry, ever conscious of the outward appearance of things, realised that they must look like two challenging hens, their heads on one side. He gave a snort that was not laughter, but mockery.

'How are we to achieve that, Mr Braxton? Appeal to Woolmer's better nature? I would as soon appeal to Judge Jeffreys.'

'We are to buy him. I think we know how to set about that.'

'Do you have to be so crude, Braxton?' Henry was unable to control his anger any more. His tone was contemptuous.

'Call it anything you like, sir, but that's the sum of it. I know you lawyers like to wrap things up in pretty paper and tie them up nicely. When all's said and done, you buy him.'

Henry could not walk away. Too much depended on it. He must co-operate with this man, and swallow his definitions. He gave a slight inclination of the head.

'Call it what you will, sir. I shall do my business my way, you do yours in your way. You must have all the plans prepared and a complete survey of the route?' Braxton nodded. 'Good. Then have a set sent to my chambers tomorrow so that I can examine what we're dealing with, together with a list of landowners and interested parties.'

'Of course.' Braxton hovered for a long time in silence beside Henry. Henry was not going to release him by making his farewells. He let the man stand and suffer.

Edward was obliged to agree that Charlie had been entirely right. The country girls were so essentially healthy that blushes rushed and roared about their cheeks in a storm. Their blood seemed to be over-laden with red juices that threatened to burst from hectic faces.

'Don't they terrify you?' said Charlie with delight. 'They are so avid, so trembling, so completely unpredictable. Sophistication is a bore! I feel like a lion tamer, don't you? One approaches them not so much for the pleasure of it as to test one's steadiness!'

'You must not talk like that!' protested Nell. 'You are unkind and uncharitable. They are ordinary local girls, and are probably much nicer and more worthy than London ladies. Men always judge things at the most shallow level.'

'Listen to their accents,' continued Charlie, provocatively ignoring his sister. 'They are broadest Kent and almost impossible to understand, so you must ask them everything twice and can't understand the answer and they *ignite* with embarrassment!'

'I think you are horrible!' said Nell.

'And when they dance! You will be laid up for days and ache in every limb. Above all, they are vigorous!'

'That really is enough, Charlie,' said Louise, who had listened indulgently. 'Some of them are both pretty and elegant. I don't feel that I am so dressed in the vogue that I can criticise, and I don't know that you cut such a dash that you can be complacent.'

'Not like Edward, you mean.' Charlie gave Edward a studied glance, holding his head back and on one side as though viewing a painting. 'I think Edward is over-dressed for the occasion, and that is bad manners.'

'I'm sure the ladies won't think so.'

Edward had been thinking how beautiful Louise looked, and as she spoke she turned and caught his eye. Both of them were embarrassed. He had complimented her too warmly on her dress, and too often. Louise was flattered and disconcerted. John had disappeared early in the evening in his agricultural clothes, presumably to work or just sit in the glasshouse. Charlie and Nell were to a degree wrapped up in their own dressing and exchange of banter, and Edward had assumed the rôle of leading man. He had taken control of her clothes and her hair, advised on simple jewellery and all the time presumed in a way that had begun as playful and delightful, but had later taken the character of concealed passion. To have a handsome young man dancing attendance was an unknown delight that Louise could not deny herself. Nor could she ignore Edward's obvious admiration. They were not advances, she told herself, but the kind of foolish gallantries of which she had read but always been starved. She knew that this

61

was a half-truth and that gallantries are only an awkward prelimi-
nary, a testing of responses. She was not very sure how she had
responded or how Edward had seen her response.

They stood just inside the doorway of a large drawing-room that
was noisy with music and chatter. The carpet had been rolled up
and taken away, leaving behind its shadow, where the sun-
bleached boards met those that had been concealed. The floor had
been waxed to a state of treachery, to the delight of the young
ladies, who had to be caught and supported. The furnishings had
gone the way of the carpet, and left their silhouettes on the
wallpaper. Chairs had been hired. They were all alike and uncomfortable and had a temporary look like soldiers on a parade
ground.

One wall of the room was made up of three french windows that
had been opened to allow some ventilation, and these gave onto
a small paved terrace and the garden. It was not at all grand,
Edward thought, but had been managed with care and thought. It
was clear that everyone had come to enjoy themselves.

'We shall have to wait until the end of this dance to meet our
host, Mr Crisp,' Louise observed, 'I can see him over there,
dancing.'

'That's country manners,' said Charles.

'Edward doesn't sneer at rustics as much as you,' said Nell.
'Perhaps you have country manners too!'

Edward found their bickering annoying. Louise had taken his
arm lightly while they watched the dancers and he felt distant from
them as he felt close to Louise. It was refreshingly unrefined, he
thought. Everything in London is adulterated or added to in some
way. The bread is partly chalk, and so is the milk. The complexions
of women are red oxide of metal. To less sympathetic eyes, some
of it might have seemed absurd. Stout ladies were tied up too
tightly and their feet crammed into shoes that were too small. Stout
men puffed about the floor with a countyman's unawareness of
others. Collisions were frequent, but were treated as part of the
occasion, not to be missed. The men wore serviceable tail coats
and trousers, but few of them fitted properly; it was the girls who
stole the show. They were turned out in shot silk and challis with
piped and lace collars, and must have spent frantic weeks with the
fashion magazines. As they passed Edward, eyes were raised
briefly, then dived away again. They missed nothing. Edward had
to suppress a smile.

'You will break their hearts, Edward,' said Louise. 'I hope you
won't flirt with them too much.' Edward looked at her, but Louise
was still staring at the dancers. He knew it was a suggestion, and
wanted to protest that he would dance with Louise. As though

reading his thoughts, she released his arm. The music stopped and the floor cleared slowly. Edward had time to become resentful. Louise advanced on to the floor towards Mr Crisp who detached himself from a small group to greet her. Edward noted that he did so almost with alarm, as though he did not wish her to be seen so obviously on the floor. Louise was being stared at. Edward could see the quick exchange of words, the slight turning of backs so that more could be said.

'Mrs Kelleway,' Mr Crisp effused nervously, 'I am so delighted you could come, and Charles and Nell.' He looked enquiringly at Edward.

'This is Mr Edward Kelleway, Mr Crisp, my nephew from London.'

'How do you do, Mr Kelleway.' Crisp shook Edward's hand. A look of undisguised relief showed on his face. 'Are you down here on business, or merely for relaxation?'

'For relaxation, Mr Crisp.'

'London is such a busy place.'

Mr Crisp was a well-built, well-dressed man with rather wavy hair the colour of weathered straw, that hung from his head in an unmanageable hank glistening with pomade. His features were small as though mere pinches of clay raised from a round ball. His nose was so turned up that his nostrils were always visible. Consequently he held his head downwards and as still as possible, as if he were suffering from a stiff neck. This made him seem more oblique than he was.

'Yes, London is a very busy place,' Edward replied, determined to give nothing away just yet. 'This is a fine room you have here, and a good gathering. I am sure I shall enjoy it immensely.'

'We try to make these things a success, Mr Kelleway. It is a refining influence, I think, to get everyone to prepare for such an occasion now and again. It is too easy, in the country, to slip into careless country ways.'

'I shall dance just for the pleasure of it,' said Edward, his annoyance with Louise making him carelessly rude.

'Well, certainly,' said Crisp, trying to sum up this reply. 'Will you permit me to introduce you to my wife and to some acquaintances? We seldom have strangers here. There is a room off the drawing-room set aside for playing cards, for those that wish.'

He was drawing Edward along with him, almost as though he had no wish to bring the others as well. Edward stopped deliberately, and held out his arm for Louise, who took it, holding on quite firmly. Crisp's manners were appalling.

They were taken round the room, to this family and to that family. To the vicar of the overgrown church, and to farmers and the doctor and retired merchants. Crisp's introductions were factual and the responses were polite. Edward saw clearly that the women had erected a social barrier to Louise. They would smile at Edward, exchange a few words and introduce their son or daughter, but to Louise they would merely incline their heads. They never included her within the embrace of conversation but, in the body language of humans, turned their back on her, averting their gaze and their mind. Louise, for her part hardly seemed to notice them, but kept one hand on Edward's arm. Edward felt a growing chill about the occasion. It was far from the rustic fun he had anticipated and that Charlie had described, and more like some ancient pagan ritual. While the women ignored her, the men shot her covert glances. He detected curiosity and lust. Charlie and Nell were treated with something of the same reserve. It was obvious that they had no friends among their local contemporaries. It accounted for their aloofness and their unkindness. He realised with fierce rage for the first time that these country people rejected Louise, Charlie and Nell because of their mixed blood, saw them as mongrels and outcasts. He smiled absently at a genial matron who was suggesting he might wish to meet her daughter, and turned away, taking Louise's arm in a hard grip. The matron tutted at him and told her husband what she thought of such manners.

'Louise, you should have told me,' he said angrily, 'these people treat you terribly. Why did you come here? I would not stand this for a second. I will go home with you now, this instant!'

'Hush. Be quiet!' said Louise.

'I certainly will not!'

'Then dance. Dance first and then talk. Give them nothing more to gossip about. Behave sensibly, like a man. Take my arm and move. They are staring at you.'

Edward started to dance. The band was romping through another waltz with stiff precision rather than flowing grace. Edward would immediately have started to speak again, but Louise caught his eye and gave a slight shake of her head.

'If I can tolerate it, so can you for my sake for one evening.'

'It's monstrous. This would never happen in London.' He would have continued but, looking at Louise, was alarmed to see that she was on the verge of tears. He almost stopped on the spot, but she gripped him tightly and compelled him to continue round the floor.

'I will not give them the satisfaction!' she hissed.

'Are they all like that?'

'No, not all.' The way she replied had such a lilt of tenderness in it that he looked at her very hard. 'You look as though you are trying to see inside my mind.'

'I am sure I should be fascinated. Whom do you exclude? You say it as though there is someone in particular.'

'You are too curious, Edward. You will see shadows when there's no sun. Smile as you dance, and don't look so concerned for my sake. Play my game with me. Pretend it doesn't hurt, because then they will ask me back again. You must see that it is a trial of strength, that they want me to break down and accuse them of ill manners, to dissolve into tears, to go away and exclude myself or commit some unsocial act that will give them reason for shutting me out of their lives. They don't have the courage to do it without a social reason, in case I turn on them. They are afraid of me. The wives are afraid of me because the men are afraid of me, and fear is a great sauce to a man's appetite. Do you understand that?'

'Of course I understand that. You don't have to ask.' Edward knew he had protested too vehemently. He must control his responses, which were youthful to his own ears. 'I can behave sensibly, like a man, as you put it.'

'I'm sorry,' said Louise, 'I didn't mean to be hurtful. I was upset, and thought you might do something to give them that excuse they want.'

All the time, they were being watched. Couples of the older generation were conspicuously absent from the floor.

'Will they stand at the side all evening?' asked Edward.

'No. If we persist in dancing, they will either have to dance or go home. Some will decide to dance shortly, then others will too. They will have made their gesture.'

'Louise, I will dance with you all night!' Edward knew that he was blushing as soon as he made his protest. He cursed himself again for his youthful tongue. Louise smiled at him, kindly. Edward's heart sank, for she was so controlled that he knew none of his passion had touched her.

'Edward, I find you attractive and I owe you a great deal for supporting me in this way. You have been charming to me all evening. You must not delude yourself, however. You are full of hot glances and trembling passions. Don't speak. I can't help but hurt you, but I don't want you, although I know you want me, whether you admit it to yourself or not. I have to be blunt, because we have no time to be otherwise. You must know I don't love John, or want him. What you must know now, is that I have another man. You don't imagine I have been able to make do with that moon's shadow of a thing, which has the form of a man, poorly defined, and none of the substance?'

Edward was silent. His face showed too clearly that he felt

betrayed. He even held Louise further from him, as though to exact some revenge from that rejection. Louise felt sorry for him, but was annoyed by the petty reflex. She drew him closer, would not allow him the indulgence.

'Edward?' Her voice was kind, and she smiled at him, but he felt that these things were only part of a mime. He could not probe behind that mask. That smile, he thought, was as thin as the glaze on porcelain, and as hard. Her kindness hurt. He maintained a formally blank expression, looking through her, avoiding her eyes when she tried to trap him with them, snare and net him into her confidence.

'It was only fair to tell you immediately. Charlie and Nell don't know. They have their suspicions, but I'm not altogether a fool.'

'I don't want to know either!'

'But you do, Edward. Don't you see? You give yourself away by your protests. If I come to London, you mustn't expect things to be different.'

'Do I have to keep dancing?'

'Yes, you have to. For two reasons now. The first as before and the second to show that you are not angry with me and are in charge of yourself so that I don't have to avoid you. You see, some of them are beginning to dance now. I shouldn't be able to stand it if I have to avoid you as well, Edward.'

Edward danced on. His face had an obstinate look that Louise associated with Caroline. She was much more confused than she appeared, but realised that Edward could not see it. For the moment everything was under control. Edward gave an ironic snort.

'I thought this would be rustic fun. Jollity. Begone, dull care!'

This, thought Louise, is the very stuff of rustic fun, with all its open cruelty.

Stephenson had stopped dancing, protesting he was too old and lacking in elegance. He had contrived to end up in the farthest corner of the room, away from the band, away from Hudson and away from Henry. He motioned to Jane to sit on a firm-looking sofa flanked by floral arrangements. She did so out of deference to Stephenson's obvious need. He tucked up his tailcoat in a homely way as though settling by his own fire. In the centre of the floor, Hudson had been joined by Wellington and Lord George Bentinck. To this collection of suns, all minor galaxies were drawn. A collective movement inwards. Stephenson watched unmoved. He saw that Jane, too, was incurious.

'It is like iron filings to a magnet,' he said. 'Aye and just as fickle. When the magnet loses its strength, the filings drop off. Wellington is a great man, don't you think, madam?'

'He is the greatest man of his sort, I think, that there has ever been.' Stephenson looked at her curiously.

'You are careful with words, Mrs Kelleway.'

'Not niggardly, I hope. That would make me dull company.'

'Not at all! I mean "exact". I have done a lot of things in my time but when I compare with the experience of the great Duke, I have hardly learned to cut the top off a hard-boiled egg.' Jane smiled at his figure of speech and Stephenson was quick to note it. 'Well, it's so. Maybe the phrase wasn't elegant. When I was a boy we used to say that a lad couldn't knock the dust out of a coal sack! Or that a man couldn't make a stack of two bricks. Homely expressions.'

Stephenson stopped, watching the swarm of railway bees that had consolidated in the middle of the floor. There was clearly more that he wanted to say and she sensed she must be patient and not prompt him. She was rewarded, for he continued in the same ruminative vein.

'You see I always thought of railways as being for the general good and had little wit to see that there was so much potential for making capital out of them and cleaning the money out of people's pockets. Railways are too precious, if you like, for the future of everyone to have them prejudiced by any one thing or person. Yet, when there is money to be made, railways seem to suck in every person, even those of highest principle.'

'Even the Duke,' said Jane obviously, immediately wishing she had not spoken.

'All sorts of persons,' said Stephenson in a tone that rebuked her. 'Last year there was a lot of criticism. Morrison wanted the State to have control of railways because of the speculative problems and Hudson fought it. Hudson took two stances on new railways as well. He declared himself equally opposed to speculation and stated that as all new lines were speculation he was opposed to them. This, madam, while he controlled a monopoly created by just that speculation. Mr Hudson argued that the existing railways were perfectly able to build any new lines. He advocated all shareholders to withdraw from new lines and put their money and power behind the existing ones, which would be sure and safe. He guaranteed returns, and paid them.'

He paused, looking at Jane anxiously. 'Go on,' she said, 'I get very little chance to find out what is happening. By the time the newspapers have turned it this way and that, it is never clear anyway.'

'You are very patient, Mrs Kelleway, but there is a reason for all this that I shall come to. Last year, taking another aspect, there was an accident at Romford on July 18, when several passengers were killed. It was put down to Mr Hudson cutting his staff to the bone. Then, when Mr Hudson made a formal reply in Parliament on the accident rate on the Eastern Counties line, he fudged the figures, madam, by omitting any reference to injuries to passengers or deaths to staff. In the same way, when challenged on the punctuality of his service, he added up the number of trains that were too early and subtracted that sum from the trains that were too late to provide a figure. These sophistries show cunning but carry no conviction. *The Times* is constantly in pursuit. Lastly, Hudson's lines charge ten to fifteen percent more than any other trunk lines. There is a stage when profit should be spread like butter, evenly.'

'What do you want me to make of this, Mr Stephenson? It is all very alarming.'

'I am confiding in you because I believe your husband can help. He can bring pressure to bear on Hudson. George Hudson has been my friend for very many years, make no mistake, and I have supported him in a hundred schemes because he has the courage and strength of mind to persist when other men get weak knees. But I love railways, not speculation, and when the latter may destroy the former, then something must be done.'

'How can he help?'

'By steering things when he can get near the tiller. It will bring him into opposition with Hudson, but I think Mr Kelleway has the humour and the experience to deal with that. He must do it, however, without allying himself to Hudson's rivals or enemies. Mr Kelleway has no alliances like that, madam. You see, I know that. He must make George Hudson see sense. If he won't, he will go under, and there will be such a crash as no one has seen.'

'You pay my husband a big compliment.'

'The world is always short of honest men. Mr Kelleway is, I think, an honest man. I pay you my compliments, madam. Now we must get up and walk about a bit or they will suspect me of intrigue. You must visit my estate, madam, and I will show you my gardens. You shall eat pineapples and melons that you have never tasted before.'

'We must rejoin my daughter and my son. They are over there.'

Stephenson looked abashed.

'Forgive me. I didn't know they were here.'

'Not at all. This has been most important.'

Stephenson took Jane's arm and they walked back, round the

edges of the room, avoiding the excited court that surrounded King Hudson.

'My daughter is Elizabeth, just eighteen, and Frederick is nineteen and bound straight for the Bar, like his father.'

'Your daughter is beautiful, Mrs Kelleway.'

'Hush! Don't let her hear you say so, she knows it well enough already.'

'The lassies generally do, and it becomes them well!' All trace of his former gravity had gone. 'I shall have two pretty ladies to hold me up now!'

Henry stood with the small group of railway men that Hudson permitted near him. Their function was to confirm his repeated questions of 'Is that not so, gentlemen?', by nods and murmurs and convincing support.

Hudson was in his element. His stance was the one he adopted at a Board Meeting. He stood square upon his feet, his bulk thrust out before him and one thumb hooked in his trousers pocket. In front of him a small space was clear as though to receive the wisdom that would fall as cash from his lips. Peers, bishops, authors, painters, physicians, scientists and statesmen all jostled for position. He excluded some from his immediate vicinity, simply by asking the crowd to make way for his favourites in his strong Yorkshire accent. Those rejected hung about the edge of the magic circle. They could not afford to take offence, but annoyed those in front of them by asking what the great man had said and were shushed or treated more rudely. It was a thoroughly Roman crowd, Henry considered, for such allegedly distinguished men. They had come to hear something of advantage, and meant to get it. He wondered why the railways had proved such a fatal attraction to such an assortment of men. The great Duke, for instance, universally admired, stood by Lord George Bentinck and the Duke of Leeds, nodding sagely as Hudson expounded. That supreme strategist was prepared to listen to the linen-draper's plan of action and entrust him with his money. Was it possible to deceive the Duke? Did the Duke sense that by investing in railways he could turn his already considerable fortune to profit yet feel it was being put to patriotic use at the same time? Or did he simply not care, treating the railways as he had treated India, as an opportunity for financial advancement. It was a puzzle. On the other side of Hudson, the Archbishop of York who had a strong predilection for the Midland line, was writing minutely small notes in a gilt-edged pocket book. It was all very unedifying to Henry in his present sour mood. Nor was he helped by the knowledge that he in particular must listen as closely as any man there, in case Hudson should let slip anything that might contain Henry's own ruin.

Hudson was continuing on the now familiar theme of the route into Hitchin for the Eastern Counties and Midland lines, trying to whip up support on the one hand and encourage outrage against the Great Northern on the other. Henry was very bored by it all. The same questions, the same answers, the same worries over yields and debentures. He suddenly thought of a plan of escape from Hudson, from the ball, and from Jane. For a few hours, a few illicit hours. He could get away to Kate. He would tell Jane, or better still tell Frederick to tell Jane, that Hudson required to detain him on business, and that Frederick had better take their party home. It was a half-truth, he told himself, because he could hardly absent himself at the moment and he knew Jane would be glad to leave. He looked quickly towards her. Did he feel guilt? She was still engaged in conversation with Stephenson. He felt excitement, not guilt, he decided, and was annoyed with himself for asking the question. He was no green youth, concerned with matters of guilt. Things are what they are. It is my damnation, he thought, that as an adult I have never been able to cast off these quick guilts, these blushes of shame over things about which I feel no shame. It is like a weakness of the bladder. Of no importance but humiliating.

Frederick, bored by the ball, bored by Stephenson's homely conversation on the vegetable kingdom and bored above all by railways, had removed himself and was circulating round the room in a lazy fashion, pretending to examine Hudson's various pieces of silver plate. Henry recognised himself as a young man in the very way Frederick walked. Like Henry, Frederick was intolerant of things that did not interest him and arrogant towards human failure. Frederick also resembled him in features. Henry, aware of the irony of the situation, compared Frederick's face with that of the Duke. As a young man, Henry had been proud of his own similarity to the nation's hero, had cultivated it to a degree. Frederick had inherited the same hawkish face and had the same rather terse manner.

It seemed a long way, in both time and temper, since his own youth as Henry made this comparison. Here he stood beside the man he had aped, puzzling over the reason for the great man's presence and planning his own escape. What was the great divide between the military and the civilian mind? Did they both require single-minded selfish persistence, and was that what drew Hudson and Wellington together? He must get away. Frederick was nearby, and the desire had become a nagging refrain. The other agitated worries only buzzed in his head because he was impatient.

The sight of Braxton's face was the deciding factor. Quite suddenly, he was relieved of the need of a protracted retreat by Hudson moving on. He was able to drop back to the fringe and then make his way out.

Frederick was rocking on his heels with his hands behind his back as though testing the weight of the floor. His back was to Henry, and he jumped when spoken to.

'Bored, Frederick?'

He turned, looking slightly annoyed, then laughed. Both reactions were characteristic, thought Henry. Too volatile.

'You caught me deep in contemplation of nothing,' said Frederick, 'Have you finished at Court?' Henry was annoyed now, but restrained himself, knowing very well that Frederick meant to provoke. He detested railways and railway speculators and particularly King Hudson.

'No, I have not finished at Court. I came over here to have a word with you about going home and taking your mother and sister back. I know this business is infinitely boring to you, as you so often put it, but why haven't you danced?'

'I did dance once or twice. Beautiful swans. But even the daughters of speculators have nothing else to do but speculate. Within a minute they want to know your capital, shareholding and annual yield!'

'That's unfair.'

'Is it? They've all asked me what lines I have shares in, and then enquired kindly after my father ... "not *the* Henry Kelleway?" ... "and has he found any particular line to his favour recently?" All the time that we dance, they gaze at me with their china-blue eyes, bosoms heaving and minds racing! Good Lord, what sort of race of female Inquisitors have we got here?'

'I have only broken away for a moment,' said Henry impatiently. 'Can you please tell your mother that I must work late with Hudson and Lowther and the Liverpool men, and will you please escort her home with your sister. Will you please give my apologies.'

Frederick looked at Henry thoughtfully, rocking on his feet twice.

'Mother is across there. I'm sure she would prefer that you told her yourself.' Henry felt himself flush with anger. He had no idea what Frederick knew or had guessed, but dreaded the idea that he should find out and treat it with complicity without Henry knowing. It appalled him more than the idea of Frederick's contempt. Was his reply complicity?

'I don't want to get involved with Stephenson.'

'How late shall I say you will be?'

71

'I don't know, sir!' Henry tried to sound irritated yet off-hand. 'I don't hang on Mr Hudson any longer than I have to.'

'I should watch Brancker and Wylie.'

Henry stared at Frederick in astonishment.

'Is this more advice? What do you mean?'

'When I wander around, no one pays any attention to me. They were arguing with John Ellis about the Leeds and Bradford. The gist of it seems to be that Mr Hudson has taken money from capital that ought strictly to have been paid from revenue. There is a lot of talk about worn rails and new wagons. Then they saw me and were exceptionally polite, even for gentlemen, which must reflect upon their consciences!'

Frederick's memory was phenomenal. It was one of the things Henry maintained he had received from his father. He knew none of the men concerned yet had got it all right. It made sense to Henry. He had to ask.

'What did you make of it?'

Frederick looked up at his father sharply.

'Are you testing me, sir? Or should I charge you a fee for this?' Seeing no response to this flippancy, he was suddenly serious himself.

'There were more bits and pieces, mainly to the effect that this is a good year and they will make nothing of it now. Ellis was very angry, hotly denying impropriety, that sort of thing. No one else heard, they were all gathered round Hudson. Brancker maintains it is impossible to understand Hudson's accounts. It all seems clear enough. The Liverpool men want an investigation, but will wait their moment. Now if the distinction between capital and revenue accounts has not been kept clear, who knows what can be in there. The least harm is that capital has been used for repair and maintenance. The greatest harm is that it has been used on dividends. You know the permutations better than I do.'

'The Liverpool men have always been at war with Hudson. It is Lancaster and York all over again. It may be nothing, some jealousy.'

'But worth some thought and some paperwork.'

'Yes. Thank you.' Henry hovered, not sure how to end this conversation. He wanted to get away, yet found himself bound both by this new obligation and the unsolved question of how much Frederick knew of Kate, or of any other woman. Betty. He could have known about her.

'I don't think that acting for Hudson is good for a place on the Bench.'

Henry was again dumbfounded by Frederick's extreme bold-ness. He had encouraged him since the age of seventeen to address him as man to man, but had never invited him to offer advice in the same way. He saw with alarm that Jane was looking in his direction and was plainly talking about him to Stephenson. Perhaps she would send Stephenson over to collect him. He found he was staring at Frederick as though he had just been kicked on the shin.

'You may be right,' he muttered hastily, 'but I can't stay here arguing the point. I am employed, and that is an end of it. Look to your own business, for you haven't made the Bar yet.'

Frederick smiled, and shrugged disarmingly, pulling a long face. He looked less than his age, a sudden reversion. It still answered nothing but it was more acceptable to Henry.

'Tell your mother that I shall not be any later than I can avoid.'

'I shall,' said Frederick, and bobbed his head slightly. It was half a bow and might have been mocking. Henry wondered if it was indeed a hint of that complicity, but could tell nothing from Frederick's eyes. He dared not prolong their interview. He turned and walked back to join Hudson's entourage, pushing his way through a resisting wall of black backs.

Frederick was left pondering. Had Henry known, there was no complicity, but rather a deep resentment at being made a party to deception. It was he who would have to take his mother home, abstracted and talking trivialities. When he had been even younger, there had been anguish as well for Jane, because Henry had always seemed totally transparent to him and he knew Jane must see. He could not bear to watch her sustained effort to keep it from her children. He had wanted to say that he knew, and it was all right, she need not pretend, but had the sense to realise that after all her effort the reward would come if he accepted the deception and encouraged Jane to believe she had succeeded.

He had always been very close to his father, and though he felt violently about his behaviour, there was no hate in it. He realized now that Henry and Jane had made a clear division. Elizabeth belonged to Jane and he to Henry. They could not even share their children properly. It summed up their marriage.

He is almost an old man now, he thought, at fifty-five. This is his last fling, or must be nearly so. It will afford him no more satisfaction than any other of his entanglements. He wondered who the woman was. He found a young man's difficulty in imagining that any woman should find Henry desirable. He imagined she would be a woman who flattered and treated the world lightly, a widow or an unattached woman. He hoped so. The real satisfaction that Henry was seeking was the Bench. For this, Frederick thought, he was an obvious choice, probably the first choice provided always that he kept his reputation clean.

Frederick decided that he must look in more detail into Hudson's affairs. He had a nose for it. There was a strong whiff of trouble about. If he could steer his father away from it and through this latest nonsense with a woman then he would be able to sit him on the Bench and relax. The devil with Henry was that he was in so many ways a child and must not be encouraged.

He returned to Jane, who was by now grateful to be rescued from Stephenson. She smiled politely and thanked him, showing nothing. Elizabeth protested that she wanted to stay longer because she had found someone interesting to dance with and Stephenson puffed round them, unwilling to lose his audience and unwilling to join Hudson.

'I shall be accosted by engineers,' he protested, 'who think they have a duty to impress me, and I shall have to pretend I know who they are!'

Only as they left the room did Jane look back to Henry. She was shaking hands warmly with the persistent Stephenson, and smiling. She could not conceal from Frederick the pain in her eyes, even in that brief glance. It was clear that she knew.

Hudson had struck an attitude. Henry thought he looked very much like a statue of himself even when alive.

'I have the greatest good news to announce to you all,' he declared to a hushed audience. 'My lords, ladies and gentlemen, it is very good news.'

This was obviously the moment he had been leading up to all evening. He looked triumphant, enunciating slowly, tasting his words. Henry was impressed, against his will.

'Her Majesty has most graciously condescended to travel upon the Eastern Counties Railway on the occasion of the Prince Consort becoming Chancellor of Cambridge University. To mark this event, which will be in early June, the Eastern Counties will have a special carriage constructed and fitted. The order has already been placed and construction is under way. I can say that the Eastern Counties will produce the most elegant Royal carriage the world has yet seen. The Great Western has lost its laurels! I look upon it as a very great honour that Her Majesty and the Prince Consort have chosen to travel on the Eastern Counties. No more need be said by the detractors of that line.'

Congratulations spilled upon him from all sides, some from those expecting the announcement of a spectacular dividend, sounding hollow. Henry's ignoble reaction was one of amazement at the barefaced audacity of Hudson. Everyone knew the Eastern Counties was a sick line, with little hope of recovery. This ploy was a piece of pure theatre, and yet it would succeed. The great gullible public would be coaxed by the glamour of Royal patronage into parting with more money to prop up the invalid. Henry found it breathtaking that Hudson should have the nerve to arrange it and see it through. Because it was so obvious a diversion, he might succeed. He was struck by the sudden thought that Prince Albert had not yet been elected Chancellor of the University. What if the unthinkable happened? Powis was said to have a solid following. He did not suppose that Hudson had even considered it as an eventuality. With Jane and Frederick gone, he had only to avoid Stephenson. The moment seemed opportune to slip away.

The dance was proceeding in a remorseless way totally lacking elegance, and Edward was not enjoying it. Louise insisted that they should continue, despite Edward's plea that he at least felt tired and would like to sit down. It was a half-truth. In fact he felt she was making herself conspicuous by her insistence. She only had one partner.

Edward was also annoyed with Charlie, who was taking a wicked pleasure in getting the local girls to blush. Not to the roots of their hair, thought Edward, but to their very dancing pumps. He whispered to them, clearly making remarks about the guests. Whatever their parents thought about his mother, it was clear that the girls liked Charlie or at least found him exciting. It seemed as though they knew him. It was something Edward meant to ask him about when they were alone.

For Nell it was different, and this stung Edward. The inequality of the situation was blatant. She sat silently on her chair, moving her fan from hand to hand and trying to smile at Edward as he passed. He smiled at her, but felt angry.

'Louise, I shall have to dance with Nell. Won't anyone else?'

'They may do. She's very pretty.'

'I can't leave her there. I could kill these people.'

'If you dance with Nell, then I shall have to sit there. Charlie should do it.' Louise's voice was hard and cold. Edward was not sure what to make of it.

'I don't know why you came,' he persisted, 'we've made our point, so we can go. Did you know it would be as bad as this?'

'Of course I knew!' said Louise with sudden savagery. 'Does it upset you?' She was no longer smiling and Edward saw with dismay that she suddenly seemed cracked and old. With anger, crow's-foot wrinkles spread like fine fractures about the corners of her eyes and mouth. It was a snarl, a baring of teeth that Edward had never seen in a woman before. He was so startled that he let his right hand drop from her waist. She held his left in a strong grip.

'I have to live somehow,' she said. 'I have put up with this sort of thing before, as I'm sure you know. The whole family knows that. Haven't you been told? Of course you have. How do you imagine it was in Virginia? Take hold of me again, properly. What have you ever had to contend with?' It was command and Edward obeyed.

Louise smiled at him again. She realised that she had exposed herself too much. She had frightened him and jeopardised her plans. He was a very young man in spite of his veneer of worldliness. But Edward was not so easily seduced, noting how cleverly she changed. It was like cloud shadow over downland, dramatic both in contrast and in speed. The softness of expression returned, relaxed and uncaring, eyes appearing slumbrous, the angry fractures of her skin disappeared. He wanted to probe at her again because he was still angry and disappointed. She had, after all, been cruel.

'This man you told me about, is he here tonight?'

Louise looked at Edward sharply. She understood his feelings.

'What makes you ask?'

'Well, he must live somewhere nearby, so could easily be here. You are being watched by the men, they can hardly take their eyes off you. When we turn, I catch their eyes and they look away.'

'I know, I feel contempt. What would you do if I told you who he was?'

'I don't know.'

'Look at them. Does it matter which one it is? Would it really matter to you? I must get to London. You do understand, don't you?'

Yes, Edward thought, his heart sinking, I understand. He looked at the stout ladies, trussed up tight, the sun-bleached boards, the homemade finery of the girls, the extravagant dancing and frequent collisions, the men with furtive eyes. He nodded, feeling it was infidelity. Poor John. And yet he had been willing for infidelity, or so he had thought.

Nell was sick at heart. She had recited to herself the poems she knew in order to pass the time. Her face felt stiff from the artificial smiles she made at Edward, and the poems had brought her near to tears because she mostly remembered Tennyson. She felt briefly sorry for Edward who clearly had not realised what he was committing himself to. They should have warned him. However, men had their own rules and women had to suffer. It was she who had not been asked to dance while Charlie was free to cavort. Louise was infinitely selfish and had prevented Edward from dancing with her, she knew. They were all monsters. Charlie was a cheerful monster and could not be subdued, Louise was a selfish monster that would not, and John, poor John, was a devouring monster to be avoided, perhaps pitied. What was she? To be the host to some sort of monster seemed to be necessary to survive. She searched in her mind for something.

Four

The house in Flood Street, in Chelsea, had changed little since William and Maria Kelleway had first purchased it. From the front, indeed, it had not altered at all except that a flourishing garden was now tending to get out of control, breaking up walls, crawling over paths and diminishing the doorway.

The house had always been too small and, while their means were modest and before their children were born, they loved it for its convenience. Maria hated housework and William disdained it. They had never employed a permanent servant, and even now had daily help only from the village. It was a principle with them, founded on solid prejudice. Neither could stand the interference of another person cleaning or tidying.

Their neighbours had also largely remained unchanged, and it was still very much a village although becoming a prosperous one. Chelsea had always seemed to owe its existence to the muddy Thames. The flat slabs of ooze appeared natural stepping stones, and deceptively firm as they glistened in the sun at low tide. The coal and grain barges still pulled up by rickety wooden quays. Big horses and cumbersome carts stood by the old wooden derricks to receive bricks or chimney pots or lime. But the quays were not being repaired now, and the carts that had once been painted in the livery and scroll-work of their owners were battered and had passed from one middle-man to another. The wood was bruised and fibrous, and the names were illegible. The barges showed the same decay, sails patched in grey canvas on red, in red canvas on grey, uncaring, and all washed out with salt and ready to tear. The very ropes were scrawny and lean with wear, the bargees older and more grizzled. Famous dogs had died and not been replaced. Big mongrels that swaggered ashore at Chelsea to raise hell and have water flung over them in their fighting and coupling had all been consigned to the bottom with a granite sett. The railways were beginning to affect trade, and the roads firmly connected Chelsea to London. Houses had grown up along these roads, and the carriers' wagons had taken up the river trade.

Larger houses of stucco and paint had appeared, replacing the modest architecture of reddish brick and rubbed arches. They looked over old brick walls and stared like strangers with no manners. Where two small houses had lived in harmony, never

78

offending each other, now there was one, land-hungry and over-staffed.

The Kelleway house retained its modest features, an elegant pediment over the front door the only decoration. At the rear, however, the demands of a family for space had forced the addition of a studio which projected into the garden. Maria hated it but acknowledged its usefulness. She hated its high round-arched windows and slated roof with north lights. William had designed it, according to Maria, and Maria according to William. In fact neither had devoted particular attention to it because both resented its intrusion.

Inside, it was full of bric-à-brac. A cast-iron stove could provide searing heat within a tiny radius but was incapable of warming the extremities of the high room during the winter. Today it was cold, still full of yesterday's ash. It was a bright day but the sun had not yet picked up summer warmth. The smell of turpentine and linseed seemed to envelop every article of furniture. There was an overall stickiness which deterred visitors from sitting down, but Maria and William seemed not to notice. William's sister Caroline was hovering uncertainly by a proffered chair.

'It's Florentine tapestry,' said Maria, mistakenly believing that Caroline was examining it. There was only a year between the two women, Maria being the younger at fifty, yet she looked ten years less. While Caroline had grown elegantly grey, Maria's hair remained deviantly glossy. It was the sort of hair that no woman deserved to have at her age, her friends said. Maria said it was the linseed oil.

'I am worrying about my dress,' said Caroline opting for the truth. 'Paint and things.'

'That chair is clean,' said William. 'We use it for sitters. Some very eminent people have steeled themselves there in utter discomfort, and some very naked ladies too! When I have an archbishop there, I like to think of all the naked ... you know!'

'Well, at least you don't change,' said Caroline, sitting down abruptly then inspecting her dress as if for instant marks. 'So you are still doing portraits? As well as everything else?'

'I like to keep my hand in. Landscapes have become too much the rage. In any case, they pay very well.'

Caroline laughed.

'I suppose you are forgiven. You know, some things about London are changing very fast, but I like coming here for reassurance.'

'That sounds terrible,' Maria protested, 'as though we are ossified. Everything seemed to us to be changing. We have our fair share, whether we want it or not. There's building everywhere.'

'But you still have the river, the eel fishermen, they don't seem to change much. You know, coming down from Highgate, there is that enormous view. It used to be all countryside. Now it seems to be nothing but brickworks and building sites. The smoke is terrible on a heavy day. There are kilns everywhere and the ground torn up to get at the clay. You can't imagine the mess. And where they aren't building houses they are excavating the most enormous cuttings for railways. I've never seen such laceration of the earth.'

'Perhaps that's why landscapes are all the rage,' said William. 'Perhaps it has to be painted before it's all gone. Some sort of record made.'

'But no one paints that sort of landscape,' said Caroline. 'They are all idealised and romantic. Where is today's Constable?'

'I find the earthworks exciting,' said William. 'I can't be your champion to the full because there are such colours and shapes and forms from the mounds and clay they throw up. It's all desecration, I know, but it has its own beauty.'

'So has war.'

William laughed uneasily.

'Touché, Caroline, I'm deflated. I can't talk anyway, as I have developed a terrible taste for the vulgar. Maria will tell you all about it. It's shameful really.' William nevertheless seemed pleased with himself. It was typical that he should ask Maria to talk for him, while he sat to one side and chuckled, making the occasional addition. In Caroline's view, Maria indulged him. She should not allow herself to be the cook while he played the master chef.

'They have even divided up Primrose Hill into formal walks. They surely can't be more vulgar than that. Everything has to be made regular and easy so that people can enjoy beauty with the minimum effort. I think they enjoy it less as a result.'

'Now, now, Caroline, that's all very Calvinist! I would say that more people get the chance to enjoy beauty.'

'You have weak fibre, William,' Caroline scolded, only half-joking. 'What is this vulgarity you've been up to? Does it give the people more chance to enjoy beauty?'

'She is astute,' William said to Maria.

'Caroline, don't let him annoy you.' Maria scowled at William, and seated herself on the edge of a greenish chesterfield. 'He is painting a diorama for Cremorne.'

'A Cosmorama,' said William happily.

'A what?'

'According to Mr Ellis who runs the gardens, a Cosmorama is

a superlative diorama, a panoramic diorama. He is advertising it on all his posters. I won't let William put his name to it.' Maria was firm.

'What does this thing show?' asked Caroline, intrigued if not approving.

'A grand Cosmoramic view of the City of Mexico, according to Mr Ellis. It is to be the main attraction. Come on William, you tell us what it is. I've never seen it. I see bits – lumps of cathedral, mountains covered with snow, whole streets.'

'It is a view of Mexico City, as though you were a bird, or in a balloon. The whole place is ten square miles and it has six hundred streets all precisely laid out north-south and east-west. There are huge sierras behind it covered with perpetual snow. In the centre is the Plaza Mayor, which itself is fourteen acres and full of fountains and gardens. There is the huge cathedral, the largest in America, public buildings, fantastic houses, convents, markets, gardens. It is an amazing place. I knew little about it, and the more I learn the more fascinated I become.'

'I should think no one knows much about it. Where do you get your information?'

'I have a list of people who lived there, street plans, lots of sketches made by travelling artists. There are etchings of the principal buildings and squares. What I have to do is to unite them all into something that is more than the sum of all the parts. I find it very challenging.' William sounded defensive.

'What he means is that he has to make the rest up,' said Maria. 'Then it all has to be fantastically colourful and spectacular. Mr Ellis has an eye for topical subjects. It will probably be a great success. He certainly must think so, for he pays well enough.'

'Well, I suppose you always had a liking for the spectacular,' said Caroline. 'By now, with your reputation, you could be fashionable and dull.'

'Dear Caroline,' said William, 'I always know where I may come to hear the truth.'

'I didn't mean to be rude,' said Caroline. 'I meant it as a compliment. So many people are becoming fashionable and dull. It is clearly where Jonathan gets it from.' It was Maria's turn to be ruminative. They had foregathered to go to Cremorne to watch Jonathan make a balloon ascent.

Jonathan was certainly not dull. Other adjectives sprang readily to Maria's mind. Vain, immature, clever, exciting to silly young girls. His ballooning was very much in the vogue and a constant terror to Maria. It attracted to it young men and women who wore clothes striped almost like the silk panels of the balloons. She pardoned his vanity because it was picturesque and rather extravagant in an overt way. It was the vanity of youth, the showiness of the spring season.

Maria wondered what Caroline really thought of Jonathan. Her utterances on any member of the family were increasingly scathing these days, but Maria thought that there was a bond between Caroline and Jonathan. Perhaps he reminded Caroline of her own Edward. They certainly had ingredients in common in their characters, a certain devil-may-care attitude towards life. Edward was much more of a gambler, however, while Jonathan merely took chances. Edward was more a man of the world, as they said of young men who were forward with women. Jonathan retained his innocence or at least remained comparatively gauche. But then, thought Maria, the real cut, the arterial wound, is that Jonathan is a Kelleway in action and appearance, and Edward is a Ware no matter what he is called.

She remembered Charles Ware as a puffy-faced, purple-cheeked man, over-weight and overbearing. Edward had his light brown eyes, and his face and jowls would run to the same flesh. Caroline had refused to marry Ware, and Maria had no idea if the man was still alive though she supposed it was unlikely from his unhealthy appearance. She wondered if Caroline ever thought of him. There had certainly been no love in the relationship and Caroline had been inexperienced and ignorant. Yet she had taken things too far in her rejection of him. Maria thought Edward had a right to know his father, not just his name. Caroline had not kept things from Edward but nor had she softened the blow, showing too clearly her dislike of Ware. Her total loss of contact with the man seemed a selfish act now, when viewed dispassionately, and it hurt Edward. A love-child is a hundred times better off than one that is born out of ignorance, thought Maria.

Now Edward was always alert for his father's name and Maria knew he had made enquiries when the hurt had been worst, but there were too many Wares in London alone to make the search more than a gesture. 'Well,' said William, to break the silence, and because he could think of nothing else, 'It's a perfect day for ballooning.'

'Windy, I should say,' said Caroline. 'There is high cloud and when I came down from Highgate it was quite gusty and buffeted the carriage. I hope they don't drift. They could go anywhere.'

'It's a southerly wind,' said William quickly lest Caroline should alarm Maria.

'I suppose you mean they won't drop in the Thames,' Caroline persisted, 'Instead of which they may drop in the Channel. I suppose it is at least cleaner and sea bathing is healthful.'

'Don't be such a kill-joy.' William was annoyed now. 'I've been

82

up in balloons twelve times, Caroline. I think everyone should try it. It's both exhilarating and humbling at the same time. Quite unlike anything else.'

'I get a splendid view from Highgate hill without entrusting my life to a lot of gas and silk.'

'It's nothing like standing on a hill. That's what everyone says until they try it. The view from a hill starts with foreground and plods on into middle distance and with total boring weariness trudges into the distance. In a balloon there is only vastness. Immediately under you, all around you. It's why I'm painting this diorama. I shall be the first man who has painted one from first-hand experience from a balloon. I actually know what things look like from above. The whole earth is a huge diorama.'

'You don't go up there clutching a canvas?'

'No, of course not! But I make sketches. You have no idea how infinitely small everything looks and how unimportant.'

'But how can you stand there with only half an inch of wicker between your feet and certain death?'

'My dear Caroline, Maria is frightened enough by it all without you expanding on the subject.'

'Yes, I am,' said Maria, 'and Fordham Hays is a heavy man.'

William laughed aloud.

'Maria, he won't upset the balloon!'

'He is heavy all the same, and the wicker creaks and crackles when he climbs in.'

Fordham Hays was courting Charlotte with all the signs of success. It seemed that no one liked him except Jonathan. Maria realised that she was privately hoping that he would fall through the basket work, and was shocked by the thought. She did not want to kill him, but somehow to incapacitate him to stop his attentions. She supposed if he was injured he would only seem more attractive. Besides, if he fell through the basket, what about Jonathan? She had a picture of Jonathan's legs waving frantically through a bottomless basket, then Jonathan slowly losing his grip and falling in horrible slow motion to earth like one of the damned in a painting by Hieronymus Bosch. How shocking a mother's thoughts are, she realised, when she is defending her young. Yet Jonathan was hardly young.

'I still can't understand what Charlotte sees in that man,' said Caroline critically. 'It will be the first high Tory we've had in the family if it ever comes to it.'

'It will also be the first rich man,' added William provocatively. He knew that Caroline saw in Hays certain similarities to Ware.

83

'I worry about Charlotte,' said Caroline as though sensitive to just that thought. 'I hope that she is sensible.'

Maria and William exchanged a suffering look, knowing what Caroline meant. William pursed up his lips in a very good imitation of citric sourness. Caroline went too far. She should look after her own.

'I'm sure she is,' said Maria very brusquely. 'Now we must think about leaving. If you are late for a balloon then there is disappointingly little to see! I have a hamper in the kitchen which should feed a small regiment and the carriage has been waiting for at least a quarter of an hour'

'Is that Simpson's hackney that I saw outside? Are we going in that?' Caroline had an acid note in her voice again.

'Yes, we are. What's wrong with it?'

'I'm sure there must be better carriages for hire in Chelsea, Maria. That thing is chipped and knocked about. It looks as though it has been shipwrecked. The leather is cracked up like dried mud.'

'Simpson is reliable and he is cheap!' declared William. 'I don't intend to go on display in it. It'll get us there and back. It is clean you know, Caroline,' he added sharply.

William carried the hamper out of the front door and down the path, ducking the bushes. Simpson, seeing him, dismounted from the seat and met him at the gate. They stowed the hamper away beneath the driver's seat, Simpson rasping with the effort.

'I hope you've been over the leather,' said William when they had finished.

'Oh yes, Mr Kelleway. Of course.' Simpson was obviously surprised and slightly offended at being asked. 'I always does.' He was an elderly man, well whiskered, who had been a carpenter until ten years previously. His breathing was the result of the constant inhalation of the fine sawdust of hardwoods.

'It's my sister from Highgate,' said William with a conspiratorial wink.

'Then I shall have to drive exceedingly careful.'

'Oh, I shouldn't worry about that!' said William cheerfully. 'It's a fine enough day and I should rattle along at a good pace. We don't want to be late.'

The sky was a uniform tempera blue with unlikely tempera clouds that moved across it quite quickly. William felt uplifted by the joys of tactlessness. He had a strong desire to clap Simpson on the shoulders.

The balloon dominated Cremorne, sticking up above the trees like a giant bald head in a hair-net. The Achromatic Camera

84

Obscura – the biggest in the world – the Chinese Walk, the Archery and Rifle Shooting and Bowls, the Electro Magnetic and Galvanic Experiments were all very well and had their devotees, but there was no doubt that everyone had come to inspect the balloon and admire the aeronauts. Naturally they were disappointed that there were to be no ponies strapped beneath the car, and the spectacle would lack the appeal of the lady who had ascended with her pet leopard, but any balloon flight excited the imagination of fashionable circles. There was always the real chance of drama, and it would certainly be covered in the journals.

Mr Ellis's Tyrolean brass band romped and bumped away, producing a powerfully unmelodic din that could clearly be heard across the river and which attracted the idlers in the Flora Tea Gardens in Battersea Fields. The competition between Cremorne and Vauxhall and Battersea was hardly as fierce as it had been a hundred years before. The battles then between Ranelagh and Vauxhall in particular had provided free spectacles for half of London, with fireworks on the river, illuminations, parades and pageants. Mr Ellis meant to renew old rivalries. Cremorne would outdo Vauxhall in everything, and the world should see it, at a shilling a head. At least, as Mr Ellis was very well aware, that part of the world that could afford a shilling a head. A strong railing, strong attendants and a screen of trees prevented the undesirable unmoneyed from intruding themselves. Like wolves they skulked round the perimeter at night, keeping to the shadows.

Within, everything was elegant and fantastic. The bandstand was a mighty tiered pagoda that could provide music for four thousand dancers rotating around it in a fantastically lit enclosure. Myriad gas jets flamed from arches, from pavilions of boughs, from the trees themselves that at night were illuminated by gas chandeliers. The Grand Cosmoramic view of the City of Mexico, when it replaced that of Venice, would be amazingly lit at night. The Vaudeville was one of the best in London, and the Casino d'Eté, with six masters of ceremonies and fifty performers, was, Mr Ellis stated, quite unrivalled.

It was still afternoon, and although some of the gas jets had been lit, it was not dark enough for the place to assume its magical blue and purple hues. At sporting activities, gentlemen could unashamedly show off in front of the ladies and pretend it was all a simple pastime, a nothing. Old soldiers, young soldiers and sportsmen of all shades and description could prove their prowess at comfortably short range with the sporting rifle. Young ladies looked fetching and pink and struck statuesque poses – quite by accident – at the archery ground. It was undeniable that, as a sport, it did so very well show off the grace of the female form. Gentlemen

85

concentrated fiercely on the targets, and were very helpful with hints on stance and aim and stood very close. Heads almost touched, hands were laid on hands to steady a certain tremble. Young ladies almost swooned at the applause as their arrows struck the back planking. Attendants grinned evilly, said the lady was so expert she must really try again, and kept well down.

Cremorne was a place for flirtation and assignation, for sighs and breathings, tears and hints and lowered lashes. It was also a place of fashion. After all, Mr Ellis had seen to it that there were serious scientific matters to be discussed by gentlemen of taste. Galvanism was explained airily by husbands to their wives and daughters, who could perfectly well understand what the man in charge of the experiments was saying. Fashion stared at fashion. Mr Ellis's army of children and dwarfs moved about among the crowds with animal diversions. Neapolitan boys with monkeys. Arab boys with monkeys that danced on the back of dogs. A dwarf pulled round in a cart by two pairs of geese. A great dane with a cat in a howdah. Jonathan hated the animals and the dwarfs. He hated the way that they allowed themselves to be laughed at, how they submitted to so many indignities with every sign of pleasure. He had refused utterly to appear before the ascent and be presented to the crowd. Mr Ellis had been annoyed at first, then had turned it to advantage, dubbing them the 'modest aeronauts'.

The two men sat in a hut disguised as a Chinese temple, Jonathan by an unglazed opening and Fordham Hays at a table. The whole area was roped off and stakes had been driven into the ground with large warning notices nailed to them saying 'The Public are Forbidden to Pass this Point as the Balloon is Inflammable and may Explode'. Uniformed attendants ensured the line was not crossed, for the risk was real enough. A strong odour of coal gas was everywhere. Rubber tubes ran from ordinary gas lighting pipes over the car and disappeared into the mouth of the balloon, which was moored to the nearby trees by six ropes attached to the ring. It seemed enormous on the ground, as if it must pull out the trees as easily as garden canes, yet the restraining ropes were slack, holding it there by their weight. The panels of red and white oiled silk moved slightly in the breeze, but curiously slowly so that the balloon deformed slowly in one direction and then the other, no longer quite round. The circular wicker car sat on the ground, dressed with flags sprouting from it at all angles. It looked like a large flower tub, and was no bigger.

Hays had been drinking brandy most of the afternoon, announcing he was bored stiff and wished to God they could get on with it. Jonathan said nothing in response. He privately believed that

Hays was frightened at the prospect of the flight and could not blame him. Hays had only been up once before, and that had been with the experienced Mr Green, veteran of over three hundred flights, and had been to a height of a mere thousand feet on a captive ascent. He wished however that Hays would stop drinking. He was already on his second bottle of brandy.

Jonathan liked Hays well enough. The man was two years older but in many ways seemed younger. Hays was an amiable companion for an escapade, rich enough to have no better occupation and able to pay for any consequences. Jonathan found his contemporaries in the legal profession too stuffy. He could not realise that he dominated Hays in wit and imagination and that Hays, besotted with Charlotte, could see no way out of it except compliance. Hays resented it, and enjoyed it by turns. At the moment he was sullen, and would have declined to go if he could have done so without shaming himself. He hated the smell of the noxious gas, that was like bad drains, and could not see why he should be risking his life suspended from a bubble just to give Jonathan pleasure. He had subscribed to the idea because Jonathan had first extolled it in front of Charlotte, and Charlotte had been impressed and frightened for him, and he had dismissed it as nonsense. He had been up before, he said. There was really nothing to it. He hated heights, he thought, and hated the rotation of the car that added to the whole dizzy sensation. He had been sick over the edge. Mr Green had charitably put it down to the smell of the gas.

'The sun is going to set red!' said Jonathan with satisfaction. 'Red at night, sailor's delight. Sailors, Hays. Over the rooftops, over the river, first stop France.'

'Don't be stupid,' replied Hays, unable to disguise his alarm, 'we are going to land in Hyde Park, or Hampstead at worst.'

'Who can tell?' said Jonathan, very serious, 'we may get a cross wind and spend the night dangling over the German Sea, hacking our way through impenetrable cloud. We must check we have an axe.'

'Oh, stop it. It's a beautiful evening. I wish you wouldn't exaggerate, Kelleway.'

'I wish you wouldn't drink so much, Hays. It needs both of us to manage the balloon.'

'Damn it, Kelleway, mind your own business! It's internal warmth. I know how cold it is up there!' Realising he had been too vehement, he tried to make a joke of it. 'I shan't share the bottle, you know.'

'Well, if you take on any more ballast, we shall be able to do without sand.' Hays stared at him, worried.

'Tell me, Kelleway, how am I to ...? Well, unballast?'

'You should have thought about that, sir. There's only one way.'

'Over the city?'

'Yes, sir, over the city.'

'Good Lord!' said Hays in tones of such astonishment that both men burst into laughter. 'You know, I never thought of that.'

The sun was gradually sinking lower and the gas jets were sparkling and fluttering. Men went from place to place with tapers, adding to the number. It reminded Jonathan of church.

'The sun is really golden now, you ought to look.' He said it to distract Hays from his bottle. Hays had his hand outstretched towards it, and understood.

'What's the sun to do with it?' he asked curtly. 'It won't affect the balloon, will it?'

'Hays, you have no soul. Imagine the effect we will make. Who wants to see a balloon in a drizzle? Think of this vast globe rising noiselessly from the gloom of the trees, rising up black into the purple twilight. The sun is down, over there, as far as anyone can see because it is lurking behind buildings and trees. Suddenly the whole balloon lights up! We are struck by a blaze of blood-red rays. We become the sun! It will be magnificent, a red globe in the purple twilight sky, drifting across London. We shall look down and see all the churches and hills and the dome of St Paul's caught in the same light, and the river like fire.'

Hays, as if unimpressed by so many fine words, helped himself to the brandy bottle after all.

'Well,' he said, 'you're a very funny fellow for the Law. Of course it runs in the family, which may account for it. I never heard another lawyer who had a scrap of imagination until it came to making up his fees. You think I'm a dull sort of fellow, don't you? I know I have no imagination. It's just as well. There isn't room for both of us.'

Jonathan, recognizing the strains of alcoholic melancholy, felt a twinge of annoyance. Hays had been heavy going all afternoon and was definitely spoiling the fun. Jonathan thought that he had been put in the position of having to work to keep the party going. He found himself looking at Hays in a jaundiced way. Did he really want this man to marry his sister? It was strange how a good companion could become a bore. Hays must be growing old before his time. He was certainly putting on weight. It must be one of the quirks of nature, he pondered, that even if you transplant a man from his natural habitat he assumes the characteristics you expect. Hays was the son of an estate owner and had the right build for staying stable on a rackety hunter. His shoulders were heavy and hunched forward as though crouched over reins. He was fair-haired, grey-eyed and red-cheeked. On the other hand, I am the epitome of the city dweller, he thought, built slightly, rather sallow and dark-haired. I would no more look right demolishing hedges than Hays would look right wheedling a jury. Charlotte was dark and delicate too. Jonathan realised to his surprise that he was jealous of her beauty and did not want it wasted on this amiable dullard.

'Fordham, you make an act of it,' he said untruthfully.

'No, I don't,' said Hays. 'That's why we've been such good companions. You have all the ideas and I have none. I may have no imagination but I am honest. I would have a dull time in London if you didn't think them up. Do you think Charlotte will be happy with a fellow like me?'

'I'm sure she will. You know that.'

'No, I mean it, Kelleway. She sees me with you, when there is a flurry of excitement in the air. I wonder if she sees you reflected in me and has never realised what a plain bit of clay I am. God, I suppose it is the brandy!' Hays sighed noisily. 'You see what a bore I am. It's written on your face.'

'Nonsense. For Heaven's sake, stop this gloom. Come and look at the gardens, let's go for a walk, listen to some music.'

'I don't even like music,' said Hays tragically. 'The more I think about it, there isn't anything much I really like, and particularly I don't think I like going up in balloons.'

'You're going for a walk.'

'I think that's probably a good idea.' Hays was immediately reasonable again. 'Walk this wretched stuff off. You see, I do know I'm a fool.'

'Let's try our hands at the rifle shooting. Pass the time.'

'Good idea.' He hoisted himself to his feet. 'You know, I do mean it. I want to know if you really think Charlotte will be happy with a fellow like me?'

'Fordham, you must ask Charlotte!' Jonathan made the coward's retort, then was ashamed of himself. It had been a genuine moment for truthfulness. Although Hays was not fully sober, he was by no means drunk; he was in a mellow and receptive phase. Why had he avoided a straight response when he considered himself an honest man?

'Can you aim straight enough to hit a target?'

Hays brightened.

'Kelleway, that at least is one of my accomplishments. You know that! No pheasant is safe when I'm around.'

Jonathan was annoyed at such a fatuous reply. He wished that he could leave Hays behind, but then they would have to ballast the balloon again. In any case he needed someone to help with the thing. Hays was now taking imaginary aim at fast flying birds, traversing the dark roof of the hut, and making firing noises. Even his noises seemed silly and unreal to Jonathan's jaded ear. He would have to do something about Charlotte. Take her aside, but in such a way as not to make her resent his interference and thus become wilful. Alternatively he could find some suitable and stupid girl for Hays. That was the best course.

'Come on then, Fordham, we'll have a small wager.'

'Let's have a big wager.'

'I can't afford big wagers, Fordham. Save them for your rich country friends.'

'Not money, Jonathan. If I win, you go up in the balloon alone.'

'You can't be serious, Fordham! Everyone's coming to watch!'

Hays sighed heavily.

'I suppose I promised Charlotte.'

The coach journey from Chelsea to Cremorne was brief, and as the road had recently been paved with granite setts for most of the way the elderly vehicle ran comparatively evenly, not lurching and swaying, but trembling with a marrow-jolting hardness.

'I don't know that these roads are an improvement at all,' said Maria, having to talk loudly over the rumble, 'I prefer a coach bouncing about on something soft to all this bone-shaking. I can hardly talk for my teeth rattling.'

'Macadam is much better,' said Caroline, 'but it must be kept in repair. This road is terrible, my hat keeps slipping off. Are you sure Simpson is driving the thing properly? It feels as if we have a three-legged horse. I wouldn't be surprised if he has cracked the springs.'

'I think we'd have noticed if he'd cracked the springs,' said William reasonably. 'We would be dragging along like a sledge.' He was getting tired of Caroline's complaints. Caroline snorted, and very deliberately straightened her 'coal-scuttle' bonnet. It was of blue silk, rather faded, trimmed with yellowish lace in a style that was ten years out of fashion. Maria had long ago concluded that Caroline intended to be ten years out of fashion as an indication that she did not subscribe to any of the ideas of today.

As if in defiant confirmation of this, Caroline gestured to some building works beside the road.

'More horrible villas. They are filling in between the places left over from the time they filled in before. This road used to have only two houses, and now they've gone. There's just no end to it.'

Despite the late hour and the low angle of the yolk-yellow evening sun, men were still laying bricks from wooden scaffolds, where the sun sought them out and glittered on their trowels as they struck and cut bricks with deft movements. The ground around the buildings was white with lime as though dusted by some extremely local snow storm. A kiln for burning bricks or lime had been set up behind the building works. It emitted from the top of its inverted funnel a yellowish vapour so hot that it shot upwards like fire from a rocket. At night, the whole of the top of the kiln would glow a dull red. Clay had been excavated everywhere and the ground was criss-crossed with barrow runs. Nothing of the former landscape remained except the severed stumps of trees, tortured further by burning out their hearts. All building is depressing, Maria thought, but that is just the human reaction to change. We should not feel that nature is being destroyed when man takes over, because man is part of nature. Ants colonise a tree stump, beetles live in its bark and consume the tree. Rabbits, sheep, deer eat the bark from trees and consume their branches and leaves.

'What do you think of it all, Charlotte?' pursued Caroline. 'London is changing out of all recognition. I think old London started to disappear when the Houses of Parliament burned down. Since then we have had nothing but more demolition and big new buildings, quite out of scale, and railway lines crashing through streets and villages to end in huge termini with iron over them and iron tracks on the ground. Everything will be iron soon.'

Charlotte, who was being deliberately dragged into the conversation by Caroline, had said very little since the coach had left. She knew that Caroline meant to invade her privacy, resenting her silence as though it were a secret that she must discover. Charlotte enjoyed travelling by coach. She enjoyed the bright yellow sun which blazed in her very pretty dark face in furious explosions that made her close her eyes. It crashed its way between the dark shadows of buildings as if it at least was determined not to be put down, or smothered. It left drifting dark green clouds of colour on her retina.

She had been thinking of Hays, fearful of his making the balloon trip but excited on the other hand that he should be doing something so bold and spectacular. Yet she was aware that she only felt these things when he was engaged in some activity. When they were together in conversation, for example, she found him different, almost unwilling to be alone and without Jonathan. It was something to ponder upon and try to understand and she did not want to become involved in conversation with Caroline. She wished Caroline would pick on her sister Margaret, but Margaret was studiously looking out of the other side of the carriage. In any case, Margaret never ventured opinions and was generally agreed to be sensible, so Caroline left her alone. She supposed Caroline was lonely and her inquisitiveness and manner were only an attempt to have interests.

'I think they are making great improvements too,' said Charlotte cautiously. 'Trafalgar Square is very splendid, and the wider streets allow the traffic to move more easily. It also allows in the sun more.'

'And all the Clubs in St James's? Are they splendid?'

Charlotte looked quickly at her mother, knowing the turn the conversation was about to take. Maria came to her rescue.

'Caroline, we know you object to them, but the buildings and the streets are handsome.'

'And this endless spread of villas? Anyone with an income of a hundred and fifty pounds a year has joined the middle class to despoil the green grass. The middle class that Brougham, who was always a stupid man, called the wealth and intelligence of the country, the glory of the British name. That can be anyone's for a hundred and fifty pounds.'

'You sounded then just like father used to,' said Maria. She did not succeed in making her remark seem light.

'Maybe I do, but I object to certain trends, and Charlotte and Margaret should as well, for they affect all young ladies. I'm old. Nothing affects me.' She glowered out of the window at an eruption of yellow stock bricks that looked as raw as new-baked biscuits.

'Lady Blessington is always complaining that ladies are obliged to study the pursuits and tastes of the gentlemen in order to find favour in the eyes of these lords of creation. It *is* a degradation of our sex and it continues to get worse. These Clubmen prefer a well-dressed dinner to the best-dressed woman in the world and, as she observes, are able to dine more cheaply in their Clubs and in more exotic fashion than they could possibly afford at home. Is it any wonder that some of them seldom see their wives? I believe this is unique to England and I'm sure every other nation thinks us mad. As for the parade of carriages in the Park every day, the men go there to canter past the ladies and *be* admired. They no longer do any admiring. I think the men admire each other more or, more particularly, admire each other's horses!'

William burst out laughing. It was meant to sound good-humoured, but conveyed nothing except a rude and interruptive noise. Charlotte was looking annoyed too and Maria understood

92

why. On all these scores, Fordham Hays stood indicted. Maria understood Caroline well enough to know that it was deliberate. She wished she would mind her own business.

Margaret suddenly spoke, demolishing the rather sullen silence.

'I don't agree that we are unappreciated.' She smiled at Maria. 'Those bricklayers we have just passed all took off their hats and were waving them to me!'

Caroline's silence was impressive, and took them to Cermorne.

The launch was a great success from the point of view of Mr Ellis. The 'modest aeronauts' had attracted the imagination of the crowds in a most rewarding manner. At the hour of six, the crowd around the roped-off enclosure was very dense indeed and must have consisted of five thousand people, all at a shilling a head. Other activities had been stopped. The Tyrolean brass band had been gathered together on a temporary stand of planks where they sat on spindly iron chairs that looked quite unequal to the task of supporting them. The brass band's knees gleamed in the gas light and their sounding brass reflected sparks of light. They were to give the balloon a triumphal send-off.

Ellis made his speech through a megaphone in his rather harsh busking voice. It was heard by only that section of the crowd facing him, but Mr Ellis thought it all added to the drama.

The sky was garish, with the low clouds like cotton wool soaked in gore, then it became diluted by distance to pink, purplish blue, yellow and green.

'Red at night,' Mr Ellis declared as though he had coined the thought, 'the balloonist's delight! The gentlemen plan to touch down before dark, but who knows where? They will try to descend in England, but who knows? If the wind and the mood take them, they may drift on over Continents!'

Ladies murmured and drew in their breath in proper admiration. Mr Ellis had made it plain to Jonathan and Hays that, if they landed more than thirty miles from Cremorne, then they could pay the cartage. If the balloon was damaged, they could pay for that too. They were to try to land back in Cremorne, and if that was not possible, in Hyde Park or Vauxhall. If none of these was possible, then everything was down to their own judgement and pockets.

The gas pipes had been detached from the balloon, which moved very slowly and very lazily, as though testing first this rope, then that. The wicker car was now suspended clear of the ground and the restraining ropes were alternately taut and slack as the balloon attempted to escape. Additional bags of sand were hung around the car like so many muslin-coated hams.

'Get on with it!' Jonathan muttered.

'If he doesn't, I shall be sick,' said Hays.

They stood slightly behind and to the side of Ellis on a raised wooden dais, painted red and gilded. It was decorated with fairground motifs and had obviously been part of something else in its past history. Jonathan thought it was an unnecessarily vulgar touch.

'You can't be sick here,' he hissed firmly at Hays. 'Not in front of everyone. I can smell that brandy from down wind.'

They had been paid a short visit by Maria, William, Caroline and the two girls. Maria was matter-of-fact as befits a mother who is hiding her fears and wants her son to know it. William was openly enthusiastic and talked about achieving new heights, speeds of ascent and other matters that terrified her more. Caroline restricted herself to a kiss on Jonathan's cheek, a remark that she was sure he was insane, and a frosty handshake for Hays. She hoped, she concluded, that this would be the last time they defied those sensible laws that had been designed by the Almighty to keep man's feet on the ground.

'I hope you will both be very careful,' Charlotte had said, touching and beautiful in her concern. She shot shy glances at Hays who shifted from foot to foot like an overawed yokel. Charlotte could smell the brandy on Hays' breath, and it made her feel ashamed and at the same time touched her. She hoped that no one else would notice, especially Caroline, and that no one would comment upon it. She wished he would not drink, would not spend so much time in Clubs, would show more admiration for her. Caroline's utterances had a habit of lodging in the mind. Margaret said to Hays, 'What do you think of her, Fordham? She has dressed especially for the occasion. This grey-blue silk is so elegant. I have such a pretty sister.'

'Both the Kelleway sisters are exceptional,' the idiot had replied. Margaret had shot Hays a scathing glance that the man was unable to interpret. He reflected that he always seemed to be in the wrong with Margaret.

They all left quite quickly because there was nothing to say. Like railway departures, Jonathan said, balloon departures are best kept brief. Now Mr Ellis had wound up his speech, praised their modesty yet again, made a flamboyant gesture in their direction, and the crowd was applauding politely. Mr Ellis's minions raised a cheer and the Tyrolean brass band stood up in a rustle of leather and horse bristle.

The two men immediately left the platform and made for the balloon car. Men untied the ropes and hung on to them, joking and pretending to be carried up into the air. The Tyrolean band continued to bump its way through military airs. Jonathan was first in the car and helped up Hays. He thought that Hays already had the look of a sailor rescued from the sea.

'Get to your side for the ballast,' he ordered.

'All right, Kelleway!' Hays sounded unsteady. 'I have had enough ordering about, y'know.' Hays steadied himself on one side of the car. Each bag of sand had a draw-string attached so that it could be allowed to trickle out. Ellis had walked across and was insisting on shaking their hands. The Tyrolean band bumped harder. Maroons were let off in the gardens at a safe distance from the balloon, and at a gesture from Jonathan, the men gradually released the mooring ropes. There was little sensation of movement, yet they were quickly higher. The car was level with the tree-tops in seconds, then above them.

'Pull in the ropes.'

The mooring lines were hauled up into the car. It could only have taken twenty seconds, but suddenly the sun was upon them. It was so brilliant they could glimpse nothing of the lights of Cremorne, and could not see the ropework of the balloon without shielding their eyes. It seemed to be alongside them and as big as the balloon. Both men were awed by its violence. It was not round, but slightly oval, distorted still by the horizon that seemed to suck at it and pull it apart in layers at its bottom segment. As they rose, these segments seemed to weld themselves back to the mother body, as though it had decided not to fruit, to disintegrate, and was pulling matter back into itself. Within a short time the sun was whole again, the sunset reversed, the horizon rejected. Below them the Thames still attracted reflections from the sky, strange yellows and greens, and slid like spilt colour to the widening mouth where it became diffused and was lost.

It was suddenly much colder. Jonathan realised that the speed of their ascent had been considerable. They had entirely lost their concentration and were doing nothing to control the rapid upwards dash.

From the ground, it had been as tremendous as Ellis had hoped. The balloon had appeared incandescent. Someone had shouted 'It's on fire!' and there was a gasp, and momentary panic. It was perfect, except that they were rising a little too fast. There appeared to be no drift yet. He hoped it would be southward so that the glowing orb would be visible for at least thirty minutes. He wondered where they would end up, shrugged off the thought and put his mind to restoring the normal activities of the Gardens. Reporters from the daily papers were clamouring for information on the balloon, gossip on who was present, on his future ideas.

The balloon had started to rotate. Caught in a high wind current in the clear sky the car at first swung like a pendulum then, as the ropes carrying the basket formed cat's cradles, wound and unwound. This movement seemed eventually to transmit itself to the balloon, and they spun silently like a carousel. Hays was sick over the side.

'Get hold of the ropes!' Jonathan was shouting. 'Hold them apart, stop them winding up!'

'Go to hell!' shouted Hays.

'It's your damned brandy!' Jonathan shouted back angrily.

'It's the smell of the gas!'

'There isn't any smell of gas.'

'Then what the devil are we going up in the air on?' Hays was sick again, vomiting wetly over the side of the car. The smell was vile and Jonathan himself began to feel sick. He wrestled with the ropes, trying to fight the winding motion. He succeeded to some extent. The whole performance of Hays had so far been predictable.

'Try to take the ropes. You won't feel sick if we can stop it turning.'

Hays did not reply, but was holding his forehead with his left hand and his stomach with his right, and groaning. Jonathan saw him shiver violently and realised his hands were becoming numb with cold. He had no idea how high they now were, and wished they were equipped with some instruments other than a barometer and thermometer. He was too preoccupied to attempt to take readings and calculate their height. He remembered vaguely that if the temperature was below zero and the barometer about twenty-three inches, then they must be about a mile and a half up. The barometer read twenty-four inches, but the thermometer was misted over with condensation. He was furious with Hays.

'Damn you, Hays, if you can't pull yourself together, we'll get completely out of control! Do something, you fool! We've risen very fast. Look at the balloon!'

The balloon was grossly distended and pushing its way through the netting. It looked like an enormous Venetian glass lantern.

'I'm going to pull the valve line,' Jonathan shouted. All their shouting was unnecessary, for there was no sound except a slight sough of wind through the lines. Down below, in the black mass studded with pin-heads of light, a train whistled. They heard it quite clearly, as though it were a field away. The sun had cleared the horizon completely, but hovered there as though watching them before slipping away to the other side of the earth. Jonathan seized the ropes that secured the car to the ring of the balloon, and reached up for the valve-line that ran through the centre of the ring, up through the balloon, and operated two spring-loaded, semi-circular shutters at the apex. When he pulled on the line, these opened, releasing coal gas. He pulled for about twenty seconds, afraid to release too much unless they started to plummet downwards. Hays regarded him balefully, holding on to the wickerwork. So far he had done nothing.

'We must find out if we are going up or down,' Jonathan shouted.

'How do you propose to do that?' Hays was resentful. He felt so ill that it mattered not at all what happened. 'Hold out your finger for the wind? I thought you were supposed to be an expert, Kelleway? This thing is a menace. You can't look after it.'

'Shut up, Hays. I don't need you being drunk and ill all over the car. Have you got a piece of paper?'

'No.'

'Think, you fool. You must have a banknote.'

'What for?'

Jonathan still clung to the ropes with one hand and held the valve line in the other. His temper took the better of him. He was numbed with cold and could easily lose his grip and fall. The bovine fool slumped like a sack of corn against the wicker basket was just so much useless human ballast. He would never let Hays marry Charlotte. It was a strange place to be assessing the situation, he thought, but peril sharpens the perceptions, they say.

'What do you think it's for?' he stormed. 'I want to send a message to the birds! Perhaps we could put it in one of your empty brandy bottles and throw it over the side, asking for help!'

'I've had enough of this, Kelleway. I know nothing about balloons, I never wanted to come up in the damned thing in the first place. You've done nothing but call me a fool.'

'You shouldn't have got drunk.'

'Damn you, Kelleway, I am not drunk! It is the spinning of this damned thing and the gas.'

Both men were illumined by the blazing sun. The colour seemed to add to their heat. Jonathan, clinging to the ropes, looked like some avenging fiery angel, Hays like a furious and disgraced demon. Below them London existed only through noises. It was a buzz, punctuated by bells tolling the quarter. Occasionally they could hear a dog bark. It should have been a moment for sublime contemplation, for a god-like view of creation, for contemplation of the violet vastness of the sky above in which stars glowed with fierce intensity. Instead, Jonathan was aware of the smell of Hay's vomit, of his pudgy face and defiant eyes, of a trickle of filth that had run down the man's waistcoat and shone in the red sun like blood. He resisted the temptation to tell Hays that he was finished as far as Charlotte was concerned. It was the culmination of a whole day of irritation. He felt he could cheerfully push Hays from the balloon. Perhaps Hays understood, because he seemed almost to snarl at Jonathan.

'You think you have a hold over me because of your sister, Kelleway. Don't you forget that she loves me. And don't you forget that I don't need all this nonsense. I have money and can do what I please!'

'Have you got a bank note?' Jonathan repeated with insulting patience.

'What sort of a damned fool question is that, Kelleway? What are you driving at?'

'Listen, Hays, I am hanging on up here with hands that are becoming increasingly numb. If I fall off, you are as good as dead yourself. If you have a banknote, please take it from your pocket, hold it at arm's length over the side of the car, and release it.' Jonathan spoke with laboured patience. Hays stared at him as though he had suggested jumping out for a swim.

'Do it, Hays!' Jonathan persisted rudely. 'If the note appears to drop rapidly, then we are still ascending, if it is stationary, then we are descending rapidly, but within control, if it shoots out of your hand in an upwards direction, then we shall both be shortly killed.' Hays looked at Jonathan as though pleading with him to smile or modify this statement, but when Jonathan merely stared back, Hays at last reached inside his coat with numb and clumsy hands. He had difficulty in extracting a note and took a long time. Eventually he held it out. Jonathan nodded, and Hays let it go. It fluttered lazily sideways at first, and seemed inclined to drift inside the wicker car. Hays flapped at it in a ridiculous fashion as though to get it back on some course. The note drifted idly away from the car, turning over and over, extending its distance from them only slightly.

'All right. We are now descending at a fairly regular speed. We rose in about twenty-five minutes, and we should descend in about the same time.' Jonathan released the valve line and ropes and settled back in the car. 'Have you got any of that brandy with you?'

'What do you mean?' Fordham Hays looked guilty.

'What I say.'

'A little.'

'Can I have it?'

Hays looked surprised, trying to judge if this was an overture of friendship. Jonathan did not look at all friendly. Hays felt in his coat pocket and produced a flat half-bottle. Jonathan uncorked it with some difficulty while Hays watched every action. He then took the bottle, poured brandy into one cupped hand, stood the bottle on the floor of the car and thoroughly rubbed both hands in it. Hays was too stunned to say anything.

'I had almost lost all feeling,' said Jonathan. His hands were blue and mottled. He rubbed at them until the discolouration left. 'We had better get out the guide rope.' He stood up from his crouching position. The bottle of brandy fell over and poured on to the floor-boards and through the wicker.

'You did that deliberately!' Hays shouted.

'I don't want you to drink any more.' Jonathan flung over the thousand-foot coil of rope that would serve as a self-balancing ballast when it touched the ground – the more rope that lay on the ground, the more the balloon would tend to rise again. The sun was now dropping over the horizon with exaggerated rapidity.

'That's none of your business!' Hays persisted, as though determined to carry this quarrel right through the flight.

'Can we just forget all that for a moment?' Jonathan demanded. 'Can we forget about everything, and enjoy the sensation of flight? Can we for a few seconds be quiet, look and listen? We may even be able to discover where we are.'

They peered over the side of the car. There were lights everywhere. The setting sun dropped over the horizon as though it had been punctured and they were suddenly in total darkness. Another dog could be heard barking, relentlessly. They could clearly hear a train but could not see it. Somewhere, it rattled across points and let out an owlish hoot. They were now quite low, and could see the moving lights on carriages.

'We're still over London,' said Hays.

'Stand away from me, please,' said Jonathan abruptly, 'You stink.' He could not concentrate his other senses because of the assault on his sense of smell.

Hay's mood changed from belligerence to pathos. Peering over the side had made his stomach heave again.

'I can't help it. You ought to feel a bit sorry for me, Kelleway. You just rant at a fellow's misfortunes.'

Jonathan ignored him. He had caught a quick glimpse of light that he did not understand, a flat flash that was diffused and seemed corrugated, forming patterns. He saw it again and then understood.

'We're over the river! We haven't drifted at all. We're coming back down where we started.'

'I can't swim!' Hays declared, panic in his voice.

'I should have guessed that,' said Jonathan sourly. 'It looks as if you'll have to try.'

'Can't you steer this thing to land?' The note of panic was rising.

'I can't steer this thing at all if there's no wind! For God's sake, use your head.'

Jonathan underestimated the desperation and anger that had built up in Hays. He was quite unprepared when the man suddenly grabbed over the side for the ballast sacks, and at first thought he had merely stuck his head over to be sick again. But Hays was not being sick, he was sobbing with panic and anger. His hands were tugging at the cords and the balloon started to yaw. Jonathan leapt at him and at first tried to drag him back by his coat. Hays was far too heavy and did not appear to notice. Jonathan was compelled to get alongside the struggling man, and tried to grab at his hands. It was futile, for Hays was so much stronger that he brushed Jonathan off as though slapping the hand of a child. He had pulled all the draw-strings on one side of the car and the sand rushed off into the darkness beneath them with a slight dry hiss. Jonathan found himself scrabbling at it and foolishly clutching two handfuls. Hays lurched to the other side of the car and repeated his performance. Jonathan yelled at him, flung the sand away and tried to scrabble and wrestle with him again. The wicker of the car squeaked and grated as they struggled, but again Jonathan was powerless to prevent the strings being pulled. He wondered if he could knock Hays down, but realised immediately that either he or Hays could easily fall from the car. Hays was so much stronger in any case that, in his present state, he might pick up Jonathan bodily. Jonathan stopped tugging at the man's thick wrists, and stood up, taking a quick look at the ground. Everything had receded dramatically, and wind whistled through the ropes. There was a sensation of rising at speed. Jonathan seized the valve line and pulled it full open. Hays was unaware of this, and still scrabbled at the ballast sacks, shaking them now, to make sure that every grain had gone. Eventually satisfied with his work, he turned round towards Jonathan, who concealed the valve line behind his back. They were no longer rising.

'You won't put me down in the river, Kelleway. You've had enough fun with me in this damned balloon. I won't be humiliated any further!'

'I haven't humiliated you, Hays. You have done that yourself. It started with the brandy.'

'Oh no! You have enjoyed yourself. I can't stand the smell of gas, and I don't like this sensation of flying.'

'Then you shouldn't have come.'

'I didn't want to, Kelleway. I made that plain. I only came up because of Charlotte.'

Jonathan stared at Hays. He was thinking that Hays would marry Charlotte over his dead body. Hays stared back at him defiantly, and grasped what Jonathan was thinking.

'You won't mention this to Charlotte, will you, Kelleway?'

Jonathan could not do it. He could not bring himself to say that of course he would, that it was his duty and he must. It was a level he could not stoop to, and, realistically, he was not sure that Charlotte would anyway put much weight on it. Two grown men, squabbling and bickering in a balloon. It was no credit to either.

'No.'

'Thank you.'

They both knew that it was the end of the friendship between them, and the beginning of strong dislike.

Jonathan had forgotten the valve line. A flapping above him alerted him. He let it go immediately. The balloon was partially deflated now and they were falling rapidly. The car was swinging like a pendulum and Jonathan could see nothing but blackness below. On the return swing he saw street lights, very low and close.

'Hang on! We're going down!'

Hays said something, or shouted, but Jonathan never heard. There was a tremendous jolt and a crash. The sky around them seemed full of obstacles. Something slapped him hard across the face and there was a thrashing, rushing noise. He tried to grasp at the thing around him, but it was like handfuls of sand again. He was upside down, falling, thinking as he fell that his leg hurt and wondering why. Then there was a tremendous blow and oblivion.

Hays was luckier. He had clung to the ropes and by his strength had prevented himself from being flung out into the tree. He could see street lights and guessed he must be some distance from the ground. A large tree, many large trees. A park. He thought he heard voices. The balloon must surely have been observed as it came down. Half of London would have been able to see it at some time during the flight. He wondered, calmly, if Jonathan had been killed. He had seen him struck by a branch and then pitched head first out of the car. He found he did not mind one way or the other. After all he was only a passenger, Kelleway was the balloonist. He would say he had been told to release the ballast.

There was a distinct shout from below.

'Is there anyone else up there?'

'Yes!'

'Just one?'

'Yes!'

'Are you all right?'

'I think so. I can't get down.' He had better ask, or it would seem strange. 'Have you seen my companion? He fell out of the car.'

'He's down here, sir. He's injured a little and unconscious. You hold on, we're getting ladders.'

Hays had every intention of hanging on. If Jonathan remained unconscious, he would have to give an account to the journals. They were sure to ask for it.

Five

Henry Kelleway arrived at chambers very early. The sun was still struggling with wisps of white mist that clung to the moist grass of King's Bench Walk. The river was invisible, beneath a coverlet, weary. Sparrows cheeped in the trees and from gutters, a desolate sound like silver coins clinking. Wood pigeons made drowsy domestic noises to one another. So it seemed to Henry, who was envious of the birds, envied their domesticity, their easy ways.

He was up early because he had woken early. Life had become as stark as that; the act of waking meant the act of rising. He was unable to bear the thought of breakfasting with Jane. He remembered her note as soon as he awoke. It had haunted him for several days and he had been unable to bring himself to deal with it, even to focus his mind upon it. It irritated him because it intruded upon those few erotic moments of fantasy between sleeping and wakefulness that he liked to savour as his communion with Kate, a mingling of the flesh with which he could commence the day. It was spoiled by the need to escape, not to linger unless he should become trapped. He wanted Kate and missed her and it was imperative to leave the order and propriety of Gower Street.

Everything about the area seemed too correct in his present mood, too solid, too orderly. Railings were always freshly painted, door-knobs and bell-pulls, letter and name-plates freshly polished by that unseen army of servants that always rose before dawn. The brickwork of the houses was severe, regular and mechanical, as though it too was virtuous in never straying up or down, never varying in coursing or bond. So much regularity was oppressive, in some way counter to the nature of the material.

He had walked part of the way, not wishing to wait for his own sleepy coachman, and had then taken a hackney, although it was an unsavoury vehicle smelling of urine. He did not want the sociability of an omnibus.

Henry glanced at the board that was attached to the wall at the entrance to his chambers. It was an involuntary act that he performed every morning, noting, as he had done for two years, that his name was now at the top; noting also that those who had gone before him still remained under certain conditions of the light, their overpainted names faintly legible. Mr Thackeray had died, and Mr Wells, bodies beneath the soil, names beneath a thick layer of cream paint that in turn hid another layer of cream paint and another. Names inscribed in the Book of Life, and then the pages stuck firmly down upon death. Or retirement. Mr Agnew and Mr Turvey had kindly left vacant the space at the head of the board where Henry's name was now applied in elegant black script.

Not only had Henry fallen heir to many of their clients, but Mr Wells had left him most of his furnishings. Mr Wells had collected carpets and, latterly, furniture in competition with Mr Agnew and it was natural that he should feel that Henry should have it. Mr Agnew and Mr Wells had loved the finest washed colours of Kerman and Feraghan. They knew the symbolism of the abstract designs and read the rugs from Trebizond and Nish as easily as the nomadic makers, arguing about which rug had come from which district. It was unthinkable that Mr Wells should so supplement his rival's collection by leaving them to him, and unthinkable that the rugs should leave the chambers. Henry knew only a little of the subtleties that had engrossed the two men, but enjoyed the continuity the collection represented. The colours were warm and pleasant. It was a far cry from his first pauper's sticks, his torn leather armchairs and bare boards, but in many respects, he reflected, there was no more comfort in it for him, because after all these years there was no more comfort in himself. The myth of possessions always struck him at this early hour. Before the sun rises the smell of baking bread is worth more than money.

Corbett, the aged senior clerk, was not about yet, and would probably be sitting on an omnibus from Stockwell. His fire had been laid the previous evening, however, and he wondered whether to light it. Feeling unequal to even this decision, he glanced out of the window at the buildings across the Walk, trying to see if any chimney was giving out smoke. He knew he was killing time, but he felt excited. He had an early morning appointment with Kate. It was the best he could manage. He would be in Hitchin for a week at least, and then in York and Bedford and wherever else the iron roads met iron opposition.

No smoke. Either there was no one in at this hour, which was unlikely, or everyone had decided it was going to be a warm day. He heard footsteps beneath and looked quickly downwards. It was only some weary counsel, eyes hollow with night reading, who still clutched papers beneath his arm with the evident pretence of continuing his reading at home. Perhaps he would. Perhaps he would return to breakfast, a loving wife, a warm bed.

Henry cursed himself for this continual refrain. He pressed his forehead against the cold glass as though sobering himself. The man was probably due in Court at eleven and was going for

104

breakfast in the Black Horse before going on to the barber. He heard the voices of porters bidding the man 'good morning'. Other steps were soon about. Tradesmen were delivering to residential chambers, shops and inns. Bread, milk, vegetables and meat. Servants were arriving, or were out sweeping steps.

The knock on his door made Henry jump. His mind had gone to sleep staring at this soothing traffic and lulled by the soporific shushing of brooms. His head was still pressed to the glass. It worried him that his concentration had so completely failed. He made quickly for the door and opened it.

The woman outside was dressed well and soberly. Her coat was brown, trimmed with darker brown satin. Her bonnet was of cream material edged with the same brown satin and tied under the chin with a satin ribbon. She was dark-haired and attractive, young for her thirty-two years, with features that might have been conventional in a Bo Peep way except for the lines of humour around her expressive mouth. She smiled at Henry, but the smile was of darting quickness, making it clear that she did not wish to linger there.

'Come in, Kate!'

Henry closed the door behind her. Kate walked to the centre of the room, equidistant from door and windows. Henry saw and understood.

'Don't worry, it isn't exceptional for lawyers to see clients at a very early hour. The clerks won't be here for another forty minutes. It's good of you to come and marvellous to see you.'

He kissed her on each cheek then gently on the lips, a mere brush. She smelled of lavender.

'The porters have seen me.' Her voice was anxious and she spoke quickly as though she was fleeing and sought refuge. There was nothing about her appearance that was disturbed, however, and Henry found that he was rather nervous. Clad in coat and bonnet, she seemed unapproachable. He had never met her when dressed so stiffly in walking clothes. Coats and bonnets he associated with his wife. They were severe, practical things that he disliked. The more Jane wished to show her disapproval, the more she took to wearing heavy, high-buttoned coats. It was a denial of her softness and her femininity, he thought. A chastity belt. He was not the man who could ever admire a woman dressed in that way or see any elegance in it. He liked his women in flowing gowns, in silks and muslins. He knew it was hopelessly immature of him, but did not care. He tried to ignore Kate's garments, for she was looking at him seriously. Her eyes were particularly beautiful, brown with light flecks that shone close to the iris like chalcedony.

'The porters see hundreds of people. Discretion is their watch-word. No, they're more than discreet, they are professionally incurious.'

Catherine Carter loosened the satin ribbon under her chin. The ends fell down to her breast.

'Please take off your coat.' Henry tried to sound polite rather than pleading.

'No, I don't really think I should. It will look better if anyone should come in.'

Henry shrugged.

'I don't think it likely.'

She looked around the room, at the rugs and the mahogany, at the supple green leather armchairs and the rows of vellum and calf-bound Law Reports.

'It is very impressive and rather terrifying.'

Henry smiled indulgently. He was pleased at her reaction.

'The Reports come with the chambers. They are just wallpaper, legal window-dressing.'

'I have never been inside chambers before. They are much more comfortable than I imagined.' She moved tentatively towards the window, as though wild animals dwelled outside, standing back from the glass where she could not be seen. 'The gardens are beautiful too. It's like a park. It seems curious, really, to carry out such grim business in a garden. It is like a battlefield. I have visited several and they are all such inappropriate spots, or so it seems. When I was a child we went to Edge Hill. It was covered with primroses, on a grassy bank. Naseby was a sea of bluebells. Where is all the legal dust and disorder that we are supposed to find?'

'You won't be disappointed. I can show you chambers next door! Hartman encourages the cobwebs. In fact I have caught him hooking them up when they have fallen down. I like things my way.'

Kate turned from the window, trying to show purpose in swinging around so abruptly, trying to assume a firm tone.

'Henry, I don't like being here, yet I want to be with you. Why do you want to see me so urgently?'

'I shall be away for a number of days, perhaps weeks. Please take off your coat?' Kate unbuttoned it, but when Henry stepped to her with the intention of helping her from it, she raised a hand to stop him.

'It must be more than that,' she encouraged. 'We have seen each other recently.'

'I can't stand being at home any more and away from you. I can't stand being in my own house in the morning. I wake and I think of you and I have to leave. Perhaps I am bad at concealing things.

106

I don't want to be in the atmosphere and surroundings of my other life. Everything in Gower Street seems another life now. I have to go there to maintain it because it is another job of work, but that's all. I get up at five and everything rejects me. Is that enough explanation? Can you understand that?'

He was much more emphatic than he had intended. It was a declaration not a gentle remonstrance. Kate took his hand kindly, beckoning like a mother for it, because Henry had stood like a small boy with both hands behind his back. He might have been confessing to writing on the blackboard. Kate was unable to decide whether he was telling the truth. It was all very well to search his face, his earnest, firm face, but she could not tell from that whether this was a lover's passion, careless about deceptions, caring only for the urgent needs of love. It was something she needed to know because she loved Henry but did not dare to say it. What he said sounded practised, but that need not make it untrue. Kate envied the man, who could leave as Henry described. She had felt just the same but had no such opportunity, had to supervise the preparation of meals, had to share breakfast with a man who was more estranged than any stranger.

There was something else upsetting Henry. She was sure of it. His dependence on her had become demanding in a different way.

'I can understand it, Henry. I am only a custodian in my own home. I know it's difficult to find enough time or even a place to meet, but I am happy, because it is a whole world better than anything I had before.'

She had hoped to probe further into Henry's feelings, but Henry suddenly became practical.

'Shall I rent an apartment? Would that solve things? We could meet there. No, I can see you don't like it, and you're right.'

'Henry, I would feel debased. My husband will be away soon. I don't feel the same about that, I feel that it is not his house anyway, he has no rights there, no meaning.'

'I still don't like that arrangement. There should be nothing furtive about us!'

He crossed to Kate to prove his point, and kissed her on the lips and neck and on the fabric that covered her breasts, as she knew he would. It was an overture, she thought, that all men used.

'I want to make love to you now,' said Henry challengingly.

Kate stroked his head. Henry was a child, eager and impractical, always seeking reassurance that he would not be rejected, always following his words with the most obvious actions, but she found it charming. Her husband, ten years older than herself, had been pre-ordained her husband from the age of eight. By the time they were married it seemed like incest. He would come to her room in his nightgown, set down the candle he was carrying, avoiding her eyes, and then blow it out and climb in beside her. He would lie still in the dark for perhaps a minute then say his prayers as a prelude to rolling on top of her. He was without any other preliminaries and, when he was finished, fell asleep without grace upon her, heavy, uncomfortable and brutish. She had always felt abused.

'I want to make love to you too, Henry, but we can't here.'

'Why not?' Henry looked disappointed.

'Only because someone might come in.' Henry smiled.

'I love you, Kate, for that answer. But what shall we do?'

Kate could not reply. She wanted no arrangements, no temporary schemes because she knew she wanted Henry. He must work it out for himself. Kate felt sympathy but no regrets for Jane. Jane and her own husband might have suited each other better, she thought cruelly. If Henry were allowed to find some temporary way of overcoming their difficulties, Kate was suspicious that it would soon become permanent. He still needed his Jane to run to, not as a wife but as an escape. She could not yet compete with that, if it was how he felt. Such a feeling was an accretion developed over many years, without any particular merit except familiarity.

'As we have done,' she said, 'and you must realise that I don't mind that we meet in my house. I finished with my husband two years ago. We are lodgers in the house. Quite impersonal. The house is quite impersonal. I keep myself and to myself. What you suggest would make me a kept woman.'

'I should love to keep you, Kate!'

Henry's enthusiastic outburst convinced her how right she was. He started to kiss her again. She was annoyed with him but flattered too. She tried to pull away but he persisted, slipping his hand inside her dress, cupping her breast. She did not pull away. Why should I, she asked herself? It is what I want, but how do I get hold of him, hold on to him?

'No, Henry, don't stroke. It isn't fair to me. Be still, just hold me.'

Henry obeyed. They were quite quiet and still, hearing the birds outside, hearing boat sirens on the river, horses and carriages. Henry could feel her heart beating and was struck by the thought that he had never felt Jane's heart beating, never been conscious of it.

'What else is the matter, Henry? You have been very upset, you know.' Henry made a face, trying to make light of it.

'Oh, just railway matters. There are problems. Standing like this, I have no problems.'

'Henry, don't be so obvious. I would like to know. It will help you to tell me.'

'It's all very complicated.'

'I expect it to be. You can't put me off in that way. Are you in trouble? People say that Hudson may be in trouble. They say a lot more beside.'

Henry withdrew his hand and fastened two buttons of Kate's dress. She thought it the most loving gesture he had made to her. Henry began to try to explain. Braxton would call for him in two hours.

The four surveyors were making the most of the trip. They followed in a rackety coach with chipped paintwork where the wood showed through. They had brought crates of beer and flasks of spirits which they passed up to their driver, a large and phlegmatic man with an unquenchable thirst. It was thirty-four dusty miles to Hitchin, following the stage road from Islington through Barnet, Hatfield and Stevenage, and it would take four and a half hours on a very hot day.

The leading coach that contained Henry and Braxton was new and very smartly turned out. It was dark bottle-green with lime-green lining. The shafts were white and the harness had the light brown colour and unwrinkled surface of new leather. It was intended to impress the inhabitants of Hitchin. Hudson had ordered it.

The liveried driver hated it, because he was very hot and his seat was unyielding in the manner of all new seats, firm where his backside wanted it to give and uncompromisingly upright. The reins were new and hard and refused to hang easily. His livery felt like a corset. No one offered him beer. His shirt was sticking to his back beneath his coat and sweat ran down his ribs from his armpits. He thought with satisfaction that the livery would probably be ruined.

Inside the carriage, the smell of leather was overpowering. There was nothing fragrant and pleasant about it. The sun shone directly on to the far seat, which both men had left vacant, and the heat had brought out all the vapours of tanning and polishing. The windows on each side were slid down to their fullest extent in an attempt to let in a cooling breeze. Instead they let in dust, and the air seemed to have come shimmering from the road.

Both men had removed their hats and unbuttoned their coats. They suffered from the new leather in much the same way as the driver. With every buck and lurch, they slid about on the polished surface and braced their legs on the floor to remain in their places. Braxton's fiery face was even redder and he was exasperated.

109

'This thing is uncomfortable! It's a wonderful advertisement for the railway train.'

He was trying to read a newspaper. Henry just stared out of the window. He felt that he would have been sea-sick if he tried to read anything. He was glad that Braxton was keeping to himself and hoped that the man would persevere with his reading. The words he had just spoken sounded too much like an overture to conversation so Henry pretended not to have noticed. Corn was ripening in the fields. The hedgerows were high with cow-parsley and meadowsweet on which butterflies gathered. Ponds had nearly dried out and were all crust and no filling. Streams were low and the watercress, instead of being a crisp green flutter in the ripples, was a rank weed with ugly white flowers and stems like hemlock. The ruts in the road were hard as rock, and the coach had to negotiate along them so that the hedge plants occasionally thrashed at the window, throwing in leaves, fragments of flowers, and insects. Henry watched a black beetle that tried to orientate itself on the carpet. It felt about itself, unable to understand what this new substance was. It tried a short run and found that nothing happened, then raced across the floor. Braxton saw it and crushed it under his boot. When he lifted his foot, the beetle had been completely flattened but still retained its shape. One leg waved.

'Bug weather,' said Braxton. Henry was annoyed. He had been going to observe that beetle, discover how it explored this new place. Braxton had intruded. 'It's going to be hot work if it keeps this up, Mr Kelleway. I remember last year in weather like this, we were surveying near a spinney and ran into a swarm of hornets. You should have seen us run! Hot weather with bugs means storms. When you see the cow-parsley covered all over with little black beetles, then there will be thunder.'

Henry could not well avoid this.

'Is that so, Mr Braxton? Perhaps the moisture gathers in the flowers.'

'Maybe.' Braxton did not seem particularly interested. He shook out his *Observer*, trying to hold it upright. 'This Woolmer is going to be a difficult man to deal with, Mr Kelleway. Have you given much thought to how you will approach him? If he will give in and sell, half the county of Hertford will follow. He has to give in and sell. Mr Hudson is very clear about it. If he don't, then there will really be trouble.'

Henry resigned himself to the inevitable. It was stupid to pretend he could avoid talking business. He had to get on with Braxton for the next few days and might as well make the best of it.

'I have indeed thought about Mr Woolmer. Our first problem

will be to get near enough to him to try to reason. I really believe that man might try to ventilate our hides as he threatened. He hardly struck me as a reasonable man.'

Braxton snorted.

'That is just a little of your legal understatement, Mr Kelleway. Woolmer will reason with us about as long and hard as he reasons with a pheasant.'

'He has to be careful. He has to avoid assault.'

Braxton's snort was even louder.

'Pardon me, Mr Kelleway, but I don't think that will worry him. Every magistrate in the country is a friend of his, and law or no law, I can't see them do more than give him a wink, which is little consolation if you are lying on your stomach while the surgeon digs out pellets from your tender parts.'

'I don't think he will shoot at a lawyer. He isn't that much of a fool.'

'Pardon me again, Mr Kelleway, but you sound as if you are trying to convince yourself.'

'All right, Mr Braxton, may be I am, but what do you suggest?' Henry was cross and sounded it. Braxton's vulgarity was intolerable. He would never ordinarily mix with such a man.

'I suggest that we stand no chance with him. We will go to the house with the plans, try to see him. Either he will slam the door in our faces or we will be shown in. Meanwhile I will have instructed the merry men to do their business, which they will set about with lightning speed. If we can get him talking, they can survey the first line in half an hour and be out of sight of the house. The trouble will be if he has gamekeepers, and he will. It's heavy work running with a theodolite.'

'He's bound to discover we have deceived him. I don't think it's a good course at all. I can't subscribe to that sort of thing.'

'This is field work, Mr Kelleway. No time here for well-reasoned argument and a nice turn of phrase. More use here for a nice turn of speed. The four merry gentlemen behind are well accustomed to it. Half the lines in England owe their existence to the amazing speed of a surveyor when under pressure from a wolfhound.'

Braxton was right. Henry knew perfectly well that they would have to cut corners somewhere and it was no use pretending that lines were built by observing strict codes of behaviour. The only question was whether Woolmer was sticking out for money or for a principle. If the latter, Henry would have to try to find out whether he objected to all railways or only to those Hudson controlled. He was empowered to offer Woolmer a seat on whichever board he cared to choose, and a substantial holding in stock. Braxton was empowered to make considerable adjustments to the proposed route to take account of any particular requirement of Woolmer's, and even to offer him a halt on his land. The cost would be high but the potential gain enormous.

'Do you think it's money or principle, Mr Braxton?'

'It's principle. Woolmer is as mad as Sibthorpe. They just hate railways because they cut through land. Sibthorpe used to claim they would set fire to the whole country. I don't think we'll budge him, and I don't think Mr Hudson will be very pleased with us if we don't. In fact, you could say I'm not entirely optimistic about it. Perhaps Woolmer will die suddenly, and we can deal with the Estate!'

Although Braxton was being flippant, he was clearly seriously concerned. Both men had forgotten about the heat and the smell of leather and the dust. They were thinking about the ominous figure of George Hudson. Braxton picked up his newspaper again, to withdraw, to allow them both time for thought. The carriage passed through woodland, and there was blessed relief from the sun. The ground, too, was soft under the trees and for a while the wheels ran quietly.

'Brockett Hall,' said Braxton.

The semi-darkness allowed Henry to think of Kate. Somehow he had not been able to create her properly in his mind in the full glare of the sun and in the heat.

She had noticed that he was worried, and he thought of himself as careful not to allow such things to intrude. Was it obvious to others? Old George Stephenson was right too. He didn't have a mind for railways in the way Hudson had. He had no heart for the thrusts and skirmishes of business, and told himself that he preferred the intellectual challenges of his profession to the physical pressures and brow-beating of commerce. It was all a hypocrisy, he knew. There was not one jot of difference between his own dissection of witnesses or evidence and Hudson's buying and bankrupting. People were hurt equally. Unlike Hudson, he could not deal with confrontations outside the measured dance of the courtroom. He had no ability to deal with the Woolmers of this world. He had no ability to deal with Jane or Kate either. He had no ability to deal with his railway shares, he had no ability to tolerate men like Braxton.

Gloomy woods, gloomy thoughts. The cool air smelled of leaf mulch and damp decay. His situation was desperate, if he stopped to consider it. He loved Kate and she wanted him. He loved Jane in the way that he had always loved Jane, on a plane of acceptance that made her an extension of himself. He could no more contemplate the loss of Jane than the loss of his own limbs or a vital organ, and yet he wanted Kate and did not want Jane. Paradoxes that are not paradoxes. The smell of leaf mulch reminds us of mortality. Man is only a mulch upon the earth when all is said and done, an expensive organism that takes a great deal that the earth has to offer and gives little back.

Kate would not be content with a minor role, and Henry realised that he thought of her at that moment as interchangeable with Jane. If only he could introduce them both into his house, he thought, there would be no problem. Was that such a shocking thought? It was immensely disloyal to Jane, in the eyes of the world, but he felt so evenly divided that he was not sure that it was not loyalty to them both. He was doing nothing about it. He was doing nothing about his financial problems, when the answer to them was to tackle Hudson direct. I have entered a Sargasso Sea in my life, he thought, where I am held firm in the cling of commitments. Why not sell Hudson's shares at a loss, and be shot of that? Answer, because he will dismiss me as his counsel. Second answer, because if I hold on and Hudson declares a good dividend, I stand to make a substantial profit.

Yet if he did not renounce Hudson, and what Stephenson hinted was true, was he going to be sucked down into some mess of corrupt dealing? His promotion to the Bench was merely a matter of course. While he was seen to act for Hudson, in fact, it was assured. Provided always that the King stayed on his own rails.

The sunlight crashed in on them cruelly, hurting their eyes. Henry shielded his with his right hand, partly in an attempt to pursue his line of thought, but it was no good. None of it stood up to such brutal nudity.

'Have you seen the train that is being built for the Queen?' Braxton asked. He had been watching Henry with curiosity during the silent trip through the wood.

'No. It can't have got very far.'

'Oh, it has. Hudson had anticipated the event to the extent of having a car almost ready. Now they are fitting it up with all the trimmings. It is to be white and gold outside, and inside it will be lined with grey satin. The blinds are all silk with tassels of gold on gold silk cord. The furnishings are to be either satinwood or mahogany.'

'I hope the Eastern Counties can afford it! I hold shares in that wretched line.'

'I don't think the Eastern Counties can afford not to, Mr Kelleway. I also hold shares in it. It will never pay. Let us be honest about it. What does it carry? Corn and cattle. Let the Queen travel on it, then sell fast and be first, say I. The shares are bound to rise, the public are such fools. What do you think, Mr Kelleway?'

'That's speculation, Mr Braxton, that's what I think.'

'Come along, sir! I won't be the only person of like mind. He who hangs on to his shares to the last will find the bottom of the barrel scraped so thin that there won't be enough money to get under his fingernails. That isn't speculation, it's prudence. And the devil take the hindmost!'

'I am a lawyer, Mr Braxton, I can't subscribe to that.'

'Mr Kelleway, I know many men in your profession, with no disrespect to it as a profession, and many o' them wear the full-bottomed wig. They talk of the law's delay, but you should see them when they want to unload a share at the top. There is nothing more savage than a judge who wants his money!'

'I can't talk about that, sir. Forgive me if we change the subject!' Henry felt he ought to restore some dignity to the conversation. The terrible thing about money was that it bred familiarity. Everything Braxton said was true, and Henry had thought about it already. Then there was the warning Frederick had given him about the Leeds and Bradford, in which Henry also had a holding. If Hudson had been taking money from capital on one line, why not on another? Why not pay dividends from capital on an ailing line to prop it up? He was heavily subscribed on the Eastern Counties, and if that stock was worthless, he was virtually ruined by it alone. If all Hudson's stock crashed, he was bankrupt. Braxton was right. He must extricate himself from a part of it.

'Anyway,' he said to Braxton, feeling it struck the proper note of calm and consistency, 'the East Coast route to Scotland is virtually complete. There is no doubting that line. Hudson plans to open the stretch between Tweedmouth and Newcastle on the first of July.'

'No, there is no doubting it, except that the bridges are still mainly timber and the work is not complete. I believe the work will be complete, but Hudson is starting to do too much for show. It is all very well, but when all is said and done, Mr Kelleway, the Midland line still has no route to London other than the one from Rugby to Euston Square and that's no good. Rugby is a disaster, the delays are intolerable. So what are we here for? We know what. To cut right across Great Northern territory and effect a link between the Eastern Counties and the Midland. At the same time we are trying to revive an old agreement that will force the Great Northern, much against its will, to let us use their terminus at King's Cross and their line from there to Hitchin. There are a lot of "ifs" and "buts" about it, sir, if you ask me.'

'But we have to succeed, Braxton.'

Henry had not meant to be so forthcoming. The remark was both innocent and earnest and Braxton immediately turned to look at Henry. The coach was passing through hedges of blackthorn which were still thick with white flower. The sweet smell blew into the carriage, too sweet, cloying.

'I know about your commitments, Mr Kelleway, if you will forgive me for mentioning it. No, I understand how you feel, and before you tell me to mind my own business, I just want to tell you I find myself in much the same position. I don't ask for your sympathy or any such thing. I just find myself in the same way of being.'

Henry's temper had flared at the man's impudence, but when the ugly red-fringed face took on an earnest expression, which he obviously hoped was ingratiating, Henry had not the heart to reject him. He did not, however, want to encourage him.

'I'm sorry to hear that. I daresay it will all turn out all right.'

'Do you really think so?' Braxton was being meaningful. His head hung forward so that his face was not far from Henry's. It weaved about with the motion of the coach. The man's breath smelled. 'I don't think there is any chance of the Midland getting this Hitchin branch and crossing the Great Northern. But I think the Great Northern will complete, and I would put my money on it. I should think about it, Mr Kelleway.'

Braxton sat back, and stared out of the coach window. He was twiddling his big thumbs, as if trying to be studiedly casual. Henry pondered Braxton's words. The stupidity of the situation was that he thought Braxton was right but could not admit it. In any case, if the Liverpool men, Wylie and Brancker, meant to tackle Hudson on the affairs of the Leeds and Bradford, it would hardly persuade the citizens of Hertfordshire to subscribe to Hudson in their territory. One acrid whiff of sweat and they would be off.

The coach was now running through fields with high hedgerows interspersed with elms. Everything still had the full green of young summer. A glorious time, thought Henry, before the dust and dryness of the dog-days. A time when dews are still rewarding. He came to a conclusion, hardly understanding what he meant until he said it.

'We must do our business here. We are duty bound to it. Then we will see.'

'All right, Mr Kelleway,' said Braxton, interpreting this in his own way, 'I agree with you. Then we will see. I think it makes a lot of sense to keep an open mind about things, and I am certain it will make money.'

Henry should have asked him what he meant, summoning up

indignation in order to establish his innocence. Instead he was silent, as if in complicity.

They could see their destination before they reached the gate-house. Woolmer's house was an example of nature aping art. There was a calm, flat unreality about the colours of its setting that immediately recalled an eighteenth-century canvas. It lay in gently undulating grassland that had been cropped to a fine turf by sheep and rabbits. The sheep stood in the middle distance where they should have stood. Trees postured; horses in a paddock struck attitudes. A sheet of water shone before the house where it had obviously been applied by a large brush. Even from this distance they could see ducks upon the surface, making neat vees as they moved. Dark hedges of yew surrounded a garden. They were the sort of hedges that spoke of centuries of struggle with that tardy wood. The hedges now represented pillars and walls surmounted by urns.

The house was of light stone in the classical manner and obviously replaced a much earlier building. Its portico of long columns was in the Corinthian style, and the columns were surmounted by a froth of foliage. The stables and outbuildings, survivors of that earlier house, crouched in the background, low buildings of humble brick and tile that had become encrusted with a sumptuous ochre lichen. The drive swept down to the house in such a way that it would always be visible. It was perfectly maintained in raked and graded gravel. A forbidding approach, defying the visitor to disturb it along its mile length.

Braxton had stopped their coach and Henry and he now stood on the road waiting for the surveyors. They had chosen a covert place to stop, out of sight of the gatehouse and among trees. The grounds of Woolmer's property started alongside the road, over a well-made stone wall. They could hear the surveyors laughing among themselves. Braxton scowled. The coach-driver stopped his horses rather too violently, so that they tossed their heads and backed up. One of the surveyors stuck his head out of the window.

'Here we are,' said Braxton sounding increasingly annoyed. 'Will you gentlemen please get yourselves together and get down. Quietly!'

Despite this warning, the surveyors seemed to fall out of their coach with a great deal of jovial noise. Two of them availed themselves of the trees at the roadside. Henry thought that the coach-driver was in imminent danger of pitching off his seat. He held the reins in one hand and was trying to conceal the fact that he clutched a bottle of porter in the other. No wonder he had checked the horses badly. Henry felt that this element of farce was ominous. Apparently Braxton did too. However his suggestions to Henry might indicate his intentions, he clearly meant to do his business properly. It was an aspect of the man Henry had not considered, and he was impressed that he had genuine professional pride. He was forced to realise that Braxton must be good at his job, might be as good an engineer as Henry was a lawyer.

Braxton was severe with the surveyors. Three of them were young men, but one of them was considerably older and obviously in charge. Braxton singled him out.

'Barlow, your lads had better pull themselves together. Mr Hudson will expect a full report of your activities, and I want to be able to give him a good one. This is not a picnic, and you all know that. You will work in silence as far as possible, and there will be no more drinking from now on.'

The surveyors all wore tall tile hats. Henry wondered if it were to see one another more clearly across the fields, some aid to identification. Now they were rather sheepish.

'We are dealing with boulder clay here, depth at least ten yards, on alluvial gravel,' continued Braxton, 'and there are several streams and sources, as you know. You've never had an easier job, so get on with it. He has three gamekeepers with dogs, so if you can't keep quiet, you will have hounds at you. If the hounds don't get you, Woolmer will be out with his pig-sticking lance and bird-shot. You had better dry yourselves out fast. Do you think these men are capable of laying me a straight line, Barlow? How much have you drunk?'

'We can lay a straight line, Mr Braxton,' said Barlow, affronted. 'Have we ever failed?' The coach-driver watched with evident relish as the surveyors unloaded their equipment. It all seemed to be either heavy or unwieldy. One young man tried to carry an uncontrollable bundle of surveying poles, another struggled with two chains that kept unfolding and escaping. The older man took the theodolite and held it firmly. The last young man gathered up a bundle of drawings, a pad and pencils.

'The coach will go round to the Manly Highway. Have you got that, driver? Do you know where it is?'

'I do, sir. I'll be there.'

'I hope you're sober, sir. Throw away that bottle!'

'I be sober, sir,' protested the coachman, throwing the porter bottle into a hedge. 'I have only had refreshment for the heat.'

The surveyors laughed, derisively, and prepared to clamber over the wall.

'You will have one hour,' said Braxton. 'You must assume

117

that's all. If you are challenged, keep working. I'm sure you can think of some excuse, like the Great Northern!'

The men in tile hats eventually got themselves and their rods and chains over the wall. Braxton waved their coach forward, threatening the driver with dire consequences if he was not in position. Henry had not said a single word.

'They may not look it, Mr Kelleway,' said Braxton, reading Henry's mind, 'but they are very good surveyors. Things are not always what they seem in this line of work. Mr Barlow is something of a geologist. He is a good man with clays. This will not be London clay, up to five hundred feet thick and full of ferruginous sand and organic remains, this will be boulder clay which is the devil. One day it is so hard it must be blasted with powder, the next it turns into fluid glue.'

'So you do think we will get this route.'

'Not for a moment.' Braxton walked back to the coach. 'Let's see Woolmer.'

The drive to the house seemed endless and, when they finally stopped on a broad sweep of gravel in front of the portico entrance, Henry was nervous, against all his reasoning with himself. They climbed down from their splendid vehicle, which was now dust-hazed and grimy. The driver had knotted a handkerchief over his mouth and nose which he quickly removed. There was a line across his face where the dust had stuck to the sweat on his forehead and the bridge of his nose.

'You had better wait,' said Henry. 'Stand the horses under the shade of a tree. We will try to get feed and water for them.'

Get feed and water for me, thought the driver, envying the surveyor's driver who would undoubtedly make a dash for the nearest inn.

Henry walked up the limestone steps, aware of the shapes and pock-marks of ancient fossils embedded in the rock. One of those homilies on humility, Henry thought, so beloved by preachers. The humble unthinking bi-valve is the foundation of great houses, the mollusc leaves a more lasting impression upon the form of the earth than man. He took hold of a brass bell-pull the size of an apple and tugged it. Braxton stood behind him. They waited, watching the large front door, which seemed to have been built to permit the entrance of a man on horseback. Instead a door to the side opened, and Woolmer himself appeared. He came out towards them, and looked at them silently, his head nodding slightly. Woolmer wore no coat, but was in his shirt sleeves and waistcoat. He seemed even heavier round the shoulders than Henry remembered, and quite capable of hurling them both down his steps.

'I knew it was Hudson's coach when I set eyes on it,' said Woolmer, 'but I didn't know who it contained. I very much doubted it would be Hudson himself. Good afternoon, Mr Kelleway, and you too, Braxton. What do you want from me now?'

'Land, Mr Woolmer.'

Henry's straight retort seemed to affect Woolmer like a physical jolt, for his head bobbed back. He looked at Henry, not unamused, then made a wry face.

'Well, I can't complain I didn't get a straight answer. You shall have one from me too. You'll get no land.'

It was Henry's turn to pause and try to assess his man.

'We have been sent by Mr Hudson to offer very good terms. I won't insult you, Mr Woolmer, by saying they're generous, because the Midland obviously considers your land to be worth it. The Midland wants this Hertford and Hitchin branch. It is an integral part of the Midland's long-term planning and strategy.'

Henry was interrupted.

'Devil take the Hitchin and Hertford branch! If you are going to pursue that hypocrisy in private, then I have nothing more to say to you, sir. What Hudson says in a meeting, or what you say, is one thing, because you must obviously support him. But don't talk to me about the Hertford and Hitchin on my own steps. When I first saw the coach, Mr Kelleway, I unlocked the gun cupboard. Then I thought it might be you and we might be able to talk some sense.'

Woolmer's face had become a mottled red. In his waistcoat he looked uncomfortably like a pugilist. Henry knew he was not being very clever, or persuasive. He must try another tack.

'Very well, sir, I won't mention that line again. But can I just touch on a matter of principle?' A connection to the Midland line will link Hitchin to Scotland through the Midland network. It must bring prosperity.'

'I have heard all about that, Mr Kelleway, and nothing persuades me that the East Coast route is as good as the Great Northern's route by the West. Hudson made his route by tying together bits of string. He was very good at it, and when railways were things that ran between two or three towns, he saw the advantages of taking over lines and extending them into things of more than local interest. But he is still left with a lot of pieces of string. The Great Northern is being built as one great enterprise. It has a London terminal, it has straight routes. Hitchin will be linked to the north, in any case.'

'But the Midland is to open direct services in July. Corn and stock can be moved direct.'

'I can wait for the Great Northern, Mr Kelleway. I believe

it will be the greater line in the end.'

'Then, sir, you are not opposed to railways on principle?'

To Henry's surprise, Woolmer laughed.

'What do you take me for? You've misjudged me, haven't you, sir, and you haven't done your homework. I know you have written me off as a local Sibthorpe, and it serves you right! Good God, Kelleway, I have a big holding in the Great Northern. Do you think I shall ruin my shares by allowing the Eastern Counties to make a junction with the Midland by crossing my land and my line? The Midland has no London terminus. It shan't get it through me!'

Henry tried hard to keep on top of the situation, but Woolmer was enjoying himself.

'I'm no fanatic, but it suits me to seem one,' he continued. 'I don't like the York grocer, the man or his manner, and you really think you can induce me to cut my throat on his behalf? You see, these city grocers think that country squires like me are all fools. I daresay Mr Hudson thinks I eat roast fox with my boots on and can't count over twelve!'

'That's certainly not so!'

'Come on, Kelleway, how do you know? Hudson detests people like me, almost as much as I detest him. So forget your offers, and save yourself an unpleasant job. Now that that is out of the way, I feel I can offer you hospitality before you drive back to London. Please come in and join me for lunch. I make one condition however, and that is that you don't raise the subject of the Hitchin and Hertford again, and nurture no ambitions that you will get your man when he is mellow with port.'

Woolmer turned about and went in through the door, his big figure stooping as though he might bang his head. This was presumably Henry's invitation to enter. Henry looked at Braxton. Braxton looked entirely blank and shrugged. Not a word had been addressed to him so far by Woolmer, and Henry found this odd. Braxton did not even seem particularly surprised and his blankness was controlled.

'Is Mr Braxton to join us for lunch?' called Henry, annoyed at being left to shout through the doorway.

'Yes, of course.' Woolmer's voice was matter-of-fact. The sun reflecting off the white stone steps was dazzling. Swallows were nesting somewhere among the eaves, and swept down and past the two men with a stiff flutter and snap. Henry was thinking fast. Thinking of what Braxton had said earlier, of what Woolmer had said now, of how he had been the man presented and served up for this occasion. Braxton stood two steps behind him, unmoving until Henry went forward. He should push Braxton aside and walk to the coach that sheltered under a tree. He hesitated and knew he had capitulated.

'You knew about this, Braxton, didn't you?'

'Yes. Woolmer is immovable, so the Great Northern will win. Eastern Counties is a hopeless line. It only survives with Midland traffic on it.'

'Woolmer is a clever man.'

'Oh yes, Woolmer is a clever man.'

'What about you, Braxton?'

'I don't think I'm stupid, Mr Kelleway. Nor do I think you are. We both have a very nasty choice. Loyalty is a fine thing but it will lead to bankruptcy. There are things about Hudson's affairs, so they say, that must in the end bring it all down.'

Henry said nothing, but walked up the steps towards the doorway. He was suddenly struck by a thought.

'What about the surveyors? Does he know about them?'

'I'm afraid he does, Mr Kelleway. He will give them an hour and then set the dogs on them to make it look realistic. They'll be all right. They are very fit men! Of course the surveyors are just doing their job.'

Henry was appalled. He tried to tell himself that he had not committed himself to anything, and that they had all been talking in the vaguest way. He had said nothing that was disloyal to his appointment. Yet he knew as he stepped through the doorway into Woolmer's house that it was an act of treason.

From the sunlight, he thought cynically, into the cold gloom. He told himself he would just listen. He had no idea what Woolmer intended next. He gave one backward glance to the coach beneath the shady elm tree. To leave would be irrevocable, to continue was not a commitment.

They had entered by some side-door into a passage. Now Woolmer led the way from this stone-flagged catacomb into the main hall. It was all that Henry had expected from the exterior of the house. A large lantern light rose in several tiers over a sweeping stone staircase. The walls were hung with paintings which appeared to be made of mahogany veneer. Here and there some light patches made a grain in the brown surfaces which seemed to suggest a nose or fingers or a glint of steel. The floor of the hall was marble in black and white checks. Rugs had been laid on it adjacent to the wall and trapped under some elegant eighteenth-century furniture. Austere, Henry thought, but certainly not impoverished. There was no sign of flowers, none of the smaller bits of china that might indicate a woman's taste.

Woolmer led them into the dining-room, which was extremely pleasant, surprisingly so after the austere hall. Evidently it was part of the older house that had once occupied the site and had been preserved because of some previous Woolmer's affection for it. The walls were wood-panelled, the floors boarded and the ceiling a glorious dark mixture of oak beams and decorative painting. It smelled of beeswax and beef. Stews and sauces seemed to have seeped into the timbers and pickled them. Fumes of wine had preserved the panelling.

'This is where we consume roast fox!' said Woolmer, adding another dimension to himself, 'I prefer it to any other room. What will you have to drink, Mr Kelleway?'

A manservant waited obediently in the corner. Henry was aware of another figure who stood at the fireplace with his back turned.

'A brandy, thank you.' Braxton asked for the same. Henry watched the figure at the fireplace, and Woolmer watched Henry, smiling slightly.

'There is someone here I think you know,' said Woolmer.

'Oh,' said Henry. If this was a trap, it was crudely done, and he would have none of it. The man turned. He had obviously been waiting his moment. There was a deal of planning about this whole thing.

He did not immediately recognise the other man, although the face was familiar. The man swallowed and his adam's apple slid up and down his long throat. In a flash of sheer irrelevance it reminded Henry of a test-your-strength machine at a fair where you drove a marker up a slide in an attempt to hit the bell. The man's ears were long and thin. The Byzantine Christ! In astonishment, Henry could only stare. It was undoubtedly Perrin, a former practitioner at the bar who had shared chambers with Henry when Henry was just a youth. Perrin and Henry had instantly disliked each other, and Perrin had provoked dislike into hate on his part. Memories overwhelmed Henry. A grey, terrifying morning when the two men had fired at each other with pistols. Pigeons flapping away from the wet grass. Pigeons circling after the two shots. Both men had missed. Perrin had insulted him and challenged him for stealing his clients. Henry had struck him at table on Grand Night. It seemed another world ago, a world which was not so ordered as it was now. Duels were virtually a thing of the past. Even Grand Nights were becoming tamer affairs, devoted mainly to gluttony. The young barristers still pursued the Porter's daughters, who did not always run too hard, but those times were times past. Perrin had not succeeded and Henry had. Perrin had been reduced to a stupid fraud on the Stamp Office, removing the marks from a used stamp and returning it to claim the cash. A fraud for twenty-five pounds because that was what he needed to survive. It had finished him of course, and Henry had been desperately sorry for the man although his offer of help had been rejected. There was in any case no way he could have helped as Perrin was guilty and had already been taken into custody and released on bail. They had parted with strange bitter words. The hate had either gone, or was irrelevant. They had formed a bond of understanding at their parting. Perrin's rejection of Henry had made him think about himself, about his own course. It was just after his father, old Thomas, had died, and perhaps he was susceptible. It was just after he had gone back to Jane.

Memories choked his brain. Henry knew that he was staring at Perrin like a madman from Bedlam. Jane. How many times had he gone back to Jane? They had been happy that time, but it had not lasted. Nothing lasted. He had reconciled himself to that, or justified himself by that, and yet here was Perrin. Enduring.

'Perrin?' he said, because he must say something. The confusion of his own emotions irritated him. He was unable to concentrate on the purpose behind things as he felt he should. What was Perrin doing here?

'Yes, Kelleway. It's I. You seem stunned. Did you think I should evaporate, suffer melting of the flesh like the Prince of Denmark?'

'How are you?'

To Henry's surprise, Perrin laughed out loud.

'You haven't changed, Kelleway. You asked that in just the same solicitous tone you used all those years ago. You live in a world where nothing changes, your decades are yesterdays. I have lived a whole life since that business with the Stamp Office. But you ask me "how are you?" in a small voice as if I might not have recovered. I am very well, Kelleway, and I know you have done very well for yourself, for I fall over your name every time I read the paper. You will make the Bench. It seems certain. But I ask you the same question. "How are you?" Can you answer that question? It is the most unanswerable question in the world.'

'I can say I am well. That is part of an answer.' Perrin nodded. His long face, long ears and black sparkling eyes had been further emphasized by fine wrinkles that sagged down his face, that hung beneath his eyes like fine threads which cut slightly into the flesh. His hair was white beside his ears. He looked fit, however, and was well-dressed.

'Don't play cat-and-mouse,' said Henry, hoping to stop this line of conversation.

'What are you doing here?' He managed to be brusque, and he looked enquiringly at Woolmer, to make it clear he blamed him for this, and that, as host, Woolmer had been silent too long.

123

'Perrin is my estates manager,' said Woolmer. 'He has been with me for years.' Henry wondered if this was true but could not challenge it politely. If Perrin was to stay for lunch, then Henry decided he would have to leave. 'The purest coincidence, Mr Kelleway,' continued Woolmer, evidently reading Henry's mind. 'I took advantage of the coincidence only to ask Perrin about you. He has told me that you are a man of the highest integrity. I wouldn't be talking to you here if I didn't think so.'

'If my integrity was as high as you say, I wouldn't be here either,' said Henry with some acidity. 'Be sure that I am not here to discuss the Hertford and Hitchin any more than you, Mr Woolmer, and I take care to repeat that.' Perrin coloured slightly. Something else he had always been prone to, Henry thought.

'Well, Mr Perrin,' said Woolmer casually, 'I believe you have some business to attend to. There is a rumour that we have been invaded by damned surveyors with their stick-of-rock poles, and we can't have it, you know. Perhaps you can entertain Mr Braxton while I have a talk with Mr Kelleway?'

'What about my coachman and his horses?' asked Henry, cutting off his last line of retreat before he realised that was what he had done.

'They'll be seen to.'

'You won't harm the surveyors?'

'Mr Kelleway, we shall have a bit of sport and no more. The dogs are muzzled, we shall fire off a few blanks, I shall gallop about on a horse and swear a bit and sweat and look the squire. I am disappointed that it needs so much for me to convince you.'

Woolmer's big hunched figure, his weathered face, his manner of dress all belied the subtlety with which Henry had been played. He prided himself on being able accurately to assess men. It was part of his stock-in-trade. He had fallen into the trap of his own prejudices against the landed gentry, and he supposed it served him right. He could not plead inexperience now. He said nothing. A final acquiescence.

Lunch was quickly served after the departure of Perrin and Braxton. Woolmer talked about the problems of his estate, of his attempts to improve agriculture, of the contribution of railways to the ease of moving produce, and also of the contribution of the railways to the drain of labour from the land into the better paid jobs in the indescribable slums provided for outworkers. They ate well, and the wine was good. Woolmer drank sparingly and Henry followed suit. He waited for his man to come to the point. Woolmer waited until they had finished eating.

'I'm sorry if it seemed to you that I was trying to unseat you by producing Perrin. I thought it better to do it that way than conceal him as though he were some secret armament. You would then have thought the very worst of me.'

Henry nodded.

'I was very surprised. It is so long ago now. I haven't seen that man for twenty years.'

A maidservant was clearing away dishes noiselessly. Port with two glasses stood untouched on a baize-lined stand between the two men. Henry wondered if the use of the word armament was meant to imply that Woolmer knew a good deal more about Henry than his legal career. It was a strange choice of word.

'I'm glad he has recovered from that business. It was a desperate time.'

'All past and buried,' said Woolmer. 'Perrin is a good manager. He has no embarrassment over the thing now.'

Perrin had made it his business to keep himself informed on Henry's adventures with women. Mrs Waters, in particular, he thought. A lady from that time in his past. He did not even know what had become of her. Woolmer must have been told something. He could not imagine Perrin behaving otherwise. It was a past that he had never supposed would catch up, and the more ironic because of his present circumstances. All that had been before his happy time with Jane. That happy time had been unreal, he had since decided. It was brief, put in the balance against all the times of friction and mistrust, yet it was like some golden summer about which he felt sentimental; like a golden summer in boyhood when small things seem a delight to overwhelm the senses. He *was* a sentimentalist, he told himself. That time could not return, not with Jane. Was it possible with Kate? He felt it should be, and if it was not, was there something lacking that would in the end destroy that too?

'Thinking back, Mr Kelleway? Happier times?'

Woolmer was looking at him carefully, as a man might study a painting. It was disarming.

'Perrin said you were a man of the highest integrity and honour, as soon as he heard your name,' said Woolmer. 'He said that might sound strange, but looking back on your differences, he was confirmed in this. He confesses to a hot temper and considerable envy.' Henry was trying to keep up with this. He was quite unable to assess whether Perrin had genuinely said this or thought it, or whether he was being seduced.

'Hum,' he said, hoping it sounded cynical.

'I don't mean to embarrass you with flattery, or woo you either,' Woolmer concluded. Henry raised a patrician hand, a court gesture.

'Then get to the point, sir, remembering our agreement.'

'The point must remain one of confidence between us.'

Henry held up his hand again.

'You know as well as I do, sir, that I am feed by Hudson, and that I can have no confidences that clash with that. My loyalties there are secured by hard cash. Bluntly put if you like, but true.'

'You can't be too blunt for me, sir. Of course I understand that. But as this is between the two of us, can we consider this as talk around the table? The confidences are going to come from me in any case, and I don't ask for any in return.'

'Then, as I ate your luncheon, I ought to listen.'

'You know that certain questions are being publicly asked about Mr Hudson's methods and about certain of his lines.' Henry said nothing.

'I am telling you on behalf of the landowners in this part and myself in particular that Mr Hudson will not get his crossing of the Great Northern here. We are raising objections to it in Parliament, and he cannot get the land. We know that is his plan, and we shall say so. I had the impression, Mr Kelleway, when we met in Hitchin, and I played John Bull, that you did not know Hudson's plan – an uncomfortable position for a lawyer. I don't ask that, only make my own observation. There is a thundercloud looming over Hudson. It is as black as all the smoke from all his engines, and full of fire and lightning. When that lightning strikes it will hit all those around him, and do untold damage to the whole railway system of this country. Hudson uses great men to prop him up. Great men are just as avaricious as cut-purses, but protest they don't need the money as they seize it. Even the Duke and Stephenson are his constant companions, but they stand slightly to the side of him these days, as I see it. I hear there is to be trouble from Hudson's own Liverpool men, who are far from happy with the way things are going. Like all lines, we thrive off other people's scandals.'

'Where is all this leading, Mr Woolmer?' He stared rather coldly at the weatherbeaten face. Woolmer even resembled John Bull. There was a battered look about his nose, chin and forehead, a certain knobbliness as though it had been in contact with gates and stiles and tree branches. Apart from that, his face was essentially round and rather shapeless. The eyes were dark and alert.

'I haven't said a word,' Henry continued. 'But you mustn't interpret that as agreement.'

'It leads me to the most delicate bit – are you sure you won't have port?'

'No, thank you.'

Woolmer leaned back and fixed his eyes on the panels set in the oak ceiling. Convolvulus and white roses were intertwined in a delicate pattern that had faded to sage, grey and cream. Henry found himself examining the ceiling as well. Neither man then had to register any reaction.

'If you fail here,' said Woolmer to the ceiling, 'as you will, then the Eastern Counties shares won't be worth an autumn leaf. The York draper will have to whistle up some wind! He may not be able to get it. To come back so hard on his shareholders for even more capital to prop up a line that runs away with it ... I don't think so. It's all throwing good money after bad. Men will be ruined who invested heavily in shares in the expectation of dividends.'

Henry did not look at Woolmer. There was no point. He knew what the man was driving at. Indeed, he thought, men will be ruined. Derailed. They could take this fight to Parliament, through the committees and endless sessions, but there was no way the Midland could manipulate itself into London without the assistance of the Great Northern.

'It's the great flaw in everything Hudson did,' said Woolmer. 'Being a Yorkshireman, he concentrated on the North and the Midlands and forgot about London. In terms of goods and the movement of coal and iron, it all made good sense. In terms of passengers, it was a blind spot. We saw it. However, my directors of the Great Northern have instructed me that they would not like to see an eminent barrister such as Mr Kelleway affected by all this.'

He paused. Henry was sharp with Woolmer.

'You mean they feel it would be bad publicity, or do you mean they don't want a fight on their hands? It seems to me they want me to change camps because that would make life most comfortable for them.'

'Yes. That's quite so. We never pick a quarrel where it can be averted.'

There was a long silence which was almost companionable. Henry tried to feel indignant, as though he could emanate waves of hostility to destroy the benign atmosphere. He ought to retain his professional position. He should respond immediately, reject Woolmer out of hand, affect indignation. But why should he? If he failed here as it seemed he would, then everything Woolmer said was true. Hudson would not hesitate to squeeze the Eastern Counties for more money. The vice was closing in on Henry and he felt an uncomfortable sensation of panic. If he could not pay, he would be ruined as far as his chances went for a place on the Bench. He might recover financially – he still had friends that he could borrow from – but the Bench would be filled. He had a mental image of a wooden bench, packed with a line of scarlet-robed figures so that the last man at each end had to clutch the wood of the seat to prevent himself from sliding off on to the floor. They were all pushing and puffing, sweat on their faces. They all stared out from their seats with intense hostility, at someone who must be Henry himself. Territorial as tom-cats. He made himself think about what Woolmer had said. The Great Northern was a respected line. These days, Hudson definitely attracted flies, for all his personal wealth.

'I should assist in bringing Hudson down?' He tried to sound mildly outraged.

'Hudson will bring himself down. They say he'll mizzle on his own lines and hit the buffers! His accounts make no sense and they are due for examination. You must see that. I admire what Hudson started. He persuaded men into the railways who would not have ridden a dog-cart. He's a showman and did spectacular things, but we're past all that now. The railways want solid, sound investment and proper management by a skilled Board if they are to succeed and continue. The Mogul Prince has had his day. Now he must be examined very fine. Put under the microscope.'

'This can't be for charity.'

'Of course not. The Great Northern don't want you fighting them, one, because that will create delays. They think you can spin it out for a year or two. Mr Hildyard thinks so, so you can be complimented.'

Henry snorted, to indicate he was not to be seduced by flattery. He was, however, very pleased. Woolmer was leaning forward now, obviously purposeful. Henry still found the knobbly face incongruous with the words that issued from the man's mouth.

'Therefore my directors would like to offer you stock in the Great Northern, preferential of course, to equal the stock you have in the Eastern Counties, and we can promise you a dividend that will allow you to dispose of the Eastern Counties stock before it gets worse. You must be suffering a hefty loss on that alone.'

Henry raised his patrician hand again, but Woolmer had not finished.

'We don't want an immediate answer, Mr Kelleway. You can't leave Hudson overnight, but there could be a strategic withdrawal.'

From far away there was the sharp sound of two gun shots, then another two. Henry looked at Woolmer sharply.

'What's that?' Woolmer gave a slight shrug of his hunched shoulders.

'The surveyors?' asked Henry, knowing the answer, and

wondering why he did not feel angry.

'Damned vermin,' replied Woolmer without rancour. 'No pellets in them, I promise. I forgot, talking like this. I meant to be out there on a horse, thumping up and down shouting view-halloo. Anyway, it's done.'

'I have to congratulate you, Mr Woolmer,' said Henry, 'You are a very convincing actor. At Hitchin I had you in the same class as Sibthorpe. It is my fault. I misjudged it. I will think about what you've said.'

'Of course. Remember, Mr Kelleway, when dealing with the landed gentry, that the great Duke himself was just a country squire from West Meath!'

When Henry returned to the coach, Woolmer accompanied him. The driver and the horses had evidently been well refreshed. When the driver climbed down to open the door, he brought with him a powerful reek of beer. Henry took a moment or two to adjust to the lack of light in the interior of the coach. Braxton already sat there. There was a suggestion of a smile on the man's face. Woolmer inclined his head to Henry and proffered his hand, which Henry shook.

'Goodbye, Mr Kelleway. I hope you have a pleasant journey back. It will get cooler soon. Good day to you, Braxton.'

Woolmer did not linger, but turned and walked back up the white stone steps. Henry suddenly realised that he had seen no signs of there being a woman about the house.

'Is Woolmer married?' he asked Braxton.

'He was. He's a widower.'

The smell of the leather in the interior of the coach had died down as it cooled in the shade. But it was still strong enough, and did not mix with Braxton's beery breath. Obviously he and Perrin had not spent all their time directing operations against the unfortunate surveyors.

'How are the surveyors?' Henry asked.

Braxton laughed.

'Hot.'

The coach jolted as the driver slapped his reins on the horses. They were reluctant to leave the cool shade of the tree, smelling the hot air with flared nostrils, and placing their feet on the gravel as if it were hot coals. The driver shouted and slapped at them again, too hot to be bothered with his whip. The horses moved off, dawdling. 'I have to look at some of the Great Eastern works,' said Braxton, 'It will mean a diversion before we get back to town, but as we've come all this way ...'

Henry nodded, secretly angry. It was too hot in his view for anything further and he would have to kick his heels. The implication was strong that it was all right for lawyers, but engineers had other things to do. Henry wanted to know what Perrin had said to Braxton, however, and this extension to their trip might give him the opportunity to find out. He wondered how to approach the subject. Braxton was consumed by his own curiosity, but was more direct about it.

'Did you have a good talk with Mr Woolmer?'

'We had a talk,' said Henry coldly. Braxton was not to be deterred.

'I take it that you don't see much chance of buying Woolmer's land? After all, he saw our surveyors off in good style with powder and shot, so you and he must have had a fair old battle, eh, Mr Kelleway?' Braxton turned to Henry and pulled down the corner of his right eye with his forefinger as he spoke. Henry stared at him frozenly. Braxton turned fiery red.

'You don't have to take offence with me, Mr Kelleway. Absolute discretion is my watchword. I take it unkindly that you treat me like you do. If you are worrying about motives and morals, think of this: what is a moral railway line? It's one that deals fairly with its shareholders and passengers alike, cuts no corners at the same time and in the end profits everyone. I was blessed by being born without the problems of loyalty, if you like. Loyalty seems to me to be a blind man's buff. For a fee, you have a scarf tied round your head! Well, I don't subscribe to it. It seems to me a curious sort of loyalty, although I know very well that it's promoted by professional men.'

'If you use that argument, then no criminal deserves a defence.'

'I don't say that. I say defend him with your eyes open. In any case, are we pretending to each other that we believe in the innocence of Mr Hudson? The world is a worldly place, and lawyers certainly know that!'

'You over-simplify everything, Mr Braxton. I can arrive at my own decisions and actions by other more subtle routes.'

'There's nothing subtle about what we've done today. It's business and it's sense. It don't need to be sanctified to be acceptable.'

Henry was defeated. He had not been talked at so bluntly in years and there was no way he could explain to Braxton the tortures he felt over his professional scruples. He wondered if he had just jumped from the frying pan into the fiery furnace. The question of Perrin would clearly have to wait. He picked up Braxton's discarded newspaper and held it up in front of him as a screen. He had just been accused of hypocrisy and double standards and had given no good account of himself. He, Henry Kelleway, barrister, candidate for the Bench, was in danger of being robbed of defences by moral hesitancy. The irony was that people put him in this position, as Woolmer had done, by identifying with his essential honesty. Essential honesty seemed altogether like Braxton's peculiar brand of amorality.

His eyes were caught by a paragraph on the left of the page in front of him. In scanning the page, part of his brain had picked out the name Kelleway from the mass of grey words. Crash of a Balloon, it said in darker type.

'There occurred an accident yesterday evening to a balloon that had left Cremorne gardens for a high altitude ascent but which came to rest in a tree in Hyde Park, tipping one of the occupants, Mr Jonathan Kelleway, to the ground.'

'Mr Kelleway was taken to the house of Mr Green, a surgeon who lives nearby, and was found to have suffered a blow on the head that has fractured his skull, and has also broken his leg. It is understood this last injury is quite severe.'

'Mr Fordham Hays, who made the ascent with Mr Kelleway, escaped unhurt. It seems that the cause of the accident was the precipitate action of Mr Kelleway in releasing too much ballast, causing the balloon to rise rapidly, which Mr Hays had to promptly correct by releasing gas. If it were not for Mr Hays' action and his prompt use of the trailing rope, worse could have befallen.'

'This incident points again to the fact that while ballooning may be a pleasureable pastime, it is not unattended by risks and should only be indulged in by those with experience.'

Henry read it through again. It made no sense. Jonathan was the experienced one of the two, and he could not see Jonathan panicking in the sort of circumstances described. Another damned nuisance. He wondered how badly Jonathan was hurt. He would have to visit him immediately he returned. As for Hays, he would want a word with him, for he had obviously given the report to the newspaper. There was more to it all than met the eye. There was more in everything at the moment than met the eye. Crash of a Balloon. Even the headline had ominous meanings.

Gower Street was dark when he finally arrived home, although the sky above it was still a luminous blue. Gas lamps were already lit, and Henry was again aware of that feeling of constriction. He was dusty and tired but had even enjoyed the visit to the construction site. The working men wore virtually nothing – a ragged piece of trouser about their loins – and were brown and shiny as shoe leather. He and Braxton had sweltered in their black suits. It was expected of them. There was a freedom about everything that he felt he himself needed. The men worked hard, drank hard, fought hard, laid track and moved on with their women, children, prostitutes, camp followers and Company store. At the end of it was an early death, worked out by forty unless they were exceptionally strong. They complained about almost nothing, providing they thought the pay was fair. Henry did not delude himself so much as to envy them, but he was tired of the stuff of his occupation where men complained about almost everything. Tired of the hot dark streets of London that shut out everything except a pencil line of sky. The houses seemed fortified, secret vaults of emotion. How did men live with their women in those tents and shacks, side by side with only canvas or straw walls? They could have no secrets, conceal no actions and passions from one another. When they were drunk, everyone would know. When they made love it would be the same. He wondered if it was any more unlovely for them than the sepulchres of Gower Street.

He looked up at his house as though he expected it to be transformed into a tomb, the windows black holes into rock, mould, running decay. Jane was waiting, watching him from the first-floor window. Constriction. She was clearly waiting for him, and meant him to see it. It would be about Jonathan. Far above, swifts screamed and crossed and re-crossed the ribbon of luminous blue. The door was opened for him before he could reach out his hand for the bell. It was their butler, Weeks, for whom Henry had considerable affection. He too was trapped in the uniform of his trade and the unyielding pattern of his life.

'You musn't anticipate me every time,' he said to Weeks, humour in his eyes blunting the accusation in his voice, 'it's too like the warder that hovers around outside a cell.'

'I saw you standing outside, sir, staring at the house. Pensive.'

'Yes, I suppose I was. I have returned because I cannot contemplate the uncertainties of life outside these walls.' Henry spoke with the toneless voice of a penitent. Weeks, a slight man with a sideways motion of his head like a tortoise, smiled gently.

'Yes sir. I have much the same feelings myself. You are awaited.'

There was again a hint of a smile, a hint of conspiracy that Henry knew he should not subscribe to. Weeks' elderly neck was thin and wrinkled, seeming to taper into his collar. His eyes were grey and faded.

'That is one of the certainties, Weeks,' said Henry, aware that he could be interpreted any way. He took off his hat and allowed himself to be dusted down. He would have preferred to change, but Jane was already on the stairway. He went up, and she immediately ushered him in to the drawing-room. She made no attempt to put out a hand to him, he noticed, nor to peck him on the cheek, and he was grateful.

'Henry, I have something to tell you. I'm sorry to bother you as soon as you get back, but it's important. Did you have a pleasant trip?'

'My trip was very hot.' He had no idea whether it had been pleasant or not. It hardly seemed to fit into that category of description. He was annoyed that she should ask such a vapid question. He poured himself brandy from the tantalus. Windows were open at each end of the room, yet it was still hot, the air unable to circulate between city streets and with that used quality as though all good things had been extracted leaving an exhausted ether. There was dust on polished surfaces, drifting in with this poor substance.

'I suppose it's about Jonathan. I read about it in the *Observer*.'

'Yes!' Jane was clearly excited about it. He found himself, yet again, regarding her dispassionately and thinking that she looked even more beautiful when excited. This evening routine, the coming home to an opened door, the brandy, half an hour of discussion before changing for dinner, was all perfectly domestic. On the face of it he was a lucky man.

'It is in the other journals too. The whole thing is a lie. I've spoken to Jonathan and he confirms it.'

'Oh. He's well enough to tell you about it?'

'His head is all right,' said Jane, 'but his leg is badly broken in two places, one at the ankle. The surgeon thinks it will be a difficult job to knit it properly. He may have a limp for life.'

'I suppose it was Hays' fault.'

'We must do something about Hays. The whole story he is putting out is a libel. Jonathan says the man went mad. He was drunk and a coward, and used the opportunity of Jonathan's injury to get his story forward.'

Henry sighed. He felt tired and could not work up any enthusiasm for Jonathan, Hays or the whole stupid business, yet he supposed he must. It would keep Jane happy, and if she was happy she would more probably remain incurious.

'What about Charlotte? Aren't they intended to marry? Anything that we do to put this matter right is bound to break up their plans. Don't you think there may be a case for Jonathan gritting his teeth and saying nothing? No one will remember anything about it in a week. After all, Jane, it is rather a fuss about nothing.'

133

He said it casually, without thinking, and realised immediately that it was stupid of him. Before he could modify his statement, Jane had rounded on him.

'Jonathan may be maimed. That's hardly a fuss about nothing! And do you think that William and Maria are going to allow Hays near Charlotte again? You can't compromise with people, Henry. This isn't some nice point of law where you find a middle course about which no one is entirely happy but it will do.'

I have found a middle course, about which no one is entirely happy but it will do, thought Henry. Jane has found a middle course in the same way. Life is entirely the finding of middle courses while we pretend that we have picked the best road, the highest road. He wondered if she realised what she was saying, and waited some seconds before answering. Time for Jane to consider. She turned away from him, but whether in anger or realisation he could not tell.

'"It will do" is not always so bad, is it?'

It was cruel of him, but he was tired of being compromised. He was annoyed to hear Jane sniff. It seemed to him that they had come to a moment of realisation which ought to be conducted at a higher plane than tears. He was prepared to discuss their problems calmly, had created a platform from the moment, that would allow them to be honest. It was almost like setting a table with cloth and cutlery, centre pieces and salts which then becomes an inescapable place for the activity of eating. The importance of time and place and atmosphere.

'Is it so bad?' he persisted. 'She loves the man from all I hear.'

'Is that so important? That will pass. All love passes, doesn't it, Henry? You've said that so often.'

'No. I have said that passion passes.'

'Ours has.'

'Yes,' replied Henry.

They were both silent. Through the open windows came night sounds. Horses' hoofs, the jingle of harness and rattle of wheels. A train whistle, far away, all sounds travelling far in the still air. Voices, laughter. The sadness of hearing laughter seemed another, deeper, dusk. The swifts still screamed overhead, their shrill metallic cries devoid of any emotion. Like the sound of our own voices, Jane was thinking. She was determined not to cry. She heard Henry get up, wondered if he were coming over to her for a moment, then realised with fierce bitterness that he was going to the door.

'Are you going to change?' Her voice was level and normal. She congratulated herself.

'Yes.'

'There's one other thing. George Stephenson called before leaving town. He is very concerned about Mr Hudson. He wanted your help.'

Henry felt rising panic. Events wound themselves around him like the serpents around Laocoon. Had he made his sacrifice to Poseidon?

'In what way? Hudson has briefed me on what he wants. It's why I was at Hitchin.'

'It has nothing to do with that. Stephenson wants nothing more to do with Hudson and believes he is on the road to a most enormous crash unless someone takes things in hand. He says everything he is doing is speculation and that he moves money from one line to another at will. He says you are an honest man, and because of that he trusts Mr Henry Kelleway and begs to ask for his help, not for Hudson, but for the lines.'

Jane stopped, because she could hear the bitterness in her own voice. It was better to leave the irony to Henry, let him search his own soul. The door crashed shut and she turned to look at the empty room. She hated the very fabric of it. Bunches of white stock in a glass vase stood in the empty fireplace. With the increasing dusk, the blooms seemed to glow with inner light. The heady, unpleasant sweetness made her feel revulsion. There was a hint of the sweetness of decay, the smell that crowded cow-parsley gives on hot days in country lanes; in graveyards. Already a brown tinge like scorching affected them. The browning of shrouds.

Henry stared at his wardrobe in the dimly lit dressing-room, eyes unfocussed. His suits were suspended in a row like so many hung men. The gloom, he thought, of a dying day, a gloom peculiar to summer when the life-giving sun departs leaving a trail of things that are finished, having given their brief glory.

He was trapped at every turn. Woolmer and Braxton first, now Stephenson and Jane. At each twist he was entangled because they turned to him for his honesty! He wondered how many masters honesty could serve. Jane had hit him in the face with that honesty and he deserved it. He wished that he could confide in her but recognised that as the final hypocrisy. He was not sure that he wanted to confide in Kate, even if she would listen, and expose himself. It would tarnish with handling the carefully preserved polish of their relationship. It was a shock to him to realise that he thought it would not survive such handling, would become dull and marked. He felt like a condemned man.

Six

Louise's descent upon London was sudden and theatrical. Charlie was the appointed herald of it, arriving without warning in Highgate, galloping up Southgate Lane at a breakneck speed that turned heads and made the dust fly. Shopkeepers stepped outside to watch him, curious about his destination. Charlie saw them and grinned.

By luck he caught Edward at home, and it was he who opened the door and saw the dusty figure. Edward looked so surprised that Charlie laughed.

'Yes, it's me. This is a sleepy sort of place, you know. Are you going to ask me in? All of Highgate has come out to stare.'

Caroline appeared, hearing their voices, and was astonished. Charlie gave her only the briefest explanation. Caroline was not satisfied.

'But is your mother here for a visit, and if so why doesn't she come and stay with the family? Come and stay here? She always liked this house.'

'She is and she isn't here for a visit. We don't really know what we shall do next, but mother says she intends to stay in London.'

Caroline subjected Charlie to a very cold look.

'You are making no sense, Charlie, and you are perfectly capable of expressing yourself. I want to know what your mother is doing, appearing suddenly like this. She hasn't written or given us any warning.'

Charlie was chastened. He was well aware of the strength of Caroline's tongue.

'We have left Kent. That is the long and the short of it.'

'You have left Kent, but your father has not left Kent. Is that right?'

'Yes.'

'Ergo, your mother has left your father and you have all come to London. That seems to be a clear explanation of things.'

'I think mother should tell you about it.'

'Charlie, I can't stand dissembling. You come galloping up to the door like a despatch rider, in a high state of excitement, and it is perfectly obvious what has happened. What do you want here? You must tell Louise she is to come and stay, if that is what she

136

wants. I don't know how I can accommodate all of you, but I daresay we can manage somehow. It's all very well for you young people, but I will have to look after the practical matters.'

'No,' protested Charlie, 'I came to tell you, and to ask Edward for help. We are trying to find a place to live. Mother says she won't impose upon anyone until she is settled herself.'

'Where is she now?'

'At Camberwell. We spent the last night there at the Anchor and Hope, not too far from the Montpelier Tea Gardens. Today I want to try to find accommodation in town.'

'I shouldn't be discussing these things with you, but as you're the only person here, I have no choice. Have you any money?'

'Not much,' said Charlie, jolted into candour.

'Is that one of the other things you mean by "help"?'

Charlie was silent. He had intended to discuss this with Edward.

'I won't ask you any other details, Charlie. I shall obtain these from Louise myself. But this question of money must be answered. Your father is not in a position to settle large sums on you all, even if he had the inclination, which I doubt. I do know that things have been bad for a long time, Charlie. I am by no means ignorant about the state of your mother's marriage.'

That is too obviously true, thought Charlie, beginning to wish that he had arranged to meet Edward some other way. They still stood in the hall, and Caroline was making no move to invite him in further.

'I have some investments that I want to discuss with Edward, but I suppose it is true, basically, that we shall be short of money.'

'Have you got any?' pursued Caroline, ruthlessly.

'Very little.'

'Any?'

Charlie looked up at her, desperately.

'About ten pounds.'

Caroline sighed.

'Very well, come in, wash, brush yourself down and have luncheon, and we will see what we can do immediately.'

'Come on, Charlie, I'll look after you,' said Edward, and took him upstairs to wash.

'What an inquisition,' Charlie protested. 'I walked into that.'

'It won't end there. Anyway, tell me quickly, what's going on?'

'We've all had enough, I suppose. It came to a head with arguments and shouting. Father locked himself in that tropical house of his for a day and a night. It's his way of not listening inside

137

his own head. He can come out of that place and pretend he has completely forgotten what happened the day before. He *is* mad, you know. Not exactly mad, I don't mean that in the madhouse sense. He is strong and fit, and moves all the time as though he is on a very short fuse. It terrifies mother.' Charlie was washing his face in the wash-bowl, while Edward inspected his dusty coat, flapping at the worst of it with a hand. He could not think of Louise as 'mother' to Charlie. It jarred and he was unable to use the word.

'How is Louise?'

Charlie paused. He had not shaved well that morning and soap suds clung to his chin. A cautious expression crossed his face. He did not like Edward using the familiar name. He had no objection to Edward admiring Louise, but things his father had said in the violent exchanges that preceded their departure had hurt him.

'As well as you could expect. She is looking forward to seeing the sights.' His tone was as guarded as his expression.

'Come on, Charlie, you said that like a professional chaperon.'

'I suppose that's what I shall have to be.'

'And I will help you, Charlie! We shall take Louise on a grand tour of everything. We shall take trains!'

'Edward ... ' Charlie started to say something and then stopped.

'What is it?'

'Father accused you of paying too much attention to mother. He said that you were just another of her suitors. He said that was why you came to Kent.'

Edward stared at Charlie, aware that he was turning red. He threw Charlie's coat on to the bed. Water was dropping from Charlie's chin on to his shirt and making a grey stain.

'Do you believe that?' asked Edward. Charlie shrugged.

'I think you do admire mother, but then, why not?'

He turned from Edward and poured more water from the river into the flowered bowl, hiding himself by bending and splashing his face. Edward said nothing until Charlie had finished. When he straightened up and reached for the towel on the top of the stand, Edward quickly whipped it away from his reach. Charlie blinked at him, wiping at his face with his hands as soap and water stung his eyes.

'Do you believe that?' demanded Edward again.

'Come on, Edward, give me the towel.'

'Do you believe that?'

'Come on, Edward, give me the thing!' Edward held it behind

his back. Charlie's eyes were watering vigorously from the strong carbolic soap.

'All right, I don't really believe it.'

Edward flung him the towel. He tried to smile but did not entirely succeed. It was a warning. He had not even been able to give a convincing denial. It was a clear indication that things would not have the same rustic simplicity about them as his visits to Kent. Charlie was going to watch him. He wondered if he really cared about Louise anyway and in the same moment dismissed that hopeful thought. Why was he so excited at the prospect of seeing her and squiring her round London? He must not fall out with Charlie.

'I shall certainly need your help; I want to have a look at this business of investment in the railways that you go in for. We shall all need money.'

'You need money to start with, too.'

'But not much, I'm told. If you have the right information, you can pick up hundreds of shares for a song.'

'You said that last time we met. You mustn't go in for that sort of line.'

'You do.'

'But only when I know that something is on its way.'

'Well, I'm only asking that you share it with me.' Charlie's boyish face was as candid as a choirboy's. Life had always seemed easy to Charlie, thought Edward. It was just a question of finding the right person to ask, relying on the expertise of others, and in this case applying some ruthless pressure. He had never given thought to Charlie's amorality until now but, looking back, he realised that Charlie cared for no one and had always used people – Nell, his mother, the country girls he treated with such contempt, and now Edward himself. Charlie had named his price.

'Of course I will share it, if I come upon anything really good.'

'From uncle Henry for example.'

'He's the sort of person who knows.'

'I know.'

'You need a clean shirt,' Edward said to hide the annoyance he felt. This was not at all how he expected things to turn out. He took one of his shirts from a drawer in the mahogany press. Both men were about the same size. It would make a fit of sorts. Edward did not care if it choked Charlie.

'And how is your father?' he pursued, hoping to spike Charlie on this subject at least. Edward had sympathy for John, when he was able to think of him in isolation and not as Louise's husband. And in isolation, he thought of him in that other isolation. Sitting in his tropical house with the warm sweat from the glass plopping on the leaves, or sitting at his own table, denying that equatorial passions had a place in northern climates. They had all left him with that devil on his shoulder he had talked about, which Charlie had fatuously dismissed.

'I told you. Not madhouse mad, but mad.'

Edward felt a strong dislike of Charlie for his casual reply. Edward had no father. John, it seemed, had no family. They all seemed so unattached.

'Why is everyone smoking cigars?' asked Charlie, gesturing out of the window of the coach. 'Is this a new fashion?'

Edward laughed, trying to be light and good-humoured. They were being taken by Edward on a tour of the City in a hired hackney, a 'tired hackney' as Charlie insisted on calling it, and had just left St Paul's. They had walked the cathedral quite diligently and had then wandered among the book-sellers and print-sellers in the Churchyard. Browsing gentlemen puffed ferociously as though trying to get up intellectual steam. Boys lingered for the cigar-ends, darting among passing carriages to rescue them and suck desperately. A jaunty cheroot seemed to be the mark of the artisan.

'It's the small things that impress, isn't it? I suppose these fashions don't happen in the country. It's what they call the "cigar mania".'

'Everything is a "mania" these days,' said Nell. 'I think manias are a mania.'

Edward smiled at Nell, pleased with her and her opinion. He had found himself staring at her during the morning and had dutifully looked away, examined the white marble of tombs of generals, admirals, some famous and many unknown, that littered St Paul's. It was inevitable that he should compare her face with the haughty marble profiles of these men who stood astride coils of cable. He thought that the English language was short of words which could convey beauty without becoming overblown or flowery.

In the Churchyard, Louise and Nell attracted a good deal of attention from the gentlemen browsers, who did not seem at all unworldly about their search for truth and beauty. Charlie had become rather annoyed that so many of them should raise their hats as they passed. Edward had instructed him to respond in the same way. Charlie had then become over-zealous about it.

Comparisons with male marble were not very flattering to Nell, Edward decided. Comparisons with the living female sex were more rewarding. Her country complexion was striking, if unfashionable beside the pallid ladies of London. Nell exuded health. It was part of her beauty, inseparable from the beauty of her face and figure. The only comparison which fully expressed it to him was that between the dull-coated weary nags which pulled City carriages and the glossy vitality of country horses in clover. Nell had that same gloss and alertness. Her hair shone as though lacquered.

Edward realised that he was staring at her again.

'Everyone has suddenly taken up cigars,' he continued in explanation, aware that he was being rather incoherent. 'So much so that the swells have ceased to indulge in the weed. There was even a report, that the journals made a good deal of, that a moustached medical student was stopped by a dustman in Regent Street and, to his infinite indignation, asked for a light. Such is the stuff of gossip and fashion.'

'Why does it matter that he was moustached,' asked Nell.

'Moustaches are going out of fashion, as you can see, and are known to be worn by the "gents" as they call them, of Queen's Bench Prison. But they are "all the go" with tailors, barbers and snobs who wish to be taken for foreigners.'

Louise laughed and Nell was fascinated.

'What strange expressions!' said Louise. 'Strange words and phrases. Is that really the fashionable way to talk?' She clearly enjoyed these trivial snippets and Edward suspected she was making a point of memorising them.

'Oh yes,' he said, 'and fashionable discussion can safely be about Mr Elias Howe's new American sewing machine, or about Sir John Herschel who is always very popular and respected. He has just declared that perfectly good bread can be made from sawdust, and that it is both wholesome and digestible as well as highly nutritive!'

'But that must be nonsense!' said Louise. 'How can wood be nutritive?'

'How can Sir John be wrong! Such a great scientist. Some of the greatest ladies of quality in London have sent out their cooks to purchase clean sawdust, and are at this moment sharpening their teeth and their appetites on baked oak planks!'

'Edward, you're teasing us,' said Louise, encouraging him.

'No. It is perfectly true. If they persist, we can all expect to be served mahogany bread and pine biscuits, believe me. How marvellous for long voyages. Biscuit will last indefinitely, and can only be destroyed by fire! In the event of shipwreck, it will even float and a man may save himself by tying enough of them together!'

Louise was still laughing. There was something about her, so totally relaxed, that struck Edward as rather vulgar. He had never seen her so relaxed before.

'What nonsense!' she protested. 'Are you telling us that there are no sane people in London?'

'Oh, there are plenty of people who are as solidly sane as the next man, but you can always avoid them and they hardly ever bother you in fashionable circles, where it is never done to be left behind.'

'You are sneering at them now,' protested Louise.

'I suppose I am, and it's not fair of me.' Edward was aware that Louise meant to be critical. 'Anyway, it is absolutely compulsory to hear Jenny Lind, in everything she does, if one is to be at all acceptable. She is really marvellous. She is to sing Susanna in *Figaro* at Her Majesty's, and that is the event of the season. You must have tickets.'

'You make everything sound compulsory,' said Charlie, who felt left out of all this. 'I'm sure I shan't find it so.'

'Fashion is only compulsory for the ladies,' replied Edward easily. 'It's fashionable that it should be.'

'I have never been to the opera,' said Louise. Her voice was full of such genuine longing that there was a pause, as though she had screamed. 'I know nothing about it.'

'Then we shall have to start immediately,' said Edward, glancing at Charlie to include him in the arrangement.

'I can't stand singing,' said Charlie.

Edward glowered at him.

'It isn't "singing", as you put it, Charlie. It is the whole theatrical experience and the music and the occasion. It is a place for beautiful ladies.'

'I can always be persuaded.'

'I have never been to a proper theatre either,' said Louise in the same tragic tone. 'All I have ever seen are country entertainments.'

Nell took her mother's arm.

'We'll do all these things,' she said, 'and we will see all the sights. That's why we're here.'

'One of the reasons,' said Louise.

They were moving slowly along Lower Thames Street towards Custom House Quay, where Edward had promised them a view of the Thames and its shipping. They would then return through the City where Edward would point out to Charlie all the places of business, and make for Mayfair where they were to look for accommodation. Louise was determined that she would settle for nothing less than Mayfair. Certainly she could not stay in Camberwell. A pearl in pinchbeck. Yet Edward was against this move to Mayfair. He was jealous, and recognised it. He did not want Louise to be outside his waning control. He did not want her to plant herself in such fruitful ground for fulfilling her ambitions.

The street was narrow and very dark. It smelled of manure, spices, new rope, tar, brewing, and fish. Edward shot an anxious glance at Louise and then Nell. He did not want to lose either of them but could not possibly be their chaperon. The helpless Louise whom he had just glimpsed did not appeal to him. She had also managed to distance herself from Edward. By turns she had been loving, appreciative and amused but had managed to remove herself by that generation which existed between their ages. He was being treated as a charming young man, a charming friend of her son's. It had happened almost immediately, and grown rapidly as Edward introduced her to this or that person. It's like Jack and the Beanstalk, he thought; I am responsible for this thing over which I have lost control. He wondered if it would grow in such a monstrous fashion. He was surprised to find that this process of losing Louise was not as painful as he had imagined it would be. She had seemed essential and he was discovering that perhaps she was not so essential to him after all.

Edward realised that Caroline had sensed Edward's confusion quickly; like a pointer she had been alert in every sense, almost quivering with concentration. He suspected that Caroline had talked to Louise about him, and meant to ask Louise when he got the chance. It was shaming, and that too extended the distance which was growing between them.

'Look, there's the river! And the ships. Hundreds of them!'

It was Nell, excited. The carriage had racketed into the open space of Billingsgate fish market. Its huge open shed was locked up at this hour, but inside were piles of empty boxes and baskets and the smell was potent. Edward reached over and shut the windows, but it made no difference. Louise flapped at the air with her hand as though this might dispel it, and made a face. Nell and Charlie held their noses and made noises of disgust. The cobble-stones were silvery with dried scales. Cats watched them pass, dozens of them from vantage points and from the shadows where they chewed at indigestible, choking things. Then they were clear of the market and on to the Quay.

They followed a procession of heavy wagons loaded with baggage and goods. Here the cobbles were worn into even deeper ruts by the grinding of iron rims and their carriage bucked and juddered. Their driver was shouting overhead, and was having difficulty in making a path as the dockers and boatmen ignored

143

him. Bales, casks and chandlery were heaped everywhere.

'Get that coach out of here!' roared a bulky man dressed in black with a tall hat, shouting at their driver. 'Foot passengers only. You can't bring horses in here.'

A derrick swung out from the Customs House to emphasize his words, its heavy, netted load narrowly missing the heads of the horses. Their ears flicked and they pranced. The bulky man stormed over to the coach and glared in angrily at the window. His expression changed comically from fury to mild annoyance when he saw the two women.

'Begging your pardon, ladies, but your driver must get this coach out of here. The Quay is already jammed – we're loading six ships and there are wagons behind you that can't get in. There isn't room for a cat.'

'Then we'll get down,' said Louise.

'I would advise against it, ma'am,' said the bulky man. 'There are all manner of rabble here. This isn't regular cargo trade but emigrant ships. I would advise against mixing with the likes of these.'

Edward glanced at Louise. Her face had become pale.

'I'll get down all the same.' There was an angry edge to her voice. The bulky man shrugged. He had done his job by warning her and was too busy to care.

'Suit yourself, ma'am. Driver, when your passengers are disembarked, get your coach away from the Quay.'

Charlie leapt down with the jaunty air that Edward had come to dislike. It attracted attention. The bulky man was perfectly correct, the Quay would be crawling with petty thieves working among the emigrants, stealing from them before they departed their petty, cherished things. A last gesture from their home country. A farewell kiss.

Six ships were drawn up at the quay, three cargo boats and three for human cargo. The cargo boats were easy to identify. Their cables were of stiff new hemp, their paintwork was intact, their sails in good condition. The emigrant ships were old with caulking bulging like starved ribs from their seams. Sails were made of bits and pieces.

'They're hulks,' said Charlie, stating the obvious.

Louise was walking along the Quay and Edward was compelled to follow her. They were watched by hard-eyed Customs men who showed in their scowls that they thought she had no right to be there.

'Louise, I don't think we should go any further,' said Edward. He was puzzled by her behaviour. She passed through the endless snakes of men manhandling boxes up the gangplanks. They stared at her, lustfully, catching one another's eyes and whispering things, but never paused. Edward took her arm and, although she did not reject him, she was wooden.

'I want to see these people, Edward.'

'But why?' The helpless Louise had disappeared.

'They are going to America. I once came from there on a ship just like these.'

'Not so bad, surely? Not crowded.'

She stopped and looked at him. It was the way she had looked at him at that dance in Kent, when she had asked what he had ever had to contend with. It commanded him to think.

'The ship wasn't full of people. I wish it had been. But I was crowded to insanity, imprisoned. I thought you could understand.'

There was a noisy commotion on the quayside directly ahead. A crowd of people of all sorts had gathered to stare up at the deck of a ship where a young woman was leaning over the rail and addressing the crowd, who responded with cheers and whistles. A man, who appeared to be the captain, stood beside her and was also shouting, trying to make himself heard. The ship's crew were perched on vantage points on the rail and in the rigging, grinning, watching. Louise and Edward were drawn to it by a general convergence. The young woman was quite striking, and had thrown back her shawl from her shoulders so that she stood with hands on hips, breasts thrust out. It was impossible to make out what was going on until the captain picked up a belaying pin and banged an iron stanchion, making it ring.

'This young woman has handed me a dot of two hundred pounds in money,' shouted the captain in a voice thick with a country burr. 'She was embarking with her intended ...' He managed to get no further, for the Woman took advantage of the silence to plunge in.

'My intended!' She spat on the deck and tossed her head. She was not a Londoner and had the looks of a countrywoman. The crowd gave a small cheer at this gesture. Men folded their arms and settled in for a performance. 'He asked me for half of it when we hadn't more'n got aboard, so I told him what any woman would tell him, that he wasn't getting it, no not likely until we had arrived in America. I saved this money and sold what I owned for it, I'll tell yous and I don't intend it should be drunk before we leave London. Well, he wouldn't have none of it, so 'e's off, ain't he. Going to give me the slip, wasn't 'e. Now what I ask is what am I to do? He ain't my intended now, and I shall need a good man in America, 'cause it ain't a place for a woman alone. What I ask is, there must be some other handsome young fellow who would be prepared to take me on!'

There were cheers and ribald remarks.

'Same conditions, mind! Whoever steps forward shall be my intended for marriage. I ain't taking just anyone, he must be a good working fellow who has a future in him.'

The crowd groaned.

'I have two hundred pounds, and I'm young enough, so don't be bashful, you young fellows, if you're free. Let me have a look at 'e. You must be healthy.'

This produced cheers, and some jostling as men shoved at each other, and some women shoved at their men. After the cheers died there was a shuffling silence. Charlie whispered to Edward.

'By God, I believe I would go with her! Isn't she splendid!'

Edward could not reply. Charlie's crassness knew no bounds. Edward felt tense and distressed. He found himself looking over the crowd, trying to find a man for this woman. Louise was watching with a curious smile that seemed to be only in the corners of her mouth while her eyes were near to tears.

'Come on,' shouted the captain, now the auctioneer, 'I hold the dot and can vouch for it. There must be someone among you lads.'

An old man, with his trousers tied with string at waist and knees, stepped forward to laughter, and threw his arms open wide.

'Not you, grand-dad!' called the woman. 'What about you, lad?' she continued, now pointing into the crowd, 'or you with the blue kerchief?'

The man identified shook his head, while his companions clapped him on the back.

'I be married!' he shouted to more laughter.

A young man who had stood silent, unsmiling and unnoticed, stepped forward quite suddenly. He carried a bag of some sort of tools.

'I'll come if you'll 'ave me.'

'What do you do, mister?' called the woman.

'I'm a mason by trade.'

They looked at each other across the timeless space that had suddenly opened up between the ship and the quay.

'You'll do.'

There was a noisy cheer which the young man ignored, stepping up the gangplank very coolly without a backward glance. He had no soles to his boots and the pink of his feet showed as he walked. He went up to the woman and stood directly in front of her. They looked into each other's eyes. The woman nodded, and they were gone, ushered below by the captain.

'Astonishing.' said Charlie. 'I do believe I lost my chance there.'

Louise started to weep. Edward noticed the tears on her cheeks and turned to her, but she started to hurry away, retracing their route across the quay. Edward walked quickly after her, followed by Charlie who kept asking her, 'What's the matter?'

'Look after Nell,' said Edward rudely. 'Don't lose her in this crowd.'

He caught up with Louise only by running.

'I found it upsetting too,' he tried. He could think of nothing else.

'She was free,' said Louise. 'It was a way that I was free once. If a man made me an offer like that, I would go with him immediately. It showed me how much I've lost over all these years, and now I'm not young! Do you understand, Edward?'

'I don't know,' replied Edward. He understood, however, how dangerous her emotions were.

They passed back along Upper Thames Street, then by New Bridge Street past the Bridewell to Fleet Street. Louise had not seen this part of London all the time she had been closeted in Kent, but she recognised it for it had changed little.

'There is even more traffic than I remember, and the variety of it!' She had recovered her composure and seemed disposed to play the spectator. They were grinding along now, axle to axle with other vehicles – gigs, tilburies, curricles, whiskies, dennets and dog carts, all mixed in with wagons and carts. Fleet Street smelled of horses as potently as Billingsgate smelled of fish. The animals sweated nervously, jostling with one another as their drivers pushed for position. Their droppings formed a smooth mat on the cobbles. A shower of rain would make the smell unspeakable and sunshine would raise a malodorous mist.

'It stinks like a stables,' said Charlie. Louise gave him an annoyed look but said nothing.

'There are a lot of beggars,' said Nell with apprehension in her voice.

'The nameless ones,' said Edward.

'Why? What do you mean?' asked Nell.

'They are, literally, nameless. I think it was Disraeli who christened them that. They forage for what they can find, but as there is an army of them, there isn't much. They are always there, always with us. Disraeli says that infanticide is practised as regularly in England as it is on the banks of the Ganges, but the Church does not care to notice. They give the babies treacle and laudanum to keep them quiet and leave them with another woman to nurse. If they are too much trouble, then a little too much laudanum will do, and who's to know?'

'That is terrible,' said Nell, her voice showing real concern.

147

'But if it wasn't so, just think how many of them there would be,' said Charlie.

Fleet Street widens generously then is nipped in firmly at St Dunstan's Church and at Temple Bar. Some drivers paid little attention to the narrowness and drove firmly into a shouting, angry wedge, taking pleasure in scraping the lacquer from a fancy coach. The stone walls of St Dunstan's were scarred with the crashing of hubs. Edward could see they would soon be at a standstill. He had no particular wish, in his present mood, to be locked in with Charlie any longer if he could avoid it.

'Down Bouverie Street!' he shouted, leaning backwards out of the window of their carriage. The driver nodded. Edward found he was so far out that his head was practically through the window of an adjoining carriage. The well-dressed lady inside gave him a haughty stare. Edward noted with satisfaction that their own driver stung the other carriage's near-side horse with an experienced flick of his whip, so that it bucked and moved over. Their carriage forced through on the inside, followed by angry shouts, and they crashed over the kerb stone into the narrow entrance of Bouverie Street. Edward had hardly had time to duck back inside, and was flung on to the floor. Charlie laughed. Edward was aware of real anger boiling up inside him. He had hurt himself and was jarred. It was certainly not funny. He pulled himself back on to his seat, aware that both the women had exclaimed and were holding out their hands. Charlie sat with arms folded across his chest, grinning.

Edward protested he was quite all right.

'With luck, we can push in somewhere behind King's Bench Walk, and go in to uncle's chambers by Temple Street.'

Finally, they descended from the carriage and walked between sooty buildings into the gardens. The change was as theatrical as ever.

A vista of grass and trees stretched away from them up the slope of the Walk to the Crown Office. Down the grassy slope the view was partly blocked by King's Bench Office, but on each side of the building was a glimpse of more trees with the river and shipping beyond. They paused, looking around. Figures moved about the landscape, either in a great hurry or at the idlest pace. Men passed them in black gowns with white wigs and faces as white as though they too had been powdered. There was an air of unreality about these men, Edward always thought, as though they had just stepped from the stage. Which in a way, he supposed, they had.

'They are like actors,' said Louise, uncannily voicing his thoughts. 'Do they powder their faces? They seem so grey and white. As though they never see the sun.'

'They're not all like that, but it is a sort of fashion,' replied Edward. They started to walk towards Henry's chambers. 'Like actors, of course, they have no formal training, so the similarity is very real. They introduced some form of examination for the first time last year.'

'You mean anyone can be a lawyer?' asked Charlie in the way that Edward was becoming accustomed to.

'As long as he eats his dinners and can pay,' said Edward, 'And even that has fallen by the wayside. In Lincoln's Inn it is enough if you only eat the oysters.'

'Then how do they learn anything?' asked Nell.

'You had better ask uncle Henry about that,' replied Edward. 'It is all down to ability and reading and watching and knowing about the Widow's Estate.'

'What is that?'

'I shan't tell you. Ask uncle Henry about the Widow's Estate.'

Nell looked at him fondly, pleased that he was teasing her, pleased that, in the interplay between herself and her mother, Edward seemed less attentive to Louise in this place. Perhaps, she reasoned, he did not want his uncle to have the slightest inkling of the emotions that crackled about between them. Edward felt immersed in her fondness. It was altogether different from any smile from Louise.

Corbett received them with practised deference, permitting just a little more warmth in his manner than he allowed for clients. They did not have an appointment, but Henry had no one with him. Corbett showed them into a bare, hot waiting-room with its windows tightly shut. Corbett himself was equally tightly clad in a black suit with a high collar and severely wound stock so that he appeared swaddled up to the neck. Seemingly oblivious of the warmth, he even kept his coat fully buttoned.

'I'm sure Mr Kelleway will not be long...' he ventured, and left them. Nobody spoke. The room defied conversation. Edward was pleased to see that it made Charlie uneasy.

Henry himself opened the door and came in. There was a reticence about this action that Edward immediately recognised. They were not to be allowed to troop through his chambers.

'Louise!' Henry pecked her on each cheek, smiling but not convincing. 'I didn't expect to see you. I know that you're in town of course, but you should have told me. I could have arranged for you all to lunch with me. How are you, Charlie? Nell? And you, Edward?'

He shook hands with the two men, and pecked Nell as he had pecked Louise.

'I must say you are all looking very well. Ladies, you are a decoration to the City! I seldom have visitors like this. What a change from my dreary procession.'

He is protesting too much, thought Edward. He is standing back from them all.

Henry was in fact disconcerted. It was predictable that Louise would arrive unannounced in this fashion. It was how she did things. But he had forgotten how beautiful she still was, and had no idea that Nell had become such a beauty. Old Corbett had given him a sly look when he announced them.

'There is a Mrs Louise Kelleway to see you, and daughter, and son and Mr Edward. I have shut the young clerks in their room, as they are inclined to lurk about in the corridor!'

'I can't ask you all to my room,' Henry was continuing, 'because I cannot seat you. Louise, come with me for a moment and tell me what you are doing. Corbett will provide refreshment for the children. Then perhaps I can show you all around?'

The finality of this was not pleasing to Charlie.

'We will have time to talk, won't we, uncle?'

'I expect so.'

'I would like a little time to talk about the railways. As you are an expert. You see, I intend some investment there.'

'I expect we can discuss it.' Henry's manner was abrupt.

'Charlie, you must not be so demanding!' said Louise. 'He has no tact at all,' she added to Henry. Henry smiled sparsely at Louise. He ushered her from the room.

Despite what Corbett had said, heads bobbed back as they entered the corridor, and doors were left strangely ajar as they passed. Henry's chambers were at the extreme end of the corridor and were thus the largest, enjoying the full depth of the building. Louise looked out of the window at the view Henry knew so well, then round at the room with its rich furnishings. There was clearly space to seat them all.

'I am impressed,' she said. She looked at Henry as she said it, and he was embarrassed and looked away. She is altogether too warm, he thought, altogether too exotic. Her eyes and hair are stunning, her skin exceptional, her age immaterial. Faithlessly, he thought of Kate, comparing her unfavourably with this overtly approachable creature, reminding himself of Kate's buttoned coats and brown satin. Louise was dressed in yellow satin that set off her striking dark features. When she moved, she moved easily, swinging around as though she were trying on her gown. She loosened her bonnet and took it off quite casually, aware that Henry was studying her figure.

'*I* am impressed,' said Henry helplessly. He had not meant to say it. Louise laughed, gay and friendly. She took Henry by the arm and led him to the window. Henry felt as though he were doing something immoral. It was the easy way she touched him, let her body brush against him. He reminded himself that this was lunacy, she was his sister-in-law, why should they not be arm in arm? Caroline had been very sour to him about Louise, but he had discounted much of it. Caroline was too critical, perhaps a little jealous.

'I like the view, I like the room, I like the gardens. In short, Henry, I like London. I am so glad I have got away. Can I tell you that honestly? There doesn't seem to be anyone else I can say it to, because I think they all criticise me for leaving John. But I was dying!'

Henry was quiet for some moments, thinking how to reply. His reactions were complex, but he knew that Louise had no interest in complex replies. Because she made this clear, she seldom got them. It was how she manipulated people.

'John must be impossible to live with. But what will he do alone? Can he manage? I shall have to visit him.'

'He will be much happier alone.'

'He will worry about you.' Louise seemed blank at this, but withdrew her arm from his. Henry found it a relief. It was easier to be to the point. He moved slightly away from her so that she could not take hold of him again. Louise immediately noticed, and part of the friendliness went from her.

'Are you going to be a critic too? What sort of existence do you think I've had, lost in the mud, amongst all those trees? Sophistication was not throwing your bones on the floor, or taking off your boots for dinner.'

'Putting something else on, I hope.'

'No! The squires of Kent are quite happy just to take them off. I was never accustomed to that. In Virginia I had everything. Then I had John, a different John so nothing mattered. It went, everything at once, John quite mad, everything quite mad, I am entitled to pick up a few pieces, Henry, and none of you will stop me.'

'What do you intend to do then? What is this picking up of pieces?'

'You ask me that?'

Henry stared at her, astounded, then angry. She was looking at him with a smile that was knowing and conspiratorial. Henry flushed, suppressing any furious retort. He would have to be careful. She was not going to be allowed to attach herself to him.

'I promised to talk to Charlie and Nell. We should join them.'

'Certainly.'

Henry opened the door for her, and stood back as she went out, afraid of contact, of her closeness. A dangerous animal. They nearly walked into Meadows, whose room adjoined Henry's and who happened to be lingering in the corridor. Henry was obliged to make introductions, still simmering with anger. Meadows was enchanted, Meadows was delighted. Louise lingered, would not move on, wished to look inside Meadows' room, was impressed by that also. Meadows would be delighted to offer Mrs Kelleway some refreshment.

'No!' interrupted Henry. The act was entirely for him. His rudeness surprised Meadows, who raised a cautious eyebrow and wondered what the devil had taken Kelleway. He thought Louise quite enchanting. He said he was delighted to have met her. Perhaps he would meet her again?

Henry drove Louise down the corridor with as much courtesy as a farmer driving cattle.

Charlie and Edward were looking annoyed when they entered the waiting-room, and were standing in an attitude of confrontation. Nell was between them, clearly trying to mediate. The scene immediately broke up, Charlie and Edward casual like naughty schoolboys. Corbett had brought tea, Henry noticed, but it had not been touched.

'Uncle, tell us about the Widow's Estate?' asked Nell. The naughty schoolboys were sulking and obviously not intending to speak. Nell's demand was clearly a change of subject. However, it brought Henry up short, absorbed as he was in his own rage. It gave him time to cool down. He thought Nell a clever girl.

'Oh, it's a legal device, a nonsense really. When a man is called to the bar, it passes as an examination. A piece of paper is delivered to you at table before you go to the upper table, and a topic is written upon it that you are supposed to argue. Perhaps it was once argued – but now the topic is always the same, "whether C. shall have the Widow's Estate." Then you must read from this slip which has over the years become so much nonsense that, if you can keep a straight face for one sentence, the senior Bencher says, "Sir, that will do," and you are admitted. If you can't keep a straight face, then you must plough through the whole thing!'

'That admits you to the bar?' Nell was frankly incredulous.

'It does.' Henry could not see Louise's face. She stood in front of him and made no effort to move. He assumed she was concealing herself from him.

'Then anyone can be a barrister,' said Nell, 'who can eat oysters and repeat a sentence with a straight face.' Nell was clearly extending the conversation.

'Anyone who has come a long way before he reaches that table.'

Charlie fidgeted. Edward darted a look of annoyance at him. Henry guessed that he was about to know the source of the friction.

'It's all really amazing, isn't it. But, uncle, I wanted to know if we would have time for a quick word on the prospects of various railways. Edward says you are too busy, and that I'm rude to ask, but I think not because I must do something. A man needs some employment, especially when he needs income.' Charlie, having said his piece, seemed gauche.

Henry looked at the three children and suddenly felt old. They were all so eager to cast him in the role of an uncle, and he was not accustomed to it. He had lectured them like an Ancient.

'The railways are dangerous for investors. It is a game for those who know them well and know exactly what they are doing.' He admired his own hypocrisy.

'Edward has always said that you are an expert and know the railways like the back of your hand.'

'That is a curious expression. No one really knows the back of their hand.' Charlie coloured. Louise turned to Henry, seeming quite composed.

'Charlie has never been able to put things tactfully. Perhaps he is like his mother in that, Henry. But you will do it, won't you?'

'We can have a stroll together and Charlie can explain his ideas.'

Louise smiled at him.

'Thank you, Henry. I'm so glad we can help each other. I knew we could.'

Henry felt he had just acquired another burden. Louise and Charlie were parasitic, were seeking a host. They must be handled at arm's length.

'Perhaps I can accept the refreshment that Mr Meadows so kindly offered,' said Louise, looking steadily and impudently into Henry's eyes, 'while you have a short stroll with Charlie.'

Henry could only nod.

Seven

Jane was worrying about what would be the correct thing to wear, and was annoyed with herself for her indecision. It was hardly an event to affect women all over London, but here and there at least other women – 'elegant females' as they would be dubbed in the journals – were faced with the same problem.

Jane thought Caroline was right, when she maintained that the position of women was worse every year.

'In the days of that fat balloon George,' Caroline had said, 'women at least held their position – and I don't mean just in bed. Mind you, Harriet Wilson had a particular sort of social position, as some rarity, some curiosity, that didn't mind breeding in public like something in the Zoo. Today, she would be shunned completely. Times change, and not for the better for us.'

Jane looked at her dresses with a jaded eye. 'Elegant females' were required to grace the royal route. Nobody cared who they were. Elegant females were one step down from the wives of nobility or Members of Parliament. Elegant females were the wives of directors, engineers, lawyers. Jane sighed, disenchanted with the whole thing. Twenty years ago they would all have been permitted their names and identities. She supposed it was because they now had a queen. It seemed that England needed a lusty king for women to keep their station.

She tried one bonnet after another, slipping on the stiff hoods of material. All her clothes felt uncomfortable, intended to subdue by their stiffness and thickness. They permitted little comfort and certainly did not allow the outline of a thigh or profile of a breast.

'Overdressed. Stuffy,' she said to herself. For the occasion she felt nothing, neither pleasure nor displeasure. She appeared from time to time as Henry's wife on behalf of one railway company or another, was introduced to this person and that person, made the usual vague social gestures which were expected of her, then was forgotten until the next time. Henry did not take her to social gatherings of an intimate nature. She had no friends among the wives. It was her own wish to keep it like that, because it would have been very easy to accept the invitations so liberally broadcast by other elegant females. She sighed again, bored with the imposition of having to choose. Frederick was whistling noisily

154

upstairs, and would be impatient at any delay. His cheerfulness masked unhappiness too, she thought, or if not unhappiness a lack of content. He was not on good terms with Henry, but then, who was? She refused to think about Henry, disciplined her mind deliberately by trying to remember a piece of poetry, and was even able to feel slightly amused that the first words that floated into her head were apt.

'A Robin Redbreast in a Cage
Puts all Heaven in a Rage!'

She repeated it to herself again and again. She could not remember the continuation, but it seemed a very sufficient phrase in itself. Hardly epic stuff, but satisfying. She shut her eyes and grasped the first dress she felt when she stretched out her arm. It would do. She supposed there was a state of unhappiness when one wanted friends. In the emergencies of grief for example. In her own continuing state of unhappiness, friends would have been an imposition, their talk providing endless contrasts between their situations and her own. Heaven certainly seemed to be in no rage about her, she thought, and yet she was caged.

'The wanton Boy that kills the Fly
Shall feel the Spider's enmity.'

Another snatch of the same thing, and complete nonsense. The spider would surely be just as keen to kill the fly as the boy.

Quite suddenly and without being conscious of it, Jane burst into tears. Her efforts to control her thoughts collapsed. Henry had left the house two hours before, saying he was needed early. She knew he did not want to go with her, but was again leaving her to Frederick. She had been trying to deny her anguish all morning and Frederick had been trying to conceal his pity and anger. She hated the woman, whoever she was, Henry was going to see first. She knew the symptoms, knew with certainty that her diagnosis was correct.

She must not let Frederick see that she had been crying. His anger might explode into the open. She stood in front of a cheval-glass and looked at herself severely, repeating the phrase in her mind until it drove out all other thoughts.

'A Robin Redbreast in a Cage
Puts all Heaven in a Rage!'

She thought it was Blake but was not sure. Perhaps Frederick would know. Anyway, her eyes were dry now, and she had chosen a dress and bonnet so there was nothing really to worry about.

'A Robin Redbreast in a Cage Puts all Heaven in a Rage!'

The Eastern Railway Company had problems of its own. The Shoreditch station was far from elegant, being little more than a two-storey brick box, constructed of raw-looking yellow bricks that had not had time to mellow before being stained with soot. The streets around the station were a good deal worse. The dark slums of the area were as appalling and frightening as anything London had to offer. It was unsafe to outsiders, a haunt of pickpockets, common sneaks, garotters and prostitutes. Shoreditch was Hudson's shame, and he had tried to disguise it.

The streets around the station were hung with bunting. Crowds had gathered since early morning, attracted by the rumours and then by the hammering of workmen who hung up the patriotic colours and erected barriers to keep back the patriots. Nothing could be done the day before as it would have disappeared overnight. The general foreman in charge of these operations had made it plain in writing to his manager that he never expected to see the bunting again and would be surprised to recover half of the wood. It was just plain sense to cover yourself in Shoreditch.

The police were worried. Shoreditch is cheek-by-jowl with the City, and they could expect an influx of spectators, all rich for plucking. They would have agreed heartily with Hudson, that the sooner he got his new station in Liverpool Street, the better.

A procession of coaches had passed by since dawn, bringing the directors, caterers, florists and other dignitaries to the Station. The wags in the crowd wanted to know if this was all for Queen Victoria, or King George. 'Long live King George!' they shouted at passing coaches, thinking it a tremendous joke and never tiring of it. They could not tell one coach from another, nor identify the occupants, so cheered Hudson without knowing who he was. He smiled to himself, gratified. It was something to be known so well by the common people. It was something to be greeting the Queen and attending her to a royal carriage on his own line to Cambridge. It would do well for the Eastern Counties. The shares would leap.

He felt a moment of utter contempt for all shares and shareholders. The man with a hundred shares who thinks he is entitled to give advice to a Board. Or the man with ten thousand shares. He would open the entire East Coast route to Scotland on the first of July – only on temporary wooden bridges between Newcastle and Tweedmouth, but open it would be. Parliament dissolved on the twenty-third of July, and he would stand for Sunderland in the next session. He was almost guaranteed to succeed, he had made sure of that, doing his groundwork thoroughly. After all, he had promoted the Sunderland docks successfully and given its control to his supporters in the Conservative Association. His York men would make sure he was well represented at the hustings. Planning conquers all, he thought. Robert Stephenson should have Whitby in the same elections. It was important to secure Robert. There was a dark side about George that was sinister. He was looking old and troubled and was critical. There was disapproval in his eyes. Young Robert carried almost as much kudos as his father, and showed no signs of failing impetus. To be over-scrupulous may be a pleasant indulgence for old age and retirement, thought Hudson, but I have no time for it now, any more than I have for criticism. He was pleased that the *Yorkshireman* had called Robert Stephenson 'the nominee of Mr Hudson'. It made a bond in advance of his winning. Too much had been slipping recently. Liverpool needed closer control. He had had a discouraging report from Kelleway on the land at Hitchin. It was crucial. He determined to speak to him about it when he arrived at Shoreditch. Kelleway was another man with a sanctimonious look in his eye and a pocket full of cheap shares. It was time some dancing was done.

The yellow brick box of the station was draped with swags of red, white and blue, and a canopy had been erected outside which successfully hid much of it. The waiting-room had been redecorated throughout and swathed with garlands of flowers twisted into fine muslin. This was to be the ante-room. Hudson had had a pavilion erected beyond, which was suitable for the occasion. The florists had been given a free hand and had encrusted the walls with set pieces. The Royal cypher had pride of place, and representations of railway engines puffed round below. The scene was chaotic and not altogether pleasant.

Beyond the pavilion, a covered walk or gallery had been constructed along the platform to the door of the royal carriage, which was the culmination of the whole setting, and the wonder of everyone who was privileged to peer inside it. Mr Bridges Adams had designed the car and Mr Herring, the Fleet Street upholsterer, had fitted it out. The bodywork was white with gold decorations and cypher on the outside. Within, the walls were lined with French grey satin, with the roof of the same material, fluted and bunched. The floor had been lined with an inch of felt and covered with Axminster carpet. Mr Herring was most proud of the blinds of peach silk with silver tassels, and of the state chair of maple, carved with the rose, shamrock and thistle. The carving was gilded and was ornamented with gimp, cord and silk tufts. Surmounting the back of this extravagance were the Crown and Cushion, richly gilded, which matched in miniature the enormous Crown and Cushion that glittered on the carriage roof, looking as though it must slide off when the train moved. The elegant ladies were to line this covered walk, were to provide the decoration to the carriage door. It was a flamboyant piece of showmanship, but it had caught the popular imagination. Jane could afford to be casual about her presence among the 'elegant females' but competition had been fierce for a place in the rows that would curtsey to the Queen.

Hudson's arrival caused as much disturbance as though it had been the Royal party. Watching with a disapproving eye, Henry thought there was more overt bowing and scraping to the fat autocrat than even Victoria could expect. He wondered why Hudson persisted in wearing a cut-away coat that so exposed his paunch. It was as if he had some primitive pride in his bulk, equating it with wealth.

Henry was nervous and deliberately hovered about in the forecourt, where he would not be seen. His report on Hitchin had been well wrapped up. It contained the survey, which somehow had been complete, and an engineering report by Braxton which was brief and admirable. It confirmed the suitability of the route. Henry had had to write the assessment of their chances of achieving it and itemise the problems of land assembly. He had been at pains to play down Woolmer's opposition, merely stating that Woolmer was unlikely to come to an arrangement at the moment as he was firmly involved with the Great Northern. He emphasized that many of the smaller landowners whom he had subsequently visited were in favour in principle, provided financial agreements could be reached with some minor changes of route to avoid severing this piece of land from that. He set out in some detail the problems they might encounter over covenants or rights of way. He itemised the compensation that these small men would seek, and listed land values as far as these were known. It would fool nine out of ten directors by its calm optimism, but it certainly did not fool Hudson, who had retorted to it by sending Henry a brief note.

'It seems, Mr Kelleway, that you have entirely failed. The seriousness of this is, I think, fully understood by both of us.'

The threat was unsubtle but expected. Henry knew he would achieve nothing by avoiding Hudson, because Hudson would seek him out. He wanted to delay the confrontation as long as possible, feeling unequal to giving a good account of himself. Jane had made him flee the house, and having taken flight he felt it was easier to keep flying. She had wanted him to tackle Hudson, to drop hints as old George Stephenson had suggested, that trouble was brewing. It was ludicrous in the circumstances. Jane knew nothing about Woolmer, and nothing about Hitchin and nothing about the Great Northern shares he now held. They could not be kept a secret for long, and Hudson must find out when new lists were published. He wondered how long he had got.

'Hudson has got a new favourite,' said a familiar voice, making Henry jump. Braxton stood behind him, hands behind his back, looking mildly amused.

'I'm sorry?' said Henry, not understanding. He could not restrain a flash of annoyance at the man for creeping up on him.

'Mr Robert Stephenson. Old George has washed his hands of it, won't even come, and has told Hudson he don't intend to take any part in any of Hudson's lines. Now we have young Robert instead. I'll bet there are a few words exchanged between those two, father to son. Young Robert is a real businessman.'

Hudson was indeed shaking hands with Robert Stephenson, making a fuss of him, and a small crowd of Hudson's personal friends had gathered.

'This is quite a performance, just to take Albert to Cambridge,' continued Braxton. 'Especially if you consider he only made Chancellor by two votes! I wonder how much this will cost the Eastern Counties? Or the Midland? Or what other dividends the expense of the whole affair will be drawn from?'

'I suppose it may make the line more popular. For a few months. Even that would pay for it.'

'Mr Kelleway, you know as well as I that the current liabilities of the Eastern Counties are thirteen and a half million pounds. Receipts are so low that Hudson should not be paying as much as one percent dividend for the first half of this year. I have just heard, talking to the directors, that he is paying two percent. It seems obvious to me to ask where the difference is coming from. From capital? Who knows. Nobody can understand his accounts.'

'What am I expected to do about it? That is a very serious allegation to make, Braxton. I represent Hudson and the Eastern Counties, I remind you. I should act against the sort of allegation you have just made.'

'Come on now, Mr Kelleway, there's no need to talk to me in that way. We understand the position everything is in. You can't pursue an allegation without provoking an enquiry, which might not be in your client's interest! It's all dangerous stuff. Any road, Hudson is telling everyone of his Parliamentary ambitions now. Maybe he will give up a seat or two on his Boards, but I doubt it. He's getting himself in really thick. And we are keeping at arm's length, aren't we, Mr Kelleway? Loyalty modified by common sense.'

'You know, Braxton, every time we meet, it seems as though

you pummel me. Why do you do it? Are you devoted to bringing Hudson down?'

Henry had hoped to disconcert Braxton, but Braxton's whiskery face broke into a broad grin.

'I am an honest man, like you, Mr Kelleway!'

'Are you a man of letters, Braxton, disguising it?'

'I don't know what you mean, sir,' said Braxton blandly.

'I am *accused* of honesty! You know *Othello*, I take it?'

'I am acquainted with it, but could hardly claim to know it.'

'"Take note, O world! To be direct and honest is not safe."'

'Not unduly cynical, Mr Kelleway. It don't say it's bad, just not safe. A pretty fair summary.'

He stopped pointedly, nodding covertly in the direction of Hudson. Henry looked and saw that the man was coming their way.

'It would be civil to walk towards him,' said Braxton.

'Damn civility!' said Henry, but walked towards him all the same. Hudson's entourage started off in tow, but the big man stopped and flapped at them to go away, much as a man would dismiss dogs. Like dogs they scattered and looked at one another, slightly confused, except for Robert Stephenson who walked beside Hudson. Henry took pleasure in noticing that Braxton was nervous and licked his lips. Stephenson was, after all, the man in charge of the Conway and Britannia bridges, the man who had advocated the use of tubular wrought-iron beams, the man who worked with Fairbairn, Hodgkinson, Brunel and Gooch, the man who had constructed the 'Rocket' at the age of twenty-six. Poor Braxton by comparison had only a few modest achievements to his name. There was nothing in embankments that caught the public imagination, or in the simple structures he had flung across meandering country rivers.

Stephenson, at forty-four, was regarded with Brunel as the greatest engineer of his time. The relationship between the two engineers was as Pope to priest.

Robert Stephenson was watched by everyone. He attracted as much attention as Hudson. He was well built, but his face was lined – a sign of his rather sickly youth. He sported a fringe of beard that stretched from ear to ear, round and under his chin which was clean-shaven, and the effect of this reminded Henry irresistibly of a head on a platter surrounded by a border of piped potatoes. Stephenson wore no moustache and his hair receded slightly from his forehead. His face was brown and weathered – a man who, like Hudson and his father, preferred to see for himself. Henry found himself automatically standing straighter, trying to be as imposing as the other two men.

'Mr Stephenson, this is Braxton, one of our engineers, whom you know,' said Hudson, rudely introducing Braxton first. Stephenson shook Braxton's hand, engulfing it in a powerful, horny fist.

'And this is Mr Kelleway, our lawyer I was telling you about.' Stephenson inclined his head but did not offer to shake hands. The old antipathy between engineers and lawyers, thought Henry. Engineers think they are the only doers in the world.

'I have been discussing matters with Mr Stephenson, Kelleway, who has been so very kind as to listen to me and give me advice. It is imperative that we secure the Hitchin route. We are agreed.'

So that is that, thought Henry. He does not want to know about failure, it is simply to be done. He has brought Stephenson along for added reinforcement.

'My report went into that in detail, Mr Hudson,' said Henry with some tartness.

'I know that,' said Hudson, his accent suddenly broad and Yorkshire as anger flashed in his eyes. He looked dangerous and piggy. 'I'm not interested in your report. What do you take me for? All that tells me is a whole load of excuses why you can't do what you have been instructed to do. I'm giving you the opportunity, Mr Kelleway, to go back there and do the job properly, as I want it done. You can find a way if you put your brains to it. This Woolmer must have a price, and surely you can isolate him by tying up negotiations with everyone else around him. We'll even go under him if that's what he wants. The man is only sticking out for what he can get, like the rest of all these gentry. You're no stranger to it, Kelleway, I can't understand your attitude at all. You seem to have baulked at the first fence and have no inclination to turn around and have another go at it. You were sent to bargain, not come back with a report that makes you look like a kicked cur!'

Henry tried to restrain his anger, but a voice inside kept asking him why he should – a fateful question because he could find no answer.

'That is no way to talk to me, sir. You can dispense with my services any time you wish. Now, if you please!'

'Nay, Kelleway,' flared Hudson, his normally colourful complexion becoming hectic, 'I haven't done with thee yet! It isn't that easy, is it? I haven't done with thee until you secure that route, or if we have done with each other I shall be compelled to make a call on your shares. I have held back, sir, knowing your situation, and I haven't been repaid in my opinion. You had better fly a more attractive kite for Woolmer, or think of some other way of prising him out. I see the long shadow of the Great Northern overcasting all this, but I tell myself that that is my imagination. I have an honest lawyer, who is good at his job, and he will succeed. You may offer this Woolmer any sum you like, within reason. His own private branch line. Make him see what a direct route to London will mean to him. The Great Northern has nothing to offer him.'

Robert Stephenson had so far watched this display of rudeness without comment. As Hudson turned to him, self-importantly, and as he was obviously supposed to add something, he took his cue.

'Railways are projects of far too serious undertaking to be held up by human wilfulness. I was in Colombia, working silver mines. An immensely valuable project. The whole thing foundered on human wilfulness. We cannot have it here.'

Henry stared at Stephenson and back at Hudson. The two men were watching him with the cruel intensity of hunters who have just shot an animal and are waiting to see how long it will be until it drops. Henry wondered what Hudson knew or guessed about the Great Northern openly to drag them in. He must, like the hunted animal, give the impression he has not been hit, that the shots were wide. He gave a bleak smile to Hudson, devoid of any humour.

'In short, I am not allowed to fail.'

'Aye, that's reet,' said Hudson. 'If you fail me, you fail with me. We both have too much to lose. We are playing high cards at this stage of the game.'

'You're putting me under duress,' protested Henry, knowing it sounded feeble.

'Nay, joost working ye hard,' replied Hudson, 'all that's just lawyer's talk. Fine in its place but precious little good when there's work to be done in the field.' Hudson turned away, followed by Stephenson, and, as the two men retreated, Henry heard them chuckle. What price my respected position on the Bench? thought Henry. He wished he had never become involved with the railways. These men treated the Law as a scullion.

'That sets a nice problem,' said Braxton needlessly. 'They say Robert Stephenson is just as tough as his father and twice as determined. I daresay Hudson can get from him the sort of support he ain't getting from old George.'

'He's a thruster.'

'Hudson is going to put him in to Whitby. He can secure that. That will give him more muscle in Parliament.'

'It's going to take him more than that to save himself from the Liverpool men.'

'Aye, I've heard about that too, and if I've heard about it, we can be certain sure that Hudson has and has already decided how to deal with it. I should have thought he would have already brought you in to that?'

'He hasn't. I shouldn't want to take it either.'

'No, so maybe Hudson knows that would be your limit.'

Henry shrugged.

'He's as slippery as a bar of soap. You think you have him, and he's gone again. He is trying to fog everything with this idea of railways in Ireland. If he can get that through, then the stampede and activity will entirely obliterate his business peccadilloes.'

'He will never persuade the Government to put up two thirds of the money.'

'He will never persuade Peel, at any rate, to part with sixteen million pounds, especially when the Irish members are lukewarm, to say the least.' Henry thoughtfully stroked his nose. 'I can only hope that the Liverpool men get on with it as fast as possible. It looks like the only thing that will save me.'

'I should have a word with them. They must know what he wants to stir up over the Irish railways.'

'I may do,' said Henry, 'but on the other hand, I think not.' He was suddenly concerned at how much he had revealed to Braxton. Braxton was a patient listener, too clever at it.

'Think on it, anyway.' said Braxton.

Victoria and Albert arrived in an open State Carriage, accompanied by two more carriages with her ladies-in-waiting. The crowds cheered, flags were waved and pockets were picked in one easy motion. Victoria wore a white muslin cottage bonnet and a satin dress embroidered with peach blossom. The sun shone – 'Hudson's bought the sun!' said some wit in the crowd – and the preparations were all that the florists and decorators could have desired.

Victoria cast an eye over the drapes and swags that festooned the frontage and was seen to approve by the reporters of the national journals. She descended, holding Albert's hand, and walked to the reception room, leaving the royal imprint of her small shoes on the pile of the new carpet. In the reception room, Hudson bowed, clutching his top hat rather low, to his stomach. It was a rubbery, pneumatic motion he managed with some difficulty.

'Good morning, Mr Hudson,' said Victoria.

'Good morning, ma'am,' replied Hudson who had overcome his nerves and was now caught up in a dream. Surely a knighthood could not be far away from all this. Albert was repeating the greeting, and Hudson again responded. It was a precious moment but soon over, as Victoria passed immediately into the pavilion, followed by her ladies-in-waiting. Hudson, who had been instructed in the protocol by an annoyingly insistent elderly man, watched his wife slip away with the ladies-in-waiting. He was vaguely aware that she too had curtsied and responded, and had managed it reasonably. The Queen was now circulating in the pavilion. Albert addressed him again. The men had spoken on a number of occasions, and Albert was impressed by railways.

'This is impressive, Mr Hudson.'

'I hope you will find the journey comfortable.'

'I see you have constructed a new carriage for the journey.'

'The Eastern Counties is not to be outdone, Your Royal Highness, in providing for the comfort of her Majesty.'

'I hear that you are about to open an entire route up the East Coast. That is a very big endeavour.'

Hudson bowed with gratification. He could see the Earl Marshal, the Duke of Norfolk, hovering impatiently, eager to get his charge on board. Hudson determined to risk it.

'It is, your Royal Highness. But even that great endeavour will seem small if it is decided that we shall build railways in Ireland.'

Albert's face remained bland, and he merely nodded. Hudson had no way of knowing if the remark had gone home, and Albert did not invite him to elaborate on the inestimable benefits and countless thousands of jobs that Hudson held out as the benefits, blandly ignoring his own potential profit. The Earl Marshal, face prim with disapproval at this line of conversation, murmured to Albert that others awaited them in the adjoining room. Albert turned from him, the Earl Marshal walking alongside, thus forcing Hudson to bring up the rear as they could not go three abreast. It had been a risk, but was well worth the gamble. Hudson rather thought that Albert might raise the subject again. He must choose some suitably informal occasion.

Within the pavilion, the important males were lined up along one wall and the elegant females along the other, so that they faced each other as though about to start the figure of a dance. The Queen and Prince Albert were now reunited and it was Hudson's job to pass down the line of important males and introduce them briefly. The men were to bow to Victoria, and only shake hands with Albert if he offered to do so. Henry, to his unreasonable annoyance, was sandwiched between Braxton, who seemed to have become attached to him, and a corpulent director called Willoughby who smelled of nervous sweat. The confused hiatus of scents from the floral display could not entirely mask it. They were rather too far down the line, by Henry's way of thinking, too much among the groundlings. Other directors, Stephenson, other engineers, were all to be introduced before him. He was sure it was deliberate, although he could not blame it precisely on Hudson as the order had been dictated by the elderly man from the Palace, whose name nobody seemed to know.

Victoria smiled upon Stephenson, Albert shook his hand, looked into his face as though seeking his essence of greatness. Hudson talked and explained,trying not to wave his arms too much.

'Britannia Bridge,' he heard, then more smiles, then another handshake from Albert.

The directors were treated in accordance with their power and influence. Here, just a nod, there a firm handshake from Albert and a murmur from Victoria. To Henry's chagrin, Victoria spent almost a minute, by his count, with Mr Bridges Adam who had designed the Royal car.

Willoughby shifted beside him, for Willoughby was next and was feeling that he might well faint when his turn came. He could feel droplets of sweat running down his temples, following the line of his cheekbones to his neck then trickling down behind his collar. To mop at his face was unthinkable, so what was he to do? He moved his head slightly so that he eased his neck inside the stiff collar. He had not quite completed this operation when he was suddenly confronted by the Queen.

'This is Mr Willoughby, one of our important directors.'

Mr Willoughby contrived to bow, while his head was still slightly askew from his contortion. The movement was not a great success, Mr Willoughby looking lunatic. There was no hand from Albert for Mr Willoughby, whose wife was now glaring at him from across the room with a look of pure shame.

'Mr Kelleway,' said Hudson. Henry bowed elegantly. Nothing else happened. He was stupefied. Hudson did not expand in any way, had not mentioned that he was their lawyer, legal adviser. Nothing. By the time he had straightened up, the Royal party was already in front of Braxton and he had been granted no more than a flickering glance.

Henry's rage was intense. He knew he was glaring at Hudson, but could not prevent himself. The insult was deliberate and calculated, and he had no immediate redress. Hudson had not even met his eyes.

'Mr Braxton is most familiar with forms of soil, and what lies beneath the green surface of fields and hills,' Hudson was saying to Henry's unbelieving ears. 'In every part of the country, the material changes, sometimes being almost liquid, and sometimes, of course, solid rock. Mr Braxton must know what to expect and how to deal with it.'

165

A smile from Victoria, expressive of interest, an extended hand from Albert. Braxton was so surprised that there was a momentary pause before he comprehended that his hand was to be shaken.

'Most essential work, Mr Braxton,' murmured Albert, and the group moved smoothly on.

At that moment, Henry caught a backward glance from Hudson. A smirk of malicious glee.

The Royal Party were not introduced to the elegant females. Victoria and Albert merely paused, looking in their direction as they prepared to leave the pavilion for the train. The elegant females curtseyed, trying desperately to catch the Royal eye, but that was already averted. They would have to be content in the knowledge that the gentlemen from the journals had requested and received the formal guest list and they could therefore expect to find their names in print in the newspapers on the following day.

Hudson escorted Albert to the train, while Victoria was accompanied by the Earl Marshal. Albert was complimentary, declaring the carriage to be magnificent, although privately thinking the colours a little too exquisite, preferring something a little brighter, a little more robust than Mr Herring could provide. Hudson, still fussing around them, had now presented the Queen with a framed, hand-drawn pictorial map of the line, and illuminated copies of the timetable of the train. Mrs Hudson had contrived to elbow her way into a position of prominence, where she could view and be part of this presentation. She was tired of being surrounded by ladies-in-waiting. Almost immediately, doors were closed, and Hudson and Mrs Hudson retreated to a carriage further down the train. He would be first out at Cambridge to welcome them at the other end. He had no intention of doing things in half-measures. There was just as much traffic required from Cambridge to London as there was from London to Cambridge.

With a short whistle the train started to move. As it cleared the station, the crowds were able to see it properly, and cheered and shouted, boys running along beside the track until it gained too much speed and they were tired. It seemed only moments before it was gone.

In the pavilion, husbands joined wives, or, like Mr Willoughby, tried to elude them. Jane saw Henry standing still in his appointed spot with a frozen calm that she knew well. He wanted no one to approach him, least of all herself. She had seen the brevity of the introduction but could only guess at what was said. She had better find Frederick, who would still be outside, having no claim to enter this hallowed ground. Henry did not even notice her leave.

'You know, Kelleway, I couldn't believe it!' Braxton was

babbling to Henry. He was more excited than Henry had ever heard him. 'I'm not the sort of man to be impressed by Royalty, but when it came to Hudson saying those things, and his Royal Highness agreeing, I was really flattered, I can tell you that. It's funny, isn't it. I mean, I never thought Hudson thought anything of me. I don't even like the man, as you know. Well, well!' He looked at Henry, who was still motionless. 'He was short with you, wasn't he, the devil!'

Henry was thinking that Braxton had never addressed him as 'Kelleway' before. This assumption of equality was as impertinent as it was abrupt. Henry wondered if Braxton considered himself to be going up in the world, or considered Henry to be going down.

'I can't say I feel any great concern,' said Henry, untruthfully.

He had arranged to meet Kate that afternoon, and had pushed all business aside. Apart from Hudson's flood of routine paperwork, he was supposed to be dealing with Hays. Jonathan's leg was not mending well, and Hays' libel dominated family conversation wherever he went. Louise was making a nuisance of herself with Meadows, Charlie was being a pest over his speculations, and Frederick was thunderous with almost perpetual disapproval. All these intrusions. He must dine more frequently in Hall, he was losing contact with his influential friends among the Benchers. Another meeting with Woolmer was imperative, to promote the long process of unravelling himself from Hudson without bringing about his own destruction. There was simply not enough time in his life.

The elegance of the Royal Train would have brought nothing but derision from the third class passengers travelling on the eleven o'clock down train to Derby. Their engine was Royal, was in fact called 'The Queen', but their carriages were more like Mr Shillibeer's buses than a State Coach.

Since Gladstone, as President of the Board of Trade, had succeeded in introducing a Bill which became law, that obliged the railway companies to convey third class passengers at a fare of a penny a mile in vehicles fully protected from the weather, these carriages had been dubbed 'Parlies'.

They were a remarkable advance on the open trucks previously used for third class transport, and the Midland 'Parlies' were better than most. Mounted on four iron wheels, each carriage was divided into three compartments by half-height partitions, each compartment being five feet long, just over six feet wide and five and a half feet high – on the principle that no one should be standing up anyway. Into each of these pens were crammed ten legal seats, but there were usually twelve or fourteen passengers.

The doors on the Midland, however, had proper droplights, and at night a paraffin lamp provided light. Of this last touch of splendour the Midland was particularly proud. It did not however indicate any change of policy from that of all the railway companies – to make third class transport so uncomfortable as to dissuade the users and force them to pay a 'proper' fare.

While it was sunny in London, the Midlands were overhung with accustomed gloom, a mixture of industrial smoke and drizzle that fell as grey as newsprint, staining the leaves on the trees and making the corn a curious colour of dirty fawn. Sometimes the drizzle was more yellow, and sometimes more red. The plagues of Egypt, they said, would largely have gone unnoticed. The cuttings through wet black rock were like the entrances to coal mines, grimed with the soot of passing engines which had formed thin crusts on ledges. A few meagre weeds survived, wild parsleys almost bare of flowers or leaves like umbrellas with only the spokes remaining.

Inside, the passengers had no eyes for this familiar scene. They were wet, or the man beside them was wet, or the woman with the child was wet and the child was sick, or the old man in the corner smelled disgusting. They must either open the window or stifle, so they opened the window and the drizzle sifted in, eagerly, searchingly.

'The Queen' belched black smoke, adding to the enveloping gloom, having just topped an incline that had made her gasp.

'Hey oop, lad!' shouted the driver.

His mate, who had been stooped double, shovelling coal into the stokehole with a steady rhythm, straightened up. His back and trousers were steaming vigorously from the heat. His cheerful face was streaked with soot and rain. He was a young man in his twenties but looked at the moment like some phantom from the mist.

'What 'er it?' he bellowed through cupped hands.

'Don't need more steam. Reckon we have to slow, this length o' track.'

'Why?' The younger man liked speed.

'Not level. Weren't last time. Rails!'

'Aye?'

'Tires woan't take it!'

'*Coom* on!' Cajoling, a tinge of scorn.

'Woan't!'

The racketing noise of the track increased suddenly and the train

168

began to judder and sway. The older man grimaced at the younger and grabbed for the steam valve, releasing pressure with a hiss that split the head, obliterated all sounds. The train slowed gradually, but still clacked uncomfortably at the junction of each rail. The steam valve was shut down again. After a while both men could hear again, the strange music of deafness clearing from their inner ears.

'Nae bloody upkeep!' Shouted the older man. 'The whole section should'er had a restriction on speed. Thon's dangerous. It's shifting!' 'Coom on!' shouted the younger man, grinning cheerfully at the driver, thinking him a right owd Jessie, a worry-guts.

The passengers in the 'Parlies' had forgotten their other physical discomforts, and were talking in alarm, asking one another the questions none of them could answer except by a shrug. What was that? What was going on? Was it all right? Babies, sensitive as hounds to atmosphere, began to bawl. The clacking became more subdued, the rocking less violent. Individuals returned to their isolation, their awareness of the smells of others.

The driver, or engineman, of the up train, 'Albion,' was late, and the engine was flat out. Sparks flew from his chimney and drifted off into the wet fields in a continuous pipe of smoke that seemed to fall from the funnel and stay there. A line of charcoal slashed across the landscape. No worries about fire, he thought, eyeing the soaked corn. Farmers will be worrying, though. No worries for enginemen, except making up time.

He leaned out from the cab, buffeted by the wind and rain, looking for the down train. He expected to pass it soon and leaned on the wheel guard of the spinning drive wheel. It shook. Everything shook. The wheel was an invisible blur of iron. He leaned out further, trying to see forward, round the barrel body of the engine. He shielded his eyes and could see or sense something in the murk.

'Here she cooms!' he shouted. 'We're not that bad, and she's on time!'

His mate, a man of his own age, wiped his face with a kerchief that had once been red, and held his thumb up in recognition. Then he held up both hands, fingers stretched wide.

'Aye, maybe ten. But we's'll make that oop!'

The driver reached for the whistle pull and gave a long and a short blast in recognition, then leaned back over the side, the drizzle coursing down his face, sticking to every hair of stubble, so that he could wave. The 'Albion' struck the up section of loose track with a series of crashes, seeming to leap. Sparks flew up between rail and tires. Before the driver could move, the wheel guard exploded upwards beneath him, the man dissolving into chunks and liquid that smashed into his mate knocking him senseless to the iron floor. The engine crashed down on to the track on its rear axle, digging deep into the broken stone, screaming across the rails, and in a second turned completely over. Fragments of the shattered tire struck the third class coach of 'The Queen' as she passed, cutting through the compartments like cannon shot, scything down people in an instant and leaving things, nameless shapes with gore and intestines. A terrible screaming started.

At the same time the carriages of 'the Albion' reared up over the engine with a tremendous smashing of glass and wood, and fell sideways, by nothing but luck, out of the path of the rest of 'The Queen.'

The driver had no idea what had happened, but he could hear the screaming on his own train and had heard the crash of the up train. He snatched for the tender brakes, but found the mate had already got there and had them turning full on. He grasped at the whistle and began a continuous burst, a signal for the brakeman to apply the brakes in the guard's van. The train was beginning to slow down.

'Oh, greet God!' the driver kept exclaiming, 'Oh, greet God!' He could think of nothing more adequate. He was shaking from head to foot.

'The up's smashed!' shouted the young man.

'Is that what? What's that screaming? Greet God, listen to it!'

'It's from us. We mist've been hit!'

'Stop! Stop!' The older man was beating on the ironwork ineffectually, willing the train to stop, trying to bring it to heel. The train continued to slide on, wheels locked, the single brake in the guard's van almost useless. The two men stared at each other and at the controls, powerless to do anything about this proud engine that had suddenly become an intractable monster.

'Soon as it's slow enough, you'll 'ave to joomp!' shouted the driver. 'Must get to Loughborough box, and get on telegraph to Derby. All help, and warn them.'

'Tell them what, an' all?'

'Tell them a smash. A disaster. Stop the trains. You can joomp now!' The younger man hung over the side of the train, trying to judge the speed and bracing himself to roll the right way if he fell. The track was bordered by clumps of brambles and he would end up in these. He leapt clear, hit the stones of the track with a jolt that made his jaws ache and fell into the bushes. He hardly noticed that they tore at him as he picked himself up and began running,

170

overtaking the engine in a few seconds. It was slowing right down now and would stop in less than fifty yards. He was grateful that he was not going back, towards the crash. He ran in stumbling fashion, with great difficulty, over the broken stone and sleepers, gasping for breath. He had never been much of a runner.

There were already people approaching the track through the drifting drizzle. The noise must have been audible for miles, and there were houses near the track. The running man paused briefly, waving his arms in the air to attract attention, then pointing vigorously, with exaggerated gestures, down the track in the direction from which he had come.

'There's been a smash! The up train has smashed. Bring help. I'm going to Loughborough box!'

'Is it bad?' asked a woman's voice.

'Don't know!' shouted the young man. 'Must get to Loughborough box!'

He ran on. Is it bad? Of course it was bad. He knew he was trembling, but the running disguised it. His stomach heaved, both from shock and exertion and he stopped for a moment, gasping for breath. He retched violently, but brought nothing up. It was over a mile to Loughborough box, but he should be nearly there. It seemed to him that he had been running for an hour. His limbs were inadequate to support his weight, his throat and chest hurt as though he had swallowed burning lead. He staggered on.

'What's the matter, lad?'

A man in Midland uniform seemed to have appeared from nowhere. He too was puffing. He must have been running towards the accident.

'A smash.'

'The up or the down?'

'The up. The down's hit an' all.'

'Jesus Christ. I'll get back to the box and telegraph Derby.'

'Aye. I coom to tell ye.'

The man turned and ran back the way he had come, leaving the engineman to follow at his own pace.

The arrangements at Cambridge were every bit as elegant as those at London, but on a slightly smaller scale. Again, much had been done with swags of material and of flowers to cover the structure itself, and a pavilion had been erected in front of the station entrance to accommodate the Queen and Prince Albert for that brief moment while they awaited their carriage.

As the train drew in, the crowds were interested to see a door open before it had stopped, and the figure of Hudson appear in the doorway of a coach adjoining the Royal coach. The moment the train was stationary, Hudson stepped down with great deftness, and laid his hand firmly on the handle of the Royal carriage, opening it. The station master, who had rehearsed this act for a week, could only look on in astonishment as he froze into immobility. The station master's wife was most put out. She had, after all, invited all her friends to this occasion.

'Your Majesty ... ' murmured Hudson deferentially, extending his arm. To his gratification, she took it, and he assisted the Queen from the train, where she stood for a few seconds on the platform while her entourage collected themselves together. The Earl Marshal resumed his proper place as her escort, and Hudson proceeded with the Queen to the pavilion. Prince Albert walked on her other side, evidently pleased by the cheers of the crowd, and acknowledging them with smiles and small bows.

'Really, this *is* beautiful,' said Victoria, half to Albert, half to Hudson. 'Is it not *most* gratifying.'

It was more than Hudson had dared hope for, and he prayed that the journals would print it word for word. He would ensure that they did. He bowed humbly towards the Queen, regretting that he could not prolong this intimate stroll and must now introduce her to the unmemorable officials of Cambridge. The Railway King was arm-in-arm with the Queen at last. The cartoonists would make fun of it, the journals would portray it, his enemies would satirise it, but nothing could diminish it.

It was after the Royal party had departed that the man in the Cambridge telegraph office got the message. He should have picked it up earlier, but had left his desk to watch the proceedings, like everyone else. He took it to the station master.

'Thank you, Mr Thompson,' said the station master unemotionally. He was cut to the quick by Hudson opening the Royal door and even more mortified that, having done so, Hudson had walked with the Queen to the pavilion without bothering to introduce him. The station master is lord of all he surveys. He is as territorial as a robin, and as aggressive. There could be no excuse.

'It's urgent,' persisted Thompson.

'Thank you,' returned the station master, not deigning to read the message until Thompson had gone. Its contents were bald enough.

'Urgent attention Mr George Hudson. Train crash Midland Rwy by Loughborough. Six fatalities certain, number of injured not known. Investigation into cause has commenced. Second train hit by wreckage from first. Train driver dead. Up line blocked, down clear.'

That should wipe the smile off his face, thought the station master grimly.

Hudson was talking buoyant business when the station master found him, and had the air of being as unapproachable as a bishop at the altar. However the station master reminded himself that this was his station and stepped up boldly enough.

'A message has come by telegraph for you, sir.'

Hudson's eyes flickered over the station master. The expression on his face remained, to indicate the trivial nature of this interruption. He took the proffered slip of paper on which Thompson had written the message in his careful copperplate, read it with no change of expression and put it in his pocket.

'Thank you.'

Hudson's eyes flickered briefly again over the station master. He was dismissed. The only satisfaction the Station Master would obtain would be in complaining to his wife.

Hudson's smile continued and broadened.

'I am giving a banquet in the Mansion House in York next week,' he said, managing to give the impression that somehow the message was connected with this piece of news. 'To celebrate this royal occasion, of course. Formal invitations will be forthcoming when I can get 'em printed, but I hope that you will all try to coom.'

'When will it be next week?' asked a stout director who looked as though he enjoyed his food. Hudson smiled indulgently at such a naive question.

'Why, *all* next week.'

In the ensuing laughter, his mind was working quickly. He could recall the stretch of line near Loughborough, as he could recall almost every mile he controlled. It had given trouble during construction due to unstable ground conditions. It had been difficult to achieve proper consolidation, and expensive. The regional manager had recently complained about the condition of the track, and lack of maintenance men and funds. Hudson had promptly cut back on them further. That might get out. It might mean trouble, especially if anyone important had been killed or injured. The reporters would love to dredge something up about bad repair. The Midland might face proceedings. Another job for Kelleway, he thought unkindly, his mind going back to their earlier encounter. The man annoyed him with his sanctimonious air. He deserved another dirty task, and then ... get rid of him.

Eight

The atmosphere in the studio at Flood Street was bitter as the smell of turpentine.

Jonathan had been feeding the stove with coal because, although it was high summer, there had been a tough, raw wind from the north which had bullied clouds around the sky, torn up leaves into scraps and snapped off wiry green twigs. It left the evening clear and bright, but with a hint of frost in it. The mud banks of Chelsea glistened as though already iced. Waders and crows ran about on them, looking for food that the boisterous water had churned up. The wind buffeted them, blowing their wings over their heads, like old ladies with big skirts. They staggered and ran, staggered and ran.

Jonathan was squatting by the door of the stove as best he could, poking vigorously at the coals with a poker which had long since burned to a point. This method of breaking up the bigger lumps was proving ineffectual.

'Do stop stabbing at it!' said Caroline tartly, expressing quite clearly the irritation she felt about everything in general.

'You should break up the coal before you fill the scuttle. Don't you have a coal hammer? Why don't you order smaller coals?'

Maria paid no attention except to glance at her and away again. It was necessary to acknowledge Caroline, or she would only continue in a similar vein at greater length. Maria was angry herself, to a degree that made her feel savage. She was watching the awkwardness of Jonathan's left leg, propped out to the side as he squatted down, and felt pain in her own leg that made her wince. Jonathan had told her many times that there was now no pain, only stiffness and awkwardness, but she knew this was not true and imagined his whole leg ached fiercely, like a toothache. The shin had been fractured and had mended badly and was misaligned. Worse, the tendons had shrunk, drawing up his heel and making the knee almost useless. He wore a special shoe and had laid the leg sideways as though it was wood.

'How can anyone have any idea where she will be?' asked Maria, returning again to the subject that had brought them together. Maria had found a note from Charlotte at noon that day, which informed her that Charlotte had left home and intended to marry Hays. She left her love, but wished the family to understand

174

that she loved Hays more, and could no longer live with the criticism and animosity that was directed towards him in their house.

Maria was thunderstruck, Jonathan was furious. William had been quiet, sensing that there was enough anger in the other two, and that his role must be that of preserving reason. He had tried to deter Maria from sending a note to Caroline, but Maria had insisted and here they all were, bristling.

'Find Hays,' said Jonathan, slamming the stove door with a metallic clap, 'and there she will be.'

'So you really mean to stop the marriage, do you, Jonathan?' said Caroline, much as a mother talks to a babbling infant. 'Human nature is an odd thing, in case you haven't noticed it. Perhaps this marriage will be the right thing for Charlotte.'

'There is not going to be a marriage!' said Jonathan loudly and vehemently. 'I shouldn't be wasting time talking. I should be out, trying to trace her. Or him.'

'To horse! To horse!' declared Caroline rudely. 'What will that achieve? Where are you to dash off to? So you charge off out of Flood Street, so far so good. Where do you go next?'

'Hays' estate.'

'I should doubt very much if you will find anyone there.'

'So you propose that we do nothing?'

He wondered what this tart old dragon knew or thought about anything. She had never been married, but seemed fluent with advice on the subject. Revenge for her own lack of romance? Vicarious pleasure? It was possible. Jonathan saw nothing romantic in the situation at all. It was a disaster, a duping of the innocent, the theft of an uncomprehending girl by a man without the least principle. The only time that Hays had spoken the truth was when he had described himself as a plain bit of clay, a bore. The thought that Charlotte, with all her beauty, should be touched, handled, fondled by such a man was so repulsive to Jonathan that he wanted to scream. His views were not mature. At twenty-two, there were many traces of attitudes which were passionately adolescent. Caroline, with her astuteness, saw it of course, but with her heartless bluntness was not prepared to make allowances.

'I think we should also inform the police,' Jonathan announced. 'The man even looks repulsive. He is a coward and a libeller. He has still got that to answer for. He has still my leg to answer for. Isn't that enough, Aunt Caroline?'

'What are the police to do?' asked William. He was sitting beside Maria on a maroon satin sofa which at his end was worn through to the horsehair. 'Are they to drag her back? She hasn't been abducted, she isn't under age, she has gone of her own free will.

175

Without permission if you like, but that isn't very much for a woman of her age. If she wants to marry, there's little we can do about it, Jonathan. That's the position. We can only try to persuade her against it.'

'I shall persuade *him* against it!' declared Jonathan recklessly. 'I shall persaude him so that he remembers.' William raised his eyebrows to Maria. She shook her head slightly. Caroline too chose to ignore this remark.

'You brought her up to have too advanced views, you know, Maria,' she said.

Maria was so astounded that she could only stare for a few moments as though she disbelieved the sense of what she heard. William, alert to imminent fireworks, got as far, in the act of intervention, as to stretch out an arm in an oratorical gesture, but he was too late.

'I daresay these advanced views are something to do with her Kelleway blood,' said Maria. Her tone was rude. 'You can hardly pretend that your life has been lived strictly in accordance with the conventions, Caroline.'

'I hardly ran off with anybody,' said Caroline with tartness. She sat very upright and looked at Maria with her patrician stare. She seemed to have gained inches, her features to have become sharper. With a little will, Jonathan thought, she could change herself into a dagger, steel to represent her feelings in concrete form. He admired her despite her sarcasm towards him.

'We must *do* something,' he said. 'I know that sounds rather weak and perhaps it sounds aimless and not very clever, but surely doing something is better than doing nothing!'

'But, Jonathan, what are you going to do?' asked Maria. 'I have to keep asking that. I know how you feel, we all know how much you dislike Hays.'

'Hate,' said Jonathan.

'Very well, hate. That makes it so much worse, can't you see. We all understand why. We know you have unfinished business with the man, but it is the nature of life that some business is sometimes left unfinished. You must not turn this into a vendetta. A vendetta is a dark thing without reason.'

'Some things may be sometimes unfinished,' said Jonathan, 'but not by me. It's all very poetic, this thing about vendettas. Dark things without reason. Instant damnation I suppose, shades of Dante. I mean to find Hays and, when I find him, I mean to have it out with him.'

'How?' asked William sharply. 'Do you know what you intend to do? Do you intend to break his leg, take Charlotte by the arm, drag her from the clutches of servants who cling to her, run a few of them through with a rapier, vault over the garden wall with her under your arm, fling her over your saddle and gallop away?' He paused. 'How? Answer me that? This is a serious matter concerning your sister and her life. Reality, not fable.'

'Don't treat me like an imbecile!' Jonathan was angry, and turned as though at bay, his back to the stove. He was forced by the heat to move forward and this spoiled the pose.

'You say in one breath that there is nothing that the police can do. You apparently intend to do nothing and, when I suggest doing something, paint me as a picture of ridicule. That is too easy!'

'Jonathan!' protested Maria, trying to keep the peace. 'That isn't what your father meant at all!'

'He keeps asking me how! How should I know how? I haven't decided how. Perhaps if we could all agree on some course of action, we *could* discuss how!'

Maria looked encouragingly at William, willing him to mollify Jonathan. William chose not to notice.

'I think we should consider very seriously what Caroline said,' said Maria quickly. All William wanted was to get on with his work. It was something basic within him, and there was nothing she could do about it. It was not that William did not love Charlotte, but he had a streak of selfishness or perhaps it was self-protection that made him impatient with emotional storms, even his children's.

'Caroline said that perhaps this marriage will be the right thing for Charlotte. Perhaps we should consider that properly. Perhaps we should be thinking of ways of supporting her. Opposition will only made her more determined, we know that. It is the common response. My instinct is to welcome the situation, welcome her news, attempt to welcome her back into the family. That will give her time to think. If she was acting in too much haste, it might give her time to pause.'

'You don't think that Hays is going to believe that.' It was Caroline. She snorted like a horse. 'Really, Maria, I understand your sentiments, but that is all as old as the hills. The first thing this Hays is not going to allow is a renewed contact between you and Charlotte. Would you, if you were in his position? She's run away because she can't face you over this matter, hasn't she? She doesn't want letters from you that tug away at her heart-strings. She won't even open them; I wouldn't. Perhaps Jonathan is right, and should try to find her, but not swinging an axe or waving a blunderbuss. He should visit his sister, as a brother should, to see if there is anything he can do, and any way he can help. That would establish a link which would not be oppressive. The difficulty is that you, Jonathan, will have to keep your head.

177

I think you can, with a bit of prudence.'

How Caroline really loves Jonathan, thought Maria. They have a lot in common, there is a bond that will mature as Jonathan matures. He will listen to her while he will not listen to me.

Jonathan was giving this statement of Caroline's serious thought. He turned, stooped awkwardly, his injured leg splayed, and picked up the poker, again prising open the door of the furious stove. He stared at the flames for some seconds, perhaps finding relief in their raging.

'I think that is a very good idea, Aunt Caroline.'

Margaret had spoken. She had sat throughout in silence and unnoticed. As she was not given to intervention in such matters, her quiet opinion was received as though the clouds had been parted and tablets of stone had crashed at their feet.

Such a pretty girl, thought Caroline, inconsequentially. A very sweet nature, but lacking in sparkle. She will make a lovely wife, a decoration for someone, and may be perfectly happy as no more than that. It was with an effort of will that Caroline considered the words Margaret had spoken.

'Thank you, my dear. I'm glad someone approves.'

'I think Charlotte will respond to Jonathan and, if she is not really happy, I think she will say so, in the same way that she would tell me. She will be too ashamed to tell mother or father what she really feels.'

'Charmingly put, my dear,' said Caroline.

She really is intolerably patronising, thought William, but Caroline is quite probably right if only Jonathan can be relied upon to stop breathing fire and slaughter.

'I agree it is a good idea,' he said, 'but so much depends upon you, Jonathan. You will have to be civil to Hays or nothing will come of it. Can you manage it?'

Jonathan's shoulders rose and fell in a shrug. He would not turn to them just yet. He was trying to imagine himself taking Hays by the hand, greeting him calmly, not cordially, coping with his emotions when presented with Charlotte. What if they were living together already as man and wife? Could he cope with that? For the sake of Charlotte. It was in his interests to woo her away, return her to the family fold, disenchanted, then he would have time to plan a terrible revenge.

'Perhaps I can.' Jonathan gave a half-laugh that held no humour. 'I can practise it, until I am versed in the part. It will be a piece of theatre, so I may as well study it as an actor. Who is to direct me?'

He turned from the fire and looked round the room. It was a curiously theatrical moment, and Jonathan was right. He was to act out a part on behalf of them all and for Charlotte. He must be trained in it.

'Are you to train me, Aunt Caroline?'

'Well, my dear Jonathan,' murmured Caroline disparagingly, 'I really think it is something for your mother to decide.'

'It certainly is!' Maria spoke more fiercely than she intended. She had had enough of Caroline for the moment. 'We can best discuss how we think Charlotte would wish to be approached.'

'That seems like a good arrangement,' said William. It had calmed everything down again. Mexico City could now continue its sprawling growth. His mind was full of ideas, of small details, of effects that would outshine anything done before. The grand Cosmoramic view of the City of Mexico would be the eighth wonder of the world. Or, if not that, at least among the top hundred. It would be preserved forever, not painted out like its predecessors. Ellis was already saying that he would find a permanent home for it in Cremorne.

'We must also contact Henry,' said Maria. 'He ought to be kept informed. He is very sensible about this sort of thing.'

Henry would not have been pleased to be disturbed. He was concentrating upon the feel of Kate's body, pressed to him as they lay satiated. He was thinking that the female body is a curious thing, so soft and yet so hard and bony. A man's body was by tradition hard, but was probably as soft as a woman's. Especially in middle age, he thought wrily. He touched toes with her, noticing how hard and dry feet are, even a soft woman's feet. He supposed he used to notice these things about Jane, but could not remember it. Kate had much better breasts. Pressed to him now, he was aware of them. They did not disappear, melt away, leaving rib in contact with rib. It was a pleasant contemplation.

Outside, the noise of horses and carriages was insistent and increasing. The idle and the easy-living were already homeward bound. It was nearly five, he estimated. The room was dark, heavy velvet curtains drawn, except for a diffused glare which escaped over the top of the curtains and illumined the pelmet. A beautiful evening was beginning to assemble itself outside. The sun already had a perceptible orange tinge. The clouds had accumulated into a puffy margin. Blackbirds were tuning up, and had stopped fighting over a snail in the back garden. The air had become soft, with only a tender breeze which breathed on all things as Kate breathed on Henry's back, for gentle sport. To attract attention without breaking spells.

'Yes?' asked Henry in a voice that was reluctant. He knew what Kate was about to say.

179

'We can't stay like this forever.'

'I know.' He made no effort to move, nor did Kate, but their minds began to surface from the warm depths of indulgence, to notice warmth and cold. An exposed part of back that was not quite comfortable. A supporting arm that had partially gone to sleep. The sharpness of toenails. Hunger. Henry had eaten no lunch and realised he was ravenous. A journey back to the humdrum, he thought. That necessary distancing from things that are exquisite. Only the youngest lovers can sustain it, and then only for a first love, and that for only a short time. Et in Arcadia ego.

Henry's mood might have been self-indulgent, but Kate's was more alert. What if her husband returned? Would he be likely to come to her bedroom, and if he did, would he care? Could things be precipitated in any way by such an event, and if so, would it do more harm than good? Henry continued to declare he loved her, and she believed that he believed it, but would not go beyond that. He still persisted with the idea of setting her up in a little house of her own, of moving her from London, even, to Tunbridge Wells or Cheltenham. That was tantamount to buying her, she had told him, and insulting, and she had burst into tears. She wanted to be beside him, needed in his everyday affairs and business, she had declared. Did he want a mere plaything?

Henry had been contrite. He was sorry he had been so stupid, and had talked without thinking. Kate had forgiven him, or pretended to, but could not ignore the obvious. He did not think of her as a wife, or even a potential wife. Not yet. Maybe he never would. He must be deprived of her and made to make up his mind. She must tantalise, give and take away, because there was a great deal of the child in Henry. Kate would enjoy the giving, and would suffer just as much as Henry from the taking away, because her love was real enough, but the pain would be worth it.

'The birds are starting to sing,' she said, lest he should note her long silence and ask what she was thinking. It sounded a particularly vacuous remark as soon as she said it, and it had the result of making Henry prop himself on one elbow to stare at her.

'My word, so they are,' he said. He looked at her carefully, removed the sheet from her upper body and looked that over carefully. 'What is the matter?'

'I said the birds are starting to sing. That's all. There's nothing remarkable in it.' She took the sheet from his hands and covered herself again.

'You said it as significantly as a Sibyl.'

'I didn't mean to.'

'You are going over what we said before. I said I was sorry. No Cheltenham, no Tunbridge Wells. I promise.'

'I was thinking about railway matters,' lied Kate. 'That shows how much you wrong me.' She smiled to soften the statement. 'I suppose you've forgotten that you came here fuming about Hudson, and paced up and down and lectured me.'

From below came the sharp jangling of a door-bell vigorously pulled. They both started guiltily.

'Who on earth's that?'

'Well, it's not my husband, he has a key!'

'I'd better get dressed!' Henry started up and flung back the bed clothes. 'What servants are in the house?'

'Only cook, and she knows all about us. She won't say a word because she enjoys the complicity so much.'

'I don't think you should just lie there,' said Henry, struggling with his clothes.

From below there came another tremendous jangling. Whoever it was was no longer satisfied with giving the bell-pull a tug, but was now shoving it out and in with some violence.

'I refuse to start an undignified scramble,' said Kate. 'I don't care who knows I'm here with you.'

The jangling stopped abruptly and two voices spoke, one female, one male.

'It's certainly a man,' said Kate, 'that's cook's voice.' She was trying not to laugh at Henry's fumbling contest with his clothes. His shirt collar was defeating him completely and one arm of the shirt was inside out.

'Let me help you.' Kate stepped from the bed, naked, and started to turn the shirt sleeve in on itself. Henry looked at her with horror.

'You can't stand here with nothing on!'

'Don't be ridiculous.'

'No, go back into the bed!'

The panic in Henry's voice was too much for Kate, who laughed.

'You have some strange ideas, Henry Kelleway. We have just been in that bed together. My nakedness didn't bother you then.'

'It's not the same!' He sounded so alarmed that Kate was touched by it. She sat down on the bed and draped a sheet around her. The voices below were quite loud now. The man seemed to be following cook upstairs. She could clearly be heard telling him to stay where he was until she came back. There was a knock on the bedroom door. Tentative, almost apologetic. Henry looked desperately at Kate.

'What is it?' called Kate.

'There is a gentleman here who insists on seeing Mr Kelleway, and won't take no for an answer. I'm very sorry, Mrs Carter.'

'What sort of a gentleman?'

'A railway sort of gentleman, he says, with urgent business. Shall I tell him to go away?' Kate looked at Henry, who was now putting on his shoes.

'Damnation, I suppose I shall have to see him,' said Henry. 'How did this fellow find me here? Someone knows, that's for sure. I didn't know that anyone knew. The secret's out.'

And that is the first thing you thought of, thought Kate to herself. 'Tell him to wait downstairs,' said Kate loudly. 'He has no business to insist on seeing anyone. Mr Kelleway will see him immediately.'

Henry scowled at Kate. There was no humour in his face, no conspiracy, Kate saw, only anger. Considering that they had just been so preoccupied with and within each other, it was an unpleasant check.

Henry was dressed now, but untidily.

'You look ... obvious,' said Kate.

'Well, help me!'

'Then, let me out of bed.'

'All right!'

Henry's voice was bursting with ill-temper but also with that note of despair of a man who cannot stud his collar. Kate stepped out of bed and straightened his collar for him, forcing the front stud through and taking satisfaction from Henry's coughing as she thrust her forefinger hard into his throat. She straightened out his shirt and coat, adjusted his waistcoat, went to her dressing-table and took a brush to smooth down his hair. Henry at first had averted his eyes from the sight of all this nakedness but Kate knew he was now covertly watching her. She brushed his hair flat, standing on tiptoe to reach, and still not able to flatten down his crown. Without warning Henry kissed her breasts quickly and lightly. Kate paused where she was, looking him carefully in the eyes.

'There now,' she said, 'that didn't hurt, did it? Now go, Mr Prude, or that man will think we're bedded down again.'

The 'railway sort of gentleman' was standing in front of the empty grate in the attitude of a man warming his breeches. The gas lights on either side of the mantel had been lit and gave a soft and very yellow glow that was still less bright than the light of the evening sun. It was not a very humble position or posture to adopt in a stranger's house, Henry thought. Besides, the 'railway sort of

182

gentleman' had a knowing look for all the deference he showed in stepping forward and proffering his hand with a little bow. Henry took an immediate dislike to him.

'I beg your pardon, Mr Kelleway, I would not have interrupted if it was not a matter of the greatest importance.'

'You have not interrupted,' said Henry in an off-hand manner, giving his haughty profile the benefit of side-lighting from the window. The Wellington pose to bring out the Wellington nose. And brow. He wondered how this straggle-haired, ginger-whiskered sycophant of Hudson's had found him.

'The name is Hussey, sir, William Hussey.'

Henry nodded distantly.

'I have come from Mr Hudson.'

The man dropped his aitches and had a strong London accent. Henry wondered inconsequentially why the family name had not changed to Ussey. Henry recognised him vaguely by appearance as one of those creatures who was always on the edge of things, a messenger boy of Hudson's. Part of the chorus.

'Well, Mr Hussey, what is so important that you virtually force your way in?'

'I'm sorry, Mr Kelleway, I had no intention of offending, but you know Mr Hudson and he was absolutely insistent that I should get you right away. What he says is the word, the law and the bond, as you know, sir, and what he said was, get Mr Kelleway on this immediately and let him get on to it promptly. He was most insistent. To the point, I think I could say. And when Mr Hudson is to the point, then he is to the point! You take my drift, sir, I'm sure. It was find you or find other employ! I was sent to your house, sir, but your wife said you weren't at home and I should try here, so I came on, as quickly as I could. I have the cab standing ...'

The man continued to prattle, apparently oblivious of the thunderbolts and sheets of fire he had hurled at Henry, but all the time his sharp eyes were alert, belying the stream of verbiage.

Henry tried not to move a muscle, tried not to think about anything for the moment except the man's declared purpose in coming. Now the heavens are raining fire, he thought, and the sentence kept repeating itself in his brain. This Hussey would certainly report back to Hudson. And there was Jane. He must listen to what the man was saying.

'What is the matter, Mr Hussey? You haven't come to the point. We all know that Mr Hudson likes things done, but what is it?' He was pleased that his voice sounded calm and precise. Amid the rain of fire. Fuel for Hudson's fire. A conflagration for Jane.

'There's been a terrible accident near Loughborough. Six killed

183

and two likely to die, they say. Mutilated very nasty. The up train "Albion," see, broke a tire. Shattered to smithereens, killed the driver – pulped him they say – and derailed the train. Part of the tire cut through the down train that was passing, killing two others. Terrible mess. Bits of people everywhere, so they say.'

'Yes, Mr Hussey. There would be. I have seen other accidents.' The man's ghoulish relish disgusted Henry. He vowed to take Mr Hussey with him if he got the chance, so Mr Hussey could see with his own eyes. Hussey looked momentarily put out.

'What is the problem then,' continued Henry, 'that has set Mr Hudson rushing for me? An investigation will have started immediately, I suppose? Has this just happened? How long ago?'

'Don't you know, Mr Kelleway? It was in the journals this morning. Haven't you seen them?'

'You mean it happened yesterday?'

'Of course. There was a lot of space devoted to it.'

The man's tone was impudent.

'I have not seen a journal yet,' said Henry. 'The court lists are generally our daily reading.'

'Quite,' said Hussey.

'You will know that I was engaged with the Queen's visit to Cambridge.'

'Yes. Mr Hudson told me.'

Henry was becoming furious. He wondered what Hudson had said. He could not imagine him being confidential with a man like Hussey, but he might have dropped the odd phrase to encourage the man's impertinent air.

'And what is the matter with the enquiry at Loughborough that Mr Hudson needs to bring me in? I should have thought that an accident report could be prepared by Mr Hudson's engineers. You say a tire fractured. That seems clear enough.'

'But they are saying that the tire fractured because the track was loose. There were important people on the train, and important people were killed. There is already talk of suing, because of bad maintenance. We have enemies on other lines, Mr Hudson says, who would be only too happy to prove it, and will stop at nothing to do so. It is imperative to have you there, Mr Kelleway, to see what the situation is and to be ready to prepare a defence, or we shall be paying out through the nose.'

'Is that what Mr Hudson says?'

'Much the same, only blunter.'

'Do you think the track was loose, Mr Hussey?'

'How should I know, Mr Kelleway? I haven't been there.'

'But you must be able to judge from Mr Hudson whether he was really worried or whether this is just a precaution.'

'I wouldn't presume to try to judge that, Mr Kelleway. Mr Hudson just wants someone there to make sure his position is protected against any of his enemies who tries to make capital out of it.'

'And I suppose he wants me to leave immediately?'

'That was his message, sir. You are to get on to it promptly. I think we really must go, because I had some difficulty finding you, sir, if you forgive me, and have already lost some considerable time. While matters are left for the engineers to investigate, and are held for your inspection, no trains can run on that track, and Mr Hudson is hardly pleased about that.'

Damn the man, thought Henry. Hudson was treating him like some working dog, to be sent here and there at a command or a whistle. First Hitchin, now this. Exerting pressure, provoking resistance, threatening a call on his shares. This Hussey had either been sent to spy on his private life or had fallen over it by accident. It made little difference, it would be retailed to Hudson and used against him. He thought again of Braxton's remarks that the Eastern Counties' liabilities now stood at thirteen and a half million pounds. Keep it at arm's length, Braxton had said. Loyalty modified by common sense. He had told Braxton that he felt that he stood accused of honesty. If they said the track was loose at Loughborough, Henry was inclined to believe it would be. Hudson's penny-pinching on maintenance, his gesturing on staff reductions to cover his huge deficits, his figure-shuffling, all of it could be open to exposure. Here was just the tip of the ear of a rabbit which could be eased from the hat. Let others jump in and sieze it. The Liverpool men. The Woolmers. Let it all come out. Kate, Jane, everything. He could contain it all no longer. If it destroyed his chances for the Bench, then so be it. If he was to be condemned and cast out, it might as well be for honesty as deceit. Hudson would bankrupt him. Wylie and Brancker appeared to mean to bankrupt Hudson, at least on the Leeds and Bradford, and that could be the beginning of the end. Perhaps the Great Northern would have him.

Hussey coughed meaningfully.

'I have a carriage outside. Shall we return to your house, Mr Kelleway, to pick up your bags? We can get a train to Loughborough within an hour.'

'No, damn it, Mr Hussey, I don't need bags. It won't be the first time I've travelled with one suit of clothes. If Hudson's in the hurry he says he is, we'd better be on our way.'

Hussey looked at Henry, puzzled by this sudden vigour and heartiness. It rang false and he wondered what he was up to.

'Go ahead, Mr Hussey. Get in the carriage. I shall join you in a moment.'

Hussey found himself propelled from the room without ceremony, and Henry followed him down to the door and showed him out, shutting it behind him. Wants to say goodbye to his lady friend, thought Hussey, smiling to himself. That had been a nice way to catch the bastard. Hudson would be pleased with him about that. No wonder Mr Henry Kelleway didn't want to go home for his bags! Hussey indulged in a large grin, and slapped his thigh with delight. Mr Kelleway was clearly on the way out, and Hussey felt that his stars were in the ascendant.

Henry's farewell to Kate was quickly made. He did not explain how Hussey had found him, although she asked. He knew that Kate wanted to be discovered, but felt he ought to conceal it. He wrote a note to Braxton, asking her to post it as soon as he had gone.

Nine

Frederick had never been to Liverpool, nor had Charlie. It had been a long journey by the London and North Western to Manchester, then a wait to change trains.

Charlie, particularly, had been full of wonder, pointing at the belching chimneys of mills and manufactories. It was a sight they knew from engravings in the journals, but the scale of the reality took them by surprise. The railway track passed close by coal pits and potteries, many with sidings crammed with wagons. At stations, the people themselves seemed to become greyer, as though their skin had been impregnated by the black grime which lay over the countryside.

'Look at the trees,' Charlie had said. 'The leaves are covered with soot. The grass itself is black. I expect the cows give black milk.'

Frederick nodded to avoid being churlish, but said nothing. He did not really know Charlie well, only as cousin knows cousin, and Charlie's prattling got on his nerves. He had had misgivings about letting him come with him, but Charlie had been insistent that he wanted to learn about railways if he was to invest in them, and must see for himself. Frederick had wondered what he was going to invest with. Words would not be enough. Frederick had paid the fares. He supposed that he had really done it to please his aunt Louise. It had been her suggestion in the first place, when she found that Frederick intended to make the trip. Frederick had chosen this moment because Henry was in Loughborough and could not question his reasons. To be honest, he thought, he had brought Charlie to buy Louise's silence, as she had immediately hit on the heart of the matter.

'I understood the railway men in Liverpool were enemies of Hudson's?' she asked, treating Frederick to one of her more innocent radiant smiles. Such a smile, Frederick thought, that would melt a polar ice-cap, but it won't melt me.

'It's all the same company, in the end,' he had said. 'It all belongs to Hudson.'

'I know he owns it all, by amalgamation, but he must have made enemies. A man like that is bound to. I understood that the Liverpool men were his enemies.'

'How did you hear that?' asked Frederick. He was genuinely

surprised at the amount of useful information Louise seemed able to acquire in a short space of time. When she had acquired it, she was remarkably indiscreet with it, perhaps deliberately. Perhaps she kept more to herself than she repeated.

'From Mr Meadows, who shares chambers with Henry.'

'Does he share his business secrets too?'

'Oh, come now, Frederick, you're being stuffy just like Henry. It's hardly a business secret. It's in all the newspapers. Everybody in London seems to swaddle themselves in cloaks of secrecy when everything is in print and can be purchased for a few pence. It is an extraordinary double standard. If it can be printed, it can be talked about.'

'Talk embroiders.'

'Talk is amusing.'

Charlie obviously subscribed to this view, Frederick thought sourly. He was now boring the other two occupants of their coach on the subject of gauges, explaining that there was a choice between telescopic axles, broad-gauge wagons to carry narrow-gauge wagons, or containers, and that, other than this, lines would have to be constructed with a third rail. He had become an instant expert on the subject. Like mother, like son, thought Frederick. The whole family swallowed knowledge like birds eating berries. The elderly man and his wife whom Charlie had trapped nodded and smiled politely.

Suddenly they had arrived in Liverpool, and buildings hemmed them in. The elderly couple climbed down with some assistance from Charlie and disappeared with some speed. Charlie and Frederick took their own bags, despite the attentions of a porter, and soon found themselves in Dale Street. The impression was one of almost total reconstruction. Liverpool was growing, building, re-building. The Exchange was too small and coming down to be replaced. Plots were being cleared. New stone shone yellow. Mica sparkled in new granite. Wagons rumbled down the street towards the docks in an unending convoy. Material seemed everywhere on the move. Heavy carts loaded with hewn stone struggled over the cobbles. Horses slipped and crashed. A wagon had shattered a wheel and lay lop-sided on one axle. Bales had fallen on to the street, and the carter seemed more concerned to keep off a swarm of children, than to right his wagon.

'Tobacco,' said Frederick, who could smell the rich pungent odour.

The carter was thrashing at the urchins with his whip now, watched by an unhelpful, laughing crowd. Suddenly a bale was slit, and the urchins were running, hands full of twisted black leaf. The man bellowed and swore, started to run, but they were gone, disappearing up a narrow alley. The crowd moved on.

'Give us a penny mister? Give us a penny?'

The litany of child beggars was common, in London or Liverpool, but here they seemed to haunt the centre of the city. Accents were strange. Lancashire, Welsh, Irish, Scottish. In the distance the Mersey gleamed, in shafts of sunlight, not blue but muddy green and choppy. Masts of big ships formed an impenetrable thicket in the foreground.

'This place is *busy*' said Charlie, stating the obvious with emphasis. 'What a port! London docks are nothing like this.'

'It was once the principal slaving port,' said Frederick. 'Liverpool merchants carried forty thousand slaves a year from Africa to the plantations. It founded the fortunes of the place. Then, when the cotton industry grew, they prospered on that as well.'

Charlie was silent for a while. Frederick's unkind reference to slavery and cotton had turned his mind inwards to his own family, to the past of Louise and John. He thought that Frederick was more ruthless than he appeared. He had chosen to remark upon that subject to put him in his place. Charlie knew that Frederick saw him as some inferior level of being, without pedigree. He disliked Frederick heartily as a result, but was quite able to conceal it, so long as it was to his advantage.

'We're here,' said Frederick, stopping in front of an imposing entrance. They walked up steps and inside, where a brass plate as big as two doors gave a list of names of the companies. The York and North Midland Railway was only one of an impressive list which Frederick recognised as being owned or controlled by Hudson. A liveried attendant ushered them up one flight of white marble stairs, and asked them to wait in a mahogany-panelled room, lined with engravings of railway works and portraits of directors and engineers.

'It's a bit like a railway carriage in here,' said Charlie, out of nervousness. Frederick found that he was annoyed that Charlie's observation was so apt. The buttoned leather seats, the mouldings of the panelling, the company carpet on the floor all combined to give that effect. Charlie had an observant eye. It was a pity he could not hold his tongue.

'I'll be seeing Wylie alone, Charlie,' said Frederick, 'to start with, anyway. I must get through the business side of things. I'll try to get you in later on, but I know they will never talk with you present. They are far too close for that. Rightly.'

'I understand that,' said Charlie nonchalantly, 'but just make certain that I *am* properly introduced. And remember I am looking for a business opportunity. Any business opportunity within reason. I have to rely on you to put me forward as best you can.'

'I will,' said Frederick. He would do exactly that. He assumed, however, that Wylie and Brancker would form their own opinions of his cousin.

'Mr Wylie will see you now,' said the liveried attendant, to the room at large, then looked expectantly from one man to the other.

'Mr Frederick Kelleway?' he asked.

'I am Mr Frederick Kelleway,' said Frederick. 'This gentleman is Mr Charles Kelleway, my cousin. He is awaiting me here.'

'Very good,' said the attendant, 'I shall arrange some refreshment.' Charlie looked at Frederick, winked and grinned. Frederick wished he would not be so raffish. The attendant affected not to notice, but Frederick knew he had. He was the type of old retainer Wylie and Brancker probably respected, might even ask for an opinion, but Charlie would never be able to grasp that.

He passed into another and bigger mahogany-panelled room. A huge area of polished table dominated the middle ground and reflected a perfect image of the large window at the far end. Mr Wylie and Mr Brancker were at first indistinguishable from the portraits which lined the walls. It was a curious sensation. Frederick thought he had them pinned down as being the substance not the representation, but with the glare of the window could not be sure. He waited for some movement.

Two of the portraits converged on him. With some sense of triumph, Frederick saw he had been right. Both men were whiskered down to their chins, both wore moustaches, but there the similarity ended, for Wylie was short and stout and Brancker almost emaciated, though of average height. Wylie made this plain from the beginning.

'Good morning, Mr Kelleway. I am Wylie, the short stout one, and this is Mr Brancker. Tweedledum and tweedledee, eh? We may look different but we scrape the same tune. How was your journey?'

'It was well enough. We were only a few minutes late.'

'Late, eh? No excuse for that. I'll make a note.'

To Frederick's surprise, this was no platitude. Wylie produced a notepad book from his coat pocket, bound in leather and held with a bright brass clasp. This he popped open and, taking a pencil from the side of the book, proceeded to write. Brancker, who had said nothing so far, smiled kindly at Frederick. Wylie stopped writing, shut the notepad with a snap and a click and replaced it in his pocket.

'Mr Wylie takes timing seriously,' said Brancker. 'I am

pleased to meet you, Mr Kelleway.'

He extended a dry, bony hand to Frederick and shook his hand vigorously. Wylie, only then realising he had not observed the formalities, stepped forward and did the same.

'You must think me a boor,' said Wylie, 'I sometimes forget my manners.'

'Not at all,' murmured Frederick politely.

'You are Henry Kelleway's son, aren't you, sir?' asked Brancker. 'I know him of course. A good man, and respected. I think he has worked for the railways nearly as long as we have now. Hudson has landed him with the problems at Hitchin. The Midland Bill is most ususual. They have made it a provision that the Midland line must terminate with the Great Northern by a junction and cannot cross it and that the Midland trains must be timed to connect with those of the Great Northern. Most unusual. Unless Hudson can get a route southwards by his Eastern Counties track via Hertford he will never get an independent route into London and will have to continue to use the London and North Western track and terminus. A very serious situation, and not one, I fear, that much can be done about. I wouldn't like to tackle this one, Mr Kelleway. There is so much going on in that part of the world – too many interests involved, too much money. The Great Northern seems for the moment to be in the ascendancy. These southerners are all playing their own game, and the Great Northern board is mostly made up of them. They don't like Hudson, as you may know.'

'Perhaps Mr Kelleway knows all this,' put in Wylie drily.

'A fair rebuke,' said Brancker, 'but I shall get my own back!'

Frederick lost patience with the repartee. The conversation was being kept on an entirely artificial level, and he wondered if he should bring it down to earth. He felt it might otherwise float away on to some other tack. The two men were waving him towards a seat at the huge table, then walked round it to the other side and seated themselves. Wylie had started to indicate the portraits round the panelled walls, telling Frederick who each notable was. Frederick nodded politely, but paid no attention. Brancker nodded, too, at this recitation, and Frederick found himself becoming increasingly annoyed. He was either being taken for an idiot, or he had been entirely misinformed. These two men were supposed to be avowed antagonists of Hudson, and two of the most astute men in the railway business, as well as the hardest. They were behaving like fools in their dotage, but all the time he was aware they were watching him.

'Gentlemen, forgive me if I seem rude, but I have not come

all this way to admire oil paintings.'

His interruption did not seem to upset them. Brancker looked at him squarely, sunken eyes seemingly buried deep in the mass of whiskers down the side of his jaw that met with his eyebrows and moustache. Without his whiskers, Frederick thought, he would be skeletal.

'Are you here on your own account, sir, or on account of your father?' asked Brancker. 'You understand we have to ask and we expect a very straight answer.'

The change in Brancker's manner was abrupt.

'On my own account, but hoping to help my father. He knows nothing about this visit, and would have tried to prevent me if he had.'

'What is your business then?'

'To try to find out the truth about some of Hudson's dealings, and so prevent my father from getting in worse than he is.'

There was a considerable pause. Wylie and Brancker looked at each other, at Frederick and at each other again.

Wylie spoke this time.

'You must know that we have no love for Hudson. That at least is common knowledge. You must also know that we here in Liverpool have been pressing him on several matters and have never had a satisfactory answer.'

'Of course.'

'Well, pressing Hudson is not like pressing grapes. We intend to set up an inquiry on the Leeds and Bradford line. Perhaps you knew that?'

'Yes.'

'Then I will tell you that we also intend to press this monstrous fruit until we obtain a Committee of Investigation into the dealings of his own darling, the Midland Railway. You may not know that the Liverpool shareholders in the Midland, who are a stern lot, Mr Kelleway, employ their own professional accountants to investigate the so-called balance sheets that the Midland produces half-yearly. The opera scores we call them. Very much open to interpretation!'

'Not always sweet music,' murmured Brancker.

'I'm a merchant,' continued Wylie, 'and you must know that Brancker is a ship owner – of some substance – and we are not the sort of men to be fooled by Hudson's pranks, no matter how heavily he huffs and puffs on us when we question anything. It's an old game that you must know, Mr Kelleway. Lawyers make much of it when they're short of facts. Bluster and bully. Hudson's accounts would shame a hawker. We know, for example, that he uses capital to pay dividends, that, when revenue is looking a bit lean and starved, he diverts from whatever source he fancies until he has the appearance right again. Furthermore, we have our suspicions on some very odd share dealing.'

'There's no secret in this,' said Brancker, ruffling about in his whiskers like a preening fowl. 'As you will have seen by the letters we have written to the journals. Not perhaps in quite such words, but making it plain we think that Hudson's judgement is unsound. Up to now he has always been able to squash our opposition. The more we criticize, the more he hands out to prove us wrong. Who wants the accounts questioned, Mr Kelleway, as long as the dividend is fat? Investigation might lead to a lean return. But as soon as he can no longer raise capital, can no longer promote new schemes, no longer keep the whole circus going, then the dividends will fall.'

He paused for Wylie, who took up what was obviously a practised exposition.

'Then we shall complain about the dividends,' continued Wylie, 'and then the shareholders will notice us. They always suspect concealment when things go down. We are not very pretty in the railway business, are we, Mr Kelleway? Fair-weather companions who run at the first drop of rain. We will get our enquiry then. Hell has no fury like a shareholder with something that isn't worth the ink! So we wait our moment.'

Frederick looked from one to the other. The sun had warmed up the mahogany of the giant table, and a pleasant smell of beeswax perfumed the air. Without knowing anything more about them than they had themselves revealed, Frederick was impressed. There was nothing ranting or hot in their manners, and they carried conviction.

'Then you believe, as I do, that Hudson is finished.'

'It will never be as simple as that, sir. Men like Hudson do not collapse like a card house. It will take a year or two, but he will run out of track and run into the buffers, to use a railway image,' said Wylie.

'Consider this, Mr Kelleway,' said Brancker, extending a long lean finger as though a touch of it might mean death. Frederick found he was steeling himself in order not to retreat from the touch. 'At this moment, Hudson is chairman of four principal railways. The Midland and the Eastern Counties who are sworn rivals of the Great Northern on the one hand, and the York and North Midland and York, Newcastle and Berwick who are all courting an alliance with the Great Northern on the other. He must resign from one or other of the factions. We believe he will ditch the Eastern Counties which is a miserable, profitless line that cannot rely on the occasional transportation of the Queen. We also believe he is preparing to do a deal with the Great Northern to link the York and North Midland to them. It won't then be a feeder line to his own Midland, and he will have sold out one of his lines to another to do a deal with a third party which is also the bitterest opponent. What price his chairmanship of the Midland then? What price an enquiry?'

'I should have thought there would be an uproar.'

'There will. We know negotiations are already underway. But that is all very fine stuff and our business. We haven't really concentrated on your business. I think I should make it clear, sir, that we have respect for your father and don't intend that anything that we have said about Hudson should reflect upon him. You say you hope to help your father. Perhaps you can be a little more precise, within the bounds of discretion, so that we understand the problem.'

'Can I speak to you in confidence?' asked Frederick.

'You can speak in entire confidence, provided nothing that you have to say touches matters which affect our lines and ought to be revealed. I'm sure you understand our position.'

'Certainly. My father is being hung by his Eastern Counties stock on which Hudson constantly threatens to make calls he knows he cannot meet. My father was not so much persuaded to take the stock, as forced to as a measure of demonstrating his loyalty and confidence in Hudson and the line. Now Hudson knows how he feels, he is determined to use my father for his dirtiest work, confident that he can wave a financial club and command service. At Hitchin for example, where Hudson is up to fast business. And in other matters about which I cannot be precise, I know my father has had to act against his conscience in order to protect Hudson's interests. If he murmurs, then there is the hot breath of ruin at his neck.'

Wylie rapped on the table top with his nails, sucking his upper lip.

'Forgive me, Mr Kelleway, but really, your father should not have got himself into it. I sympathise, but he is where he is because he took the job and Hudson, as we know, pays well. I wouldn't be speaking my mind if I didn't say so. If you run with the hare, then you have to keep running with the hare. There is no way that you can turn to the hounds and plead your case. I'm sorry if that sounds hard.'

'No, it doesn't sound hard,' said Frederick. 'It is however the easiest thing on earth to say that a man in his position deserves it. I'm sure that will be the world's opinion of the matter. I had hoped that, as you both know how Hudson operates, you could take a more charitable view of the difficulties of breaking away from the man. It is almost impossible, as it is almost impossible to get to grips with his accounts. Everything is concealed, covert. Any questions are rebuffed. Hudson brushes aside reason and never hesitates to use financial pressure. My father can no longer, in conscience, serve the man. He must quit.'

'Then what do you want from us?' asked Brancker. 'It seems you have a clear view of the subject. On the morals of the matter, I can't see that Henry Kelleway should concern himself overmuch about failing to continue in Hitchin. Hudson will never secure a route linking his lines as he wants, with or without Henry Kelleway. That game is over. As for the Eastern Counties, if I were Henry Kelleway, I would get rid of my shares for what they could fetch. I still don't see, if you forgive me, what you want from us. We would assist, within reason, if there were anything in particular that you want.'

'I hoped you could advise me on what was best to be done.'

'In the long term, what is best to be done for all of us and for the railways in general is to dethrone the king. If Henry Kelleway is a man of real conscience, then, rather than quitting, that is what he should be thinking of. Then perhaps we would have something to talk about. As to the rest, he can take the alternative of selling up and quitting. If he takes the real path of conscience, I am sure he can devise some way of hanging on. It cannot be impossible to serve the company without serving Hudson. That must be his own battle and he must use his own skill. I'm sorry to be so forthright, sir, and I hope you are only using us to sound these matters out, for I'm sure they are as clear to you as they are to us.'

'Perhaps not so bluntly put,' said Frederick.

Brancker made an apologetic gesture, extending his two bony hands.

'We lack assistance in London,' said Wylie, thoughtfully.

'I didn't come here, of course, to make any promises on behalf of my father. In fact, as I have said, he would be furious if he knew what was taking place here.'

'I think we understand that,' said Wylie. 'I'm sure you won't take offence if I say that it is obvious that this is a spur-of-the-moment visit. One where you have no really clear object in mind but would like to explore possibilities.'

'Am I as inexperienced as that?' asked Frederick ruefully.

'Well, I think you had not considered things through,' said Brancker with a dry smile. 'Rather fishing than casting a net.'

'I concede,' said Frederick. 'I really had no idea what I was trying to discuss. I apologise for taking up your time with things that are really my personal affairs, as you have so politely indicated.'

'You did hear me say that we lacked assistance in London, didn't you, sir?' said Wylie. 'I wondered if you had fully taken my meaning. We in Liverpool are on the west of this country, and if Hudson is about to sell us out for a route up the east, that is no profit to Liverpool. The Midland is at least down the middle. The Great Northern will kill us if Hudson makes a deal with them. He is from York. York is the east. He has no interest in the west, and none in Liverpool. It is the old, old story. Lancaster and York. We will fight for the Midland and fight to rid ourselves of Hudson. If Mr Henry Kelleway, or you as well, sir, cares to consider the true well-being of the line, then I think you will see it is the right way for the company, its employees and the shareholders. It is the way of conscience. Not quitting.'

There was a silence. Wylie and Brancker studied the portraits on the walls, careful not to catch Frederick's eye. Frederick, who had not known what to expect, was rather taken aback at such forthright advice. He had been seeking a retreat and was being invited to take part in an evangelistic campaign of some fervour. The world turned upside down again, he thought. Henry cast as the man of conscience. Henry being dressed up in armour, clothed in white and pushed out in front. In this particular instance, Henry would be well content to be a camp-follower running away at the rear. Frederick told himself that he had not committed anyone to anything, but had an unpleasant feeling that Wylie and Brancker were the type of men who followed things up as a matter of course. Henry would indeed be furious.

'I will talk to my father about this conversation when I get back. But very cautiously. I don't yet know how I shall put it.'

'We would like you to mention our point,' put in Wylie gently but persistently. 'That, with a man we respect who shares our views, we would be pleased to meet and talk about matters.'

'No doubt you will not wish to put it any stronger than that,' said Brancker and both men nodded, in time. Tweedledee and tweedledum. Frederick found that he too was nodding and stopped. The earlier frostiness and caution in the atmosphere had thawed and both men were looking at him with a sort of avuncular approval. If it was a business stance, thought Frederick, it was well done. He congratulated himself on still being able to be detached despite all this flattering faith and fellow-feeling. There was a lot in this for Wylie and Brancker, and there might be a lot in it for Henry. Not to speak of Charlie. The recollection of Charlie's presence was like a plunge in a cold river.

'I will probably put it no stronger than that. This has been a most interesting conversation. I must say I had no idea we would arrive at this point. But it is a very good point. My journey has been very worth while.'

Recognising these as closing words, Wylie and Brancker pushed back their chairs and rose to their feet.

'What about my companion, Mr Charles Kelleway?' said Frederick, 'What can we do with him? I took the liberty of promising that I would properly introduce him. He is most insistent that he is interested in the railway business up here. I think he hopes to make his fortune.'

Frederick passed it off lightly, judging rightly that it was the most acceptable course.

'Has he any capital?' asked Wylie.

'Not much.'

'Has he any experience of railway matters?' asked Brancker.

'Not much.'

'Then he would be better off with the Eastern Counties,' said Wylie, and both men chuckled.

'No, we don't mean to be unkind,' Wylie put in quickly, still smiling.

'We will do what we can with the young gentleman. I take it that he can be a bit of a nuisance?'

'Well, he *can* talk,' said Frederick wryly.

'That will be our bargain,' said Brancker. 'You talk to Mr Henry Kelleway, and we will talk to Mr Charles. We will see what we can do.'

He extended a hand and they all shook on it. Even as he did so, Frederick realised that things had become suddenly formal, and that this shaking of hands was by no means to be treated lightly. A deal had been made almost without his noticing, and he was committed to it. Henry was to be brought to their side, and was to stay with the Midland, and he, Frederick, was to try to achieve it. No wonder Wylie and Brancker smiled on him so kindly!

It shimmered with heat along the railway track. Wispy mirages of the visible horizon rose and dissolved in the vibrant dance of nearer images. Heat-loving flowers – mallow and knapweed that had rooted themselves in the crushed granite ballast – contracted and sagged.

Temporary accommodation had been built at the side of the tracks for the men, but was unusable. The walls were of timber steeped in creosote and the roof was of the same timber covered with tar-paper. The tar-paper dribbled black stickiness in the sun. The smell of creosote was numbing. Crickets and grasshoppers kept up an infuriating buzz which seemed in the heat to rise to a continuing scream. The steel of the tracks burned the hand. Even

197

lizards lay and panted. In adjoining fields, cows stood in a stream, mute.

'I don't agree with your point of view at all, Hussey. *Because* the track was loose, the tire smashed.'

Henry had taken off his coat as a concession, but still wore his tall hat to protect his head. A small group of men stood in conversation together, Henry, Hussey, three directors, two senior engineers, Braxton. Two of the directors were fully clad as for the board room. They had all been summoned at short notice.

Behind them, and down the track, a gang of platelayers were stretched out, one man to each sleeper, with crowbars and hammers. They disappeared into the heat haze, leaving curious illusions of floating torsoes and heads. Perhaps a hundred men. At intervals there was a shout, a concerted ringing of steel on steel, of ballast on shovels, then a pause for surveying and levelling.

'It wasn't the other way round, as far as I can see.' Henry was hot and annoyed. So were the others. 'The fireman on "the Albion" was quite clear about what happened, and it was confirmed by the driver of "The Queen." The tire shattered, killed the driver, the fragments cut through the coaches of "The Queen," "Albion" ploughed on and was derailed by virtue of the smashed tire. We've all seen the marks of the axle cutting through the ballast.'

'You can't say that!' declared Hussey. 'Surely, as a barrister, you can't just turn around and make these assumptions when they amount to an open admission of liability. If the track was loose, and I don't believe it, then we shall be sued for want of care and maintenance. Negligence, Mr Kelleway, as you know very well. Damages could be very high indeed.'

'We would be completely exposed if that were the case,' said Lewis, one of the swaddled directors, a man Henry had met occasionally in the past. 'We can't have that, Mr Kelleway.'

'Independent engineers have already examined the wreck,' said Henry. 'They will have seen what we have seen. Don't harass me, gentlemen. Ask Mr Barlow, ask Mr Braxton. They are the engineers, they have seen the physical evidence and they must have come to their own opinions.'

Behind them and to the side of both tracks lay the evidence. The engine of the 'Albion' lay where it had fallen, with its funnel and front wheels embedded in the ground. It had not toppled completely over, but was wedged in the slight embankment alongside the track. Two of the carriages were shattered, the raw ends of timber showing white like broken bones through the thick lacquer of the coach-work. Glass, upholstery and buckled iron were entangled. Clothing remained here and there, scraps of dress material, a hat, a shoe. In places the ballast was dark brown, almost black, where blood had dried. A policeman stood beside it, perspiring in full uniform and thinking only of pints of beer.

'I have asked Mr Barlow,' said Lewis.

'So have I,' said Henry, 'and it seemed to me that he agreed with me.'

'It seemed to me that he agreed with *me*,' said Hussey.

'Well, shall we ask Mr Barlow?' demanded Henry, exasperated.

Mr Barlow did not seem to welcome this predominance. He too had shed his coat and wore a tile hat and waistcoat. His eyes had the bleary look of a drinker, a kind of gelatinous layer over the pupils. His nose was veined and pitted with dark pores, and the nostrils were abnormally hairy. Appearances were all against the man, thought Henry, who had already decided he did not trust him, however good an engineer he might be. Mr Barlow produced a spotted handkerchief, and wiped his face.

'I don't know what you want me to say,' he offered tentatively, as though hoping by this very feebleness to make everyone dismiss him and go and ask someone else.

'We want you to tell us what happened, in your opinion, as a skilled engineer and a servant of the Midland Railway,' said Hussey bluntly.

'Not forgetting either part.'

'Just give us your honest opinion,' said Henry, doubting the possibility but being gentle as the cooing dove.

'Well, my opinion of what happened is that it is quite difficult to say what happened. We know the tire shattered and we know they do, from time to time, due to some weakness in the metal that is invisible to the eye.'

'But what about the loose rail?' asked Henry.

'Now that is difficult to say,' said Barlow. He seemed to have withdrawn into himself. 'The rail could very well have been properly fixed. It has been torn out by the derailment.'

'But what about the statement of the fireman?' Henry pursued.

'He could be mistaken,' said Barlow, who like some birds, now seemed to have a second lid to his eyes. 'If the tire was breaking up, it would produce a bumping effect until it smashed.'

'Yes, but the fireman says that they all knew the track was loose, and had been for months. It was not an isolated instance.'

'I couldn't say about that, Mr Kelleway. All I can say is that the cause of derailment was the disintegration of the tire, and the derailment caused the deaths on the "Albion." Those on "The

Queen" were definitely caused by fragments of the tire hitting the carriages of "The Queen." I would say that, when a tire breaks up like that, it is more an Act of God than anything else and cannot be negligence. The tires were nearly new and had recently been replaced.'

'Really? I was informed they were old and worn,' said Henry sharply.

'Who informed you?' demanded Hussey.

'The engineering workshops.'

'Oh, no! You're quite wrong there!' said Hussey loudly and rudely. 'I don't know where you get this information from, but this is ridiculous. We have the labour dockets, don't we, Barlow, for the fitting of the wheel?'

'Aye,' said Barlow.

Henry was dumbfounded. His information was the contrary, but he had no reason to doubt it.

'So what you are saying is that the track was properly fixed, and that there is no cause for alarm there, and that the tire was nearly new and there is no cause for alarm there either.' Henry's tone was disbelieving.

'I don't like your attitude, Mr Kelleway, and I don't mind saying so,' said Barlow. 'I am an experienced engineer, and don't like my word being doubted.'

'No one does, Mr Barlow,' said Henry, 'but, if I am to advise the Company properly on whether or not they have a case to answer, then I have to get to the facts. It seems to me that the fireman and other drivers I have talked to are saying one thing, and you are saying another.'

'Well, who would you rather believe?' demanded Barlow angrily. 'Firemen and drivers will always talk. They complain about everything and they have their superstitions and myths and legends about this stretch of track and that, about this tunnel and that incline. I've heard it all, Mr Kelleway, over a great number of years. Riddled with superstition. Like sailors. They're all sea-serpents and rubbish. On the Midland and on every other line in the country there are supposed to be haunted tunnels and unlucky bends, good track and bad track, rogue engines and good engines. They say a Derby engine will always speed up as it approaches Derby! Do you believe this sort of thing? Preposterous. I base what I say on more solid grounds!'

Barlow concluded with a snort and, having worked himself up so well, took the opportunity to storm off and distance himself from any further probing.

'It all makes sense to me,' said one of the directors, to whom Henry had been introduced, but whose name he had forgotten.

'Certainly it doesn't seem that there has been any slackness on the part of the Midland Counties.'

'I certainly agree with that,' said Hussey.

'It should be our case from the evidence we have seen, if we have to defend ourselves,' said Lewis. 'It seems to me that you have a very good and simple defence. You should be well satisfied with it, Mr Kelleway.'

There was a nodding of heads, an expectant pause while they waited for Henry to concur.

'When I am satisfied, I shall let you all know,' said Henry. 'I'm not yet satisfied.'

'Preposterous!' said Lewis. 'This is not at all a satisfactory state of affairs. You are taking a very curious stance, if you don't mind me saying so, sir.'

'If you don't mind me saying so,' said Henry, 'you have tried to dragoon me into the conclusion that you want me to reach, and I won't be treated in this way.'

'Damn it, sir,' shouted Lewis, 'who employs you, eh? Mr Hudson won't be pleased by this. You had better recollect your loyalty, I should say. You have an open and shut defence and you seem to be looking around to shoot holes in it!'

'I hope you are not going to be difficult about this,' said Hussey in a threatening tone.

'What do you mean, sir?' demanded Henry, trying to stay calm. The question was impertinent. Hussey eyed him carefully.

'I explained to you that Mr Hudson wanted you to be sure to protect our position. Those are his wishes. You will remember I conveyed them to you when I managed to find you.'

'So I do, Mr Hussey.' Henry was now so angry that he thought it better to say little. He contrived to look grave and dangerous. 'I understand Mr Hudson's wishes.'

He nodded briefly to the other men and walked off down the scorching ballast. Small blue butterflies had been sunning themselves, and dashed in front of him only to alight again a yard or two in front. Henry's anger was huge and consuming. This was the end. He recognised it for that. Here was a place he was not prepared to go, a course he would not take. My dignity is a pretty tattered cloak, he thought, but I am not prepared to tear it off and throw it away for these lepers and parasites. As for Hussey's threat, it followed on Hudson's threats, and he was not prepared to be threatened by them or anyone again, whatever the cost. Clearly the Midland had failed to maintain the section of track. The drivers all knew it was loose. Engineers advising the prosecution would soon find that out, no matter what Hudson did to try to muzzle his men. I cannot support the unsupportable, he said to himself, watching the blue butterflies. When they closed up their wings, the undersides were brown, and they became invisible. I am like the blue butterflies, he thought, I never get out of the way, I just advance a few more paces until the same problem catches up with me again. The butterflies have not got the wit to stay still, brown and unnoticed, and let me pass, taking that slight risk that I may tread on them. They take to flight again and reveal themselves.

He heard steps behind him and ignored them. Braxton caught up with him and walked beside him in silence for some moments. They stopped with mutual accord to watch a host of cinnabar moths which overlay a profuse clump of knapweed.

'It's the weather for them,' said Braxton. It immediately cast Henry's mind back to the coach journey they had shared to Brockett Hall.

'Bug weather, eh?'

Braxton looked at him sharply, trying, then succeeding, to recall. He smiled briefly.

'I like insects, all sorts of them. They have tremendous strength, are marvellously functional. Nothing can beat them for colours.'

'You gave a display of remarkable silence just now, Braxton.' Henry's tone was accusing and rude. Braxton's reply was calm.

'I thought it better to hold my tongue.'

'Is that so? Am I to take it you think this wreck was due to a fault in the tire, an invisible fracture in something that was nearly new?'

'No. That was why I said nothing.'

'I could have done with your support.'

'I wanted to see what you would do on your own, without being aided and abetted.'

'Damn it, Braxton, don't play games. You can see the position I'm in. "Recollect you loyalty," says Lewis! By God, I won't be brow-beaten or threatened!'

'You are bound to act for the Midland though.'

'Only this once and last time. I am not bound to pretend that it was an accident when it was not. I shall advise the company to settle out of court and admit liability.'

'You will be finishing yourself with Hudson.'

'Damn Hudson!'

'He will go for you.'

'I know that. I will have to be ready.'

'And then? Off to the Great Northern?'

Henry turned to Braxton. His voice was sharp.

'Damn it, man, have you no idea of tact, or propriety? Is this the place to say things like that?'

'No one can hear us.'

'It is still not proper. I am acting on Midland business. What else have you said? Do you make a habit of this sort of careless remark?'

Braxton was annoyed by this attack, and his face, already red with the sun, flushed further. This, with his ginger whiskers, made Braxton the colour of a turkey's wattles, thought Henry, and his skin just as coarse.

'I never make careless remarks, and I take exception to your remark,' said Braxton. 'I was speaking to you in confidence, and, I thought, as a friend.'

Henry was touched by Braxton's hurt dignity, and touched despite himself at Braxton considering him as a friend. In a friendless world, it was moving to find anyone who would ally themselves with him in adversity. He wished Braxton could somehow be made more attractive and presentable, and in that thought saw his own arrogance and ingratitude. He smiled wryly at himself, caught Braxton's eye again and realised that the smile might be misconstrued as further rudeness.

'Forgive me, Mr Braxton, I wasn't smiling at you, I was laughing at myself. It takes a special sort of fool, I suppose, to protest his virginal innocence, as I do, when he is, so to speak, pregnant.'

'I have spoken to no one else about the Great Northern. My lips have been sealed like a Pharoah's tomb.'

'I'm sure they have.'

A sparrow was hopping closer to the cinnabar moths, watchful. Hopping and waiting, uneasy at the presence of the two men. It sprang quickly into flight, pecked up one in its beak without pausing and flitted away. The moths dispersed, flying among grass stems, wings folded.

'You seldom see that,' said Braxton. 'The red colouring of the moth is a warning that they don't taste good, or so they say. Birds seldom eat cinnabar moths.'

'Maybe it was an immature sparrow,' said Henry, amused and intrigued by the man's continual interest in such things.

'Well, we ain't immature sparrows, are we, Kelleway?' said Braxton, smiling at Henry. Henry smiled back but said nothing as they turned and walked towards the platelayers. He thought that Braxton looked like a pantomime pirate when he smiled.

Jonathan had stopped his horse in the shade of an ancient elm that grew out of the hedgerow of the narrow road he was following. He doubted if this was the quickest route, although they had assured him it was at the stage office in Derby. The road was almost overgrown in places and, although the brushwood had been hacked back in places, he doubted if it was used by anything more than farm carts. Two deep ruts had dried as hard as rock, and the horse had to keep to the central strip. Beyond the hedgerow on each side of the road was a stone wall, and more walls ran off at right angles enclosing farm land. He had passed mills with tall chimneys, and what he took to be mines, but the character of the countryside was changing. There was more grassland ahead, and he could see the house in an area of parkland where it was partly concealed by trees. It was a landscape with which Jonathan was more familiar than he was with the curious conjunction of corn-fields and smoking chimneys.

His left leg ached and he tried to ignore it lest it should stir up the anger he had rehearsed himself to suppress. On horseback, he was at least mobile. He wished the hot weather would end or that it would become overcast. The horse shook its head and stamped. The flies were a nuisance. As hired horses went, it was a good enough animal, but bony with a lurch in its gait. Like me, thought Jonathan. He was not able to relax properly in the saddle.

He took his left foot from the stirrup and let it hang, moving it gently to ease the ache, while he tried to rehearse his manner and his opening words. Hays would be in no doubt as to how Jonathan felt about him, as Jonathan had made that plain in writing both to Hays personally and to the journals, making clear the true circumstances of the accident. His letters had been printed without comment, and it gave him little satisfaction. After several discussions with Henry, they had decided there was no point in pursuing Hays legally. It would prove nothing, alter nothing.

If, as he imagined, he encountered Hays first, he would not shake hands, that was ridiculous, but would wish him good morning and say that he had come at the request of his mother to pay a visit to his sister. It was all he had to say. Hays must respond somehow and he would have to be polite but firm. He would like to speak to Charlotte alone.

What if Hays forbade this? Or if Charlotte was so besotted with the fool that she refused?

Jonathan shrugged. It was no use, he would have to get on with it. He eased his left foot back in the stirrup and moved the horse on.

The small overgrown roadway almost immediately stopped, and he found himself on a broad gravel drive that crossed it at right angles before sweeping round in a bend and away from him between a formal avenue of mature trees. Looking back from the gravel drive at the road he had just come from, he realised that it was indeed a short cut and that the drive approached the house from the north. He passed through massive wrought-iron gates, properly hung from limestone pillars. They were well painted and he noted the oiled hinges. No genteel decay. The horse did not seem to possess enough intelligence to realise it was on a different class of surface, for it still pecked along as though trying to avoid ruts. He thumped it with his knees and induced a canter of sorts. He did not want to spend ten minutes in plain view of the house. It would give Hays too much time to organise anything he was considering doing, and too much time to talk to Charlotte.

The house was huge, and mostly of limestone with some brick. Jonathan, who knew nothing about architecture, saw only that it had been built in two entirely different styles and that the bigger portion which formed the main frontage seemed to be the newer. There were stables at the rear and a large stable clock. Formal gardens stretched in front of it and he was vaguely aware of water beyond the box hedges. He found he was suddenly very nervous and his heart was thumping hard. Where was he to dismount? Large houses are the devil, he thought. Where do I go? Pray God, I don't make a fool of myself, and go to the wrong door. He made for the main entrance which was fronted by a sweep of stone steps, hoping that it was not some architectural ornament, and quickly dismounted. Now he had to wait, or get rid of the horse and approach the door on foot. Looking around desperately for somewhere to hitch the horse, he could only find a massive ornamental urn that sprouted spiky leaves. He looped the reins to one of its projecting handles, hoping this showed a proper style, and strode up the steps as best his aching leg allowed. A visitor to one of these places was always at a disadvantage. To his relief, there was a brass bell-pull and he tugged this firmly and waited.

A manservant in livery opened the door, after only a brief pause. Jonathan was so relieved that it was the right door that he was not as coherent and poised as he would have wished.

'I have come to see Mr Hays. My name is Kelleway. Jonathan Kelleway.'

The man's expression was immediately wary, and he paused too long before opening the door further and stepping aside.

'If you will stay here, sir, I will see if Mr Hays is in.'

Jonathan was left standing in a large hall, elliptical in shape and floored with white marble which was cut in segments to converge on a central roundel. This roundel of dark red marble inlaid with white showed a centaur wrestling vigorously with a maiden. It made Jonathan feel the rage he was trying hard to control. He stared at it as though it were a deliberate insult, then stood on the centaur to obliterate it. He looked round the hall, which was decorated with classical allegories in plaster, seeking further signs of depravity and annoyed that the figures seemed to be dancing muses linked by garlands. The man walked up the staircase which led from the hall in a measured tread that allowed him plenty of time to watch Jonathan and try to sum him up. Jonathan scowled up at him, to prove he was not cowed, and knew he was being assessed. Jonathan's heart was thumping again. His leg ached. He wished he was somewhere else altogether.

He heard not one but two pairs of footsteps start down the stairs. He did not immediately look up, because sunlight fell from a lantern-light which illumined the hall and shone full in his eyes.

'Good afternoon, Jonathan. This is a surprise, but I suppose it isn't unexpected.'

Charlotte's voice was nervous and trembled. She coughed when she finished the sentence. Jonathan looked up. She had her arm through Hays' and they had paused on a half-landing. Jonathan said nothing, but watched them. Charlotte seemed to urge Hays on, and they continued down the stairs. Hays seemed to have lost weight, but apart from that had not changed at all. It surprised Jonathan to see and remember that Hays was handsome in a florid way. He had been decidedly unattractive when being sick over the edge of a balloon basket, but when groomed and set in these surroundings, where he was obviously at ease, he was presentable. He stared at Hays, but Hays looked at him briefly, caught his eye and looked away. The couple stood in front of Jonathan. Jonathan looked at Charlotte, looked into her eyes, trying to see any message that could be read there, trying to ask the question that was obsessing him, and had been all the time without his daring to acknowledge it. Was she a virgin, or had she and this man done all those things together that made them husband and wife? Jonathan himself had no experience of such pleasures and his curiosity was agonising. He wanted to know this more than any other thing, and he forgot his mission, his rehearsed role, in his confusion.

'Hello, Charlotte,' he croaked. 'Are you all right?'

Charlotte had blushed red under this fierce appraisal. With quick instinct, she knew what Jonathan wanted to know and felt pity for him. They had been close. Jonathan was jealous. Sexually jealous. Someone had stolen his sister, stolen his own virgin bride, had given her pleasure with his body, transformed her with passion. Jonathan could not bring himself to believe it, was obsessed. She would have to be very careful with him.

'Yes, Jonathan. I am happy and well. I know everyone must be anxious for me and I do regret that. I'm very pleased to see you. How did you get here?'

'By horse from Derby. I took the railway to Derby.'

'Yes, of course. The railway does make things so fast. How are mother and father and Margaret?'

'Missing you.'

'Oh, Jonathan, that's too short and tells me nothing and I think_ it is supposed to wring my heart. Please say hello to Fordham. You haven't so much as glanced at him. We must have that out of the way so that we can talk.'

She smiled encouragingly, and Jonathan was hurt by her beauty.

'Good afternoon, Jonathan,' said Hays. Jonathan was obliged to look at him. He struggled with an answer, could find nothing polite to say, and burst out, realising as he did so that this was going all wrong.

'What do you mean "good afternoon", Hays? You steal my sister, my leg hurts like the devil, you are a canker as far as I am concerned! Why did you say those things to the papers? You let out the sand and you broke my leg. You're a coward and a liar as far as I'm concerned, and if it weren't out of fashion, I would challenge you!'

'Oh, Jonathan,' Charlotte shouted, stamping a foot on the marble. 'Stop that! Things are as they are. Don't make them worse. If you have come here to do that, then I don't believe you have come from mother and father. What is the purpose of this visit? To make sure that you and I never see or speak to each other again?'

Jonathan looked as though he had been hit by her. He seemed even younger. 'On the matter of the balloon,' Charlotte continued, quietly, 'Fordham was afraid. Is there some crime in that? He hates heights. Everyone is afraid of something. As to the reports in the newspapers, you corrected them thoroughly, so can't we leave it at that? Fordham is desperately sorry about your leg. It was an accident. There have been enough hard words about it all.'

Jonathan looked at her, and at Hays. There was a loathsome smugness about Hays' expression, he thought. A man who has found not just an ally but a convert who can see things only as he sees them.

'Can we talk alone somewhere? I have messages from the family.'

To his annoyance, Charlotte turned to Hays, who nodded. 'Certainly.'

Charlotte withdrew her arm from Hays'.

'We can go out into the garden.'

'I shall go up to the library,' said Hays. 'You can find me there. I have accounts to see to.'

Charlotte walked to Jonathan, and took his arm. He made a slight movement, she felt, as though to take it away, but she held fast and he relaxed. They walked out of the front door together, down the steps and across gravel to the formal garden with its maze of box hedges. Jonathan's horse was being led round the back of the house by a groom. Jonathan tried to concentrate his mind on the approach he was supposed to make. Support, offer help, re-establish links. He was unnerved by Charlotte because she had changed. She was confident, suddenly woman of a house. She led him down this path and that, with the ease of familiarity and ownership, pointing out plants and shrubs. In a short space of time she had a new world that did not involve him at all. The familiarity of brother and sister was there, he decided, but there was a distance in the affection.

'I *am* happy,' said Charlotte suddenly. 'We intend to marry soon, in France.'

'You are getting married?' asked Jonathan stupidly.

'Yes.'

'Do you love him?'

'Jonathan, I know this is all very difficult for you. We were always a close family, but family cannot come first forever. I know you don't like Fordham for what happened and that it turned everyone against him, but that doesn't affect me. I love him, faults and all. Only in romantic literature has love anything to do with perfection. Of course he makes mistakes.'

'Does he still drink too much brandy?'

Charlotte looked at him evenly.

'That is a cruel way to talk about him. The answer is yes. From time to time. As you are cruel and vindictive in what you say from time to time. However, he drinks less and less.'

'Why are you getting married in France?'

'To avoid embarrassment.'

'Won't you come to see mother and father? Before all this, I mean.'

'I don't think so. You will all combine against me. I would rather present myself when I have become an honest woman, as they say.'

Jonathan shot a glance at her. Charlotte suddenly stopped.

'Don't keep giving me that look, Jonathan. Do you think I'm some sort of courtesan? I'm not ashamed of anything. We have been living as man and wife, do you understand, and I feel no guilt. Why should I? You don't understand love, Jonathan. Not yet. I don't know if you know what you want. Do you want to protect me, in which case you are protecting me from myself, or do you want to deny me things for your own selfish reasons?'

Jonathan turned on her as though she had suddenly bitten him, angry and hurt, ready to strike back. Then he turned away. He suddenly ached with a great tiredness in the hollows of his bones beneath and behind his eyes, along the sinuses of his nose. An attempt at tears he could not manage. His main feeling was desperation in his heart.

The water he had earlier glimpsed was a basin or pool of sculpted sandstone around the centre of which danced a crown of jets. Goldfish or carp lay passive, waterlogged, it seemed, not creatures of the watery element. Jonathan stared at the immobile fish, at the hard rim of stone as high as his knee, the ordered box hedges, raked gravel paths. He felt bereft in a nameless adolescent way, casting about for symbols to identify his grief, aware he was being self-indulgent but enjoying and sustaining it. He was resentful when Charlotte interrupted.

Charlotte saw him as very young then, an overgrown boy. She talked to him as she used to talk to him when they had been perhaps six or seven years younger.

'When you love a girl, you won't care whether she's perfect, a proper angel with folded wings. You may find you prefer her not to be.'

Jonathan stooped and picked up a handful of gravel. He threw it pebble by pebble with all his strength at the passive carp, which insulted him by treating them eagerly as food, sucking them in and blowing them out with a puff of dirty water.

Charlotte watched him, and laughed.

'Go on, stone them to death! Do you find it helps?'

'Shut up, Charlotte!'

In a moment they had both fallen back to earlier years. Circumstance and maturity were cast down like a cloak.

'Why is it such a thin thing?' asked Jonathan, 'this taking-on of another life?'

'What did you expect it to be?' asked Charlotte. 'You are a hopeless romantic. What sort of a lawyer will you ever make? Lawyers must learn not to become involved with their clients. You know that. You came here as a sort of lawyer to everyone, didn't you? You must be a cold fish, like Henry. Or the goldfish, they're cold fish! They don't care about your stones. You put all that violence into throwing them, and they don't even notice or understand.'

'Oh God, Charlotte. I'm no use at this, am I! I'm supposed to be a go-between, but I only hate Hays!'

'Then you must leave. I can't have you here.'

'Is that all?'

'Yes.'

'I don't forgive him.'

'That's your affair. I wish you would and I'm sorry about it, but it won't make any difference to me. You should try, for the sake of yourself.'

But Jonathan turned with a snarl and was gone. He ran back through the garden, kicking down the box hedges, trampling through beds of flowers, stumbling over tough clumps of dusty lavender. A ridiculous Minotaur breaking through this maze that was as much in his mind as around him. He ran towards the side and rear of the house, towards where he had seen his horse being led away. He found himself in a large stableyard paved with blue bricks and surrounded by loose-boxes. His horse stood, nose down, still saddled.

Hays was in the yard. Obviously he had not gone to the library, but to a point where he could observe the garden. He had seen Jonathan's ridiculous exit, and there was a look on his face which Jonathan read as a sneer of triumph. Jonathan's limp made him stagger like a drunk as he ran and the shame of it and of being watched by the man he held responsible exploded into irrepressible rage. He tried to fling himself at Hays with a yell, reaching out wildly, then trying to punch the sneering red face. Jonathan was too slight, too hampered by his leg, and Hays was strong. He seized Jonathan's flailing arms as though he were seizing a frantic child. The indignity and powerlessness of this was calculated. Hays drew Jonathan nearer and nearer to his red, bleary-eyed face. Jonathan kicked out with his one good leg, but he might as well have kicked the trunk of an oak. He could hear Charlotte running across the gravel now, shouting 'Stop!', but who was to stop, he had no idea. He cursed Hays, trying to discover words to express his loathing, but found abuse a useless currency. Hays was holding him until he weakened. The final humiliation was inevitable. He stopped struggling and cursing.

Hays let him go, as Charlotte arrived. Jonathan turned for his horse, realising that the tears he had earlier sought were now running down his face and shaming him further. He led the horse out by its bridle, and mounted it without too much difficulty, as he had learned to do. On the horse he towered over Hays, at last.

'You are a bastard, Hays, and I shall make it my business to finish you!'

Hays watched him, not hiding his contempt. Jonathan slashed at him with the loose rein, hitting him across the face, and seeing

210

Hays clutch at the weal. He rode around Charlotte, who stood still and horrified. There was no kindness in her eyes for Jonathan.

'Go and stone carp, Kelleway!' he heard Hays shout. 'Take on something you can handle!'

'Get out, Jonathan,' said Charlotte.

'I never knew my sister was a whore,' said Jonathan.

Charlotte looked at him steadily.

'You are a fool to have said that. You and I are finished now.' Jonathan spurred on the horse, which obeyed his frantic kicks and bolted down the gravel drive in a cloud of yellow dust. He rode at full speed until he came to the iron gates, then reined in the horse and turned it into the uneven lane by which he had approached. He dug his heels into the animal's sides again and sent it crashing through the overhanging hedges, scraping itself and its rider, gashing them with blackthorn, hawthorn and sloe, directing his hatred at himself. Trying to mortify his flesh, hurting the poor animal.

Charlotte clung to Hays, weeping, filled with despair at the disastrous encounter. Hays was more simple-minded. The hate that Jonathan felt he repaid completely and would have his revenge.

'Look here, Mr Kelleway, I've worked on this line as a driver for fifteen years and I know every foot o' track from Peterborough to Leeds, and I know every engine and reckon I know every carriage. That track were loose and that's an end on it. And it were loose for best part o' six months, don't you say?'

The driver, a neat, handsome man with a face tanned like a brown shoe, turned to his companion, the driver of 'The Queen', who had sat pale and silent, uneasy at the interview, suspicious that this was the end of his job.

'Coom on, lad,' urged the neat man, Mr Thorpe. 'Do tell him, Peter. So we shall lose our jobs, but at least we won't have blood on our hands. So we don't tell him, we shall. What happened can happen again, and if it can it will. Think on Watkins the driver of "the Albion," and what chance he had. That engine weren't fit for service neither.'

Peter Tomlinson swallowed and nodded.

'Aye, that's so. I suppose this will all coom up in Inquiry?'

Henry nodded.

'Aye, well like I knew it would. I suppose it will show it were none of our fault at least, and we should be able to get jobs on another line. That track were so loose I had to let steam pressure drop right away or else I reckon we should have coom off rails ourselves. Both sections were loose, up and down. She were

211

threatening to jump. They'd been like that for months.'

'Was it reported?'

'Reported!' The neat Mr Thorpe was scornful. 'We reported that track I should think every day, and sometimes twice a day. We can't make time if we have to reduce speed, and if we're late we din't half get it at the other end.'

'How do you report it?'

'It goes in the book.'

'Who keeps the book?'

'In the first place the station master, but he is supposed to pass it back to the track or line manager, who passes it back to the engineering section in this case. But, you see, Hudson had sacked the maintenance gangs. He were pressed to make savings to put up the dividends, we heard, and every time that happens, he gets rid o' men. I doubt but that we have two gangs to look after the whole track from here to Leeds!'

'It's not for shortage of labour,' said Peter Tomlinson. 'We have that many Irish roaming the countryside looking for work and as will work for nowt but bread, every piece of crushed stone could be hand-shaped. It's all show. The man don't understand. He may be very clever at buying and selling lines and junctions and branches, but he don't understand that you must never cut down on maintenance and engineering. Engines wear out, so does the track.'

'You see,' said Thorpe, 'we reckon he keeps over-extending himself, like. Always buying on to something new, never going back on what he has already built. He's after the railways in Ireland now, so they do say, but only if he can get himself nicely set up and financed. Why is that? Well, we reckon it's because he's had enough of some o' the lines he's already built. You can't tell me the Eastern Counties makes any money. So where does he pay for it from? The Midland. So we have cuts on the Midland. That runs down, so where does he go next? To raise more capital in the north-west or Ireland.'

Henry was not surprised by this analysis of Hudson's affairs. All the railwaymen he had talked to had shown a quick grasp of Hudson's problems from intimate knowledge of the exact state of all his lines, the condition of the rolling stock and the volume of traffic. They seemed to know much more by word of mouth than any of the directors.

'What about the Knottingley Curve, eh?' said Peter Tomlinson.

Henry looked blank.

'What is the Knottingley Curve?' he asked.

'Perhaps you shouldn't speculate on that, Peter,' said Thorpe, his sharp eyes slightly alarmed. Henry saw and was even more interested.

'I give you my word that, as this has nothing to do with the train smash, it will never be repeated.'

'No offence, Mr Kelleway, but we have been given the word by many gentlemen on many occasions.'

'Now you've mentioned it, Mr Tomlinson, I can always ask elsewhere, so why not tell me? I can only repeat that I will not be indiscreet.'

Tomlinson looked at Thorpe. Thorpe shrugged.

'I suppose it's an open secret.'

Henry was fast finding that these open secrets were very close indeed.

'Well,' said Peter Tomlinson, 'Hudson has just obtained Parliamentary consent for a connection between the York and North Midland line and the Lancashire and Yorkshire Railway.'

'I know of the Bill,' said Henry. 'For my pains, I had my part in drawing it up.'

Tomlinson and Thorpe exchanged significant glances.

'Well, don't stop there,' Henry exclaimed. 'It is a logical enough junction. It links two of Hudson's lines and should double the traffic.'

Tomlinson and Thorpe looked at each other with pursed lips.

The performance was annoying Henry.

'What is it then?'

'Well, Mr Kelleway, it is the general talk amongst us railway men that this link is not what it seems,' said Thorpe. 'It seems to us that this link is a way to connect the York, Newcastle and Berwick line to the Great Northern, and that Mr Hudson, while pretending this is all for the best for the Midland, is selling the Midland out, or preparing to do so, to the Great Northern.'

'I think that's stretching a point a bit far,' said Henry, his mind racing. 'You don't have any evidence for believing that!'

'Then why does he have discussions with Denison, the Chairman of the Great Northern?' demanded Thorpe.

'Because, Mr Thorpe, you can't expect the chairmen of large companies not to meet and talk about matters of mutual interest and commercial gain.'

'I think he is about to sell out the Midland,' said Tomlinson darkly, 'and we are Midland men, through and through. Maybe we don't count for much, and Hudson can fire us and replace us any time he likes, but this is our company and we've seen it grow up. If we've spoken out of place then I reckon we're sorry, but that's how it is.'

'Not at all, gentlemen,' said Henry, 'I won't repeat a word of

213

this. I thank you for the information, and sincerely hope your worries are unnecessary.'

Henry had almost forgotten the purpose of his interview, and had to concentrate upon bringing them back to the original problem.

'To return to the crash, you say that the tires on the "Albion" weren't new?'

'The tires on that engine were as thin as barrel hoops!' said Thorpe.

'There is a docket that says they were new.'

'A docket!' Thorpe almost laughed. 'There'll be a docket all right. Have you seen the tires, sir? You must have at the wreck. Never mind dockets, look at the metal!'

'I'm no expert. I just saw fragments of wheel.'

'How thick were the tires?' asked Tomlinson. He held up his hand, finger and thumb measuring about half an inch. 'Like this? That's how they should be. I would like to get my hands on a bit of that wreckage, Mr Kelleway, I really would.'

So would I, thought Henry, and I will. He had only been able to get the two enginemen aside through Braxton's influence, and no one knew of the interview. By the same means, he would get physical evidence.

'Well, I won't keep you longer,' said Henry, and stood up. The two men stood up as well and opened the door, jumping down and waiting for Henry to follow. The interview had taken place in a coach discreetly placed on a siding. Another piece of Braxton's work, another bond.

'I really had no idea that Henry was away,' said Louise, 'or I would not have imposed.'

Corbett, who had been hovering at the door, heard this remark and smiled grimly to himself. A very obvious lady, but very obviously welcome to Mr Meadows. The place was becoming no better than rooms for secret assignations, what with Mr Kelleway, and now Meadows. He wondered if Mr Kelleway knew about Meadows. He shook his head. It seemed that this sort of folly did not cool down with the natural ageing of the frame. He had little time for it himself. He felt momentary regret, and repressed it. His mind, like his body, was strictly swaddled, laced up and buttoned down. It was a way of living.

'I am very glad to see you, very glad indeed,' said Meadows, offering Louise a chair, and aware of wafts of perfume. He was slightly alarmed at her indiscretion at coming straight to chambers, but after all, she had come to visit her brother-in-law, or so she said.

214

'Have you found some accommodation then? You said you were looking for a place in Mayfair.'

'Oh yes, Mr Meadows. In Mount Street.'

Meadows raised an eyebrow. He had fine eyebrows, he had been told, dense and expressive, so he used them whenever possible.

'A very good area, and expensive.'

'Yes,' said Louise dismissively, not making plain which aspect she referred to. She did not want to divulge that Henry was paying the rent for her. For the time being.

'I shall be entertaining soon, and you simply must visit me.'

'I should be delighted,' said Meadows, flattered and flustered by such warmth. Louise was looking at him in a very favourable way, and his feelings about pretty women were not complicated.

Louise looked exceptionally fashionable, and had obviously been shopping. Nothing she wore seemed more than half an hour old. She put a hand on Meadows' arm, a light and affectionate gesture.

'I did enjoy our little conversation last time, Mr Meadows. It was so pleasant. Coming up from the country, I have missed the art of conversation very much. It was so dull.'

'That's very kind of you, but I wouldn't hold myself out to be a great conversationalist.' Meadows tried a deprecating laugh.

'Now, now, Mr Meadows! Let me be the judge.' Louise looked round the room carefully, or appeared to do so. 'You have so many books. All lawyers do. I don't know how you find anything.'

'The truth is we never use them,' said Meadows, 'but we have them just in case. It impresses. Perhaps we are showmen.'

'That is just what I was saying about you lawyers when we last came here. I think you are all like actors. You dress up and wear powder and play parts.'

'We also know our jobs!'

'But, of course you do. I accept that you must, but why do you like to dress up to do it?'

'The usual answer is that it is tradition.'

Meadows was standing beside her chair, very aware that she had not removed her hand from his arm, but kept it there, restraining him close to her by this gentle means. He prayed that no clerk would interrupt. The situation was promising.

'I don't think so. I think you are all vain. Henry is vain.'

This sudden indiscretion made Meadows start. Louise felt it, and was amused at her success.

'I don't think he would be very pleased to hear you say so.'

215

'But don't you think so? He poses. He strikes attitudes and shows his profile.'

Meadows was obliged to laugh, but with a touch of nervousness.

'I really must not talk about my fellows.'

'Well, what about you, Mr Meadows? You have your eyebrows. See, they have shot up!' She laughed, and Meadows was dumbfounded. At their last encounter she had plied him with questions and found out a lot about him. She had a capacity for being frank that disconcerted him, but Mr Meadows was not married and had in his time enjoyed the company of the female sex. Latterly he had devoted more time to work. At the age of fifty-eight, he found money a considerable obsession. As for the ladies, he knew a discreet and accommodating address. He prided himself on being well preserved and well groomed, even handsome. Flirtation was not his forte however.

'You are disconcerting me, Mrs Kelleway.'

'We agreed last time that you would call me Louise.'

'So we did.'

Louise released his arm and made a dramatic clutch at her heart.

'Then I am devastated that you have forgotten.'

Meadows smiled, a little uneasily. There was a hint of wildness about all this that excited him, and at the same time prompted caution.

'Where are the children?' he asked, not intending that the question should be such an obvious bucket of water. He need not have worried, for Louise responded in the same vein as before.

'They are hardly children! I would have thought you had noticed that. Nell especially – I find that men do notice her. At least they like to think themselves grown up. As a matter of fact, Charlie's off to Liverpool to try to do some business. He has ambitions. Nell is at home.'

'What about Edward? The young man who came last time. The one who said he was squiring you about London. I must say I thought that was a little presumptuous of him! Has he finished squiring you around?'

'Oh, Edward! He is charming, and has made himself so useful, helping me hunt for accommodation.'

'But rather possessive?'

Louise flashed a glance at Meadows that was partly amusement, partly a dazzling smile.

'Yes. How very observant of you.'

'Well, I must say I thought he was inclined to hang on to you.'

216

'He wanted to be my chaperon.'

'A chaperon!' Meadows laughed, but the sound was not convincing.

'To tell you the truth, there has been a little difficulty with Edward,' said Louise, looking beautiful and thoughtful. 'I found him a little too attentive. You understand.'

'I see,' said Meadows.

'He is charming but a little bit jealous. Ridiculous, but there you are. He is a young man.'

'I hope you don't hold it against me that I'm not?'

Louise smiled at Meadows, deprecating the thought. She was well aware of the game she was playing. Meadows was fascinated and like a fish would follow the lure, suspecting it but having to snatch at it.

'Young men have fancies. Didn't you? It's that gallant age when you imagine yourself in and out of love, without bothering to ask the other party! A gesture sets them clutching their bosoms in undying adoration, at least until breakfast.'

'He seems a little old for that state.'

'Well, you mustn't worry, Mr Meadows. Currently he seems to have fallen for Nell. Head over heels.'

'She's his cousin.'

'I'm his aunt! He'll get over it. Nell needs a gallant and adoring escort.'

'I see.' Meadows found this conversation deliciously exciting, erotic. He had never talked to a woman in this way before. Visions of all sorts of excitements and possibilities were already crowding his mind.

'Nell is very beautiful, isn't she?' pursued Louise.

'Yes, I suppose she is,' said Meadows.

'Of course she is! Don't worry, I shan't assume that you will seduce my daughter, just because you admire her!'

'Louise!'

'I like to talk frankly, don't you? It seems to me that there is too much talking round everything these days. Any man with a drop of red blood is bound to admire an attractive girl. I don't mean in any abstract fashion, but as a sexual object. Hypocrisy to say otherwise. I have been in the galleries now in London, and seen the parades of men who collect before nude paintings, admiring the technique, the tones! If there is a landscape by the same artist alongside, you can be sure it gets scant attention. They say nothing about its technique and tones. We are all covering ourselves up, Mr Meadows, physically and mentally. When I was a girl, we wore so much less, showed so much more. We talked with much more freedom. People are becoming prudes.'

217

Meadows seemed intoxicated by this aphrodisiac whirl of words. He was one of those men who really enjoyed perfume on a woman. The combination was heady stuff, and he was aware of embarrassing stirrings in his loins. He tried to concentrate his mind elsewhere. This woman was kin of Henry Kelleway, caution murmured. It could be difficult.

'Maybe you're right. They don't change their ways though. Not what we see of them. I should imagine that Henry will be away for several days. He has to make inquiries at the scene of a railway accident. You won't even find Frederick Kelleway. He called in to leave a message that he was going to Liverpool. I was supposed to give it to Henry, but couldn't, so sent it on to his home.'

'I know. Frederick has gone to Liverpool with Charlie.'

'What a clutch of Kelleways! And all out and about.'

'Perhaps you will have to look after me?'

Meadows looked rather paralysed. His words had been taken from his mouth.

'Well, certainly, of course....'

'You are very kind.' Louise paused for a moment, smoothing out the silk of her dress. 'What do you make of Frederick Kelleway? It's no secret that he and Henry are often at logger-heads.'

'Well, he does seem to give his father trouble,' said Meadows cautiously. This was a new tack, and was getting off the exciting subject. 'He is a very censorious young man.'

'So I gather. I hope he has no reason to be?'

'I don't know of any,' said Meadows too quickly. 'No, certainly not.'

She did ask too many questions, but he supposed that was just a woman's failing. She could not actually know something, not so soon. Or could she? Maybe it was known and talked about within the family. To his relief, Louise smiled at him.

'I'm sure not,' he said more firmly.

'No man is perfect...' said Louise pensively. She thought Meadows transparent. Henry was up to his old tricks again and Meadows knew about it. The very stuff of successful intrigue. She stood up, brushing casually against Meadows, noticing that, far from retreating, he moved cautiously nearer, so that their shoulders touched. She looked him full in the eyes, disappointed by his lack of boldness, for his eyes slid this way and that rather than lock them in a visual embrace.

'Now, Mr Meadows, you must not be shy of me. I'm sure that you are not generally shy of women. Where shall we go, if you are to look after me?'

She extended her hand again, resting it on his forearm. It was trusting, thought Meadows, rather like the action of a dog that gives you its paw.

'I suppose I can abandon work...'

'I'm sorry, I didn't stop to consider how busy you must be.'

'It's no problem, really, Louise. I have two opinions to write, but they can tide over until tomorrow. It would be my pleasure entirely to show you those sights you haven't seen.'

'I am most obliged.'

Something inside Meadows whispered that this was all a little overwhelming and a little obvious, but he pushed that aside, closed his ears to the whisper. It promised to be intriguing and enjoyable. What a woman to make love to! He wondered briefly what had happened to the husband.

PART TWO

The Scales of Justice

Ten

Caroline's illness was unexpected. It had the effect of drawing in the blown threads of the family.

She had always seemed so lively and observant about life that she seemed to be apart from ageing or sickness. That she should be seriously ill from pneumonia without warning was a sobering shock. Her housekeeper had found her in a high temperature after some spirited excursion in the rain and from there matters had got worse, until the doctor, increasingly showing his concern, had hinted that her chances were no more than even. Maria had been quick to pounce on this euphemism. She had organised the family.

For this reason Edward found himself making the ride down into the Weald of Kent. Maria had written to John again and again since Louise had come to London, inviting John to visit her, but had received no response. Now she had received no reply to her last letter advising him of Caroline's illness, and felt that John must be made to attend. His burdens were great enough, she thought, without being absent from Caroline's sick bed. What if Caroline should die? He should not be allowed to assume further causes for reproach. This sorry illness, she thought, would be an opportunity to reunite them, when above all they seemed determined to fragment and weaken what slender bonds they still had.

Edward did not want to go. His last visit had been unnerving, tense with undertones. However in the end, he had been persuaded by the others who had pointed out that John truly liked him despite his caustic attitude. The potency of a visit from Edward, whose own mother it was that was struck down, was undeniable.

Maria had wondered if Edward had any inkling of the nature of the bond she saw between them. John liked Edward for his illegitimacy, for being, as he saw it, another of life's unfortunates with whom he could identify. Perhaps not a good basis for a relationship, but apparently the only one John could manage at the moment. John saw himself as a man not in control of his destiny but at the whim of events.

Edward had plenty of time to consider things. He did not hurry the horse, but was satisfied to enjoy the cavernous beech woods where the mulch was so soft that the animal moved without hoof-beats, and the transition to hop-fields and orchards as the great bowl of land flattened out. It would soon be time for the hop-pickers, he thought: the army of Londoners who would swarm over these fields that were like cathedrals of greenery and pull it all down, the delicate tracery, the roofs and spreading columns.

His route took him beside these wonders of string and wood and greenery. The smell was strong, swooning, unpleasant. The alleyways formed endless perspectives filled with bees and hovering flies. When Edward reined in the horse and listened, there was a deep and constant buzz, fulsome and heavy as the smell, an overpowering noise that he found strangely frightening. It was a noise which obliterated the sound of the birds, and seemed to have an angry tone as if the insects knew and resented that this was all to be torn down. Pure fancy, he told himself, and perhaps because he wanted to prove it, or perhaps because he wanted a brief rest or perhaps simply because he was attracted by the beauty of a world roofed in green, he dismounted, leaving the horse to graze, and stepped some way into the enchanted world.

He realised, when he was a few paces inside one of the endless caverns, that it was comparable to being inside a greenhouse. John's greenhouse, with its jungle roof of fronds was much the same, but of a harder coarser green. It was a shock to discover that he had been attracted by the same allure.

There was a strong feeling of claustrophobia about these green tunnels. They were mazes without end, where the unexpected might appear from any direction. A fear of the forest, he reflected, panic, perhaps the oldest fear. He found himself glancing back to the sunlight whence he had come, being reassured by the sight of the horse cropping peacefully. The hop-flowers hung down from the ceiling in a strange perfection, as though they were formal decorations placed there at the command of some potentate of immense wealth. The bees that clambered over the flowers were so laden with pollen or so drowsed with the smell that they were unable to fly properly, but dropped off the flowers, falling some way before regaining their strength or their senses and blundering off. Their sacs bulged, weighing them down.

Edward walked on into the green interior, his mind full of the coming confrontation with John which the green tracery had so strongly evoked. Louise had rebuffed him cruelly, now she had settled in London and had other men to dally with, and yet at the same time she held him captive by using him as her guide. She stressed their kinship to deny their closer association. It was like beating away a dog you held on a lead, but knowing it was no help. He was in love with Nell, he decided, but not to the exclusion of other possibilities. This last was a defence, because Nell was besieged by suitors. He knew what the rest of the family thought of all this, but did not care.

There was a new urgency to know and find his father. With Caroline ill and the chance of her death seeming real, the last link in this chain was in danger of being lost. It was important to his relationship with all the Kelleways that he should know by personal experience what his father was like, if he was still alive. Perhaps the man had changed from what he was. The image he had been given was not flattering, but was so detailed as to have the solidity of truth.

It was not his illegitimacy that worried Edward, as Maria imagined, but this lack of a point of reference by which to examine himself. The frustration of having a life which was like a book with the first chapter torn out. Never knowing the beginning but only the after. Missing the first delineations of character, unable to assess what was inheritance.

He was sorry for John. How could he tell him about Louise? Yes, she is well, Charlie and Nell are well. What does she do? She flirts and philanders, is danced attendance upon by half the barristers of the Inner Temple, has particularly formed an association with a Mr Meadows who shares chambers with your brother Henry.

Louise shares chambers with Mr Meadows.

The thought could not be repressed, and had the power to wound. Edward could have sat down in the heavy-scented solitude and drowsed like the bees. Hops make fine pillows for those who cannot sleep. But he had lost sight of his horse which had wandered on, chopping the grass at the foot of the enclosing hedge, and was gripped by an irrational anxiety that sent him hurrying up the green tunnel. It was with real relief that he saw it had only moved a few yards. He had never considered himself to be a fanciful person but his mind had become crowded with imaginings.

It was only a short distance into the village and past the church to the entrance to the house. Since his last visit, more weeds had taken root in the knapped flint wall, finding some scrap of succour in the lime mortar of the joints. Toad-flax and stonecrop hung in bunches, beautiful but destructive, forcing the joints open and leaving them exposed for the action of winter. The gate was open as before, the black paint peeling, the lock a mass of defoliating iron.

Edward had expected the house to be ill-kept, but it now looked uninhabited except that curtains still hung from the windows. Slipped tiles had not been replaced and swallows had made their

225

nests all round the eaves, covering the walls with white droppings as if they too were certain the house was a ruin. Other nests projected untidily from behind rainwater pipes, collections of grass and twigs. Only the last remnants of paint clung to the windows which were now silvery-grey, the colour of weathered wood. The drive was a meadow of weeds.

Edward reined in the horse in front of the house, and dismounted. Weeds grew on the steps where they had accumulated pockets of earth and now spread their roots sideways to survive. He was uncertain what to do. He led the horse behind him and walked round to the rear of the house, noting that the greenery had been hacked recently with a sickle crudely but with some attempt to keep nature in check. It was the first sign of life. He stopped and listened, trying to locate any noise of human activity.

Hearing nothing, he released the horse, and approached the back-door, hammering on it with his fist.

The silence was broken only by the sound of birds; not the shrill domestic twittering of native sparrows, but raucous shrieks. Edward knew immediately, although he had never heard such a noise before, that it must be the macaws John had talked of. He made for the greenhouse, noting that a path had been slashed here through the two-foot-high grass and willow herb.

He was very nervous about what he would find. John had clearly not got better, but was he now entirely mad, or was he just in deep retreat? Neglect of material things on this scale was commonly thought to be madness, but Edward remembered his conversation with Charlie and Nell in the big glasshouse. The seeking after permanence, the immovability of plants. The care and dedicated attention that John gave to the glasshouse itself was a very disciplined thing. He was not in this respect disappointed. The glasshouse was in excellent condition, the paintwork maintained, the glass entire. It seemed about to burst with the pressure of foliage from within, which reached up and touched the glass as boys press their noses to shop-windows, getting as close as possible to what they desire. Of John there was still no sign. Edward decided it would be polite to call, to forewarn him. Whatever condition the man was in, he should be given a civil opportunity to prepare himself.

'John!' he shouted. 'Uncle John! Are you in there? It's Edward!'

The macaws screamed, and Edward had a glimpse of scarlet moving about inside. If the macaws were alive, he thought, then John was alive and somewhere near. He must be inside the glasshouse. He opened the door, and stepped inside, bracing himself for the assault of heat and humidity.

'John! Are you in there? This is Edward. I've come to see you!'

'I'm in here!' shouted a voice. Edward jumped slightly, but was reassured by the normality of the reply. In his fanciful imaginings he had half-expected John to leap out of a tree.

'Where?'

'Come straight down the central brick path.'

Edward followed it through the dripping forest of huge leaves and rotting wood upon which other plants lived and fed. It was difficult to breathe. The variety of foliage was so extensive that it covered every permutation of texture, shape and pattern which could be imagined. Edward realised that it was a true collection. The labour put into it must have been enormous for one man. Orchids suspended from rotting boles filled with water, or clumps of moss and fronds. A macaw watched him, its eyes surrounded with lines like a monkey's, shifting from foot to foot.

John Kelleway was standing in the clearing Edward remembered having seen before, where the glasshouse soared up to provide height for palms. He had let his hair grow, and his clothes were those of a gardener, down to his knee-patches and leather apron. Rather from ill-use than choice, thought Edward, for the clothes had once been good. The jacket was part of a military uniform, the trousers had been part of a suit. In the clearing, there had been a garden seat, white-painted and slatted, and a table. Now there was a timber house.

It was too big to be a mere shed, having three windows and a door to the front with a projecting verandah. The roof was covered with wooden shingles supporting a lurid green moss interspersed with brown and pink orchids which looked carnivorous.

It was bizarre and unexpected, more so than John himself, who was watching Edward nervously, as though he might flee. A Robinson Crusoe. Shipwrecked indeed.

'It is really you. What brings you here?'

John's voice had not changed. The tone was challenging and half-hostile. He was looking Edward up and down. Edward for his part was staring at the house. It was evident from the domestic clutter which lay about that John was living in it, at least in the daytime.

'Do you like it then?' demanded John. 'Come inside.'

The strangeness of going inside a house inside a house was irresistible. Edward nodded, and John made a sweeping gesture, inviting him in. He clomped up the wooden stairs, across the verandah, and entered. It was dark, after the glasshouse, and looking out from the windows, the impression of jungle isolation was complete and startling.

'Good, isn't it?'

'It's amazing.'

This seemed to satisfy John, who sat down in a cane chair, waving to Edward to do the same.

'I need a fan,' he said. 'There is very little draught, and it can get hot.' Edward wondered about the use of tenses. It was so humid and steamy that his trousers were stuck to his legs. He shuffled uncomfortably. 'What is it then? This is a long way to come, just to pay me a visit. Have you come from Louise? I don't think so, that's not likely.'

'It's about Caroline. Maria wrote to you. Didn't you get the letter?'

'About Caroline. Oh yes. Yes, I got the letter.'

He was talking in brief sentences, and chewed his lip at the end of each.

'You must come to see her. She is really very ill, you know.'

'Do you like the macaws?' asked John.

Edward was annoyed by the evasion, but told himself to take it calmly.

'They certainly look splendid. I don't know if I like the noise. Were they Charlie's idea?'

'They were mine!' John's reply was vehement.

'It's only that Charlie mentioned to me that something living would be a good idea.'

'He was repeating me.'

'Well, they're a magnificent colour.'

'Redcoats. That's what they remind me of, you know. Very smart. Well groomed. Well drilled. They march along a branch.'

Flying redcoats indeed, thought Edward. John had shied at the mention of Charlie.

'How are things?' he asked, thinking this a sufficiently obscure question to make John unwind.

'Well enough,' said John. 'I have my disappointments, some things won't take, you know. There is a lot of parasitism among jungle plants, yet curiously they are the most difficult ones to get started. I suppose it is rather like mistletoe. When I was a boy, I remember smearing berries in the dark cracks of old trees. Choosing moist ones with that dark mulch. Where you get woodlice. None of them ever grew. It was quite a disappointment. Tree orchids are the same.'

He paused and looked at Edward in a manner worthy of the Ancient Mariner.

'How are your railway interests, sir?'

The mental leap-frog from parasitism to railways was not

lost on Edward. He treated it coolly.

'My interests are sound enough. Some of them slow to start like your orchids. Slow but steady. Things have settled down to the predictable. A lot of the excitement has gone out of it, and Company reports make pretty dull reading. Boring, really. There was a time when you never knew a yield until the second the chairman opened his mouth, then there would be a tremendous din. Cheers or catcalls – half a dozen suicides – I exaggerate of course, but now everything is such a certainty we know it all in advance.'

'That could be a definition of life.'

'Come now, that's a pretty cynical remark.'

'It may be for you, but what have I got? And I don't want any pity from you, young man. What is Louise doing?'

'Seeing the sights.'

'Don't give me that bland reply.' He turned abruptly away from Edward, staring at the plants. 'What is she really doing?'

'All right, what she is really doing is buying new clothes, and going to social gatherings and seeing the sights.'

John stood with his back turned for a few seconds, then wheeled round on Edward, his eyes on Edward's.

'Is she seeing men?'

'In the normal course of ... '

'Never mind that!' John bellowed so loud that the macaws screeched, and thrashed through the palm-trees. 'You know perfectly well what I mean.'

'I know what you mean,' said Edward hotly, 'but I resent the fact that you don't listen to my answer. What do you take her for?'

'Can I rely on you to tell the truth?'

'I resent being talked to like this. If you want to assure yourself, you had better come to London rather than hiding in this jungle!'

'Damn you, sir, I'm not hiding in a jungle! This is one of the finest collections in England.'

'In my opinion you are still hiding in a jungle!'

John, furious, advanced a step towards Edward. Edward was reminded again how fit and tough he was. He was no physical match for him.

'Can't you see this is a collection? Have you no eyes in your head? Is it all lost on you? What do you think I am, some sort of aboriginal pygmy? Only the Royal Botanical Gardens can show anything better!'

'I'm sorry, I don't mean to insult the collection. I mean a jungle in your mind.'

'I see.'

This seemed to mollify John, who looked much less threatening. About personal insults he obviously cared very little, but no one must criticise the collection.

'We seem to have got right away from it, but what I came to see you about, is why you haven't replied to Maria. Mother is very ill. It isn't some slight summer cold. The doctor only gives her an even chance of getting well. It's all very distressing. She wants to see you, you know. You're dear to mother. Perhaps you've never understood that.'

'Don't chide me. No, please don't chide me. That's something I can't stand.' John's chewing of his lip had become more frequent, his manner more agitated.

'Don't you know that I know I should come, but that I can't from sheer cowardice. I can talk to you like this because, although I don't like all your smart business, and I don't like the way Louise dotes on you, you are like me.'

'Am I?'

'Of course you are! Have you never seen it? Not knowing your father is rather like not knowing yourself. Isn't it? I feel it is.'

The intensity and directness of John made it impossible to take offence. He was so matter-of-fact that Edward simply considered the statement. No one had ever discussed this matter with him, yet it was always with him and in his mind.

'It's part of my concern over mother's illness. I have been thinking about it on the ride down here. Should she die, I have lost the link with my father, in a way. I would like to see him. Can you understand that? I don't care what I feel about him, or what he is, but it is very important to see him. I don't even care if I talk to him.'

'You see, I was right!' John exclaimed. 'We're both lost. You have your own jungle.'

'But it's different.'

'If you wish. But much the same. I can understand it. I look at myself, and I can't find anything that I recognise. A stranger stares at me from the mirror. Most people accept themselves. Have you ever stopped to examine the face that looks back at you, and thought, what is that? What is there there that I recognise as myself?'

Edward could not follow this morbid trend, and did not want to.

'That's self-pity. You are simply what you see. That's what others see of you, at least.'

'But they see so little, and it is so meaningless.'

'Well, no one can see another man's soul.'

'That's not what I mean! You don't understand my point.'

'No. I don't understand it.' Edward was curt, almost rude. John threw up his hands in a histrionic gesture, then clasped them behind his back and began to pace up and down the verandah, his feet clumping heavily on the boards.

'I must come to see Caroline, mustn't I?' he said. Edward nodded. John glancing quickly at him, nodded too, pondering.

'I am really not mad, you know,' he said suddenly.

'I can see that,' said Edward, disarmed.

'People will think so.'

'Of course they won't.'

'You see, I know all about Louise. I know what she is doing. I can feel it. I don't need reports. She is a child. London is a big box of confections. She will eat them all. She will have other men. Tell me she hasn't!'

John had stopped abruptly in front of Edward, and thrust his face close. His clothes smelled of earth, his breath of onions.

'I can't tell you what I don't know,' lied Edward.

'If I come to London, I am bound to find out. Isn't that a good reason for staying away?'

'Not if you want to look in the mirror and see what you look like.'

John stopped dead, leered at Edward, pursing his lips, nodded his head to one side.

'You have me, don't you. I have nothing to say.'

'Then we're going?'

'Yes.'

Edward was uneasy. He had been made to persuade John, when John should want to come as a matter of love and duty.

'It will mean a lot to Caroline,' he said.

'And you, sir, how are your ventures going?' asked John, changing the subject. 'How are your railways? How is your tyrannous invasion of the English countryside?'

'It's not *my* invasion.'

'Splitting hairs. You pay for it by investment.'

'As to an invasion, it has brought easy transport and freedom of movement to the remotest places. The economy has been transformed.'

'I know all that, and it's cant.'

Edward shrugged.

'Well, in short, I am doing well enough. Things are settling down, and there is much less speculation. In some ways it is less exciting. The railways are becoming almost respectable. Still, there is plenty of competition, and that is where the fun lies. I make a living of it ... with a little help from Henry, and a few others.'

231

'But you have no steady employment?'

'That is my steady employment.'

'Not in the way I look at it.'

'What would you call your steady employment?' asked Edward acidly.

John clasped his hands behind his back, and pulled himself upright. Edward was again made aware that John was fit and physically strong. He had the build of a man of half his age.

'I was a soldier. I think I shall become a soldier again.'

'You can't!' Edward had not meant to protest so vehemently. John's face showed resentment.

'Do you think I'm too old?'

'The army might.'

'Then I shall lie about my age. With my past record, they'll be glad to have me back.'

'But why?'

'Don't you see why?' There was an intensity about his tone that was unnerving. 'There's nothing for me here. There never has been, it was all an illusion. I have never fitted into this life, not from the beginning. I don't think I've ever understood anything. There's a devil on my shoulder you know, a real one. It has always been there, grinning at me. I should never have brought Louise from Virginia. It was a stupid transplant – do you know, I only seduced her because it would shock and appal and because I hated myself so much I wanted to be hated by everyone in the same way. That must shock you. I have never told anyone that before. Perhaps it isn't all the truth.'

John looked at Edward, darted a glance at him, perhaps expecting to see some violent reaction, apprehensive. Edward was too confused with his own emotions to do anything but stare at John unmovingly.

'She was so very beautiful, you know,' said John, as though lamenting the dead, 'and she reminded me of other girls. I used to know a lot of other girls, dark-skinned girls, dusky girls. I like girls with dark skins, you see. White skin always seems to me to be unattractive, funnily enough. Have you thought of it?' John gave a slight laugh that was not a laugh.

'White skin is a sort of incomplete covering, when you look at it. You can see the veins and the blotches, the workings of the system as though it is only a transparent cover, do you see? There is a silky texture about dark skin, do you understand? Does that shock you?'

'No,' said Edward because he could not think of anything else to say, and was afraid to provoke John further in these embarrassing revelations. John had become quite animated, his eyes were alive, and he walked about quickly, to and fro, turning on his heel, too active.

'I've lived by a sort of honesty, eh? It may not be the sort you would recognise, but I know I have. The trouble is it doesn't fit. I have loved women because I loved them, and not because I wanted marriage, a home, possession of them, possession of things, marriage gifts, carriages, the crystal and the silver and the gimcrack burdens and reminders that are heaped upon two people so that severance becomes a division of spoils. Love is a passion to me, Edward. It may endure, or it may be quickly spent. I came back here with Louise and fell into the trap that I knew was waiting for me, stepped into it knowingly. It hasn't worked. I am as unsuited for work as I am for marriage. Perhaps work has to be a passion for me too, but I have never discovered what it is.'

'What about all this?' said Edward indicating the palm house.

'Yes, well, that's a small enough thing,' said John, dismissing it imperiously. 'You see, I should have stayed in Burma and died there and then I would have been happy. That's the devil on my shoulder. I should have died. Instead, she died, of cholera. I wanted that girl to be everything for me, and when she died I hated her so much I wanted to consign her to everlasting hell because of her mortality. I took her gold and sapphire necklace, you know. I told myself it was no longer any use to her, that she would have wanted me to have it. You see how I have been allowed to pile up guilt. Now I have such a mountain of it, it threatens to crash down on me!'

'Does nobody know about this?'

'No.'

'Not even Louise?'

'She only knows snatches of it. She never wanted to know.'

He stopped his quick pacing and looked into Edward's face. What he was looking for, Edward could not guess, but what he saw was the face of a man that seemed dead, with the muscles contorted in a grimace. The eyes had no expression.

'Do you understand any of this, Edward? I think you must, not knowing your father. Don't you feel like I do that you have been put down here on this world in an unfinished form? I don't know who Louise is, either. She is just someone else I have touched, changed and destroyed, passing through. I believe some people are born unsuited to this world. A joke. From God. Who must have a sense of humour, wouldn't you say, Edward?'

John started to laugh, clapped Edward on the shoulder, then clutched his own shoulders and began his endless pacing again,

233

laughing without humour. There was still no expression in his eyes.

'All right,' said Edward, thoroughly uncomfortable and wishing he could escape from this madness, 'I do feel as if I have a section missing from my life. No beginning to it, which is ridiculous but is how I see it. But I have no feelings of guilt.'

'But it *is* a feeling of being incomplete? Of lacking something that you can't place but know must be important?'

The questions were too eager.

'I suppose so,' said Edward reluctantly.

'I am the most incomplete man you will ever see,' declared John. Edward was appalled to see that his eyes were filled with tears. 'I love my plants, I have to have them, but, do you know, I don't really know why! Isn't that ridiculous! I can't tolerate human beings.'

'Then how could you join the army again?'

'Oh, there aren't human beings in the army! There are soldiers. Soldiers don't have guilt. It isn't allowed. Everything is certain, routine, regular. Thinking isn't allowed. A good place for me, don't you agree? The outside world goes its way, you go yours. The contacts are so slight, they are not important.'

Edward felt a heavy weight of depression. John was certainly as bad as Charlie and Nell had indicated. How would he fit in in London? He realised he was afraid of John.

'They need men like me in India,' John declared. 'The Sikh troubles that all the reports are about.'

It might even be an answer for the poor wounded devil, thought Edward, if the army would have an ageing madman.

'I can see what my prospects are when I'm in London,' said John with false naivety.

So this was the way he had been persuaded to visit Caroline. Edward was angry that he should treat his mother, John's own sister, as no more than an excuse. The man was tricky as a serpent. Edward was fearful of what would happen when John met Louise. It could not be avoided, he supposed, but ought to be controlled, even supervised. He sighed, supposing that would be another of his tasks.

'If you are coming to London, you had better come now,' he said to John with more than a trace of impatience. 'Have you a horse ready?' He really meant to ask John if he had a horse at all but rightly judged it would be taken badly.

'Of course I have. A military man always has his horse ready,' said John. He had heard Edward's impatience, and the glance he shot at him was sly. Edward was shaken by it. There was a glimpse of the madman peeping out, the man who has things

234

prepared that he conceals from others.

'You mean you have it ready?'

'Yes. Ready to go.'

So John had been prepared. Edward looked again at the 'military man's' leather apron and ancient uniform jacket. He reminded Edward of a straggler from the turgid corner of some Napoleonic oil painting. He only lacked the up-rolled eyes and blood-stained bandages round the brow.

'God Almighty!' Henry stormed. 'Who do you think you are, sir, to take such liberties? You have the nerve to try to excuse yourself by saying it was on my behalf! What damage have you done, eh? Have you stopped to consider that? God knows what will be broadcast about. The whole thing could be trumpeted everywhere. You may imagine it seems harmless enough, but think of the interpretations that can be put upon it. Henry Kelleway's son goes to Liverpool to see his employer's devoted enemies where they discuss his business and how best to bring down that employer, including how best to get rid of his shares. It makes Henry Kelleway seem a fool and an incompetent, don't you think, as well as a professional rogue, or haven't you considered that, sir?'

It was unusual for Henry to use profanities. Frederick was shaken by the outburst he had just received, but which seemed now to be drawing to a close. This last was all repetitive. But Frederick was himself full of resentment and was angry, simmering rather than over-boiling, but very conscious of the injustice of Henry's attitude. For the time being he held his tongue. Henry was definitely winding down.

'Haven't I got enough to worry about, sir? Your aunt Caroline is seriously ill, as you know. Your cousin Jonathan has displayed about as much tact, competence and general worldly ability as you have. Your uncle John is about to descend, or alight on London like the wild man of Borneo, I imagine. His wife is treating the Inns of Court in general and my chambers in particular as Madame de Pompadour treated the Palace of Versailles. Hudson and Hussey and half the Midland Railway are intent on ruining me or humiliating me or both, and what do you do?'

Henry paused for breath. Frederick had to admit it was an impressive list.

'You go to Liverpool. And Brancker and Wylie lick their lips and can't believe their luck and run rings round you. You come back here meanwhile, jolly as a sand-boy, and tell me it was all on my behalf. It's a bit like Brutus whispering it to Caesar, isn't it, sir? What commitment have you made – real or moral, eh?'

235

'I made none, I've told you that. How could I possibly commit you to anything? You know perfectly well that Wylie and Brancker wouldn't listen to any undertaking from me anyway. It goes without saying.'

'Oh, wouldn't they! You entirely underestimate them. They would listen to the daughter of the son of the second chambermaid if they thought they would get a whiff of information. Frederick, they are very clever men, and they led you by the nose.'

Frederick was not prepared to be patronised.

'I deny that!' he declared hotly. 'I know what they want, I'm not an entire fool! But what they want has got to be to your advantage. Particularly now, particularly with respect to Hudson. They are quite clear that Hudson is preparing to deal with the Great Northern and ditch the Midland in the west.'

'Frederick,' said Henry in a modified tone that conveyed his superhuman control over his outraged sensibilities, 'don't you think I know all about that?'

It was the second time Frederick had been called by his name instead of a barrage of frosty 'sirs'. He was encouraged.

'Do you really think that I'm such a deaf fool as well as a blind fool? I keep my ears open for gossip in my own way, and I don't have to go to Wylie or Brancker for that sort of news. Rumour floats up from workmen just as reliably as it descends from directors. More bubbles come from the bottom of a pond than ever found their way down. Have *you* ever heard of the Knottingley Curve?'

'No', said Frederick.

'Well then, you don't know some of the best of it.'

Henry was determined to show Frederick the error of his ways but at the same time he had to admit to himself that he was very touched, as his anger cooled, that Frederick should have taken all this trouble for his sake. There was no denying that he had done it with the best of intentions. Quite unselfishly. That made him feel uncomfortably emotional too, and he suppressed the thought. Frederick must be discouraged from any future adventures. The situation was too delicate for anyone but himself to gather in and hold the strands. He would tell Frederick, however. Give him the details, take him into his confidence. It might stop him doing things on his own.

'The Knottingley Curve is Hudson's latest attempt under guise of assisting the Midland, to connect another one of his lines to the Great Northern. I agree with Wylie and Brancker. Hudson is preparing a path for himself to ditch the Midland altogether, and that before long.'

'But what is this curve?'

'Only a small loop, by which the York and North Midland, instead of serving as a feeder line to the Midland, may become a connecting link for the Great Northern. He has been having a number of negotiations with Denison of the Great Northern and keeping very secret about it. Concessions are being bandied about as though it is all some sort of horse-fair. At the same time he holds his hand to his heart at every board meeting, swearing his eternal loyalty to the Midland.'

'But, if this is generally known, how does he get away with it?'

'It isn't generally known. I learned this gem from two enginemen at the Loughborough crash. Quite by accident.'

'And what's going to happen about that crash?' asked Frederick. 'There's a rumour that the track wasn't properly maintained. Hudson saving on labour again.'

Henry did not reply, but fished in his coat pocket and produced a small heavy piece of metal. It glinted in the sun that shone through the window of his chambers.

'Have a look at this.'

'What is it?'

'A piece of an engine tire. From Loughborough.'

'What am I supposed to make of it?'

They both stood by the window now, Frederick examining the metal. Henry's anger had spent itself.

'Look at the thickness of metal here.'

'On the rim?' asked Frederick.

'Yes.'

'It's about as thick as two pennies.'

'It should be half an inch.'

'So the tires were too worn.'

'Yes. And the track was loose and flapping up and down. On both the up and down lines. And had been for six months, according to the men.'

'What are you going to do?'

'Frederick, the problems are really too complex to tell you that. I shall advise Hudson that the company should pay up and agree damages. Accept liability and try to avoid the bad publicity he will attract if he goes to court and loses. Which he will, if he does.'

'Hudson won't like that.'

'No. He won't. In fact I'm banking on his rejecting my advice and making a fool of himself. If I play it correctly, he's bound to do it.'

'But where will you be? It's another excuse to kick you. He'll insist you defend him.'

'I shall decline.'

'Then that's the end of you with Hudson, and he'll go for you.'

'Exactly. And that's the complicated area. Where I don't need unsolicited assistance. Hudson has finished with me, and I have finished with Hudson. We are both looking for a way to do it, that's all.'

Frederick nodded, and there was the suggestion of a smile about his mouth.

'Perhaps you will have to see Wylie and Brancker. It sounds to me as if you will need any friends you can get. And money. If Hudson has finished with you, he won't want you going anywhere else. He'll do his best to sink you without trace.'

'That's all too dramatic. Assuming I take up Wylie and Brancker's game of assisting the company by dethroning the king, then I ought to take the Loughborough case to court and act out my part. If Hudson ruins me first, I shall not be in a position to dethrone anyone, shall I? What do I do? Refuse the case as a man of conscience, or play it cleverly as a man of conscience for the ultimate good of the Midland? If the latter, how do I reconcile myself to the truth that the tires were worn and dangerous and the track a disgrace? I might even be able to exonerate Hudson. There would be minimal compensation to the victims. Hudson would be delighted, and I would be reprieved for the moment. That's the course that Wylie and Brancker would recommend. Do you recommend it, Frederick?'

Frederick stared out of the window. The leaves on the plane-trees opposite were beginning to fall. They had not yet turned yellow, but were sere at the ends of branches. The grass underneath the trees had died from lack of rain. Pigeons had made dust baths in the earth. The two options were clear enough, but Frederick could not decide which path he would take if it was his decision. He supposed that personal injury ought to come first, but if the company continued to be run in the same way, what else could happen? He voiced his thoughts.

'I suppose that in the long term it is better to have the company put in order. Not just because of the financial aspect of it, or even for the future safety of passengers of the Midland, but for the whole future good of the railways. If you think that the case for the plaintiffs at Loughborough will be open and shut, it looks to me as though there is a middle course, where you defend Hudson but lose the case.'

'Deliberately lose it, do you mean?'

'Yes,' said Frederick, looking directly at Henry. 'That's what I mean. Is that so bad?'

'So I don't take the Wylie and Brancker course? Hudson is not impressed by near misses. I either win or I don't as far as he's concerned.'

'But it gives you time to get to court, and he can never be sure that you have done it deliberately.'

'Hudson will be sure. He's bound to know. I should have to suppress evidence, like this worn tire, which he'll know I've done. Do you seriously propose that I should do these things? I've never in my life taken a case into court unless I was prepared to fight it through, tooth and nail. I can put up a good defence for Hudson. He has his engineers as witnesses who will swear that track was ripped up in the collision. He will make sure the enginemen are bribed to keep their mouths shut. Dockets will be shown that prove the tires were almost new, and that there is sufficient tolerance in the castings to permit wide variations in metal thickness of the wearing surface of the tires. Experts can be produced to say that hair fractures in castings are invisible under the most careful inspection. Everything you would expect.'

'Then it's up to the other man to challenge them. You can't take the case for both sides! What sort of dilemma are you saddling yourself with? You may as well take the Wylie and Brancker line. They see it as the course of conscience.'

Frederick had not meant to speak so baldly to Henry. Indeed he had never spoken to him in such a vein before.

'Damn their course of conscience! They see it as the way they will make most money!'

Henry was shouting again. Frederick knew he had led Henry to the edge of a great abyss and had succeeded in making him look over and down. He must not destroy this triumph, by allowing Henry the indulgence of anger.

'I'm sorry,' he said, 'I'm a fool. I only understand part of it all.' He spoke with such conviction and without any tinge of duplicity that Henry could do no more than stare at him in surprise. He felt closer to Frederick than at any time since he was a boy-child to admire and embrace.

'No, Frederick, you're not. Certainly not a fool. I haven't told you one portion of all the material bits and pieces, but there is no doubt in my mind that Hudson must go, and I agree with Wylie and Brancker. It isn't easy for me to choose, because it would be simpler in many ways for me to play the game of high conscience, but I've finished with that game. This is a practical matter. Hudson must be prised out or frightened enough to take himself off. The Eastern Counties will probably collapse, but that is only a question of sooner than later. I won't martyr myself on that. I'm taking out everything I own, in small amounts, selling out at a loss, but getting out. The Midland Railway must not collapse. It's a good line, as the Great Northern is a good line. They complement each other. I shall pick up shares in the Great Northern instead. I'm not such a fool as to bankrupt myself on a principle, and I have an offer from them that doesn't conflict with anything to do with the Midland.'

'How is Hudson to be prised out?'

'The Liverpool men have employed professional accountants for the last year and a half to investigate Hudson's balance sheets. It will come to that in all business. Accountants are a growing breed. They also sustain a systematic campaign against Hudson with letters to the journals, suggesting his accounts are not what they seem. That's the way to get at Hudson, not through his neglect of track and carelessness with lives. But show him to be careless as to how he uses other people's money, and we shall have him. I shall talk to Wylie and Brancker. In my own time, but soon.'

'What about the Loughborough crash?'

'I shall advise Hudson to pay up.'

'That should be interesting.'

'He can get legal advice from Richardson, the man who writes his reports to shareholders. He's supposed to be a lawyer. I've nothing to lose by taking the fight to Hudson.'

Frederick looked quite amazed. The change in Henry's manner to this aloof decisiveness was a thing he had never seen before. He was forced to consider that Henry must have powers of decision to have got as far as he had. He remembered family stories of Henry's duelling in his youth. Of his coolness when pressed.

'Do I amaze you?' Henry demanded suddenly, reading Frederick's mind. 'Your mouth is hanging open and you're looking at me like a codfish. I remember a night at a ball when you told me that acting for Hudson was no good for a place on the Bench. Well, sir, I have taken your advice, if you like!'

Frederick was confounded. He remembered that evening, too. He remembered Henry making his escape for his woman, while he took Jane home, pale and withdrawn.

'You made your decision so rapidly. Are you certain about what you are doing?'

'I reach most decisions slowly enough and this is no exception. It's overdue, Frederick. I have a lot of overdue decisions.'

Frederick did not want to be drawn into this line of conversation. It had clearly flowed from Henry's recollection of that evening, and he felt he could not cope with any revelations.

'You've heard the rumour that Hudson is due to pay back to the banks a sum of four hundred thousand in August. They say he can't do it except from capital.'

'That has never worried Hudson before,' said Henry, looking appraisingly at Frederick. He knows I am shying away, thought Frederick, and he will let me. We still understand each other on our old plane as well.

'He must think up even more schemes now,' Henry continued, 'more amalgamations, more exciting dividends, as he runs faster and faster to stand still. He's a very fat man for all that running, but he'll keep going until we have something of substance to trip him with. A real plank.'

'You think we can get it?'

'I'm certain. This thing must be tackled from London as it is tackled from Liverpool. We need the accountants too. He shan't go to earth here. We want his books spread out and dismembered for everyone to see. If there is enough rumour, he will be forced into an enquiry. I don't think he could survive that.'

'If you get shot of the Midland, and get shot of Hudson, you can start canvassing for your seat on the Bench. Have you thought about that?'

Yes, Henry had thought of it, but as a receding prospect. He thought too of Kate and Jane and had a momentary feeling of drowning.

'What is it?' asked Frederick anxiously. Henry had actually shut his eyes and swayed. He looked very weary, not at all like a Wellington, more like a depressed Punch.

'It's all a damned burden,' Henry replied, unwilling to elaborate. He needed to see Kate, he thought, but had things to do first. He must fit in a visit to Caroline, must ask her if he should advertise in the journals for Charles Ware, with all the attendant problems they could expect of impostors. First and worst they would have to accommodate John. He could not stay at Caroline's house, so would presumably stay with them. Jane would complain. Jane always complained. He ought to see Woolmer immediately and Hudson very soon. Escape seemed a marvellously attractive idea. But where to? At least he could escape from the bonds that were put upon him by this continual harking on his conscience.

'I shall have to deal with Hudson promptly, then at least I shall know where I stand,' he said. 'You mustn't tell anyone – I don't want Jane alarmed. I shall advertise for Charles Ware, asking them, him, to write for collection at the Post Office. I can't bear to give my own address. Just tell Caroline for me that it has been done, Frederick. Edward will be back tomorrow with John Kelleway, tell her that too, her memory's not too good.'

'Where are you off to?'

'I'm preparing for battle, I suppose. I feel as if I have been under siege for years, Frederick. The drawbridge has been up, and I have been defending myself against every sort of assault while life inside my castle becomes more and more untenable. I'm starving, in many ways, and the time has come to break out, make an attack, burst through it all. Do you understand?'

'I think I understand.'

'Then forgive me if I hurt people we love ... or should love. Perhaps love at one level.'

Frederick nodded.

'I know.'

'I will try not to,' said Henry, and stalked out of the room, feeling he had already said too much.

His first visit was to the Post Office, where he arranged the receipt of letters addressed to himself, and having purchased paper and an envelope and seated himself at a mahogany table wrote a letter to Wylie and Brancker. He had a feeling of exhilaration at the danger of what he was doing. Something he had not felt since he was a much younger man, something, he reflected, he used to feel in his affairs with women, but had long since lost.

'Dear Sirs,

I feel that a meeting might be to the advantage of all parties. I know what has been said between you and my son Frederick, and cannot disagree.

It is likely that my own matters will come to a head shortly, and release me to act. I believe that the appointment of an experienced and reliable accountant at the London end ought to be an early objective, and wondered if you had given this prior thought.

I look forward to your early reply,

Gentlemen, I remain,

Henry Kelleway.

As he passed the letter over the counter for the clerk to affix the familiar black stamp, he felt that he had cast the die. He was possessed with energy, no delay was tolerable in this rush from the siege. He walked to Fleet Street, hot with haste, where he hired a horse from a livery stable. He had no desire to confront Jane and explain his actions, which he knew to be instinctive rather than rational. This was a time for wielding weapons, not for treaties. He set out on a reasonable animal for Hitchin to see Woolmer. He would cast the second die.

There had been a spate of rain in the mid-morning, and the day was suitable to the season with hints of autumn in the feel and smell of things and in the failing, middle-aged power of a corpulent sun.

242

It made riding more pleasant, for the dust had been laid without forming puddles. He would make a better time. The hedgerows still dripped and Henry made no attempt to avoid the soaking rainbursts from gusted trees as he rode through Islington, even reached up and shook branches as he passed, smiling to see his horse start away, enjoying the cold shower on his own head and face.

He would arrive at about three o'clock and estimated that he would be back home, changed, and ready to see Hudson by eight or nine the same evening. It would still be light enough for him to make good time at least to the lit outskirts of London. If it were not for Woolmer's damned stubbornness, he thought with irony, there might already be a train service, reducing his journey to under two hours. He urged the horse along, resisting a temptation to jab it into a full gallop, shout and beat at the hedges.

Woolmer did not appear upon Henry's arrival, and Henry was disappointed. He had fairly clattered up the drive and flung himself from the horse. He felt he deserved more. On his feet, he realised that he had resumed his real age. His legs and backside ached and his neck was stiff.

He was shown into the hall with the stone staircase and glazed lantern, then through into the dining-room where the man told him that Mr Woolmer was working. Henry shrugged his shoulders and rotated his arms as he followed, easing his aches, vowing he should take more exercise. He felt none of the qualms he told himself he ought to feel. Instead he felt almost brash.

Woolmer was sitting at the dining-table, papers before him and a glass within reach. A tantalus occupied the centre of the table. Woolmer got to his feet, big but not ponderous, head nodding, eyes alert. As before, he wore no coat but was in shirt-sleeves and waistcoat. He extended a hand across the table and Henry shook it.

'Good to see you again, Kelleway. Sit down and have a glass of something – there are glasses somewhere.' He gestured towards a sideboard, and Henry took one and put it on the table.

'Have you eaten?' asked Woolmer.

'Yes,' lied Henry. Woolmer nodded.

'Well, then help yourself. I can recommend the port. Brandy's passable. What can I do for you?'

Henry poured himself a port, very deliberately. The beef and beeswax smell of the room was rich as a sauce. Henry felt hungry. He sipped the port and looked thoughtfully at the convolvulus strangling the white roses on the ceiling.

'The rose of York?' he said carelessly. Woolmer gave a short snort. 'Fanciful, Mr Kelleway! The grocer of York is no flower, and certainly no rose. Are you here on his business, I wonder? Not the Hitchin and Hertford, I hope? Mr Hudson can't afford it, can he? Not with Brassey giving him a price of ninety-five thousand pounds to build it. And I hear he has been making a further mess of things. Has to pay four hundred thousand back to the banks and can't raise the whistle, I'm told. We're all waiting to see what he'll promote to cover it.'

Henry was annoyed by this.

'I haven't come to gossip,' he said. Woolmer made a face, indicating that Henry was being churlish. Henry felt encouraged rather than otherwise, and ploughed on. 'I've reached a decision on some of the other matters we spoke about last time, and have come directly here to see if the substance of it still holds.'

'And you seem to be in a hurry.'

'Yes, damn it, I am in a hurry!' said Henry with quite unusual vehemence. He put down his glass and walked up and down the length of the table, watching Woolmer, who in turn watched him from the other side.

'Pleased to hear it, I'm sure,' said Woolmer stiffly. 'However, I don't see why we can't share a glass of port first before we pitch in with it.' Henry paused, then pulled out a chair and sat down.

'I'm sorry,' he said. 'I didn't intend to be rude.'

'Of course, you didn't,' said Woolmer, cheerfully. 'Long ride, short temper. Always the same myself. Have another glass of bone oil! Anyway, the Eastern Counties is going from bad to worse. That one is so shored up now that the timber is worth more than the building, so to speak. But I don't imagine you have ridden all the way here to discuss that. Or the Royston and Hitchin. At least not directly?'

'It's direct enough about the Royston and Hitchin. You may as well know I shan't be opposing you here.'

'Very wise,' said Woolmer after a pause. He smiled and nodded. 'Very wise. Is this what you have advised Hudson?'

Henry in turn could not help but smile ruefully at the immediate way in which Woolmer came to the point.

'You don't beat about the bush, sir.'

'No, we country squires crash through all the foliage.'

'Then you've guessed that I shan't be fighting you here because Hudson will have dispensed with my services.'

'Will have, Mr Kelleway?'

'Will have.'

'I see. And does he know this yet?'

Henry laughed out loud. He was enjoying himself, enjoying

244

Woolmer's dry approach.

'I'm sure Hudson knows it, but he hasn't told me yet.'

Woolmer's large head nodded up and down again.

'I had reason to believe that you were going to save his backside from a kicking over this crash at Loughborough. A bad business that, for confidence in the railways. Five passengers killed and an engineman. Two still very serious. Loose track, worn tires, eh? We all know Mr Hudson's favourite way of making cuts. When pressed, save a maintenance gang or two, eh?'

'Your intelligence is very good.' Henry was surprised.

'Oh yes,' said Woolmer, grinning cheerfully again. 'But it's no secret now, you know. It's in the journals.'

Henry was even more surprised.

'Is it?'

'You haven't seen one then?'

'No.'

'It says you will be acting on behalf of the Midland. At least one of the directors says you will, and that there is no question of negligence as has been implied and that rumours of that nature are completely unfounded and the work of enemies of the company.'

'I've never said that,' said Henry angrily, 'I've never uttered a word to any of the directors and what's more I don't intend to take the case!'

'I'm afraid someone has been assuming things,' said Woolmer mischievously, 'A Mr Hussey, who seems to feel he can speak on your behalf. The Midland has also issued a statement on its safety record. A pity no one told you.'

Henry had not expected this move, which was tantamount to committing him without consultation. On the other hand, he was still employed by Hudson, and Hudson could expect him to do as instructed. Until dismissed.

'Hudson will not be pleased,' Woolmer went on, 'especially after making statements about it. When do you propose to tell him?'

'The sooner the better I should think, don't you, Mr Woolmer? You're goading me, sir, aren't you!'

'Never, Mr Kelleway. Encouraging, maybe. Goading never! Have another glass of bone oil and continue until lubrication is complete.' He sipped at his own glass. Henry did as he was bid. The port was heavy and sweet on his empty stomach and he felt pleasantly light-headed.

'Now I suppose you will get rid of your Eastern Counties shares?' continued Woolmer.

'I certainly shall.'

'And what about the Midland? You have a good holding in that.'

Henry felt quite cheerful about the man's impudence. He was enjoying himself.

'If you tell me so, Mr Woolmer, who am I to argue? I shall hang on to them and have no intention of giving them up.'

'Keep your seat at meetings, eh? But you'll be selling at a loss on the Eastern Counties. There is no confidence in that line at the moment. Hudson is bound to declare a good dividend, raked up from God knows where, or it will collapse.'

Henry shrugged. He accepted he would be selling at a considerable loss, but it was better than letting Hudson call on the shares.

'You must sell your Eastern Counties in small amounts,' said Woolmer. 'If it came out that you were selling them up before ditching Hudson here at Hitchin, it would look like a manoeuvre. Take your time. The Great Northern will meet your Eastern Counties holding, share for share.'

'What? The Great Northern shares are worth four times as much!' Henry was only half-protesting, half-acting. He expected an offer of some sort. This was more generous, however, than he had imagined. 'I hope you don't expect me to protest, express indignation or any of that damned stuff,' he said quickly, seeing Woolmer grinning again.

'Not at all. It's a deuced good offer and I should accept it if I were in your position. It's a good investment from our point of view.'

'How?'

'Because we believe your resignation from Mr Hudson's affairs will end him more speedily. It can't go unnoticed. He can get in another man of the law – no insult intended – but people will still smell a rat. You have a high reputation for integrity.'

'Up till now. My reputation might not survive this little bit of business we're discussing!' Henry enjoyed his little jibe.

'Rubbish, Kelleway. We're talking about integrity, not canonisation! The soup plate with the gold leaf comes in the after-life, and it's no good now. I believe you have every intention of pursuing Hudson, anyway, and that's a matter of integrity. For myself, I think it's even worth a soup plate!' Woolmer roared with laughter, helped himself to the port and passed it to Henry again. Henry abandoned himself to the prospect with a growing feeling of pleasure and relaxation.

'What do your spies tell you about me and Hudson?'

'Well, it may appear to the stupid and bovine public that the two companies snarl at each other. A useful display. It's like grouse, all territorial, but we talk very earnestly to each other as I'm sure you know. We have a common interest in the growth of prosperity of both lines, in the increase of traffic that will generate, and in the removal of obstacles like Hudson. So of course we co-operate in these matters. And I'm told that you do too.'

'The Liverpool men!' exclaimed Henry.

'Exactly,' said Woolmer.

'A neat circle,' said Henry, beginning to form a picture.

'And one we all hope you will join. What my spies tell me about you and Hudson is simple enough, then. But we must be sure that when Hudson crashes he doesn't bring us all down.'

'There's bound to be an almighty crash overnight in shares. It will wipe out millions of pounds.'

'That's why his exposure must be so carefully managed. Lines that were artificially propped must go. Good lines must not be damaged. That's why we must all be so closely in touch.'

Henry found that he was nodding to himself. Woolmer had presumably been in contact with Wylie and Brancker for some time, heard about Frederick's visit. He would shortly know the contents of the letter that Henry had just written.

'It's a conspiracy,' he said with mock seriousness.

'Oh yes!' said Woolmer cheerfully. 'Gunpowder treason and plot! Only we mean to succeed.'

'Then I suppose you may as well know that I've written to Wylie and Brancker, asking them to recommend a reliable accountant to look into Hudson's books at this end.'

'They'll only come back to me anyway. You need Mr Prance. He's a member of the Stock Exchange and very good at ferreting out a set of books. He has shares in at least one of Hudson's companies, and is of the same persuasion as ourselves. Mr Robert Prance, he's your man.'

'I'm much obliged to you.' Woolmer pushed the port to Henry again. The talk rambled backwards and forwards. Henry noticed that he had not heard himself refuse the Great Northern shares. I've taken to watching my own actions, he thought, as though removed from them.

Perrin had listened to most of the conversation outside the door. His long face wore a smile that was like a wound.

Henry's buoyant spirits fell as he clopped back through Bloomsbury. Gower Street was a stern and ugly canyon, he thought. The effects of drink had at first been delightful. Woolmer had eventually produced some food, and he and Henry had eaten slices of beef as thick as boot-soles, picking them up in their fingers. They had followed this with half a pheasant each, scattering the polished table with debris and dishes. Both men were happily drunk, and it took Henry a huge effort of will to leave the table and get back on to his horse. Woolmer supplied him with a flask of brandy, slapped the rump of the horse, and sat down heavily in the gravel as it galloped off. Henry heard his loud guffaws ringing out behind him as he skeltered down the gravel drive, only just in control. He could not remember when he had enjoyed himself so much.

He had been elated until he re-entered the outskirts of London. Then his mouth felt dry and foul from too much wine and brandy. He had finished the flask quite early on.

Now he was dejected and apprehensive. He was not afraid of Hudson, he decided, but was terrified at the prospect of meeting Jane. He contemplated not changing his clothes, but saw that in the careless euphoria of his ride he had spattered himself with dirt. His boots were caked and his clothes crumpled. He did not want to face Hudson at a sartorial disadvantage. Burrs stuck to his coat and trousers and to the coat of the horse. Jane is a burr, he thought unkindly, as he dismounted. The stable boy would have to take the exhausted animal back to its own quarters in Fleet Street. He looked at it for a moment with maudlin affection, for it had shared his day, been part of his pleasure. The door opened and Weeks the butler came nodding down the steps to take the reins from him and loop them temporarily over the front railings.

'Is the mistress in, Weeks?' asked Henry. Weeks, the knowing old rogue, shot Henry a quick glance. He could smell the stale reek of brandy.

'Yes, sir.' Henry nodded curtly. He had seen Weeks' slight smile and was in no mood for confidences.

Jane caught him in the hall. It was always her habit and he supposed she thought it correct and welcoming to descend down the stairs in formal fashion and greet him. It was too much like the stoop of a hawk, he decided. Why did she force herself to be attentive when it only made him feel more guilty? She had even dressed for him. For dinner, he supposed. It provoked in him a streak of cruelty. He would not be staying for this dinner she intended! The thought was immediately followed by shame. It was always so.

'Henry, you look as though you've had a long ride. Where have you been?'

'Hitchin,' he said, tight-lipped. He could hear she wanted to lure him into conversation, soften him with words. His mouth tasted awful.

'That's a long way. You must be very tired.'

She stood close to him. If she smelt the brandy, she gave no sign of it. Her face was white and strained and unattractive. She had tried to improve it with some colour here and there, when she would have been better to have left it alone. There was no mistaking the misery and reproach in her eyes. The words that came from her lips were a veil to her feelings, used until she should be able to get him captive. That was what he dreaded and why he could not stay. 'I have to go out again,' he said, not looking at her.

'Do you?' It was not a formality, it was a direct challenge. 'Do you have to, or do you want to?'

'Jane!'

'It's a very fair question. You come here to sleep, and that's all.' And not always that, she thought to herself. We pretend you have been here, and perhaps you believe that I have been deceived. Henry was trying to edge his way round her, to escape up the stairs.

'I have to see Hudson at his house this evening.'

'I see.' She managed to convey total disbelief.

'It's to do with my trip to Hitchin!' he protested. 'Are we going to have an argument in the hall?'

'Does it matter where we have it? It makes a change from the bedroom.'

Henry coloured. She seemed to want the servants to hear.

'I have to see Hudson to tell him I can't take his case. Do you understand? Do you realise what that means?'

'No, I don't suppose I do. To me it means that you will be out again all evening, and I don't suppose you know when you will return?' Henry said nothing. 'I have had dinner prepared for us. I suppose you have no time for dinner?'

'I have to see Hudson immediately.'

'Do you?'

Henry sighed loudly.

'At least come into the drawing-room for a moment!'

'All right,' said Jane.

'It's not fair to attack me as soon as I come home,' said Henry when they had gone in and closed the door behind them. 'What I have to do next could very easily ruin me. I have to tell Hudson that I've finished with him, and decline to take any further business from him. Do you understand what a step that is?'

'No. You've never encouraged me to understand your affairs. I imagine it will be unpleasant, but you have other things to do instead.'

'I hope so, or we all will be in a pretty state!'

'Henry, you are exaggerating. I hear from Frederick that a number of good words have been put in for you to the Lord Chancellor. If you gave up all this railway work, I'm sure you would get a nomination for the Bench.'

'Is this the next thing that Frederick is engineering?'

'He's engineering nothing! He simply heard of it. I would be very pleased if you gave it up. I've never seen less of you. I have asked myself often recently if there is any point in keeping up this charade. What do you think, Henry?'

She was standing in front of him, confronting him with a bleak reasonableness as brittle as February ice over a running stream.

'Do you think there is any longer any point in my dressing up for dinner, in my coming down to meet you, any point in pretending? It's all pretending, isn't it, and a waste of time? For me, because I still organise things around you, discuss your meals with cook, discuss when you'll be here. For you, because you feel trapped. What do you say, Henry? Wouldn't it be better if we gave up the pretence?'

It was the sort of moment Henry dreaded. His heart sank, he could think of nothing to say. He was saved by Jane. The brittle ice gave way and tears flooded down her face. She clasped her hands to it, as though wounded, the tears squeezing through her fingers like blood from some terrible injury. She rushed from the room. Henry heard her footsteps drumming up the stairs, her door slam. He stood staring at the flickering fire, then turned his attention to the gas lights. Each jet burned like the petal of an iris. The furniture was well polished, and shone. Warmth, soft glows, a comfortable room, which meant to him absolutely nothing.

He had looked at Jane just now and felt only fear at her tears. No pity. Now he felt irritation that she should always choose moments such as this for her emotional displays, moments when he needed support, when he experienced some weakness.

He wondered if she really meant what she said. What was she proposing? To move elsewhere? A house in the country would be ideal, he thought. That would be a way if she would agree.

He decided he simply could not give the matter more attention. First, deal with Hudson. Change his clothes, and grapple with that monster. He wished he had never come home.

There was no such thing as a quiet evening at home in Albert Gate. Hudson was never without some company or entertainment. If Mrs Hudson objected to the constant swarm of railway men and their endless earnest talk, she swept up a statesman or two who were hoping to get inside information, stirred them together with a few actors, financiers and clerics and insisted they entertain her.

Henry had the advantage of being well-known to the footmen, and was permitted to walk past them while they stood at attention like Hanoverian guards in silk breeches and white wigs. He trudged up the long marble staircase, wondering at his own calm. He had no idea who to expect in the drawing-room, but was reassured by the amount of noise. It sounded very much like one of the regular levees. Hudson must surely be more constrained in a crowd.

The flunkey who opened the door stepped forward and announced him. Henry looked round, his heart beating faster now. He told himself it was the climb up the staircase.

If Hudson had heard the announcement over the din of chatter and a string quartet, he gave no sign of it. He was immediately identifiable by his stooped bulk and central position in the room. Around him clustered a thick knot of men with that intensity of concentration or curiosity which characterizes a crowd at an accident.

Mrs Hudson had gathered a lesser constellation, a loose-knit affair which tended to fragment at the edges as though sucked in to the sun that ruled all their planets.

Henry was delighted to see Braxton, looking bored, annoyed to see Hussey close to Hudson. Braxton had seen him come in, and gave him a slow, solemn wink, although making no immediate motion to join him. Just as well, thought Henry. Braxton must stay his distance tonight. Lowther was there and John Ellis and many other familiar faces. He thought it better to linger by Mrs Hudson until the present conversation broke up. Hudson would surely want a word with him when he deigned to notice.

Mrs Hudson was complaining to her audience in her strident voice. She was having difficulty in retaining them and she was a little annoyed. She had been lampooned in the journals again.

'It is really most unkind,' she was saying, 'when they are unkind to me because they oppose George. That dreadful paper the *Yorkshireman*! You know what they reported!'

There were polite murmurs of sympathy. They had all read the article.

'Well, I'll tell you what they said. They wrote a piece about me, saying I delayed the express from Darlington to York for twenty-seven minutes to bring me a pineapple from Newby Park! What a scandalous tale! It's perfectly true that I had a pineapple put on the train, but it couldn't have taken a minute. The train was probably late, but they said it was all my fault.'

'Newspapers are beasts,' said an ex-Lord Chancellor, 'I always found them so.' He was rather cross himself at being dragged away from an interesting discussion on a twelve percent line.

'They pry so,' said Mrs Hudson. 'They pry into what I wear, and what I buy. Really, they give me very little privacy.' A note of satisfaction in her tone detracted from her protests. Henry saw

Braxton moving from the group in the centre and sidled cautiously towards him.

'Didn't expect to see you here,' said Braxton softly. 'I don't think you've come at a good time. He's going on about the stupidity of landowners again, and I think he means at Hitchin. He was flashing looks at me!'

'Well, he won't be at all pleased at what I have to say, Mr Braxton, so if I were you, I'd run for cover.'

'Is that so?'

Braxton looked at Henry calmly, and Henry realised he had offended this stoic man, as he had done on other occasions.

'I didn't mean it that way, I'm sure.' He moved further away from Mrs Hudson, and Braxton followed. The movement caused Mrs Hudson to look up peevishly, flashing a look of annoyance at the two men.

'I don't know! My husband seems to monopolize everything so!'

This unwitting remark was received with so much laughter that she smiled with pleasure at her own cleverness, tossing her head at the turned backs of Henry and Braxton.

The slim and rather dandified young man from the *Observer* made a note of it for the morrow.

'Are you here for what I think you're here for?' asked Braxton. The bright light supplied by the multiplicity of glass globes shone through his side-whiskers. Braxton's face looked as though it had been roughly sand-papered and the loose fragments not blown off.

'I expect so,' said Henry.

'Then you don't expect me to miss it, do you? You're going to tell him the truth about the Loughborough crash?'

'Yes.'

'Well, let me warn you that Hussey and Barlow have got in first. They've already told him the sort of pack of half-lies he wants to hear.'

'Charming.'

'I don't think friend Hussey likes you.'

'I think he made that plain.' Henry managed to intercept a servant who was passing with a tray of glasses. 'Brandy punch,' he said in disgust, after sniffing it.

'Never mind, it warms the belly. I should have a few, if I were you!' Braxton followed his own advice and drank his glass off in one. 'Now, why should I run for cover? Watch out, here comes Barlow!'

Braxton took Henry's arm and they turned together and walked off in an oblique direction. Braxton was in time, for Barlow made an irritated face after them, knowing their evasion was deliberate, and returned to the group around Hudson. Henry and Braxton were now uncomfortably close to the string quartet. A man nearly as large as Hudson sawed at a cello, his eyes fixed on the central chandelier. It seemed impossible that his arms could reach around his own girth and play the instrument as well, and they seemed always to be a little short so that he shrugged his shoulders forward from time to time as though to lengthen his sleeves.

'At least we can't be overheard!' said Henry loudly.

'Damn it, I can hardly hear myself!' Braxton glared at the fat man unkindly. The fat man shrugged his shoulders forward.

'I shall tell him he had better pay up and withdraw,' said Henry. 'That's why you had better keep out of the way.'

'I don't care what Hudson has to say, Kelleway. I have been called most things by most men in my time. It accounts for my happy smiling face and baby's bottom complexion.'

Braxton's grin was gloriously wicked and Henry felt he could hug the man for it.

'You're just what I need!' he said.

'I very much doubt that,' said Braxton with amusement, 'You're in enough trouble already! By God, I wish this fat fellow would tone it down a bit.' He made a gesture of cleaning his ear with his forefinger. The man looked straight through him.

'The thing is,' said Henry, having to speak from a point at Braxton's shoulder, 'that you should try to keep your own position as clean as possible. Without me, we shall need you even more.' He was sure that Braxton was less than sober.

'I understand all right,' said Braxton. 'And what I need is another drink. Do you know, they mix perfectly good brandy with white wine and other rubbish to make that stuff!' He clapped Henry on the shoulder. 'Don't you worry, I shall get the inside information. There is a gathering of clouds on the horizon as far as Mr Hudson is concerned. A distant sound of thunder. A great test of loyalty, such times.' Braxton stopped abruptly, his thoughts erratic.

'George Stephenson isn't here,' he said, peering about. 'Hasn't been seen with Hudson for months and months. I know they say his health is not that good, but it's more than that. They're breaking up now, Kelleway, you'd best watch your moment.'

Henry saw that he meant the central throng. Hudson was on the move, his acolytes following.

'Here we go then, Braxton.'

'Good luck, Kelleway.'

Hudson admitted to seeing Henry only when Henry was a few feet in front of him. The admission was no more than a meeting of eyes. Hudson was on his favourite subject of Irish railways.

'The population of Ireland is eight and a quarter million,' he was saying, 'while the population of Scotland is only two and three-quarter million. That makes two point one acres per head of land in England, two point five in Ireland and seven point two in Scotland. And the country is easy for railways if you exclude the West. Of the one thousand, five hundred and twenty-three miles now sanctioned, would you believe that only a hundred and twenty-three have been constructed? Do you know that the Ulster and Dublin and Drogheda Railway carried more passengers last year than the London and Birmingham, yet still there is no investment?'

He paused for effect. Lord George Bentinck, an ardent supporter, nodded beside him. Hussey was just behind again, trying to stay in contact in the crowd like a swimmer seeking to gain a rock in strong currents. He too nodded. Everyone nodded, like pecking birds. Which is exactly what they are, thought Henry.

'Mr Hudson will no doubt want a word with you, Mr Kelleway.'

It was Hussey, at his elbow.

'I hope you have a clear picture of matters,' said another voice behind him, rather slurred. Henry glanced round and saw Barlow the engineer. Barlow was staring at him with eyes as gelatinous as a seal's. His face and complexion were those of a drunkard from a Jan Steen painting. Henry allowed himself to be edged slightly aside. Barlow's coat was covered with dandruff at the shoulder, and he puffed at a cheroot. Whatever Henry had to say was going to be contrary to this man's opinion.

'I think I have, gentlemen, but I would rather talk to Mr Hudson about it first.'

'We didn't expect you here tonight,' said Hussey.

'Oh,' said Henry.

'I hope you agree with us,' said Barlow.

'I don't know what you have decided,' said Henry.

'Well, we know what you have decided, don't we then!' said Barlow aggressively. His voice was rather loud, and Hudson picked it up, cast a glance at the group and decided to disengage himself.

'Well, if you will excuse me for a moment, gentlemen, we can continue this subject later. It is so dear to my heart I am in danger of boring you all with it anyway! I must give some brief consideration to other matters, if you don't mind ... '

Hudson nodded calmly to those around him, his hands held up at chest level, making small twirling motions. The end of the audience. He moved heavily towards Henry, eyes hard and alert in the fleshy face. It was like a charging bull.

'Well, Mr Kelleway? I didn't think I was expecting you.'

Hudson carried on walking, so that they were obliged to follow, until he was out of earshot of the group he had left.

'I understand from Hussey and Barlow that this little matter of the crash is all cut and dried.' Henry knew he was agitated because his Yorkshire accent intruded more and more. 'The Company has no grounds to be worried, I'm told. The newspapers can try to make what they may of it! Another of their campaigns they like so much. That's so, isn't it?'

He had stopped and turned, looking at Henry challengingly.

'I don't agree,' said Henry quietly, feeling his heart racing.

'You don't agree,' repeated Hudson thoughtfully as though tasting the words. 'Then what do you agree, eh? Mr Hussey and Mr Barlow are quite clear on all points. Aye, and they told me right that you were inclined to be difficult.'

'Difficult?' Henry was unable to disguise his anger at Hudson's casual insult. 'I have no idea what you mean. I have seen things for myself, as you wanted. I have read the statements, talked to people involved and come to my own conclusions. As instructed.'

'Well, let me have your conclusions, sir, and then I shall decide if you are being difficult.'

Hudson stood stock still, legs apart, his small fat hands clasped together in front of him. His pursed lips were pink and petulant, his whole stance bullying. Henry tried hard to control his voice. A heated response would only precipitate matters.

'I have no interest in anything but the truth, nor has the Company,' he said coldly.

'I don't like being prated at with talk about having no interest but the truth, Mr Kelleway, I tell you straight. In my experience it is too often a preface to the very opposite.'

'Maybe it is, but in my case you will have to make an exception!'

Hudson snorted. Hussey interrupted.

'We saw it as well,' he cut in with his strong London accent. 'It was all clear enough. A clear accident, a million-to-one chance. A fracture in the tire, it was, a flaw in the casting, invisible to the naked eye. What do you call that now? You saw it yourself!' His tone was rude and hectoring.

'I would say that would limit the Company's liability if it was all that was wrong, but not entitle the Company to avoid it.'

It was Hussey's turn to copy Hudson and snort.

'Is that what you say, then?' he demanded. 'Is that the considered legal view, 'aving carefully considered everything?'

'No, it is not,' said Henry in a voice he managed to make calm. 'It is my view that the accident was caused by the negligence of the Company's servants and that there is full liability. I strongly advise that a settlement should be made with solicitors acting for the injured and deceased and the matter not allowed to go to court. Damages will have to be paid, and ought to be paid, and the Company should see to it and avoid the adverse publicity any other course will encourage!'

There was a pause. Hussey and Barlow looked at Hudson, waiting for his response. Hudson stared at Henry's shoes. Henry avoided the temptation to look down at them himself. The string quartet scraped to a halt and there was a scatter of applause.

'And how do you imagine the Company's servants were responsible, Mr Kelleway?' asked Hudson, not lifting his eyes. His voice was that of a poisoner encouraging his victim to drink.

'The track was loose in my opinion and had been for some months. This is substantiated. The tires were worn, and I believe that the fracture was a result of wear, not a faulty casting, from what I have seen. There were no restrictions placed upon speed over these sections of track, which is the normal practice. The drivers knew the track was loose, and themselves considered it dangerous. Most of them were in the habit of slowing down out of caution, although they had no instructions. Maintenance on the loose sections was almost non-existent. The records show this. Gangs had been paid off and there was only one working on a stretch of nearly sixty miles. Put that in the hand of lawyers acting for the deceased, and we will see what happens.'

'That is your opinion?'

'Only a very small part of it, but yes, it is.'

'Well, damn your opinion, Kelleway!'

Hudson's head shot forward like a tortoise's, his eyes flicked up to Henry's. Henry had expected them to be full of anger, but was unprepared for the venom in the other man's eyes. The force of it was like a slap in the face, and he instinctively drew back.

'I've had enough of you, sir, and your wishy-washy opinions! I don't know what your game is with our matters, sir, but I'd like to know whose side you think is paying your fat fee? You were bumbling at Hitchin, sir.'

Hudson pointed at Henry with a pudgy finger, jabbing it at him.

'You can't afford to take high and mighty airs with me, sir, shall we be quite clear on that? What did you achieve at Hitchin? What did you *do* at Hitchin? What did all this legal experience achieve? Where's our route, Kelleway? And where's our defence now, Kelleway, on this crash? As far as I'm concerned you have shuffled some paperwork before Parliament, done some convey-ancing, no more, and I have paid richly for that. As to your recent opinions, I would rather listen to an experienced engineer. This has to put an end to things, sir. It just is not good enough!'

'It does indeed!' said Henry.

'Then be sure, sir, that the Company has from this moment dispensed with your services.' Hudson turned to go, but turned back again. 'Furthermore, you will not expect any preference on the matter regarding your shares. A thing you have no doubt borne in mind.'

He charged away hunch-shouldered, immediately engaging those nearest to him in conversation, his face again affable, his manner condescending. Henry was relieved. It had been easy so far. There would be a war, that was clear, but the declaration was over. Hussey and Barlow were looking at him like hyenas who have seen the lion depart.

'You will not of course consider doing anything *against* the interest of our companies,' said Hussey. Henry looked up sharply. The man's tone was threatening. While Hudson was one thing, best tolerated, Hussey was definitely another.

'I shall act as I please, Hussey,' said Henry.

'But you will not,' said Hussey emphatically.

'What the devil do you mean?' demanded Henry with the anger he had so far kept in check.

'You will not unite with any of Mr Hudson's enemies either inside any of his companies or out. Nor let any of your knowledge of company affairs be known to others, will you, sir?'

'I shall do as I think fit. Do you think you can muzzle me?' He glared at the straggle-haired man, expecting this tack, half-dread-ing it, half-anxious to provoke, to see how far he would take it. It was better to know than suspect.

'I don't know about that, but I think you would be well advised to be sensible.'

'That is a threat. I won't be threatened.'

'Take it as you like to take it, sir. If you sees a threat, then take it so. Let me put it this way. Mr Hudson 'as vast enterprises at stake and 'as collected his share of enemies. The money involved is enormous. Things are a little delicate at the moment, as you know, and the balance don't want to be upset. Mr Hudson 'as no temper to put up with interference. He would consider that personal, and I would think you would not want a personal attack on yourself any more than Mr Hudson would, that so, Mr Kelleway?'

Henry had to make himself stand rigid and unmoving. The urge to hit this man in his long twisted face was very strong.

'If you hope to influence me in any way or have any hold over me by these veiled threats, Hussey, then you are very wrong.'

'Where's the threats? I was just pointing out that Mr Hudson would take it very personally if you were to turn against him.'

'You meant more than that.'

'Alas, Mr Kelleway, what you thought is up to you. A man who has nothing to hide is very fortunate indeed, I always say.'

'Hussey, I should infinitely prefer that we never spoke or met again!'

'No doubt, Mr Kelleway, no doubt!'

Henry was shaking with an effort at self-control as he walked away. It was entirely as expected, but the expectation had not blunted the sharpness of the dagger. He was outraged at being threatened, outraged even more at being threatened by a man that looked like a sanctimonious undertaker, outraged that his personal life should become anyone else's property. It was like being burgled and then having the burglar smile at you and explain he was only taking this just now, but would be back for more. He collided with someone, and looking up to apologise, saw it was Braxton.

'You did it then,' said Braxton. 'I can see from your face. I watched the nasty little gang. I should come out of here before you do someone a mischief.' He took Henry by the arm. He smelled terribly of drink, but Henry was deeply grateful for his presence. 'Look on the bright side, what's done is done. Fini. You are finished with Hudson. Now we can really get to grips with things!'

It was the most heart-warming 'we' that Henry could remember, but he had a pang about Braxton's cheerful energy. He had enough presence of mind to grasp Braxton by the coat as he threatened to tip forward down the marble stairs.

'You know, I only drank all this for your sake!' said Braxton cheerfully.

He was always able to make Henry smile.

In leaving promptly, Henry missed Perrin, who arrived hastily and finally managed to talk himself in to see a director of the Midland. It was not long before Hussey was summoned. He was soon beside himself with rage.

'He won't be back at all tonight,' said Kate. 'There isn't even a chance of it.'

Henry was edgy, about to take flight at any moment like a wary pheasant.

'He could get back.'

'He's in Bristol. How can he possibly get back?'

Henry shrugged.

'This is all very gallant of you,' said Kate sarcastically. 'I feel quite swept off my feet with your passion and love!'

Henry turned suddenly and scowled at her. There was petulance mixed with annoyance on his face, and Kate felt angry herself at this sudden juvenile mixture of expressions. He could become a schoolboy. Arrogant and selfish. Why should she be so accommodating? Or why at all? She had welcomed him warmly, held him to her, felt such joy when the maid had discreetly brought up his note. The reality was less charming. 'Don't you think I ought to feel angry when you reject me? How many women can you go to, then, that will offer you their bed for the night?'

Henry gave an impatient snort. He never liked her candour. It shocked him.

Yet she pleased him at the same time because she had made him wait in the drawing-room while she disappeared, to return in a light silk dress with her hair down. Almost a state of undress. She looked very desirable and he wanted her, but not this demanding mood.

Kate was irritated by his snorting. There had been no expansion of their small life together. It was a snatched existence, and those snatches they had gave her no time to approach the most important questions. She knew he intended if possible to keep it that way. They had not touched upon the question of their future for several weeks, and Kate felt she was losing ground. Their brief meetings were spent with present woes, present passion. It was not enough, and with familiarity had become almost tedious.

She suppressed that thought, because the hurt it gave her was likely to be destructive. She needed him at that moment. To have him there was better than not to have him. Looking at him now, she remembered how Henry had made her cover her naked body when they had been surprised by Hussey. It was a fastidiousness she had thought about since and found both disturbing and rather disgusting. Henry insisted they cover themselves with a sheet, blankets, when they made love, while she had no such reservations, enjoyed the freedom of nakedness and the sight of their bodies. At first she had thought him merely modest, but now disliked it as prudery. When he lay upon her, she would take the sheet from his back, but he would grasp it firmly and hold on. It had seemed funny, but no longer. It was no game.

She moved away from him and sat down on the sofa, wishing she could be innocent of such thoughts, and looked at him. She was in love with him but not without reservations, like some silly girl. But would these reservations grow to such an extent as to overwhelm love? She certainly loved him more than she had ever loved her husband. Within Henry there was a stifled being that was full of charm. Her heart ached at the impossibility of reaching it.

Henry seemed to sense her unhappiness and came over to sit beside her. A fire burned in the grate and the room was lit by two gaslights turned low. It was comfortable and homely. Kate had been writing at a desk which lay open, with a scatter of papers. Domestic business. There were dried flowers in two Chinese vases, one on a small table, the other on the mantel. Signs of Kate's taste and attempts to maintain her own life. Henry was touched by it, yet irritated at the same time. The homeliness seemed an imposition, a subtle trap he could not help but reject. The dried flowers had an autumnal look that disturbed him. Like dried flowers in glass cases they reminded him of death and funerals. Death reminded him of Caroline, reminded him of mortality. He felt suddenly morose.

'Oh God, I'm no sort of thing, am I?'

'Don't be sad. I don't need a sad lover!'

Kate managed to smile, managed the soft words. Henry put his hand on her thigh. He was as suddenly penitent as he had been petulent.

'I'm sorry. It's all this Hudson business and everything else. I didn't mean to be churlish, Kate.'

'Then, please stay.'

'Do you want me to?'

'Why do you think I ask?'

'I don't know.'

'You do know. I want you to stay with me like a husband, just for one night, but you want to go back to your Jane!'

Henry's hand was immediately withdrawn. Kate knew she should not have said it, but had had enough of avoiding it.

'Don't speak like that!'

'Why not, Henry? What if I become pregnant? What will we do then? I'm not too old, and you're not too careful!'

Henry leapt to his feet as though stung.

'Please don't speak like that, Kate!'

'It can happen to me, it happens all the time. Cause and effect are very well known! What happens if we have a child? Will you love it and add it to your life as I shall? Will you add me? I shan't be swept away as a mistress.'

'Oh God, not now, Kate. There are so many things!'

'There are always so many things.'

'This is my island of peace, don't turn it into a torment.'

'Is that how you really see it, Henry?'

Henry turned away, stared into the fire, looked into that small torment of flames. There was always this unavoidable moment of self-examination, of putting things in the scales that could not properly be weighed. He did not love Jane, yet could not imagine a life without her. Selfishly, he could not face the disruption. It appalled him to contemplate it. Why could this woman not accept this half-life? He loved her as much as he had ever loved a woman and yet it was not enough. They always sprang their ambitions on a man when he was most vulnerable, he thought bitterly.

'I cannot leave Jane,' he said, not turning, feeling a coward as he did so.

'Then what is there for us?'

The expected question. He must give the trite reply. The expected response. There was nothing else for it, whatever it provoked.

'Why can't we continue as we are? It's a kind of happiness, isn't it? It's better than no kind of happiness.'

Kate was silent. They both thought over these barren words, picked at them to see if they were really stripped as bare as they seemed, as commonplace. Words that had been picked over by millions of lovers, that reduced their love and passion to the mundane. Levelled it.

Kate was clear in her mind that she wanted more and could not settle for what Henry proposed. She had to decide if by prolonging things there was any hope of changing his feelings and his mind. She felt a huge tiredness, but pushed it away. This was not the moment for that final confrontation, she would let it lie for another time.

That huge tiredness was an omen of the ending of things.

'It's a kind of happiness,' she said. She got to her feet and went to him, laying a hand on his shoulder, and gently turning him towards her. Henry looked at her. He seemed afraid. Taking his hands in hers she placed them on her breasts, held them there with her own hands.

'It *is* a kind of happiness. Don't talk. You will make us both sad.'

In her passion Henry thought he found confirmation. Kate found refuge from all thought except that this loving and caressing was at least a parting gift. Memento mori.

Eleven

Edward was bitter, frustrated and confused. He was in a continual outburst about something, however trivial, and Jonathan could do or say nothing to get him to modify his mood. It was all he could do to make him keep his voice down so as not to disturb Caroline. In desperation, Jonathan had tried taking Edward out of the house. They had gone walking, drinking, to parks, but Edward would grow bored within ten minutes, fidget and find fault with the very flowers.

The advertisement placed by Henry in the journals had asked for a Mr. Charles Ware to write to the Fleet Street Post Office, care of Mr Henry Kelleway, for the communication of important news. Much as Henry had expected, they had received not one reply but several. To date, seven Charles Wares had presented themselves, and they had been obliged of course to see them all.

This had proved so nerve-wracking to Edward, that he had taken to hiding when each man arrived for his interview, trying to get a quick glance from behind curtains, or looking down over the balusters of the stairs. The interviews had taken place in Caroline's house, since it meant a journey from central London, and Henry thought this would deter some of the pretenders. He believed it would also make it easier to ask questions about items of furniture and other details if it came to it. The interviews were carried out by Henry and Frederick, with Jonathan coming and going with Edward when he could steel himself to it.

Four Charles Wares had been easily disposed of, one being a genuine mistake, a man of the same name and age, the other three too young or too improbable – confidence tricksters with glib and facile answers about their lack of years. Henry had seen them off the premises with threats of reporting their activities to the police. They had departed with speed, watched by Edward from an upper window.

'How can people do this?' he kept demanding, knowing the answer perfectly well.

'Are you sure you want to stay here at all?' asked Frederick. 'If it upsets you as much as it does, you ought to go away for a couple of days. We can at least eliminate the obvious frauds. I don't see why you should put yourself through that.'

'But I *must* see everyone, don't you see! Suppose you elimi-
nated someone as a fraud and it just was Ware? I might have a sixth
sense about it, even if all the facts were against him. It is just
possible.'

They had to agree that, as long as Edward felt like this, he was
better off in the house. So he lurked like an escaped criminal, or
a madman, flitting to and fro up the stairs, listening behind doors
and peering out from behind curtains. It surprised everyone how
much it mattered to him. They had casually supposed that it was
a matter of interest, of some concern to tidy up loose ends. They
were all unprepared for the passionate anxiety which had gripped
him. Edward's normally casual manner, his charm and general
good humour had deceived Henry, who was inclined to be irritated
by all this strange behaviour. He found it difficult to see below the
surface, to realise that insecurity could breed the charm and
sociability he had always associated with Edward. Frederick and
Jonathan had done what they could to explain, but Henry had been
impatient, short on time and temper, his mind full of other
things.

Three pretenders remained about whom they had come to no
positive conclusions. This had produced an even greater agony for
Edward, which had driven him out of the house. William and
Maria had been called in to help, but were unable to assist in any
positive identification, and Henry had transferred his irritability
to William, who was hopelessly vague and always inclined to talk
about himself and his current work.

'They're all roughly the right age,' said William, 'and the bone
structure would be more or less correct. The fleshiness was such
a feature, though, and of course that can change so much in
people's faces. I mean, I have painted people in their twenties and
been unable to recognise them in their forties, let alone their
fifties.'

'Oh, damn the bone structure!' said Henry rudely. 'All this
painterly stuff is all very well. The point is that none of them can
answer specific questions, and none of them strikes me as being
like the man I remember!'

'But they wouldn't!' said William crossly. 'You ought to listen,
Henry. I know a good deal more about the changes that time can
work in the human face than you do. Bone structure is the
foundation.'

'I want to see a man who shouts out from his appearance that
he is Charles Ware. I think it should still be there. He wasn't a
pretty fellow, to say the least, and I think we ought to be able to
spot him!'

'I don't think that is necessarily so,' said Maria quietly. 'It is

263

possible for people to change beyond recognition.'

They were all gathered in Caroline's drawing-room: Edward, Frederick, Jonathan and William and Maria, while Henry presided. Jane had declined to attend these proceedings, saying there were quite enough of them involved already. In any case, she had to look after John, who was now installed in Gower Street. Someone had to talk to him. Henry certainly was not doing so.

'What about his voice?' asked Edward. He looked rumpled and worn. His eyes were baggy from not sleeping well and he seemed quite ill.

Rain gusted against the windows, making the occasion even gloomier. The sky was heavily overcast and it would be dark by late afternoon. Lamps had already been lit, but no one had attended to a fire. Maria would stay on that night, but with the exception of Edward all the others would go. The house was already losing the feeling of being a home, had the organisation of a hospital with everything centred on the room upstairs where Caroline lay. The two servants had retreated into themselves as though they awaited the inevitable, resenting this invasion of privacy, annoyed at the disruption of all these comings and goings, of irregular numbers to feed and cater for.

Caroline was unaware of all this. They had decided to tell her nothing until they had either succeeded or given up. To raise her expectations would have been unwarranted, they agreed.

She lay propped up in bed in a state of semi-consciousness, oblivious of time in a normal way. She dozed and woke and it was either dark or light. People visited her, sometimes talked or sometimes sat. Waking at night, she had been aware of Maria sitting or sleeping in an armchair by the bottom of the bed and found this calm companionship most soothing.

Her vision was affected so that she seemed to be looking down a tunnel of some sort that blocked out all but a small area of vision. It was a tunnel with vague edges which were sometimes wider, sometimes more constricted. It was an effort to swing around this tunnel and to change her field of vision. The deep concentration required was like shifting a physical weight by power of will and she felt unnaturally tired. There was always a pain in her chest but this had become such a constant companion that she had grown accustomed to it as people who live by the sea become accustomed to the crashing of waves and no longer hear them.

She noticed that she could hear quite well, and concentrated on this, listening to the clopping of horses on the road outside, the cries of street vendors. Doors opened and shut often, but she was not interested enought to wonder who it might be. They either came to see her or did not. The evening blackbirds persisted because the weather was still mild, and listening to the rain on the window she could still hear them singing. The sort of wet evening they loved. They would be turning over the fallen leaves on the lawn, chasing and scolding one another. Far off, a train squeaked thinly, then another answered. Trains which meant so much to some of the family and which she detested.

She could still think lucidly for periods between dozing and hoped it would stay like this until the end. She was in no doubt that she was dying. Yesterday she had had feeling in her right leg, now there was none. The tunnel of vision seemed smaller, less easy to wield. She spoke to herself, trying out her voice. It was important to keep that exercised. The sound was not recognisable as the voice she remembered, but it was intelligible and she could still be understood.

'Three blind mice, three blind mice.'

The repetitive phrase took over her mind and she wished she had thought of something else. The three blind mice were the Bishops of Oxford. She concentrated on that. Mary had burned them. The farmer's wife. That was it. Which Mary she could not remember.

She supposed that the Kelleways were really three blind mice. Henry, who could not find happiness, clever and stupid by turns. William, whose promise had been overtaken by vanity and who, when that was punctured, had not had the courage to concentrate upon his real talents. A painter of scenery. Successful in the popular eye but nothing as an artist. Yet Maria had accepted it and they seemed happy and that was a measure of achievement she should not scorn.

John. John who was coming to see her. She did not know what to make of John. Was he really one of the blind mice or did he see things in a different way? Was his vision impaired or heightened?

In all this, it was Jane who had suffered, and she would see to that. Jane was trapped. A spring had shut fast about her neck.

The rain on the windows was soothing and she dozed, contemplating the freedom Jane would have with the money she would leave her. Financial escape. What would Jane do?

Downstairs, Edward was making it clear he had had enough. He had not realised the toll that the whole business would take upon his emotions. His expectations had soared, and the importance he placed upon finding this elusive father had soared with them. Old, sick, rheumy - it had ceased to matter.

This intolerable situation of having three suitors for the post was driving him to the edge of an emotional breakdown.

'It's terrible,' he was saying. 'I wish we'd never started it! At

265

best, two of them are rogues and liars, at worst they all are. What do you propose? Some Judgement of Solomon! They all disgust me! I *am* being divided up, can't you see that!'

Maria had her arm around Edward. None of them had estimated how deeply distraught he would become.

'How are we ever to know?' he demanded. 'They can't *all* have forgotten all details.'

'The trouble is, we none of us know many details,' said William. 'None of them can remember the colour of their coach. Is that significant? I don't think any of us saw the man more than once or twice. It's a long time ago.'

'But surely someone can remember something!' shouted Edward. 'The only thing we seem to be sure of is that I'm looking for a bloated drunkard! Anyone can apply! What do you want me to do? Draw straws from a hat and say "You'll do?" Get rid of them all, for the love of God! Leave me in peace.'"

He shrugged himself from Maria's arm and rushed from the room. They heard the front door slam.

'Well?' asked Maria.

'Perhaps he is right,' said Henry. 'I can't think of any way.'

'I still pin my faith on bone structure,' said William injudiciously.

'By God, you'd choose a horse, you're so stupid about your bone structure!' said Henry. 'Get rid of them all. He'll get over it.'

'That's a very stupid assumption,' said Maria. 'You'd better go after him, Jonathan.'

John had been shocked by the decline in Caroline. Only Maria had been in the house when he arrived, and she had hugged him unreservedly. Perhaps this had led him to expect a similar greeting from Caroline. He was not prepared for her limp weakness. She had not been able to lift her arms from the bed-cover, and her head only trembled although she was clearly making an effort to move.

He had not been allowed to stay long. Caroline was clearly delighted, and they had talked fitfully and painfully slowly about how she felt, how he was, how long he was staying in London.

John had replied he would stay. Of course he would stay, and Caroline had seemed content. He held her hand until she slept.

Now he sat with Jane in the drawing-room in Gower Street. They drank tea as a diversion. It gave them something to do while they explored each other cautiously, testing attitudes, coaxing out news.

'There's really very little hope, is there?' asked John. 'I've seen

266

enough of sickness, you know. She can scarcely move.'

'No, the doctor says there is hardly any chance.'

'She was pleased to see me. At least I could tell that.'

'Of course she was pleased to see you, John. She always loved you.'

John paused and examined this idea. It was a shock to be loved. He had not thought of it, and it disturbed him.

'I didn't mean to leave it so late. Until this.'

'I know. You mustn't start to reproach youself. You've come as soon as you can.'

John's clothes were old and worn-looking, his hair too long. Jane was surprised how fit and spare he looked, and surprised above all at how lucid and reasonable he seemed. There was no sign of the overt madness she had imagined. He was cautious and circumspect, but that was to be expected. He had not yet mentioned Louise. That caused her the greatest misgivings. Surely any normal man would have asked after his wife immediately and yet John had been with her for nearly two days and said nothing.

'You really look very fit, you know. You must have looked after yourself well. You don't look a day over forty.'

'Well, I hope not,' said John.

Jane looked at him quizzically. John flashed her a smile that was completely artificial.

'It's important to me,' he said.

'Why?'

John fiddled with his tea cup. The hand that held it was hard and calloused and it seemed improbable that he could grasp it without crushing it.

'It is,' he replied evasively. He looked at the tea, which he hated, and longed for brandy. He must buy his own, wouldn't drink Henry's. It seemed never to occur to Jane to offer him alcohol. Poor Jane. She had tried to make the most of herself and she was really quite a good-looking woman but she had about her such an overwhelming air of melancholy that she hardly seemed flesh and blood. He had heard Henry come in in the early hours, go to his own room, and guessed the rest. She had the air of a widow or a spinster, he decided. A woman without a man. Here he was, a man without a woman. He suppressed the sudden angry thoughts that crashed into his mind. He would not, could not, think of Louise. Not just yet. Not until he was prepared for what he thought he would find, and had already planned and secured his escape.

'How are things with you?' he asked, turning the conversation upon her personal affairs. It was safer than contemplating his own.

'You can see,' said Jane, making a small gesture, inviting him to look around at the outward show of things.

'I don't mean that. I don't mean your pretty green silk frock and your well-polished furniture and your Persian rugs. You know I don't, Jane. What about all the rough-sawn things inside? I mean, how are things with you and Henry?'

Jane did not appear to have heard. She sipped at her tea without answering, suppressing her panic.

'I don't mean to be tactless,' said John. 'Perhaps I've grown out of tact, can't afford it. Tact is a prerogative of the rich, who never use it, and the complete and rounded people of this world who roll over you with it, flatten and pulp you with crushing tact. I can't do any of that. Jane, I heard him coming in late – or early – and going to his own room.'

'Why do you have to pry?' asked Jane in a small weary voice. 'And I suppose that even saying that gives you your answer. I am so weary with it. If I don't tell, then someone else will.'

'I'm sorry.'

'So am I, John.'

'For a time everything was well again. That was what I was told.'

'I suppose it was briefly, but he never really changed.'

'There's no such thing as change.'

'That can't be so, John. That would be too depressing. Life is continual change.'

'Only ageing,' said John with a certainty that brooked no argument. 'I think the brandy is put in the cask at birth. Laid down and the lid hammered on. We're coopered and hooped.'

'That's very gloomy!' protested Jane mildly. She was worried by John's assertion. There was a glimpse of his frightening world, the Caliban that crawled on the floor of his mind.

'It's not gloomy. When the facts are known, then there is a chance of enlightenment. The clouds roll back, just a gap, above there is the blazing awesomeness of your own self. Not in splendour but in colossal selfishness.'

'I don't think I understand you, John.'

'You haven't got selfishness on my grand scale. Or Henry's grand scale.' He pulled at his nose, a gesture Jane remembered well. It was a preface to more direct questions.

'Has Henry got some other woman?'

'I won't put up with this, John!' She started to get to her feet, more acting anger than feeling it. She was torn between shame and a longing to unburden herself shamelessly to this man who cared nothing at all about shame.

'Louise has got another man, hasn't she?' John demanded. 'I know it, I sense it. Tact as subtle as the serpent surrounds her. Tact is being lit to send up clouds of smoke. Autumn bonfires are burning to prevent me asking the most obvious questions. We can talk, Jane. It's an unholy alliance if you like, but we've both been to the same well, both drunk the same water. I wish I'd fallen in and drowned. Sit down, Jane.'

Jane sat down. John still stroked his nose, pulling at it between thumb and forefinger, his head slightly bent forward so that she could not see his eyes.

'And what about Nell and Charlie?'

'Charlie's doing well enough. He's been doing some smart business, I believe.' She was matter-of-fact. He would have to assess them for himself.

'Where does his money come from? He hasn't got any.'

'From Frederick, I think, and from Henry.'

'So Henry's playing the philanthropist all round, is he? My eternal gratitude!'

'Well, who else was to provide? You certainly haven't. You can't afford the luxury of resentment any more than I can.'

John shrugged.

'I suppose not. And who is this man that Louise has enmeshed? A better bet than me, I hope. Rich as Croesus? Station?'

'A barrister.' For the moment, she thought.

'Another lawyer!'

'In Henry's chambers.'

John laughed. He seemed genuinely amused, but there was no laughter in his eyes.

'That's really very good. And how is old Henry taking that? He's paying the rent for her to disappear decently in Mayfair, and she comes back to his orchard to steal the plums! And what sort of a Lothario is this lawyer? Young, dashing, treading on Henry's heels?'

'John, do you want to talk about it?'

'Why not? It's what I deserve, isn't it?'

'John, you must stop that nonsense!'

'Why? Do you think it matters to me?'

'Of course it does.'

'Does Henry matter so much to you?'

Jane tried not to consider the question, but was stricken. Tears welled up in her eyes and she hid her face in her hands. John was horrified, got to his feet and stood over her, reaching out a hand as though to touch her, taking it away again. He turned away, unable to be of use or to find the right words.

'I cannot stand it!' he shouted. 'I cannot stand the way that words become the bullets of the brain! It should be possible not to give pain. I don't mean to give pain!'

His anguished shout alarmed Jane, arrested her tears. She looked up at him. His hands were crushing each other behind his back, moving and strangling. Inflicting pain.

'I know you don't, John,' said Jane, coaxing, comforting the child.

'I am going to join the Army, you know. I shan't be a nuisance. They will have me. They need men in India, and they aren't too fussy about their age. I'm not too old, you know, and I can always lie about it. I have enough money for a Commission. Captain, I should think.'

'You mustn't do that!'

'But it's obvious!' John said loudly. 'I always knew it was. I have kept fit. Very fit. Fit for nothing else, I suppose they will all say!'

'But suppose they won't have you?'

'They must. They really must.'

His voice had risen, and was demanding. He was giving his orders to Life. Prepared to consider no argument. Mad, thought Jane.

'But what about Louise? And Charlie and Nell? Can you just leave them?'

'*They* have left *me*. They are a lot happier for it, I expect. Nell will do well under the tutelage of her mother! They have a lot in common, those two.'

'What a disaster we are.'

'Oh no! What a success everyone is, except us!'

'John, what rubbish! You must promise me you won't try to join the Army. Come here, don't stand with your back to me. Look at me.'

John turned and came to stand in front of her.

'I can't promise you that.'

'You must see Louise. You must promise me that at least.'

'I will see Louise. But what will you do?'

Jane was spared the need to answer by the sound of the front door slamming and footsteps running up the stairs. The two moved apart as though they were guilty lovers. Frederick rushed into the room, still in his topcoat, rain running off him on to the polished boards. He was spattered with mud and out of breath.

'You must come quickly. Caroline is worse. The doctor says she is sinking.'

'Oh no!' said Jane. 'Is it really that bad?'

'Yes, I think so. Hurry.'

The coachman's haste was useless. He was an experienced driver and tried to skirt the most formidable ponds of mud-soup

270

that drained into the roadway, but still he got stuck and had to back up and wheel, the horses slithering and panting. The yellow-brown mud was as sticky as a brickfield. The coach steamed up inside, Frederick's clothes contributing to the mess. He wiped and wiped at the windows, complaining at their progress.

When they finally dragged up the hill to Highgate, Jane peered at the house through the spattered panes and saw that all the curtains were drawn. John had sat silent throughout, staring at the rain, brooding. He threw the door open before they had stopped and was first out, splashing through puddles.

Maria opened the door to them. William stood behind her, his face sombre, and Jane knew immediately that they were too late. She took Maria's hands. John, not waiting for words, dashed up the stairs.

'Wait!' shouted William, but John paid no attention. There was no sign of Edward, Jane noticed.

'We're too late, aren't we?' asked Jane. 'We came as fast as we could. It was very difficult.'

'I'm afraid so.' Maria put her arm round Jane. Frederick hovered in the hall, uncertain what to do. He still wore the same filthy, wet clothes and they had begun to steam.

'I'll go up with him,' said Jane, looking anxiously up the stairs towards Caroline's room. 'I don't know how John will take it.'

'Are you all right?' asked Maria. 'You're very white. Perhaps you should wait. The doctor has left, you know. There's nothing to be done.'

'Is she laid out already?'

'Yes.'

'It's so soon!'

Jane's eyes filled with tears, but she felt little grief. Perhaps it was shock, or perhaps it was that she had a surfeit of grief. She supposed that she had known that Caroline's death was inevitable.

'You wait here and William will get you something warm to drink. I'll see to John. Frederick, you take off that soaking coat!'

'No, I want to go up with John,' said Jane. She did not really know why, but she wanted to be there with him. Maria nodded, seeming to understand.

'Henry isn't here yet,' she said. 'Jonathan went to try to find him.'

'Where's Edward?'

'In his room. He wants to be by himself.'

'Poor Edward. You never did find Charles Ware.'

'No. And I don't know if it's a blessing or a tragedy.'

271

Jane nodded and climbed the stairs. The door of Caroline's room was open and admitted most of the faint cold light which just made it possible to see. The heavy curtains pulled across the windows shut out almost everything except a thin horizontal band that crept under the pelmet. John was sitting on a chair at the head of the bed and Jane could not see Caroline's face without moving round beside him and looking down.

Caroline seemed no different. The illness had already deprived her of essential vitality. There had been no spark to extinguish. She merely looked asleep except that no breathing person could have slept so straight, straight legs, straight arms, straight neck. Straight sheets, pulled tight and firmly tucked.

John continued to sit and stare. Jane saw that another chair had been placed on the far side of the bed, and walked round to sit on this. John appeared not to notice her at all, but continued to stare into Caroline's face. They had loved each other as children, and now perhaps John felt he had left it all too late. They had been able to confide, had had a bond that precluded the others. She knew with sick certainty that if any last grain had been required to tip the balance and set John on a course for the oblivion of a uniform, then this was it. They sat in silence for a long time, each lost in his or her own thoughts. Thoughts that seemed to Jane to batter at them with the confused fury of the rain on the window panes. Each thought entire, clear, like drops of water, then suddenly diffuse, trickling away into greater and greater shapelessness. Drops to form puddles that would form rivulets that would form streams that would form torrents.

John stood up.

'I think I will go down now,' he said in a flat voice. Jane rose too, feeling there was nothing else to do and aware that the vigil over the dead had no meaning for either of them. There was nothing to be gained. Grief would come later, stealthily, not as a storm but as a mist lying heavily.

Downstairs, Maria showed John into the drawing-room where William was waiting with brandy. Frederick had been well provided for and was drying out. Instead of ushering Jane in, Maria held her back with a restraining hand on her arm.

'Leave the men for a moment. I have to speak to you.'

Jane nodded, and Maria closed the door.

'In here.'

Maria opened a door across the hall and they went into a dismal little room that had always been some sort of unused reception room. Jane thought with surprise that she had only been in it once before. It was the sort of room that is left over in a house because it is too small, ill-lit and ugly. Being on the ground floor it had no obvious use except for waiting in. A large laurel pressed up against the window adding to the classic gloom. There was no fire lit in the grate, which was far too big for such a little cupboard.

'I wanted a word with you alone,' said Maria. 'You can try sitting on one of those chairs. What a depressing little place this is.' She dusted at a leather-seated dining-chair that stood against the wall, and sat down. Jane followed suit. They were now looking at each other across a mahogany table whose polished top seemed black in the weary light.

'What is it?' Jane was unable to keep her voice calm. She felt nervous and uneasy at Maria's formality.

'Oh, don't be worried, Jane! Quite the contrary.' Maria smiled. 'No bad news. Caroline died very peacefully, you know. She fell into a sleep, and at some stage she must simply have stopped breathing. I was sitting with her at the time – her breathing was always very slight these last few days – and quite suddenly had that suspicion, not from anything tangible, that she had gone. The silence somehow seemed more dense. And she had. I had been concealing a small mirror in my dress, you know, for several days just in case. I felt terrible about doing it, but I was glad when the time came. Just slipped away. No noise at all. Not like a flame going out, as they say, because the flame had already gone. I suppose it was more like an ember finally fading – for a long time it is alight but looks quite black, then at some stage there simply isn't enough heat there to revive it. I thought you ought to know. It was like that.'

'Thank you,' said Jane. She had wanted to know, she discovered, without knowing it.

'That was one thing,' Maria continued. 'The other is something that Caroline asked me to do when she was still able to speak to me. She asked me to tell you that she has left all her money to you. The house and some small sums to Edward, but all the money is yours. It's a big sum, because she hardly touched father's money. The interest has built up.'

'Oh no!' Jane's cry was of pain. Maria was astonished. 'She thought you deserved it, Jane.'

'I know what she thought! She was sorry for me! Oh, Maria, I don't want it. It's so I can make my own life, because she thinks with some money I can get away from Henry and be happy. It's so terrible, it's charity. It's putting a price on the failure of my marriage!'

'It is not!' said Maria with a conviction that she did not feel. 'It is a sensible provision, seen from Caroline's point of view. She made her own life that way, and obviously thought there was a similar way to help you.'

'It's terrible!' said Jane. 'It's the last thing I want. Now I'm some sort of deserving cause!'

She was shaking. Maria quickly came over to her and put an arm around her. Jane cried bitterly, not like a child but with an awful keening grief that was like the howling of a dog. Maria, trying to give comfort, was deeply worried.

John stood in the secret gloom of a shop doorway, trying to conceal himself yet at the same time not to make it obvious this was what he was trying to do. He must look respectable or the police would want to know his business. He had waited until the shop closed, choosing a saddler's. Other shops, the milliners and bonnet-makers, furriers and silk-binders, would all remain open to pursue their own trade or that second trade the shop-girls carried on in the rooms above.

He was unsure what he intended to do. Wrapped in a coat that fell to the middle of his calves, he still felt cold from inactivity. His vigil had started since before it had begun to grow dark, and the night was clear and starry. At first he had walked up and down, mingling with homeward-bound pedestrians, but not far, measuring his distance between two lamp posts and turning at the end of his beat like a sentry, which in his fancy he was. He was afraid that something would happen when his back was turned.

The lamplighter had passed like Don Quixote unhorsed, tilting at the dangling hoops beneath the gas lamps with casual expertise, missing none. They flared up, then settled, casting a light like melted butter. The streets in this area of London were relatively clear of the usual sort of vendors and beggars, but as early as five o'clock men started to arrive who seemed to know the way and passed into lit shops without even a token glance in the windows. John watched them slip quickly in, saw them walking through the shops to the back door and was consumed with a Puritan contempt and rage. The furtiveness of prostitution seemed the true vice. A desolate piece of mechanics between male and female, putting man well below any animal. He had no reason to congratulate himself, his own sexual appetites had destroyed but had been full of passion, of love, of a dark thing in the blood, if that was what it was, which overwhelmed, transcended the mere machinery of copulation. He preferred the ladies who openly walked the pavements in their silks and bonnets, but was terrified, glancing at their faces when they turned to smile at him, that he might be confronted with Louise.

It made him tremble to think of it. He knew it was a ridiculous thought, but even as he banished it, it was succeeded by one more evil. It might be Nell. It was in the blood, in his blood. Bad blood.

Sensual and impetuous. He had fought to contain it all these years. Locked himself up. He ducked back into the darkness so that rustling ladies should not see him. It was not as busy here as the Haymarket or Regent Street with their assembly rooms, cafés and Turkish divans. He had walked there earlier and it had already been thronged. It had stunned him to see how overtly busy the trade was, how elegant and expensively dressed the women were. They had spoken to him, brushed close, even bumped against him. He had fought through as though stifling in their perfume and their softness, and they had made remarks after him that he must forget. Remarks that might be true, he did not know, did not want to think about it.

The windows of Louise's house were curtained, but light shone through them dimly. The lamps had been lit when he arrived, and he had no idea if Louise was at home. She must have some servant who could have attended to them.

He pondered whether or not to cross the street again. He had done so earlier to look at the front door and assure himself that it was the right number. There was no other sign of identity on the door or beside the bell. He hoped Jane had got it right.

At first he had wondered if he should walk boldly up to the door while he still had the courage and ring the bell, but he had found he could not do it. He was too afraid of the effect upon himself and unable to imagine what he could say if Louise herself answered. Yet he had to see her and had to know whatever there was to know. Now he skulked like a felon.

Jane had made no attempt to stop him going out, and he doubted if she knew or cared. Since Caroline's death the day before, he had only seen her for one brief moment on the stairs, when she had looked over as though trying to decide if it was safe to come down. As soon as she had caught his eye, she had retreated, white and wordless. He did not know what had so upset her, because she would not speak at all in the coach on the way back. He had become impatient with her, and his concern had soon given way to exasperation, then to indifference. He would have discussed his consuming obsession with her, had she asked, but she did not. It was selfishness, he knew, but the selfishness of self-preservation. A man with a grave wound has no concern for others, and I am clutching my very entrails, thought John.

Carriages had been coming and going, obscuring his view of the door, and it was with a sudden shock he realised that one had stopped. He could not see properly because the passengers were alighting on the other side. The man seemed elderly, he saw whitish hair. He was handing down a woman, waiting by the door. It was definitely a man and a woman. John moved out of the doorway, his attention concentrated on detail as though he peered in the objective of a microscope. The carriage moved off, and he saw it was Louise.

She was no different. Exactly as he remembered her. There was no transfiguration to some creature from the pit, marked with pox.

She smiled, and he heard her laugh. She opened the door, and the man with the whitish hair stood back to allow her to pass. She looked beautiful. John watched paralysed as the door closed behind them. He had done or thought nothing. Now the moment had slipped from him. He would have to approach the door again. He could not bring himself to move. Other people passed, other carriages. Some curious glances were cast at the man who stood stock still, staring. Perhaps he was blind, lost? No one would stop to ask. Time passed. John was not sure how long. It could only have been minutes, it might have been nearly an hour. The door opened again and he saw Nell come out with a young man. She wore a heavy shawl over a green silk gown, and he took her arm as the door closed. She smiled at him, but John could not see the man's face. They talked together, walking some distance along the pavement. He thought there was something familiar about the man, and stepped forward with curiosity, thinking he might follow them, might look, but the man hailed a hansom cab and they got in. It moved off. He had no opportunity to see that it was Edward who tucked her shawl around her and held her hand tightly.

He had no right to interfere. Any right had been forfeited long ago when he had first and so ruthlessly assumed control of Louise's life, knowing he could not control his own. Louise had got a man, perhaps several. So had Nell. What they did, how innocent or otherwise, was no longer any concern of his.

He walked slowly on to the pavement, not looking back at the house and its lit windows. In his coat pocket he fingered the stiff piece of folded paper he had been handed that morning in Albany Street Barracks by an unsurprised officer. They had treated him gently as a babe. There was no novelty to them in old soldiers returning to the fold who lied about their age. They assured him his Commission would be confirmed and took his money. For the Indian service. They had walked him round, talked of the old times, of new times, the Sikh War. They had drunk port together until his head spun and then had gently escorted him out of the gate. The sentries on duty had saluted and he had returned it. The deed was done. He had felt an intense relief. A relief from life that must, he imagined, be almost like death.

He had only come to watch, to take a last look like a returning ghost that can only observe but cannot influence. He had become invisible.

'Hello, sir!' said a female voice. 'You nearly walked into me.'

John concentrated on the figure in front of him, trying to give it form.

She was grinning, looking at him expectantly.

'Lost your way, 'ave you? I can show you the way!'

She laughed again. John stared at her stupidly.

'Just across the road,' she said temptingly. 'Nice place. You're a fine figure of a man to be all alone like this. I'm not cheap mind. No dollymop neither!'

'Leave me alone!' roared John, in a voice that rang down the street, making heads turn. He pushed the girl away so hard that she fell over backwards with a scream. John turned and ran.

'He's a bloody maniac!' shouted the girl. 'Bloody shoved me over. Look at me clothes!'

John ran long after he need have done, ran to make his lungs hurt, to bring pain to his body to obliterate the pain from his mind. He wanted to be out of this world and its hideous surprises. He wanted to feel as innocent as he had felt that morning, with the relief that was like death.

Robert Prance had asked permission to call in his friend and fellow stockbroker Horatio Love as soon as he knew what Henry's business was.

'It will save us all having to repeat things, Mr Kelleway,' he said smoothly. 'Love and I work hand in glove on this thing. We are both in the same position and feel the same about Mr Hudson. You've certainly said enough to interest me. I think we may have something to interest you too.'

Love was shown in. Henry saw that both men dressed in the formal cut expected of their profession. Both wore sidewhiskers and moustaches, both wore silk cravats of dove-grey. Both watched him assessing them, revealing a sense of humour Henry found surprising.

'Yes, we are very conservative in our appearance, Mr Kelleway. You must not assume it is a privilege enjoyed only by men of the law.'

Henry smiled.

'Some members are more flamboyant.'

'Then I should not buy stock from them!'

Love sat down. He was plump but not fat. Prance was lean and saturnine. He judged them both to be the same age as himself.

'You know who Mr Kelleway is, Horatio?'

'Indeed I do,' said Love. Henry inclined his head politely.

'Indeed I believe that you are likely to assume a place on the Bench,' said Love. 'At least, it is an open secret, Mr Kelleway.'

'And like many secrets may be more rumour than substance.'

'I think not.' Love smiled. His face was frog-like, lips as pale and thin as worms, but his eyes smiled, a network of wrinkles appearing beside them. Henry inclined his head. Deprecating.

'Woolmer has told us about you,' continued Prance. 'We know a good deal about what has been going on. Besides, it is our business to keep a close eye on the railway companies. We can lay our hands on the records of all transactions very quickly. We hold shares ourselves in many companies so it's all self-interest as well as good practice.'

Love sat down, placing his hands before him on the table. The room they occupied was stacked high with documents that were thrust into pigeon-holes. Each pigeon-hole had the name of a railway company beneath it in hand-painted gilt lettering. The little wall space left was covered with maps of lines, coloured in pinks and greens and blues. The paper was unruly, curled up at the edges, projected, gathered dust, threatened to cascade on to the floor. The end of the table was piled with red morocco ledgers forming unsteady columns. Henry was almost afraid to move in case he started an avalanche.

'Mr Kelleway and I have been having a general discussion about one or two matters of Hudson's business,' Prance continued, putting a yellowing heap of folded plans on the floor and sitting on the chair they had occupied.

'He had directed my attention to a matter I hadn't noticed.'

'Then that must be interesting,' said Love. 'He doesn't miss much, Mr Kelleway. Don't be taken in by all this mess. He has it all up here.'

Love tapped his forehead, and crinkled his eyes at Henry.

'Maybe I keep too much up there,' said Prance. 'This one I should have examined.'

'Which one?'

'York, Newcastle and Berwick.'

'We have shares in that.'

'Exactly. You explain again, Mr Kelleway.'

'Let me explain, Mr Love, that I have severed all my connections with Hudson,' began Henry. 'Or more precisely, we have agreed that Hudson can dispense with my services.'

Love raised his hands, palm up from the table.

'Of course. News travels faster than trains!'

'I wanted to clear my position. What I have to say is in no way privileged information. I suppose I have ignored it until now out of sheer pressure of business, not out of any loyalty. I believe in the railways, gentlemen, not in any man's empire, or any man's personal gain or craving for power. I found I could no longer assist Hudson, for many reasons, which I gather you understand.'

The two men nodded. They did not seem particularly interested in Henry's motives. Love had started to fiddle with his hands, very slightly. There was to be no baring of chests here.

'What I started to tell Mr Prance about is the purchase of the Great North of England by the York, Newcastle and Berwick. The purchase was ratified in Parliament in July '46, and is to be complete by the end of '50. Obviously they, that is the directors, started to purchase the North of England stock immediately, waiting until such times as the market was low. In order to find the capital for the purchase, they raised a subscription for a new capital stock, in which I had some small part, which is at a guaranteed interest.'

'I know about that,' said Love.

'Yes indeed,' said Prance. 'You bought as much as I did!'

'Good sense,' said Love. 'Nothing wrong there.'

'But wait!' said Prance. 'I didn't know the rest.'

'The problem is,' continued Henry, 'that I know that the capital raised for this purpose has been used by Hudson to finance the construction of new work on the York, Newcastle and Berwick.'

'What?' said Love. His hands flapped up and down on the table.

'Exactly,' said Prance.

'Are you sure of this, Mr Kelleway?'

'Yes. I had to deal with the purchase of land for the new works. There was no doubt where the capital came from. In fact I believe it was generally known, but no one questioned Hudson's judgement. He trampled over questions and shouted down any disagreement. If the money was at the right price, he said, he would use it where he would serve the company best.'

'But how has he covered the deficiency?' asked Love.

'My friend Love has a knack of coming right to the point,' said Prance with a dry smile. 'A marksman.'

'Has he borrowed it?' asked Love, his eyes never leaving Henry's face. His thin lips were pressed very tight together and were white, almost like bone, and drawn down at the corners. A caricature of disapproval.

'I believe so.'

'Then we've got him!' Love declared, slapping the table and

279

leaping to his feet. The smile reappeared and he looked exultant.

'He'll have had to borrow at a pretty rate of interest, so how's he to explain that?'

'Let's have a look at who holds shares in the Great North of England,' said Prance. He surveyed the pigeon-holes with a practised eye, and pulled out a pair of folding library steps. He was excited, Henry saw, pointing like a gun-dog. He located the correct papers quickly, and placed them on the table, untying the ribbon around the bundle. Love could hardly restrain himself from taking half the papers, but Prance put out a restraining hand.

'Here we are,' said Prance, almost immediately, extracting a closely printed list. 'There's a few men here I can ask about this. Good God!'

His sudden shout made them jump. It was out of character for the man, out of character for the room.

'Well?' demanded Love.

'Hudson owns shares in it!'

'Show me!'

Henry, too, was round beside Prance. In the list of subscribers, George Hudson was clearly listed with two thousand, eight hundred shares. Love whistled through his thin lips.

'He's buying his own shares!' said Henry, shocked despite all he had suspected. He had always been ready to assume that Hudson moved money according to his whims on a grand scale and with no regard to the shareholders, but the petty nature of this implication was breathtaking.

'And for how much, I wonder?' murmured Prance.

'He can't know about it, it's too petty,' Henry protested. 'Hudson must have shares in every company under the sun.'

Prance straightened up, his saturnine face severe. Henry felt rebuked.

'It's the petty little things that get 'em in the end, Mr Kelleway. This is our world. Huge edifices delude the public. They assume that the men who run them live in a rarefied atmosphere, a world of grand designs where they have no time for underhand deals. They assume that their only blunders, like a general's, will be strategic. But we know, don't we, Mr Kelleway, when we think about it, that generals can sell off the rations, divert the stores, select the best bit of booty for themselves.'

'Yes, I know you're right.'

'And I expect we shall find that the Railway King has made sure that his own shares have been bought first with whatever capital he has borrowed,' said Prance.

'A nice piece of knitting,' said Love with grim satisfaction. 'We shall tug out the loose end of it at the next shareholder's meeting and he will have to answer up. Mark my words, Mr Kelleway, we have studied him for a long time, and this is only one small part of it. Let the public get hold of the end of wool, and they will strip it off willy-nilly! Strip it all away, leaving Mr Hudson a very naked man. It will take more than the support of his friends to come back from this. Stephenson is ill, and won't leave Chesterfield, and all the Lords and Dukes in the world won't help him now. A whiff of this, and we won't see their backs for dust.'

Henry stared at the shareholders' list. His emotions were complicated. He felt he had not fully understood what he was letting himself in for. Within the cold constraints of court, a man was given the full benefits of defence, eloquently argued, controlled by the steel fist of law. Hudson would be thrown to the mob. These soberly dressed brokers would consign him there without a second thought. To them it was the natural trial. Much like Nero.

'You know what this will do to him? And everything he controls?' He knew he sounded shocked, he knew they were right in their way. Hudson, it seemed, had swindled the public and should be the last man to complain when they bayed after him. He had not envisaged this alien fate, this mortal combat that Prance and Love intended.

'We know, Mr Kelleway. It always surprises me to see a legal man's sensibilities upset, if you'll forgive me for saying so. He won't be stoned to death, you know, and he'll escape with his life. Life is cheap in the law courts, and for infinitely less than Mr Hudson has stolen, here and there in his grand larceny. Disgrace and ruin are not such very high prices to pay, and he will only be beaten with abuse. As for the lines he controls, if all this is proved, he will have to give them up and if they are good they will recover. I am not a cynical man, Mr Kelleway, but I do know that, in our business, the best weights used in the scales of justice are gold troy ounces.'

'What do you want from me in all this? As you understand, it's not really my field.'

'Nothing more,' said Love. 'We must get down to work now, in the finest detail. We shall sift away and see what else we can find. We invite you to attend the next shareholders' meeting.'

Henry was shown out politely, but Prance and Love were obviously eager to start that moment. They were excited, tense, had done with him.

Frederick was waiting for him outside in Cheapside. He had insisted on coming too because the signs of tiredness and strain were increasingly evident on Henry's face. Henry had that morning put in hand the arrangements for Caroline's funeral and Frederick had also gone with him to the undertaker, and stayed with him all day. The presence of John in the house drove Henry out early, and Jane's strange behaviour and failure to appear had clearly upset him.

He is looking old, thought Frederick, when Henry emerged into the lit street. A gas-lamp cast shadows from above, emphasizing the slackness of Henry's cheeks, the bagginess beneath his eyes. Frederick had never considered it before, he realised. The haughty look had crumpled as though distorted in a warped glass.

'Did it go all right?' he asked anxiously.

Henry was not disposed to answer readily, nor to move off. He seemed reflective, disposed to stare at his feet. Frederick waited, knowing Henry was trying to sum things up. He shared Henry's anxiety over Jane, not without censure, but with understanding. He also understood the misgivings Henry felt over his recent actions, sensing that he found them distasteful at the least. Henry had had to steel himself for this last visit.

'I feel as though I have just unleashed something barbaric,' said Henry. 'The laws of civilisation have not been adjusted to deal with the full venom of commerce. Hudson will be thrown to the wolves.'

'Isn't that what he deserves?'

'I don't know. I feel I have been pushed into it all. First Woolmer, then Prance and his friend Love I have just left.'

'You have not been pushed. It was inevitable. Hudson is the author of his own destruction.'

Frederick took Henry by the arm. Henry looked up at him quickly.

'You know, Frederick, I have just begun to realise the connection between my actions and their consequence. I'm a bit long in the tooth to see that for the first time. Until this business with Hudson, I suppose I have never really made my mind up about anything. I have always been at the whim of others.'

'That's an exaggeration.'

'No, it isn't. I have always allowed myself to be taken with the tides. I have deluded myself, and deluded others that somehow this made me a man of conscience and honour. These are the very words I have used to myself. But I served all masters. Not just in my work, in my heart too. That makes me a whore, and it makes me a coward.'

'You're being unfair on yourself! You have been under too much strain. Let's go and have a drink together.'

'No, Frederick, I don't want to dull my understanding. It is arrant selfishness not to make the connection between cause and effect. I strut about like a saint because I refuse to come to grips with the real red gore of things. Hudson should be brought down. That is a reality. He will bring untold misery and harm. All that is plain. But I want to leave it to others to do it, although it is my own will. I can't come to grips with it. I want to spectate. I throw the dogs into the bear-pit and then won't watch them fight. Worse than that, I shrug it off and say it's nothing to do with me, it's in the nature of dogs to fight bears. I haven't the courage to watch!'

'But coming here wasn't like that! You've pitched yourself in with the dogs!'

'But only now! So late. You must understand what I'm talking about? I'm not talking about just Hudson, my work. I have never really dealt with anything in my life!'

Frederick took his arm firmly, made Henry walk with him on to the pavement. Henry did not resist.

'I have to get back to chambers,' he said. 'Please come with me.'

'Of course I will. Do you want to walk?'

'Yes. I feel I can talk to you better when we walk. That's another evasion. I had to make myself look you in the face just now, yet you understand me better than anyone, I suppose. What a terrible thing that is to say! Do you hate me for the way I've treated your mother?'

Frederick did not pause in his slow pace. It was like steering a blind man.

'I suppose I have at times. But only at times.'

'I hate myself for it, but I won't do anything about it! I wait for it to correct itself, like some ship's captain who has stuck his command on a mud bar and waits for the next spring tide. We only have one spring tide in our lives, Frederick. I'm waiting for something that will never happen. I seem to have spent most of my life waiting.'

He paused, proceeding some distance in silence. People walked around them, looking at the two men curiously. They were so intent within themselves, concentrated so hard on the pavement that they might have been drunk, yet they seemed steady enough.

'You know all about my affairs with women, I suppose?' asked Henry.

'I don't know if I know all about them,' replied Frederick calmly. 'I suppose I know a good deal.'

'I convinced myself there, too. Convinced myself it was a kind of happiness when it has all really been a kind of unhappiness. We are very good at invention, we rationalists. It is all a limbo with no possible progress and no end. I despise myself at being shocked by Prance. Of course he's right. He deals with things however unpleasant the consequences and those have to be the right rules. I'm wrong. Do you know, Frederick, I love Jane, I always have. Forgive me if I shock you by my directness, but this last woman – never mind her name – she clearly wanted me to marry her. Everything was steered towards it. I didn't want that ...'

Frederick did not know what to say and prudently kept quiet. They had skirted the huge looming blackness of St Paul's, passing the bookshops in the Churchyard, and were walking down Ludgate Hill. The Churchyard had been quiet, reflective. Ludgate Hill was jammed with traffic. The din made it impossible for Henry to say more until they reached Fleet Street. Henry was walking mechanically, aware of where he was, yet unaware.

'It's all a terrible indulgence!' he shouted, above the noise of passing carriages and buses. 'I pretended I wasn't really hurting Jane, wasn't really hurting anyone. Don't you think that's what Hudson's been doing?'

'I suppose so!' shouted Frederick. 'Let's get off this street!'

He was afraid that the overbearing noise would interrupt this mood before it had run its course. His arm was shaking with the effort of steering Henry, but it seemed desperately important to maintain its contact. He willed Henry on with an intense anxiety, realising how much it hurt him that Henry had obviously not considered these matters properly at all. He had assumed that Henry had at least come to some arrangement with Jane, some agreement about the situation. He was shocked that this was obviously not so.

They turned into Salisbury Court, leaving the din behind them. Frederick felt he had to broach this subject. He wanted it to be clearly known between them.

'You've never discussed any of this with mother?'

Henry sounded startled.

'No. I certainly haven't.'

'I always thought you must have.'

'I couldn't. It would have hurt her deeply.'

'But she knows! It must hurt her just as deeply to know and yet have to pretend she doesn't! It's no secret, is it?'

'You're judging me very harshly, sir!'

Henry sounded angry now. He pulled away from Frederick's steering grip, and tried to walk ahead. Frederick stayed beside him.

'You said the other day before you went to see Hudson that you felt you were living under siege and that you must burst out. Well

284

you have now. Isn't this pretence between you and mother all part of the same siege?'

'Maybe you're right, sir, but I don't want to talk about it!'

'But if you love mother, then for God's sake tell her so and act! No matter what else goes on, that will give her some certainty.'

Henry stopped dead, looking furious at being spoken to in this way. They had reached the silence of Salisbury Square, and there were few people about.

'Why do you choose this time to attack me? It's because I have so many other worries.'

'It's because it's time!'

The anger faded from Henry's face.

'Yes, I suppose you're right. There is so much to attend to, Frederick. I need to be kept to it. My life's like a house that has been occupied all these years without being properly maintained. Suddenly, everything needs doing.'

'And this can't wait.'

'No, Frederick, it can't.'

They walked on again in silence and had reached the corner of Water Lane when they became aware of two men coming up behind them, overtaking them. Frederick glanced round immediately. It was sufficiently dark and deserted to arouse his immediate suspicions. He did not recognise the men, but was reassured that they were respectably dressed. He was shocked at Henry's reaction. Henry stopped dead, his face suddenly grim and white as though he had suffered a stroke.

'Good evening, Mr Kelleway,' said one, with a long face and rather pointed ears. The other man was enveloped in a halo of gingery whiskers picked out by a street lamp.

'What are you doing here, Perrin?' demanded Henry. His voice was very alarmed. 'Why are you with Hussey?'

'Oh, I think you can add up and arrive at the score,' said Perrin.

'Perrin?' demanded Frederick incredulously. 'Aren't you the man that my father ...'

'Had a quarrel with?' asked Perrin smoothly. 'Oh yes, I'm that man. We fought a duel in our hot youth, if you could call it any sort of duel, when we both missed.'

Henry's mind had been racing and he had indeed arrived at the score. If Hussey and Perrin were in this together, then Perrin knew about Henry's conversations with Woolmer and had related them. He wondered whether Perrin was motivated by money or hate. It astounded him that hate should survive all these years, but the manner of the man was triumphant and vindictive. He supposed it must be so. With these two together, he was on very dangerous ground. He was surprised by the deep anger he felt at Perrin's betrayal. He told himself to try to remain calm.

'Mr Perrin is in Mr Woolmer's employ,' said Henry. 'He manages his estate.'

'Used to, Mr Kelleway, used to!' Perrin grinned.

'I see. When did this end?'

Perrin turned to Hussey and smiled. Hussey too was smiling, without humour, playing cat-and-mouse.

'Who is this?' demanded Frederick, indicating Hussey. His voice was openly angry, and he stepped forward to see Hussey better.

'Oh, sparks flying!' said Perrin.

'This ... fellow ... is Mr Hussey,' said Henry. 'One of Hudson's men.'

'A director, Mr Kelleway,' said Hussey rudely. 'Proper titles!'

'So you see, young Mr Kelleway,' said Perrin, 'We have put two and two together in more ways than one, and we know of Mr Kelleway's plans to harm Mr Hudson. I was able to tell Mr Hussey of the arrangements that Mr Kelleway is proposing to make to embarrass Mr Hudson. Arrangements that he commenced when still in the employ of Mr Hudson.'

'I would never have believed it, Perrin,' said Henry. 'Do you hate me after all these years? I thought bygones were bygones. I am astounded!'

'Oh, what a shame, Mr Kelleway. You seem to have jumped to conclusions. I wouldn't say I hate you, because that would sound too strong and perhaps unbalanced. But, if you must have an answer, I dislike you quite as much as ever!'

Frederick grasped Henry's arm again.

'Come on,' he urged Henry. 'We have nothing to say to them.'

'I should listen,' said Hussey threateningly. 'I think it would be unwise not to.'

'How did you know we were here?' demanded Henry. It had been troubling him deeply, and he thought he already knew the answer.

'We have followed you from Mr Prance's offices.'

'How the devil did you know we were there?' Perrin's smile was broader than ever.

'Your wife told us, Mr Kelleway.'

'You've been to my home!'

'Oh, indeed. We were looking for you to point out that it might be better not to involve Mr Prance, but it seems that you already have done. It would be better if Mr Prance was told

286

to turn his attentions elsewhere.'

Henry was beside himself with rage. He knew Frederick was right, and that they should walk on, but he had to find out just what damage had been done, and what further damage they intended.

'You are threatening me. You understand what you are doing?'

'Oh, huff and puff, we're not threatening you,' said Perrin. 'We don't want any nasty words like that, I'm sure. We just thought you ought to know how grave the consequences might be.'

'And what might they be?'

Perrin looked to Hussey. Hussey took his cue.

'Well, firstly, as you are no longer in Mr Hudson's employ, he will make a call on your Eastern Counties shares, I'm sure, and you have only paid up one pound, ten shillings on twenty-five pound shares. That is just a commercial transaction, but it could go very hard, I'm sure.'

'What else?' demanded Henry grimly. 'Well, we are very concerned, Mr Kelleway, that a man in your position, who has, we hear, every chance of being offered a position on the Bench, should use information that he gained, shall we say, inside.'

'Now that's slander!' Henry declared. 'What else?'

'I hope it isn't slander,' said Hussey, 'but it does seem to Mr Hudson that if there is any dealing or trading that makes use of knowledge gained in the employ of the Midland or any other of his lines, then it should be considered as a most serious matter.'

'How dare you, Hussey!' Henry exploded. 'I deal only in public knowledge!'

'I'm only reporting Mr Hudson's feelings! You asked me, Kelleway.'

'What else?'

'Oh, you know what else, Kelleway, I won't mention it,' said Hussey vindictively.

'What the devil are you driving at?'

'I won't mention it here,' said Hussey significantly.

'What won't you mention here?'

'You know what I mean.'

Henry suddenly understood. He felt his heart thumping, his fists clench.

'What have you said to my wife?'

'Now, Kelleway, we don't need to get excited about that in the street.'

'What have you said to her!' Frederick held on to Henry by both arms now.

Perrin looked alarmed and had backed away slightly. Hussey

too was unsure of himself. They had not bargained for Henry's fury.

'You've told her about that day, haven't you, Hussey!' yelled Henry.

'We were just asking where you might be,' said Hussey, now defensive.

'Don't you lose your temper!' shouted Perrin injudiciously. 'There's nothing been said that can't be kept between us like civilised men.'

'By God!' bellowed Henry, wrenching himself from Frederick's restraining arms and hitting Perrin full in the mouth. Perrin staggered backwards and sat down hard, then fell over. He was unconscious.

Hussey took a menacing step forwards, fist raised in defence or offence, it was not clear. Henry was shaking his fist and grimacing at the unexpected pain. He glared down at Perrin as though cheated. Frederick seized Hussey's arm and wrenched it up behind the man's back so that he yelled out.

There was sudden silence.

'I am going to let you go,' said Frederick to Hussey as though giving instructions to a child, 'and, if you move a muscle to do anything, I'll stretch you out beside him!'

He released Hussey, who seemed unable to recover the arm from behind his back and stood in voluntary surrender. Frederick stooped over Perrin.

'He'll be round in a moment.'

Frederick pulled Perrin into a sitting position, standing behind him and holding him there against his legs. Perrin was snuffling, blood running from his nose and mouth.

'Well, that was a good one,' said Frederick to Henry. 'He won't be chewing apples for a bit.'

'Leave him,' said Henry grimly, 'I must get home to Jane. Leave him in the gutter where he belongs.'

'You have done a very foolish thing,' said Hussey venomously. 'Now it will all come out. There's no going back from here.' Hussey still kept his arm behind his back, as though this guaranteed his safety.

'Damn you, Hussey, do what you please!' hissed Henry. He was massaging his right hand with his left and looked ominously as though he was preparing for a repeat performance. 'There's nothing you can say or do that will harm me. Take a message to your master that we shall be having a very thorough examination of his affairs.'

'Come on,' said Frederick. 'Hussey can look after this carcase.'

The carcase opened its eyes and focussed on Henry.

'Damn you, Kelleway,' Perrin mumbled.

'And damn you, Perrin,' said Henry. Frederick led Henry away, leaving Perrin sitting upright.

'We must get home,' said Henry.

'Immediately,' agreed Frederick. They started back the way they had come towards Fleet Street where they could pick up a hansom cab.

'Do you blame me for that?' asked Henry, hurrying along. 'History repeating itself.'

'Not at all. I'm full of admiration. If you hadn't hit him, I'm sure I should have.'

'I'm supposed to be a lawyer.'

'You had just finished telling me you hadn't the courage to fight!'

Frederick put his arm around Henry and gave him a brief hug.

'Thank you, Frederick,' said Henry. 'For your help and for everything.'

They caught a cab almost immediately, and sat staring out of the windows as it fought its way through the traffic. Both men were lost in their own thoughts. Frederick knew he had said enough in any case. He could only detract from the situation. He would slip quietly away when they had got to Gower Street, choosing his moment. He wondered what Henry would do about the real financial threat of the Eastern Counties shares. He would not have enough money to meet them without borrowing. The financial problems seemed very secondary to the present situation in both their minds. Reduced to a proper significance.

They were met at the door by Weeks, before Henry could put his key in the lock. The elderly man looked dishevelled and his head swayed about more than usual. There was no formal greeting.

'You'd better come in, sir,' he said. His eyes were alarmed. 'Something has happened.'

'What do you mean?' demanded Henry, catching the mood immediately.

Weeks was spared the need to answer by the appearance of Maria, looking tired and worried.

'That's all right, Weeks. You go, I'll explain.'

'Explain what?' Henry and Frederick were both thoroughly alarmed now. Maria ushered them into the drawing-room, closing the door behind her.

'Why are you here?' asked Frederick.

'I had to come down from Highgate because I got a message from Weeks. Apparently Jane has disappeared. We don't know anything for certain, but it may be so.'

'She's disappeared?' repeated Henry, stunned into stupidity. 'What on earth do you mean?'

'I know you'll find this hard to believe, but she left the house telling Weeks she wasn't coming back.'

Henry and Frederick stared at her in confusion.

'It may be nothing,' said Maria lamely, 'but that's what she said.'

'Why?' asked Henry. It was a wail of anguish rather than a question.

'Perrin and Hussey,' said Frederick.

'Oh God!' Henry sat down suddenly, all strength gone.

It could not be more of a disaster at this time, thought Frederick. If every weird Fate had conspired with every other they could not have concocted a worse, more calculated piece of demonic puppetry. He found that he was standing outside the situation and was watching Henry, waiting to see his reaction. Henry had been under so much strain that this latest blow might tip him into an unreasoning hate for Jane, precisely for adding a new burden. For snatching away her own hand when his was extended. Maria was trying to explain again, repetitive from sheer anxiety, adding nothing more, nothing new. The facts were as scant as stardust.

'We *must* find her!' Henry said, hauling himself back on to his feet, and Frederick was reassured.

Jane stared down the black slope in front of her, trying to judge where the ground was. Everything was black as felt.

She knew it sloped because she had to step forward and downwards to feel the soft wet tussocks of grass. A long way downwards, further than taking a step, and then her foot was slipping away from her. It was steeper than she remembered it, and it would be easy to fall and tumble right down. It would be a hideous joke of fate, she thought, if I fell and broke a leg or ankle. Here I would lie stranded until the morning, an object of ridicule of vulgar curiousity. She imagined the trains going by, the staring faces, her helplessness.

The night was clear but only a sharp sickle of moon gave light. It was like peering into a bottomless pit and she felt herself swaying with vertigo. Panicking, she looked up at the stars to steady herself, but it made matters worse. She sat down just in time to prevent herself from pitching forwards. The grass was wet and immediately soaked through her clothes. I will be muddy when they find me, she thought. And much worse besides. Muddy and bloody. She put the thought out of her mind.

She felt calm again, now she was seated. It was nonsense to worry about her clothes. It was just possible to see the lines now that she looked properly. They were much nearer to her than she had expected, confirming the steepness of the embankment. She must have been staring at the opposite side.

There was no sheer drop, she knew, because she had often seen this particular spot when travelling north to Highgate. She had even seen the construction of it, the swarms of men and horses carving a great scar out of the brown mud. The scar had turned green, overtaken by sown grass and then weeds. It was only separated from the road by a brick wall, an easy thing to climb. Children stood upon it in the daytime, dancing along it and waving as the trains went by, hooting and shrieking.

She had changed quickly into dark clothes so that she could not be seen. Then she had taken a cab to beyond Camden Town, walking the remaining distance in terror of the dark road. That had been the worst part. The last street lamp had seemed like a friend and she had kept turning to look back at it long after it was passed. It had made her eyes more blind.

A train had passed down the track before she had reached the spot, and she had peered at it over the wall, marvelling. She had never seen an engine at night before, showering sparks and bathed in incandescent steam. The engineman and his mate seemed wreathed in corposant fire. She had suppressed the thoughts that sprung to mind. There was no time for allegories. She had summoned up the pain of despair that obliterated all other feelings.

Now she summoned up that pain again, using it as a spur to continue down into the unknown blackness. She got to her feet, with her right arm extended, right hand pressed into the grassy slope, and edged downwards at an oblique angle. Caroline would surely forgive her.

Caroline had judged wrongly, she supposed. Perhaps not. Perhaps Caroline had wanted to precipitate some plan that she had not been able to reveal. What she had revealed to Jane was her own desperate inability to make use of anything in a life that already seemed to have no purpose. Was she supposed to go away with the money? Leave Henry? What for? For miserable hermitage in some seaside town, for terminal solitude to review endlessly her failure? She had, years ago, imagined that it might be possible, but then she had envisaged a new life. She had even imagined that absence might eventually bring Henry back to her, that by giving him his total freedom he would burn himself out, spend his passion for other women and recognise in her the steady love she had felt and tried to show all these years. It was all vanity, a delusion that Henry had eyes to see. Given the wealth of Croesus, there was no way of recovering happiness. Caroline had shown her that, with her thoughtful, tender gift. Loving unto death.

She was weeping now, noiselessly, not sobbing. Why can't I even cry properly, she thought. I am left with this emotionless wetness. Even the relief of unrestrained grief has been denied me. I've forgotten how to cry, from stifling it in case I made Henry hate me. She was angry, tried to make herself sob, could not.

The humiliation of Perrin and Hussey's visit fed that anger. Perhaps she should be grateful to these loathsome sneering men. She had been drowning but still trying to swim. They had added another weight. There was such pleasure in Perrin's eyes as he declared that, if Henry was not at home, then they knew a little nest where they could find him.

They had watched her, avid for her dismay. Reptilian eyes, heads forward, poisonous. They had got no pleasure from it. She had looked at them haughtily, or so she hoped.

'Then go and find him and leave my house.'

'You know about the lady then?' asked Perrin, licking his lips as a snake darts out its tongue. Scenting. She should have been demolished by his audacity, but instead had felt nothing but contempt.

'I am immune to your poison, but it will destroy you. Your sickness is beyond treatment.'

She had left the room. Perrin and Hussey had hovered for some moments, disarmed at simply being left. Then they had gone, cheated, having to let themselves out. Jane had changed into her dark clothes and left less than half an hour after. Immune from their poison, not immune from her own despair.

Her feet touched loose stones, chippings, she realised. Ballast for the tracks. She took her hand from the bank and cautiously stood upright. She had reached the tracks. The rails were now quite visible and, looking to left and right, she was surprised to see lights which had previously been masked. Signals. She stepped over the first rail on to firm stone. The granite sleepers. She was directly in the path of any train.

Jane stood for some time, quite still but filled with a sense of excitement. It seemed a quiet and peaceful place. Owls hooted nearby, hunting. It was a strange idea to choose your place of death. Was there some ideal to be striven for? The ancients had cared about it. Hemlock, the opening of a vein, epicurean feasts of quails with aconite, sweet music. Was she satisfied with this dark and rather mundane spot? She decided she was. It suited her situation. She had never stopped to consider any other way. She knew that trains killed and killed quickly and it had seemed appropriate that the engines of so much turmoil should provide her with peace. She stooped and felt the rail with the palm of her hand, surprised that it was icy cold.

She realised she had no idea what to do.

Was she just to stand there? Stare it in the eye, as it were, until it hit her? Would the driver be able to see her? Would he be able to stop? Should she dart out? Would it really kill her? She was suddenly terrified of being maimed but left alive, by the side of the track with no one knowing. How did these people die who were hit by engines?

She heard a strange noise, a subterranean murmuring that had a twanging note. She could not locate its source as it seemed to be all around her, vibrating in the air yet associated with the ground. It rapidly became a heavy metallic rumble that she could feel as a tremble beneath her feet. She suddenly saw the train. It was thundering up the opposite track. She struggled blindly towards it, feet slipping and scrabbling in the loose chippings. It had never occurred to her that the first train might be on another track. She seemed to see herself in slow motion, legs of lead, arms flailing uselessly, as if trying to run in the sea. Her right shoe slipped sideways then caught, falling off. The sharp edges of crushed granite hurt her foot. She hobbled, hopped and fell on to the stone.

The train crashed past, out of reach. She hugged her head in her hands, feeling the whole world shake, the ground heave and judder as though the earth was suddenly old floorboards. Its hot breath enveloped her, a spark stung her hand, then it was gone.

She lay still, listening until the plangent noise of the rails had become a barely audible murmur, the sound heard when children hold a shell to their ears. The pumpings and corpuscular murmurings of the blood. She began to cry, sobbing at first and finding these real convulsions of her body, concentrated upon them, coaxed them and abandoned herself to heaving, wailing grief like a child's, but whether from the bitterness of failure or relief, she could not tell.

She became aware that she was shaking and that she was very cold. The cutting was a sink for dew that settled in her hair like fine drizzle. She sat upright, aware of her shoeless foot, of the discomfort of the sharp stones. Not thinking what she was doing, telling herself to be governed by that ruling part which had taken over, she got up, balancing on one foot while she felt around for her other shoe. Recovering it, she put it on and stood upright, triumphant that she had survived. She felt as though she were picking herself up from the field of battle, surprised and elated to be unhurt and profoundly grateful to be alive.

Jane looked at the rails with alarm. She stepped quickly over them, avoiding them as though very contact would kill. She scrambled up the bank some distance, sliding and slipping in her haste. She could hear the sound again, the murmuring rumble and whispering singing of the rails. She must be safe where she was, she thought, but there was still an uncertain terror that she had misjudged it, that another deadly shaft of steel ran beside her. She searched blindly up the bank with her hands. No, she must be safe.

A train approached on the down track, seeming to hurtle towards her, then veering past in a blaze of flame. She did not seem to hear the noise, but felt the warmth of the steam. It was dream-like, watching the train that should have killed her, her executioner. The train gave a scream from its whistle, perhaps cheated, and racketed onwards with a string of dark wagons, a juggernaut hungry for sacrifice.

The following silence seemed absolute. Jane considered the condition of her clothes, her appearance. She had enough money to get home, but how could she avoid the ridicule of discovery? She pushed the thought away as unworthy. She didn't care. She didn't care about Perrin and Hussey. Why had she allowed it to concern her? They told her nothing she didn't know, so why had she put any value on it? The ridiculousness of her present situation seemed worse than that. The fear of death was fresh and alive to her, a taste in her mouth, a smell in her nose. She damned her feebleness and her weakness. Why should she submit? She had been pushed very close, but had not submitted.

At the top of the embankment the night air smelled sharp and alive. The owls still hunted, oblivious of her unimportant problems. She was able to smile at her ridiculousness as she clambered over the wall, dragging her skirts behind her. The wall was an old friend. It marked the way back. She would be walking towards the light, towards the streets now. Despair had been left where it belonged in the blackness below, listening to the singing rails.

She obtained a cab from a rank, keeping herself withdrawn into shadows so that the driver could not see her mud-stained clothes and dirty hands. The driver opened the door, leaning down from above, casual and lazy. Jane knew he would not have been so inattentive had she looked more elegant, and was pleased. The man seemed surprised when she told him to go to Gower Street, giving her a curious glance, but she was already inside and safely hidden away. During the journey she rubbed at her clothes with a handkerchief, wiped her hands and shoes. She might be able to slip in unnoticed when she got home. She enjoyed the ride, feeling an extraordinary sense of security in the dirty construction of wood, leather and glass. Relief brought exhildration.

Getting out in Gower Street, she was quick enough to avoid the driver, who was still struggling to get down from his perch.

'Wait there, I will send someone out to pay you.'

She had brought no money with her to pay for a return journey.

Her ring on the bell acted like an alarm in a citadel. Instead of Weeks, the door was thrown open by Frederick, ahead of Henry and Maria by only a moment. They stared at her, frozen with shock at her appearance.

'Let me in,' she said, feeling no shame or embarrassment. She saw Henry was yellow as parchment, his eyes wide. It gave her a wild hope. They started talking at once, touching her as though to reassure themselves of her reality, patting her.

'There's a cab outside. Will someone pay it?'

It surprised her to hear how calm she was. Frederick went out to attend to it.

'But where have you been?' Henry was asking. 'We've been trying everywhere we could think of. You're wet and muddy. What's happened?'

'She must change,' said Maria, ever practical, sensing that this was not the place to ask for explanations. 'You are well and safe, aren't you?'

'Yes, I'm well and safe,' said Jane. It seemed ridiculous that these people all needed her reassurances. It made her laugh, tears starting to run down her face.

Henry might have stood staring if Maria had not pushed him gently, unseen by Jane. Henry put his arms around her, feeling her wet hair, holding her tightly, patting her back. Jane cried.

'Come,' said Maria, 'we must put her to bed.' She steered them both to the stairs, plucking at Henry's arm. Henry turned, giving her a puzzled look.

Maria put a finger to her lips. Henry nodded. His face was full of concern. Elizabeth appeared, coming down the stairs. She kissed her mother on the forehead. Maria repeated the same gesture for silence. Jane was escorted upstairs.

As though we are carrying our wounded, thought Frederick.

Twelve

Caroline's funeral seemed to Henry to be very much a repeat of
their father's. He had chosen the same graveyard of St James's
Chapel off the Hampstead Road, not because he felt it essential
that they should be buried near each other, but for the same
practical reason. The city cemeteries were high mounds of scarcely mulched putrescence. Each excavation revealed the rotted
remains of some other corpse. The grave diggers were uncaring of
the bones and skulls they heaped around them to refill new voids.
Coffins were broken up and burned because they took up too much
room.

At St James's Chapel, Caroline would be assured of her own
neat cut in new clay, decently clean.

They waited in Highgate for the family to assemble, and in turn
were watched by a crowd of children and of the curious. The
children hung around the carriages and dared one another to go up
and touch the black lacquer of the hearse, sniggering but awed at
their own disrespect. It was even the same hearse with cut-glass
windows draped with deep plum velvet. Four black horses with
plumes nodded and champed in their traces, accustomed to
waiting, chosen for their patience.

The private carriages had been drawn up for some time now, and
it was getting late. The weather was fine and the sun warm. An
inappropriate day for their cold business, Edward thought. He was
staring out of the drawing-room window, waiting and watching.
They had all arrived except John, Louise, Charlie and Nell, and
no one knew what that family was doing.

John had declined to come with Jane and Henry and the
children, saying he would prefer to come alone.

Louise had said she would come separately with Charlie and
Nell. She had sent a note to Edward and to Henry that was the
barest confirmation.

'Where on earth are they?' asked Frederick impatiently. It had
become his litany as their time of departure had come, then gone.
They were now ten minutes late. He had visions of a gallop for the
graveyard.

'Shall we allow them a few more minutes?' asked Henry.

Edward nodded. He wanted Nell to be there. He was furious
with John after he had taken so much trouble with him, but saw

296

no point in voicing it. The room was crowded, everyone was fidgeting, tense with their own thoughts. The funeral clothes smelled of mothballs. The smell pervaded the room, mixed with sherry. A clock ticked to remind them further of mortality and the passage of time.

'Well, at least it isn't raining,' said William, and wished he hadn't as Jonathan and Maria shot him a furious look. He sipped at his sherry glass, but it was already empty so he put it down on a mahogany table. Maria tutted, and stood it on the mantelpiece, wiping at the table with her black gloves. Everyone watched. It was a distraction.

Below, the undertaker's men exchanged glances. They had another funeral that afternoon and hoped there was going to be no difficulty.

'Should have brought the cards,' said one. They eyed the coffin as a suitable table. The door was locked.

'I have,' said another. They sat closer to their burden. The cards were shuffled on the polished mahogany.

Henry stood beside Jane, her arm through his. It had been agreed that William, Jonathan and Margaret would take one coach, allowing Maria to go with Edward. It might have been more proper for Henry to have gone with him, but Maria would be more comfort, and Henry did not want to be separated from Jane. There was a tenderness between them that could be felt. Every motion of Henry was of solicitous care. A wrapping around of her black fur collar.

'How far behind you was John?' asked Edward testily. 'He can't have got lost.'

'I'm so sorry, Edward,' said Jane. 'John was determined that he should come in his own carriage. After all we are four, and I don't know what he was thinking. I can only imagine he had some idea about Louise, but he wouldn't say.'

'He was dressed and ready,' said Henry. 'We couldn't wait much longer, especially as he seemed determined that we should leave before him. You know John, it isn't always very easy to know exactly what his reasons are.'

'But after coming all this way!' protested Edward. He felt uneasy about it. He loathed the idea of a confrontation between Louise and John and knew that was possible. He prayed for good sense to prevail.

'We shall have to go ahead and let them catch up,' said Jonathan. His attitude to John was not sympathetic. 'Don't you think so, uncle Henry?'

Like the others, except Maria, he was curious about Henry and Jane. There was something between them that he had never seen

297

before. He decided they were behaving like lovers, which was certainly odd.

None of them had been told of the events two nights before.

'Yes, I suppose we must,' Henry replied, looking again at his watch.

'We are nearly a quarter of an hour late now. What do you think, Edward?'

Edward nodded. There was a gathering up of gloves and hats. The women put down their veils. Edward went downstairs to alert the undertaker's men, who opened the door to him as solemn as six butlers.

'We're ready, gentlemen.'

The journey was taken at a pace to make up time. It was perceptibly a little too fast.

'Do you think John means not to come?' Jane asked Henry. 'I'm worried.'

'Yes, so am I, but I didn't want to say so. If he's late, he may come directly to St James's.'

'But if Louise isn't coming either ...? Does it mean he's gone to her?'

'I don't know.'

They stared out of the windows. Pedestrians, horsemen, coachmen, all raised their hats as they passed or were passed. It was warm and they were overdressed in the heavy black. Jane sat with her hand in Henry's, content with his gentleness and his conversation. They had established a foundation on which to build. Like Henry, she wanted that building to be slow and the stronger for it. She knew that Elizabeth watched them covertly, but it was natural that she should. It might seem odd to a young girl to see her parents as lovers but it must enlarge her comprehension. She had seen little enough of it until now. Frederick was taking it all very much in his stride, enjoying it, but she supposed that was the difference between a man with all his freedom, and a woman. She wondered briefly what Frederick knew about women, but hurriedly dismissed the thought as inappropriate to the occasion. She would think about it later, she promised herself.

She should be giving her thoughts to Caroline who travelled before them all in isolation, as she had done in life, Caroline whose generosity had contributed towards her own crisis, but somehow the present pressed in upon her in an unashamed way. She felt Caroline would have approved, and looked down at Henry's hand in hers. Frederick caught her eye, saw what she looked at, and smiled. Jane felt herself blush.

William for his part was trying to entertain Margaret and Jonathan, and they were wishing he would not.

'I'm not depressed by funerals, papa,' said Margaret.

'I get depressed talking about them,' said Jonathan sourly.

'I wasn't talking about them!' William protested. 'Not in the real sense, but as a piece of ceremonial. In other religions white is the colour of mourning. I just wondered if they saw white as a gloomy colour as a result. After all, white is the colour of light and day. It ought not to be gloomy, don't you think?'

'Frankly, I don't care,' said Jonathan. 'I was just thinking that Charlotte should be here with us and that we haven't heard from her for weeks, and have no idea what she is doing. She obviously isn't coming.'

'I didn't expect her to. I wrote as a courtesy. These things have to be given time, as your mother always says.'

Jonathan snorted.

'Give Hays to eternity, and it won't change my opinion of him!'

'But you will have to, for everyone's sake,' said William tartly.

'It's hardly a harmonious composition, to use your terms, is it?' demanded Jonathan rudely. 'Unless you have a penchant for all things allegorical. A kind of beauty and the beast.'

'You shouldn't hate him so,' volunteered Margaret. She was so seldom critical that it took Jonathan aback.

'Why not?'

'Because hate is self-consuming.'

'That's sampler philosophy!'

'Don't be rude to your sister,' said William sternly. 'Are we going to bicker all the way to the churchyard?'

'Everyone has the right to be afraid,' said Margaret. 'Particularly friends.'

'And to lie?' demanded Jonathan. Margaret said nothing.

'I shall invite them to the opening of my Cosmorama,' said William. 'It would be a start. An occasion, if you give us the chance, Jonathan, to try to make amends.'

'I didn't know it was finished,' said Jonathan obliquely.

'Oh yes,' said William. 'Quite finished. Mr Ellis says it is the finest thing he has ever seen. There is to be a grand opening with fireworks and all the usual sort of thing. I can't tell you how glad I am to be finished. It has been one of the labours of Hercules.'

'What will you do next?' asked Margaret. 'It has taken such a space out of your life.'

'Next?' William stared out of the window for a moment, watching two dogs that ran for some time beside the carriage before they decided there was no fun to be had, and fought with each other instead.

'Next, I shall return to portraiture. These giant things are all very well and they please lots of people, but I can't convince myself about them. I feel ready for a real challenge. Portraiture, or perhaps landscapes with figures. You wait and see.'

'If Louise comes, you won't be cross with her, will you?' asked Jane, breaking the silence in their carriage. 'She might turn up at the churchyard, just as John might.'

'Why should I be?'

Jane was hesitant because of Elizabeth. She judged rightly that Frederick must know all about it anyway.

'Because she has been a nuisance in your chambers.'

'You mean Meadows,' said Henry bluntly. 'I hope no one is going to mention anything like that in front of John if he does turn up.'

'But are you angry with her? Not for John's sake, but for your own?'

Henry's mind filled with unwanted images. He remembered his meeting in his own chambers with Kate, the unbuttoned dress, his hand on her breast, the soft feel of her in his fingers. She had beautiful breasts, more firm, better formed than Jane's. He had kissed them. He remembered it, but it was no longer erotic, only curiously remote. Forsworn. At least, he believed so and wanted it to be so. The price was too much to pay. Kate won't wait. No more than a memory, a haunting like the remembrance of good summers that palled at the time with their own kind of sameness.

'Well, Henry?'

He could not be that much of a hypocrite. Jane knew he couldn't. They had their own love to build on, he had her breasts to hold, he had a kind of peace.

'I'm not angry, but I don't think that this thing with Meadows will last. Poor Meadows.'

'Poor Louise. That's not so shocking, Henry. Think of it. Poor Louise, and poor John, too.'

The hearse pulled into the churchyard, the horses familiar with the way, nod-nodding as they hauled up the slope. The following carriages stopped once they were discreetly within the massive iron gates to allow the mourners to get down and continue on foot. The appointed place was marked with a mound of new brown earth, a fresh cutting beyond the ranks of white marble and gilt-lettered granite.

Louise stood with Charlie and Nell, to the left of the mound and some distance away. She did not move, although Charlie and Nell immediately walked forward through the lush graveyard turf.

Edward intercepted Nell, and Charlie made for Frederick.

'You go to her,' Jane said to Henry. 'Make her welcome. There's no sign of John.'

Henry nodded, and walked over to her. Louise was properly dressed in mourning, but even the veil could not hide her anxiety. She looked beautiful and Henry could not prevent himself from thinking that she knew it very well. He noted her figure, almost by habit, and was angry with himself. Old habits die hard, they say, or perhaps never die at all.

'It was good of you to come, Louise.'

'Thank you, Henry. Is John with you?'

'No. We don't know where he is. He was supposed to follow us to Highgate but never arrived. We imagined he might have gone to collect you.'

'I was afraid he might, but he didn't.'

'You can come and stand with us.'

Louise looked surprised.

'Are you sure? I am perfectly prepared to stay here. I only brought Charlie and Nell.'

'Louise!'

She lifted her veil with both hands in order to study his face better.

'I thought you would be angry with me.'

'I don't think I have that right, do you?'

'I don't know if I can answer that question.'

'Then don't try. Just join us.'

They walked back to the others, Louise inclining her head uncertainly. Henry noted that Nell had hooked her arm lightly in Edward's and that Edward smiled at her. It struck him with a shock that they seemed like lovers. He glanced quickly at Louise to see if she had noticed. She met his eyes and gave him a cool, quick smile.

'Do you mind?' she asked.

'I don't know,' said Henry.

Jane shook Louise's hand.

'I've asked Louise to join us,' said Henry.

'Of course,' said Jane. 'We had all better go in now.'

The service was brief. Henry was struck by the inadequacy of it as a punctuation, the ending of a whole volume; but then no matter how long the work it ends with no more than a full stop. Caroline's life had not been so full, when he thought about it, any more than his own. It was an appropriate reflection as the heavy clay hit the coffin lid.

It appeared that none of the family felt deep grief. Loss and sorrow were more appropriate than any rending of raiment. They moved away, leaving Edward to pay his last respects, with Nell still by his side.

'They were always fond of each other,' Jane said to Henry. 'Poor Edward has really lost both parents now.'

'We shouldn't have advertised for Ware,' said Henry.

'Yes, we had to.' Jane was firm. 'It's better to resolve things. Isn't it?'

She looked at Henry, requiring an answer. Henry nodded, acknowledging the reproach.

'Yes, it is.'

'Excuse me, sir,' said a man who stood beside the carriages at the graveyard gate, 'are you Mr Henry Kelleway?'

'Yes.'

'I have brought a letter for you from Mr John Kelleway. I arrived during the service but thought I ought ...'

'Yes. Quite right.'

Henry took the letter, glanced at the front of the envelope which bore his name in John's hand, and opened it, turning some little distance from the messenger with Jane and Louise taking an arm each.

'Shall I read it out?' asked Henry, looking at Louise.

'Yes.'

'"Dear Henry, I could not, after all, bring myself to come to Caroline's funeral. I intended to, and I write this still dressed in mourning, from Gower Street. I don't think I can face you all, and I feel that I have already paid my respects to Caroline and can't add anything by attending. If Louise attends, please be kind to her. I will write to her separately and she will get the letter at her house. I have no right to interfere in her life, nor in yours or anyone's. Jane has been kind to me and I thank her for looking after this difficult individual well and with love.

'"I must now tell you that I have managed to buy a Commission, and when I have finished this letter I shall change clothes and leave the house with my baggage. I shall be going to barracks before taking ship, and I shall not tell you where in case you are tempted to try and find me. Please don't. I want to slip away quietly.

'"Will you look after my affairs in Kent? I leave the house and everything there to Louise to do with as she thinks fit. Please take this as a letter of instruction. I'm sorry it cannot be more formal, and I hope it is enough to act on in the eyes of the law. I make one condition, and that is that if the property is sold, one half of the money shall be given to Nell. Charlie seems to be able to look after himself, and I think it will encourage him not to have money to spend immediately. Of course I shall also be writing to them.

302

"'Well, Henry, I seem to have very little to say, when all's said and done. I don't seem to be one of life's great assets, do I? By removing myself in this way I feel I will spread a benign influence, which is enough of a commentary in itself. I look forward to army life. It was a mistake for me to ever leave it in the first place. Be assured I will be content.

John.'"

Henry handed the letter to Louise, who took it mechanically, but made no move to read it again.

'Louise, I'm so sorry,' said Jane, 'What shall we do?'

'Will you all blame me for this?' asked Louise, quite calmly.

'No!' protested Jane. 'It is nothing to do with you.'

'But do you blame me for that?'

'No. It's John's own decision. He's leaving all of us, Louise, not only you.' Jane looked anxiously at Henry for his confirmation.

'I think it is probably for the best, Louise,' said Henry. 'That sounds very hard, but what John says is right. Do you want to come back with us to Gower Street and bring Charlie and Nell? How will you tell them?'

'I don't think I want to go there so soon. You understand? But thank you, Henry. May I have this letter?' Henry nodded. 'I shall tell the children on the way home.'

The family were getting into their carriages, glancing curiously at the group of three and at the waiting messenger.

'All the rest of us are going back to Gower Street,' said Jane. 'They are sure to ask about the messenger and about John.'

'That's another reason I can't come,' said Louise. 'But please tell them. I must go now.' Louise was composed, seemed peaceful. It struck Henry that it was as if there had been two deaths in the family and that they had just buried John as well. Louise was mourning quietly, as though she had lost John after a long and painful illness from which death was a blessed release.

'You have both been very kind to me,' said Louise as she turned to go. 'Don't be disappointed in me, Henry. I am what I am. Don't hate me if I can't change.'

She walked away to her carriage. Charlie saw and followed, sensitive to the fact there had been some development. It was Edward who escorted Nell, and helped her in. Henry and Jane watched, allowing the others to come to terms with their own farewells. There was no coldness towards Louise.

The messenger gave a reminding cough and shifted from foot to foot.

'Yes?' asked Henry.

'Mr John Kelleway said I would be paid on delivery.'

'Of course,' said Henry, giving the man half a guinea, which was far too much.

'I suppose he hasn't even enough money to pay,' he said to Jane.

'You haven't enough money to give away half guineas.'

Henry looked at her sharply, a hint of anger in his eyes.

'That's only a temporary problem. I shan't be hunted by Hudson.'

'But I have enough money now to pay off Hudson. Have you thought of that? Caroline has made me a wealthy woman.'

'That's your money. I have never thought of it. I shall raise it by borrowing.'

Jane put her arm through his, and would not let him pull away.

'No, you will not. If you will take it, I will see it as a pledge, Henry, and how can you refuse it? It's a burden to me. Can't you see it's something I can contribute?'

'Come on, we must be going back ...'

'Henry, don't brush it aside!'

'I'm sorry,' said Henry. He was confused by his feelings. He knew he was hesitating at this final link because it was a complete commitment, a binding signature, and he despised himself for the hesitation. He had thought of it despite his denial. The completion of a new contract.

'I should have to pay it back to you as soon as possible.'

He had managed to sign. It was done. Jane held his arm tightly as they walked to the carriage. It had been a strange burying.

Thirteen

Late summer had given way to autumn, had given way to winter, had given way to wet February, but the seasons had failed to make their mark.

Although the weather had been featureless, the events of the period were green in the minds of everyone assembled in York for the shareholders' meeting.

Stephenson's death at Tapton in August had robbed Hudson of one of his props of credulity – a prop who had latterly withdrawn support, but refused to the last to condemn. Stephenson had retired, 'to vegetate among my vegetables,' as he said, but had contracted a recurrence of the pleurisy that had laid him low in Spain four years before. After what the doctors described as an intermittent fever, he had died from 'an effusion of blood from the lungs', which the sopping weather had made it impossible to fight. His funeral had been almost a state occasion and was taken to mark the end of an age of pioneering invention, and perhaps the end of an age of innocence.

The De Grey Rooms in York were noisy as a cattle market and rank with tobacco smoke. An air of expectation and hostility marked the meeting as something other than the usual occasion for bland platitudes and customary congratulations. Little knots of men talked amongst themselves, glaring fiercely at other groups, wondering where their loyalties lay. Newspaper reporters from the *Yorkshireman* smiled like sphinxes at the men from the *Yorkshire Gazette*. In the eyes of the *Gazette*, Hudson could do no wrong. The men from the *Yorkshireman* knew different, and licked their lips and waited. Prance had taken them into his confidence, and they had been told what to expect. They had occupied prime positions at the front, notebooks ready, accustomed to being treated as pariahs and this time enjoying it.

Prance, Love and Henry sat in the middle ground where the smoke was thickest and the shot and shell were likely to be worst. All around them, strong Yorkshire voices struggled for verbal supremacy, shouting greetings, discussing the obvious business in hand but keeping to themselves their excitement. Some had vowed to speak up and be heard. Others would watch the fun.

'By heavens, they have powerful lungs,' said Henry unnecessarily. He was to be a listener. They had agreed their tactics in advance, and as Henry had no interest in the York, Newcastle and Berwick, it would have been too easy to shout him down. Prance's standing as a considerable proprietor in the company could not be questioned. Love would press the point.

'I hope they use their lungs if we are pushed to it,' said Prance.

'Wylie and Brancker were fairly shouted down at Derby!'

Hudson had won that battle, the opening skirmish of his war for survival. Aided by his old ally, Ellis, they had rolled Brancker aside. Ellis had relied upon insinuations that Brancker was the author of anonymous letters which criticised both Hudson and himself, even producing one which imputed that mineral lines were being concocted to assist mine owners; and, as only Hudson and Ellis were mine owners, Ellis hammered away, the indications were clear. These letters sought to destroy the chairman and himself and so the company. He defied Brancker to prove it.

In vain, Brancker had protested that he was not the man to prove it as he had not written the letters. He was accused of mischief by Ellis, and Hudson had leapt upon the fact that Brancker insisted in all his questions that he had mentioned no names when asking for an inquiry into the Midland Railway.

'I only wish you had,' Hudson had stormed, 'we then should have had some tangible means of getting hold of you!'

The storm of emotion had blown in favour of Hudson and the inquiry had been rejected by a large majority. No one in Hudson's camp saw it as a victory, however. It was the opening salvo of civil war and they knew very well where to expect the next attack.

Hudson sat on the raised platform reserved for the directors and other company officers. He gave an appearance of monumental calm, occasionally exchanging a word here and there, or looking through his report. His eyes flickered without emotion over the reporters, seeking and finding those he knew to be rebels.

He had primed his own supporters, of course. It had proved less easy than usual, because he could not say much except that those elements which sought his ruin would no doubt try the same tactics here as they had at Derby and he looked to their good sense to deal with such nonsense and give it no room.

'We will hear from this Prance, I have no doubt,' he told his friends. 'A stock broker from London, no less. It may cross the enquiring mind to wonder what he knows or cares about railways. They never built an inch of track, never spanned a river or dug a cut, but they are very good at dismantling the business of those that do. I won't call them leeches, because the leech does good, nor vultures, because vultures leave things clean picked. They are intestinal worms that grow and grow and destroy a robust constitution. That man Kelleway has joined them with all his vast stock of learning about the law which he put to so little use for us, and no doubt has become an expert overnight in all those things he could not do.'

'I have everything down,' Prance was now reassuring Love. He waggled a closely written piece of paper. 'I even took the precaution of having it copied so that the *Yorkshireman* will have it verbatim.'

'I must say I feel nervous,' said Love.

Henry felt nervous as well. It was the atmosphere of the arena, the inevitability of combat. He was impressed by Prance. As a barrister accustomed to addressing the public, jury or bench, he knew the tension that builds up in the stomach. Prance seemed very calm. Henry hoped he could really deal with the verbal battering that he could expect if he did not win immediate sympathy and attention from the majority.

The company secretary Close rose to his feet at a glance from Hudson, and held up a hand, waiting for the din to subside. The noise fell away so rapidly that he was surprised. It was an omen of things to come. He ploughed on with the company report.

Henry scarcely listened, and it seemed to him that perhaps half those present were listening no more than he was. It was a place of darting glances and averted eyes, but everyone watched Hudson.

Close gave a report on the total receipts on account of revenue for the half-year ended, on the raising of a loan at very reasonable rates, on proposals for branch lines and negotiations to get in to Newcastle. Henry heard the stream of facts and figures as though they were a distant waterfall. Occasionally there were cheers and applause, as some good news or fat prospect was announced. There was no doubt that the line itself was doing well enough. Would they be able to unseat its master? Nine hundred and twenty-two thousand, four hundred and ninety-one third class passengers, said Close, two thousand and sixteen horses, six hundred and thirty-six carriages, three thousand and eighty dogs, one hundred and sixty-four thousand, six hundred and ninety-six tons of goods, fourteen thousand, nine hundred and nine tons of lime. The list seemed endless. Fifty-three thousand, eight hundred and sixty-seven sheep. All the time Henry watched Hudson's face. The man was composed and, apart from being unusually unsmiling, gave no outward indication of concern. Close stopped and sat down. Hudson rose and started to speak.

It was a model speech of its sort, full of platitudes with a few well-considered pieces of bait dropped in here and there. He described the need for negotiations to continue to gain access to

Newcastle, he explained with every sign of compassion and pride that the York, Newcastle and Berwick was going through an impoverished area due to the failure of the banks which prevented the inhabitants from being able to travel. The proposed line would benefit both Yorkshire and Lancashire, be a boon. He spoke with justifiable pride of the temporary bridges now thrown over the Tyne and Tweed and pushing ever further north.

'You know, Kelleway,' whispered Prance, '*I* feel proud of our line when he speaks!'

'It is a good line, no question of that,' said Henry sternly, fearing that Prance was wavering. 'It's the man we're after.'

Prance smiled at him, and gave him a nod. Henry was surprised at what he had just said, and Prance was enjoying it.

'I would conclude,' said Hudson weightily, 'by assuring the shareholders that nothing will be wanting on the part of the directors to secure the best interests of this company.'

He sat down to warm enough applause that was artificially sustained by a group at the back. Henry took Prance's hand, and shook it briefly. Prance rose to his feet, and the applause died as though throttled. Hudson put both hands on the table in front of him. His round, balding head and broad fleshy face were the focus of attention, the moon to all the faint stars around him. He looked full at Prance, as though challenging him to speak.

'The chair recognises Mr Prance,' said Close in a voice that sounded as if he had swallowed his tongue. The hush was painful.

'I wish to call the attention of the meeting to a subject which is of vital importance to the interests of this company,' Prance opened gently. 'The directors have very properly put into the hands of the shareholders some days ago a statement of accounts. In those accounts there was a charge of seven hundred and forty-seven thousand, seven hundred and eighty-five pounds invested in the shares of the Great North of England Company. The one hundred pound shares were stated to have been purchased at an average two hundred and thirty-four pounds, fourteen shillings and one farthing, the forty pound shares at ninety-four pounds, six shillings and six pence farthing, the thirty pound at seventy pounds, eight shillings and three pence and the fifteen pound shares at an average of thirty-four pounds, nineteen shillings and nine pence.'

'Hear, hear,' murmured a section of the crowd, who clearly did not understand where this was leading. The effect on Hudson was very different. His head came up smartly, and his voice was hard and tense.

'There is an error in the last item. There is an omission of two thousand, eight hundred pounds which has been paid on those shares.'

Prance held up his bundle of papers.

'I have in my hand an extract from the official list of the London Stock Exchange which contains every transaction from October 1846 to December 1848, from which it appears that the fifteen pound shares were being sold at an average of sixteen pounds, fifteen shillings. I would be inclined to say this was satisfactory, but there was something about these fifteen pound shares, something so extraordinary as to induce me to ask for further explanation.'

Prance was overtaken by loud applause from the centre of the hall. They were enjoying it, and Prance was clearly getting into his stride. His delivery was precise and not histrionic and he had won them over. Hudson's face expressed polite impatience. He twiddled his thumbs openly to display his impatience and lack of concern. His fellow directors took it less stoically and whispered among themselves.

'What was the condition of this fifteen pound share?' asked Prance. 'They were created with a small deposit of thirty shillings. Unlike the larger shares they were not to receive ten per cent dividend but only five on the instalments which were to be complete by June 1849, when they were to receive ten per cent, and when they were paid off the company had a claim to be paid off at the rate of twenty-two pounds, ten shilling premium. Add interest over the years and that will make twenty-five pounds, thirteen shillings and nine pence. The details are important, for who in his senses would raise money at six per cent to invest it at one and a half per cent? These fifteen pound shares have been bought for a great deal more than they are worth as they have never stood higher than twenty-one pounds. This seems to me irreconcilable. I disclaim all animosity or hostility towards the directors in bringing this matter forward, which I have done from no other motive than a sense of duty.'

There was loud applause now, that Prance allowed to die away.

'I am sure,' he continued gentle as a dove, 'that no more than the odd hundreds of these shares have been sold to the public so that *someone* has received great benefit by selling them at this extravagant price to the company.'

Prance sat down to a tremendous din. Some applauded feverishly, some shouted inaudible questions at Hudson. A minority protested, or openly booed Prance. Prance folded his arms, glanced at Henry and Love, made a relieved face and waited. The mob would do it for him after all. Hudson got to his feet like

Leviathan breaching. He was furious now and made no attempt to disguise it. His jowls shook as he shouted out a reply, too loud.

'I have not the books here and therefore I cannot inform Mr Prance who is the seller, as the company has bought a great many lots from different parties, but if there is any mistake, the books of the company are open to all shareholders who can examine them as minutely and as fully as they think proper!' He put both hands on the table, leaning forward, becoming more calm.

'I will tell you candidly that I had two thousand, eight hundred of these fifteen pound shares. That is all I had of them. If I have disposed of them to the company at a larger price than I ought to have done, then I am disposed to do whatever the shareholders think just and fair. I believe I got the estimates from Mr Plews for these shares, and that is all I can say about it.'

There was a catching of breath in the hall, at the admission and the audacity of the plea of ignorance. A shareholder from the rear called out.

'Mr Prance ought to be content with the assurance of the chairman, who has been candid!'

This provoked a relieved ripple of laughter. Prance rose to his feet again, not smiling. Henry knew he was largely acting this grimness, but was himself impressed. If stock brokers were barristers, he thought, we might all be out of a job.

'I am still of the opinion,' said Prance loudly and firmly, 'that my question is not answered. The question is not one of money, but of reputation!'

It was an astonishing cut of the sword. Hudson's face was furious and he glared at Prance as if no one else existed. They were stalking each other now, and everyone else was a spectator, of no consequence to the outcome. It appalled Henry as he had known it would, yet he found it exhilarating. A blood sport with all the uncaring exuberance of the chase, no concern for the quarry.

'I bought and sold the shares as I thought at a fair price,' stormed Hudson, his eyes never leaving Prance's face, 'but if Mr Prance thinks me entitled to a vote of censure, let him put it to the meeting and carry it if he can!'

'I move the appointment of a committee of five shareholders to examine into the matters and to report to an adjourned meeting,' replied Prance, staring back at Hudson. There was thunderous applause from big red hands that were tiring from being beaten together, enjoying it. A man was shouting from the rear and could not make himself heard. Eventually the meeting shushed itself to silence.

'I think we ought to know what interest Mr Prance has in the undertaking so as to be able to judge the motive which induced him to bring this question,' said a voice in ripest Yorkshire. 'I think this is all like a stock exchange job!'

Prance smiled, and nodded briefly in the direction of the voice.

'I am a large proprietor in the company.'

There was a bleating of 'hear hears'. Prance stooped momentarily to Henry.

'It is all coming out precisely like the script. We must not have a vote of censure!'

'I don't know what the honourable proprietor requires,' continued Hudson with deadly irony. 'I have told him I have sold my shares and the question is whether I have done right by selling them.'

'No, no,' shouted the supporters of Prance. The Yorkists applauded.

'Several hundreds have been sold at that premium and the inference on the Stock Exchange is that an extravagant price was given for them to get a quotation,' said Prance, sticking to his man like a limpet.

'That is an imputation of motive and is unfair,' roared Hudson. 'I have bought large lots from private individuals that were never on the Exchange at all and in some cases got them lower than others. I am however quite willing to abide by the decision of the meeting as to whether I am justified in selling them!'

Prance hesitated, seeking another way to get a hook into his man.

'It's like trying to scoop up an egg with a fork!' he hissed at the other two men. 'He keeps sliding back to the same point!'

Henry leaned over to Love.

'Second the motion for a committee. That'll sink him!' He winked at Love, and Love got to his feet as though on springs.

'I second the motion for appointing a committee!' he declared loudly, and sat down again, winking back at Henry. The timing was just right. The Yorkist faction were shouting and protesting at the rear.

'I condemn this proceeding,' shouted an angry voice. 'It is an insult to Mr Hudson and will tend to disparage the company!'

The remark produced a barrage of rude noises. They were winning, thought Henry. It must be full cry now. Hudson too seemed to realise it. He made a visible effort to calm himself and even tried to nod as though in consideration.

'I may have gone wrong in the early stage of these share transactions,' he said with unconvincing humility, 'but, if I have made an error in this instance, I have been right in many others.

I have never directed my attention to this particular transaction and, if I have made an error, I am ready to refund the money. I will take all the shares back, if you like, and pay all the interest on them.'

Hear, hear, chanted the middle ground, not seeing the danger that it would all come back to the issue of repayment. A man to Love's left, who was in the confidence of Prance, got up looking very hot and angry.

'This isn't a matter of money!' he said rudely, 'No repayment can put a satisfactory end to the enquiry, sir!'

The applause that followed was deafening. Batter away, thought Henry, this is crude work now.

'Repayment *is* the question,' insisted Hudson, his bombast returning, 'as there is no doubt I was perfectly justified in selling the shares; the only point is whether the price was too large!'

'There is no doubt about the price being excessive!' called Love, not bothering to rise. There were cheers now.

'Then let it be put right!' bellowed Hudson in a rage of frustration at being unable to escape. Denison, a director and friend of Hudson's, had been looking increasingly anxious as the exchanges became more openly heated and reiterative. He could see what would happen if they were allowed to continue. He tried to intervene.

'As there are seven other directors beside Mr Hudson, they could all have put their veto on the transaction had they thought there was anything wrong in it.'

'That's a nice try,' said Henry to Prance, who was still standing, refusing to abdicate his position at the centre of the stage.

'I beg there is no motion of censure,' said a shareholder from the Yorkist group, trying to fill his words with sweet and persuasive reason. 'Mr Hudson is said to have sold the shares above the market price and his answer is that, if this is proved, he will refund the money and, after that pledge, I for one am satisfied.'

The plea was not well received, and a robust-looking man two rows behind Henry snorted so loudly that he could be heard around the hall. He got to his feet, fingers stabbing out, pointing at the directors as if to spear them.

'Thompson of Moat Hall,' murmured Love. 'One of us.'

'In order to clear up the chairman's character,' Thompson rolled out in round Lancashire vowels, 'and that of the other directors, it is very desirable, I should think, that an inquiry should take place!'

With a final, all-embracing stab directed at all eight of the directors, he sat down to thunderous applause. So much meat slapping together, thought Henry, seeing the pounding hands around him. Trial without jury. They must not seem to take it too far. He leaned over to Love again.

'Put it to them that they deserve an inquiry in order to *clear* them,' he said urgently. 'That will win.'

Love rose again.

'Gentlemen, I think it is as much due to the credit of Mr Hudson as to the shareholders that an investigation should take place and that the committee should report without favour or affection towards any parties.'

Yes, yes, yes, they chanted. The din continued, on and on. It was the inevitable end, and Hudson recognised it. If he did not bow and hope to fight again he would be broken on the spot. He got to his feet, grim-faced as a man sentenced to death.

'If the shareholders wish it, I have no objection to a committee.'

He sat down, refusing to look at the hall again. Prance grasped Love by the hand, then Henry. Others gathered round to pat them on the back, bellow congratulations in the din of jubilation.

'We've done it!' said Prance, excited. 'He very nearly got away. He's like an eel!' and he laughed at the inappropriate analogy.

'It's the beginning of the end,' said Love. 'I can't say I feel any pity for him at all.'

Henry could not share Love's view. He found that he was sorry for Hudson despite everything. The bear had been pulled down by the bull-terriers. Yet he had enjoyed the fight, had helped to orchestrate it. At least, he thought, I feel capable of living with it. It is necessary if not nice. I have learned.

The committee was appointed. Prance and Love were elected, with Denison and Clayton and Shield. Clayton was of the Yorkist party, and although a late attempt was made by the shareholders to oust Denison and Clayton, there the matter rested after more uproar. The meeting broke up spontaneously before it was called to an end, as shareholders made their way out, talking excitedly about events and leaving the directors to preside over an emptying hall.

Henry's last view of Hudson was of a man turned to cold marble. A Napoleon defeated.

'We still have the Eastern Counties meeting,' Prance was saying excitedly as they stood on the steps outside the hall. 'Mr Cash will push for an inquiry there, and with one underway the chance of getting it has got to be doubled. Hudson can hardly weather another one like that. They may be able to force his resignation. That's your chance, Henry. You have enough interest in terms of shares to sway it all. There can only be a paltry dividend to declare, and that in itself will be enough to start the hue and cry. The maladministration of the line is a legend now!'

'I don't know if I want to be in at the kill,' said Henry doubtfully. 'I have other things to attend to, you know.'

'Your promotion to the Bench,' said Prance. 'Of course.'

'I don't think it will do me any good to be seen to bring down the axe. I think I have done enough now.'

Prance raised his eyebrows.

'I can understand about your position on the Bench, but I always imagined you would steer through the Eastern Counties meeting. You have a special interest in that after all, and no reason to love Hudson over it.'

'No, Robert. I have often been accused of being a man of conscience simply because I could not make up my mind.' He stared across the grey cobbled street at the grey stone houses opposite. 'The answer is no. I cannot go further with you, I'm afraid. I know that will be a disappointment and you may not think the better of me for it, but I'm sorry, it will have to be that way. I have so many strands to pull together that I can't devote myself to the spirit of this chase. I have had enough of railways. Perhaps I haven't the stomach for the kill. What we have set in motion will run its own course without me.'

Prance and Love looked at each other, disappointed. Love shrugged, pinched up his mouth.

'It's not what we'd hoped,' he said.

'Nevertheless, it will have to do,' said Henry. 'This is where we must part company. I've made up my mind, so shake hands, gentlemen, and accept my congratulations on your achievement.'

'This takes the edge off it,' said Prance rather sourly.

'Nonsense!' said Henry cheerfully. 'You have had a brilliant success and the whole inquiry is underway.'

He reached out to each of them in turn and shook hands, which they did with a shade of reluctance.

'Now, you see, I'm a free man,' said Henry.

They watched him go, in incomprehension.

'Lawyers!' said Love.

Henry heard the exclamation, and smiled to himself.

Fourteen

Henry was busy, and was being inefficient and irritable with himself because he was working against time. A grand family reunion had been arranged for the evening to celebrate the engagement of Edward and Nell, and it was to be held in Gower Street. They had never had so many people at one time. In fact, thinking it over, Henry realised they had never had a family reunion to celebrate a happy occasion. Only funerals. He was annoyed with himself for being nervous at the prospect, and could not concentrate on the matters in hand. Papers that started well enough turned to gibberish half-way down the page, and he had to stop and resume at the beginning. He stared at the Persian rugs, losing himself in their abstract intricacies, and might have passed from that trance into sleep if Corbett had not tapped at the door.

'It's a good job you came,' he said to the aged clerk. 'I was in severe danger of falling asleep. There seems so much to do.'

'Well, sir, elevation brings increased responsibilities, they say. I think it only brings more words. Longer ones, too. Say what you may about the railways, but at least they always used the language of mere mortals.'

Henry looked at Corbett and smiled. Corbett was secretly delighted that Henry had been sworn in as a judge. It added to the lustre of the chambers, and Corbett lived for them.

'There is a lady outside to see you.'

Henry's stomach gave a heave. They were words of doom dredged up from the past.

'Who is she?' he asked, convinced that Corbett had only put it that way to frighten him.

'Mrs Louise Kelleway.'

'Oh. Are you sure she wants to see me?'

'She didn't ask for any other gentleman, sir.'

'Corbett, you are a rogue!'

Corbett permitted himself the least hint of a wintry smile.

'That's as may be, sir. Shall I show her in?'

'Of course.'

His feeling of relief was enormous. He had immediately anticipated Kate, for he had not seen her again and she had made no effort to contact him. He wondered what on earth Louise was doing here when she should be preparing to go to Gower Street with Nell and Edward. He rose to his feet and stacked up some of the folders on his desk to give some degree of tidiness.

Louise was dressed elegantly in russet silk edged with brown fur. She was obviously prepared for the evening and she held out her hand formally to him.

'I'm sorry to disturb you when you're working. I must congratulate you on your appointment. Frederick always told me it was just within reach. He was right.'

'Please sit down. Thank you for your good wishes.'

He knew he was being rather stiff and formal, but he was puzzled and in any case Corbett still hovered by the door, curious as ever.

'That will be all, Corbett,' he said significantly. Corbett inclined his head and backed out. Louise smiled at Henry.

'He likes to listen, doesn't he?'

'I'm afraid so. He also has a weakness for the female sex. Even at his age.'

'I know.'

Yes, thought Henry, I suppose she must. Louise's visits to Meadows were not infrequent, and Corbett always made it his business to tell Henry although Henry never asked and made it plain he would rather not know.

'Why this visit, Louise? I thought you would be getting ready for this evening. Have you come to see … '

Louise smiled again, briefly. She looked well, and very attractive. He could see what men saw in her. Viewed dispassionately, he thought, she was just the sort of woman he used to …

He suppressed the thought.

'No, I haven't come to see George Meadows. He isn't in, anyway. I have come to see you. You know, Henry, this really is a very nice room. I have always admired it. Will you be staying here?'

'I certainly shall. It's home in a way.'

'In a way that Gower Street has only just become?'

'Louise!'

'Don't sound so shocked, Henry. You may have concealed it from yourself, but you haven't succeeded in concealing it from me. I'm in no position to pass judgement on anyone, so you mustn't take offence. I'm so pleased to see you happy with Jane and Jane happy with you. I have never wanted to play the role of conspirator in these things, but of course I heard this and that, and I have eyes to see.'

'I would rather you didn't talk in that way,' said Henry angrily.

'I'm sorry, I didn't mean to offend. I'm not very adroit. You have been very good to me. I only meant to say how pleased I am about you and Jane.'

'You mean how pleased you are that my last affair is over!'

'If you like. You make me sound even more inept. Please don't trap me up in words. I seem always to encounter pit-falls. I can only express myself as I know how.'

Henry snorted peevishly and went back to the chair behind his desk where he sat down pointedly, picking up a paper and staring at it.

'Well, what have you come to see me about? Nothing we've said so far.'

'I've had a letter.'

'Well, you've had a letter.'

'Please don't snap. It's about John.'

Henry looked at her sharply.

'About John?'

'Yes.' Louise did not look at him, but rustled about in the brown silk bag she carried. She took out a folded piece of paper, turning it over in her hands.

'He's been killed.'

Henry stared at her stupidly, unable to think of anything to say. Louise rose quickly from her chair and with a swift gesture, as though she was discarding it, put in front of him the folded paper. Henry picked it up, and opened it. It was a handwritten letter on thickish yellow paper like parchment, bearing a regimental crest. The writing, in a scrawling copperplate, begged to inform Mrs Louise Kelleway that as Captain John Kelleway's commanding officer it was his very painful duty to have to convey to her the news that her husband had died at Chillianwalla while charging the enemy guns with all the true bravery of a real soldier, an inspiration to all those who knew and respected him.

It continued in the same vein with the usual condolences, but Henry hardly read them.

He stared at the piece of strange yellow paper as though it had been responsible for John's death. The signature of the officer was undecipherable. Surely it could not make the difference between John being and not being? Who were these people who knew and respected him? Where was Chillianwalla?

'Where's Chillianwalla?' he asked Louise. 'I've never heard of it.'

'Somewhere in India,' she replied. Her voice was calm. She returned to her seat.

'I suppose this must be true?' asked Henry, testing the idea on himself.

'Yes, it's true. The lists were in this morning's newspapers. The post takes so long to get from India. It all happened over two months ago.'

Henry hauled himself from his seat.

'Louise, I'm terribly sorry. This is dreadful. Why didn't you tell me immediately?' He was not sure whether to put an arm around her or not.

'I don't know,' said Louise. 'I suppose I didn't really want to tell anyone. At least it was addressed to me. Last time he wrote to you. But he asked you to look after his affairs, so you must read it.'

'Haven't you had any communication from him?'

'No. Nor shall.'

'I'm most terribly sorry,' said Henry again. He put an arm around her shoulders, looking at her anxiously, expecting imminent collapse. She looked into his face.

'Don't worry, Henry, I'm not so terribly upset. It's all right, do you understand? You must try to see that it's what he wanted and he got his way. It's all right. You mustn't tell Charlie or Nell or anyone else, not when we're celebrating Nell's engagement. That's the most important thing to me, not this piece of paper. I have had plenty of time to prepare for his death, you know. It seems as though it already happened a very long time ago, years ago, and this letter has been on its way all along.'

Henry realised that she meant it. He was more upset than she was. She had been resigned.

'It does seem as though he has kept an appointment,' he said.

'You must try to feel glad for him, it's what he always wanted. I prevented him all these years.'

'No. You mustn't look at it like that.'

'I would rather deal with the truth.'

Henry looked at her calm face and found she was regarding him with pleading eyes. She was really very beautiful. He took away his arm, feeling there was something too intimate in their closeness, then cursed himself for his guiltiness. He stooped and kissed her on the cheek.

'You're right of course. Not that you prevented him or that it was your fault but that it was what he always wanted. I think we all knew that. I won't mention it to anyone, until you're ready.'

'Thank you, Henry. And thank you for the kiss.' She reached up and kissed Henry on the lips. He did not pull away.

'That doesn't make you a satyr, does it?' she said.

'No,' said Henry, finding that it did not.

318

'Come along then, we must be on our way to Gower Street. I don't believe all these papers of yours mean a thing!'

'Yes, we must be going. It has been quite a shock to me.' Louise was quick to hear the flatness in Henry's voice.

'We can grieve for John slowly, Henry, but not now. I have used up all my grief and must find a new store. I think we all will. Slowly, as we see things properly.'

In Gower Street, things were in an unaccustomed uproar. Weeks had tried to rise to the occasion but, as Maria had remarked to Jane, it was rather like the raising of Lazarus. It was quicker if the women did things themselves and Maria had assumed command of the table, leaving Jane to play host to the men. Elizabeth and Margaret rushed around to Maria's commands, to the clear disapproval of Weeks who saw it all as a professional slur and wandered about behind them and among them tutting, straightening cutlery and polishing the glasses.

'Where is Henry?' asked William from the calm of the drawing-room where he reclined lazily in an armchair, sipping sherry. Jonathan sat in an upright chair by the window, withdrawn slightly from the others. Frederick and Jane sat side by side on a sofa in happy collusion, staring with some amusement at William.

'He'll be here,' said Frederick. 'He has been down to his chambers this afternoon to clear up some work. You ought to know he works hard. He's always late.'

'I suppose this elevation will mean he is an important man?' observed William with a hint of envy. 'A knighthood to come?'

William was rather extravagantly dressed, his waistcoat too bright and embroidered with silk flowers.

'Oh, I don't know!' protested Jane.

'But very probably,' said Frederick cheerfully, determined to put William in his place. He did not have much time for William's leisurely and foppish ways and certainly was not going to stand for any envy when there was fun to be had from it.

'Oh, well,' said William soulfully, 'that's the way of the world.'

'What is?' asked Frederick conversationally. Jane shot him a glance that was intended to quell him, but Frederick only smiled sweetly back.

'Honours come more easily to the professions,' said William. 'The arts are seldom rewarded on the same basis. A certain type of popularity may be, but not ordinary endeavour. We have no hierarchy that says that after so many years of honest splashing of paint we should be shot to the top.'

'I should hope not,' said Jonathan drily. 'I would not have *all* artists shot. That would be barbaric. They should be shot according to merit!'

'Jonathan!' exclaimed Jane, but Frederick was roaring with laughter. William scowled at Jonathan, exceedingly put out.

'That's all very trite and facile, sir!'

'I'm sorry, father. You're quite right.' He made a penitent face and clasped his hands before him as though in prayer. Jane wondered about Jonathan's mood. It was certainly not free of malice. No Charlotte, she thought, and perhaps he is jealous of Edward and Nell. His foot was stuck out awkwardly from the chair, a reminder of those things. Frederick, sensitive to imminent danger, got to his feet and filled William's glass again.

'But look at the publicity you artists get,' he said. 'Everything you do attracts huge attention from the public. That must be your reward. You have to admit it's more rewarding than honours.'

William sighed deeply.

'Look at your Cosmorama,' pursued Frederick. 'What a huge success it was, seen by tens of thousands.'

'Hundreds of thousands,' said William.

'Well, there you are.'

'But it is all to be whited out, as I told you. It was in the contract, and do you know I never even knew. Never looked at the thing. This is some new form of art, isn't it, when they white it out and paint it over. A sort of layer cake, a geological formation composed of the sediment of dead artists!'

'I think it's dreadful,' said Jane.

William held up his arms in a grand gesture, and let them fall, forgetting he was holding his sherry. It splashed on his waistcoat and he brushed at it angrily.

'They have employed this idiot,' he bellowed, 'this decorator, to paint Athens all over it. Athens! I ask you! What dreary hack stuff. All blue sky and columns and superficial shepherds sitting around with fat ladies by ponds. Shades of Claude and Poussin, forgive me! It's been done so many times before.'

'I thought your Mexico City was a marvel,' said Jane. 'I think it's a crime that it's to be painted out. It should be kept forever.'

She had indeed seen it, and considered that it was very good, of its kind. As to keeping it, she had her own opinions. William must not be allowed to get too wild or drink too much.

'It *was* good, wasn't it,' said William ruminatively. 'But after a while, everyone has seen it, and there is nowhere else to put it. So under it goes. It's all so fleeting.'

He sighed again, deeply, expressing the anguish of a true artist.

'I thought you were going to go back to portraiture, uncle

William,' said Frederick. 'At least human vanity works in your favour. People don't paint themselves out, or even their dead relatives. There it has the edge over the Cosmorama. All those Renaissance painters knew that, and look how well they did out of it.'

'But where are the patrons of today, dear Frederick? In any case they don't want you to paint themselves, they want you to paint their horse, and I can't stand horses. Or they want mobs of silly spotted dogs or piles of dead birds. There's a great living to be had from dead birds if you have a mind to it, but where's the art? No, it's not for me. Ellis is my patron and I have to make the most of it.'

'But I really thought you were going to go back to portraiture,' said Jane. 'You did say you were.'

'Did I?'

'Well, I thought you did anyway.'

'I have decided not. As Jonathan knows, Ellis has promised me a huge commission so soon as this fellow has got his Athens off the walls and they can be put to good use again.'

'I didn't know that,' said Frederick. 'So you've settled for it?'

'Frankly, he offered to pay me so much I couldn't resist.'

Frederick glanced sideways at Jane and was delighted to see that she was smothering a smile. She was so much happier these days, so pleased to have the family around her and even to be bored by William. He supposed he should be tolerant of William. He had made up his mind that he had found a fair compromise for his talents. It was easy for others to criticise. He wondered if he would find a fair compromise for his own.

They were spared further examination of William by Maria bustling into the room, followed by Elizabeth and Margaret. The men all leapt to their feet.

'They're here!' she said. 'We'll let that old tortoise Weeks open the door. Then he'll think he's done his duty. I could stick a fork in him!'

'I kept piling up the fruit, and it kept collapsing and rolling over the table,' said Elizabeth. 'It was driving him mad!'

'Is Henry here as well?' asked Jane anxiously.

'Yes,' said Maria, 'They've all arrived together.'

The inrush was cordial and noisy. Nell was delighted and pink with embarrassment at being the centre of attention. Edward held her arm as though she were a captive.

'I'm so pleased about Edward,' Maria confided to Jane. 'After all the business about Ware he was so depressed. Nothing better could happen. I hope it wipes all that slate clean.'

'Well, he doesn't intend to let her go!' She excused herself and moved over to Henry, who stood outside the circle that surrounded Edward and Nell, sensing that he seemed withdrawn.

'Is everything all right?'

'Yes, of course it is. Is everything here all right?'

'With Maria in charge? Of course it is. I'm no expert hostess, but she has chased us all around and the girls have been absolute slaves. Did Louise come with you?'

'Yes. She wanted the young people to come together. They're in great high spirits.'

It was a harmless evasion and near enough the truth. He hoped Jane would forgive him later.

'I'm so pleased to have the house full of family,' she said. 'Take my arm, Henry, or I shall make a fool of myself.'

Weeks appeared at the door, bearing a silver bucket with two bottles of champagne. He still looked offended.

'I'll take these,' said Henry. Weeks gave him a pained look.

'Are you sure you wouldn't like me to do it, sir?'

'Of course,' said Jane quickly. 'And stay with us for a glass.'

'Bravo,' said Frederick in Jane's ear, 'you've quite cheered him up.'

'I had better admire the arrangements too,' said Jane. 'Louise, bring a glass with you, we will view them together. It's for you as well.'

Louise had been left on the edge of things by the children and Jane felt sorry for her. She knew perfectly well that Edward had always admired Louise in the past, but he had no time for her now. Louise nodded, grateful. They went downstairs and wandered round the long table, counting. Maria had seen to it that there was nothing to do.

'You must be very pleased about Nell and Edward,' said Jane.

'Yes. I am.'

'You must come to see me when all this is over. I should have asked you sooner, but we've been preoccupied.'

'It's very kind of you, Jane, but you don't have to.'

'I want to. I wanted to have a few words with you alone. We haven't been very kind to you as a family, have we? We must try and start again.'

'I'm not very respectable, am I? I understand.'

'Louise!'

'You know all about George Meadows, don't you? Henry has told you?'

'Yes, I do.'

'And you don't approve.'

'I don't approve or disapprove. John is no sort of husband. I know that.'

Louise wondered whether to tell Jane, but decided against it.

'I may not change, you know. I have been a captive and now I've been released. I won't willingly go back.'

'Then we shall have to accept you as you are!' said Jane cheerfully.

'Warts and all.'

'What nonsense. You look marvellous.'

'You know what I mean.'

'You will come to visit me, won't you?'

Louise thought about it carefully, considering her answer.

'Yes, I shall. Thank you.'

The dinner party went noisily from course to course. William spouted nonsense and drank too much and the children talked across everyone, shouting to make themselves heard. Jane, sitting at the far end from Henry, watched his growing enjoyment. He had been tense at first but had now relaxed. He is the head of the family, she thought, and has assumed the garments. He has acquired us all, and enjoys it. She supposed that, while Caroline was still alive, there had been a division, Henry had devoted scant time to family matters while Caroline had always been available and ready to become involved. It was the first time since the children had been very young and filled it with clamour that the house had felt fully used, extended as a home should be. She had lost so many years, but what was the point of being bitter about that? She must not look back like Lot's wife and become that pillar of salt, a mortal mourning for youth. Louise had lost so many years too and she had gone forward from them on her own course, undeterred. Whatever the morals of it, it was admirable, she supposed. John had been no sort of husband, and now he had gone, renouncing any residual claim.

'I would like to propose a toast,' said Henry, getting to his feet. 'To Nell and Edward.'

They all stood, Frederick assisting William who seemed to be having a little difficulty in disentangling himself from the table-cloth.

'May you both be very happy. The world is a very changed place from when I was a boy, and things go at a breakneck pace. May you both prosper. Nell and Edward!'

They all raised their glasses and drank.

'I would like to propose another toast while we are here in a family gathering. We have never had the opportunity to do it, and I'm sure that we should. I propose a toast to Charlotte and

323

Fordham Hays, hoping that their marriage is happy and that we will be able to welcome them back into the family before long and despite the differences of the past. Charlotte and Fordham Hays!'

Jane glanced at Jonathan. He did not raise his glass and drink. Instead his face flushed suddenly and he looked angry. He's so young, so very young, thought Jane. He will have to learn to accept things as they are and make the best of them as we all have had to, but for him it will be a long lesson. He has an unforgiving nature, and will find it difficult to live with. How long will it take him to discover that it is arrogance not to forgive weakness in others?

Henry sat down and the conversation was slow to resume again. Henry's second toast had been a reminder of rifts when they had seemed so complete. Henry was right, nevertheless, thought Jane. We must keep our eyes on reality. Perhaps as a family we have been slow to grasp it and have been over-fond of illusion.

They returned to the drawing-room leaving the wreckage of dinner behind them, to talk and play cards. Charlie had been hovering by Nell, waiting for an opportunity to draw her aside in the general noise and chatter.

'Nell, come with me a moment, drag yourself away from Edward. Don't forget your brother. Let me get you some raspberry wine?'

Edward looked enquiringly at Nell.

'Do you want to go with this ruffianly fellow? I don't like the looks of him!'

'He's afraid I shall take you aside and tell you about him!' Charlie replied. His eyes were serious however as he looked at Nell.

'Oh no!' said Edward. 'You mustn't believe what he says!'

'I shall gloss over the worst,' said Charlie cheerfully, but he took Nell's arm to emphasize his purpose. Edward released Nell with a curious look. Charlie took her over to a side-table by the window, away from the others. He poured her some wine and helped himself to port, more to give them a reason for being there than anything else.

'What's all this, Charlie?' asked Nell. 'You're looking serious.'

'Talk quietly. There's a little thing I want to tell you.'

'What is it?' she asked in sudden alarm.

'It's to be a secret between us just now. I've always told you everything, and I would have told you in the carriage but I didn't want to speak in front of Edward. There's nothing to be alarmed about, in fact it's very exciting, it's something new, and you should be proud of me. You know what an idle fellow I am!'

'Don't be so mysterious. What is it?'

'Well, it's just that I've enlisted in the army. Isn't that exciting?'

Nell stared at him.

'It is, Nell. I think it's what I've always wanted to do. I shall travel, and have a proper career. I have to tell you now, because I'm off tomorrow and don't want anyone to know about it. There would be such a fuss and I know mother will try to stop me, but I must go. I really want to.'

'Charlie, what a shock. You must have enlisted some time ago! What a time to tell me!'

'I did. But I couldn't tell you sooner in case you let it out. I didn't know we were going to have this dinner party tonight and got caught out by my own secret. I couldn't go without telling you. I'm joining a different regiment from father's, but I'm bound for India too, and I expect I shall find him there. Won't that be marvellous? Please be pleased for me!'

'But what about your railway business?'

'Oh, that. It's been a disaster. I don't think I've a feel for it.'

'Is that a reason why you're going?'

'One of them, if you like.' Charlie made a face at her. 'You don't seem as glad for me as I would like.'

'I don't know what I feel. I shall miss you dreadfully. When will you tell mother?'

'When I'm safely away. I shall leave a note and I shall write. Wish me luck.'

Nell looked at his face. He was so eager to be praised, so concerned to be absolved from thoughtlessness.

'Of course I wish you luck. I just wish you'd chosen another time and place to break the news. I think you've done this deliberately so that I can't protest.'

'But I don't want you to protest, I want you to be happy for me!'

'I'll be happy for you, for your sake,' said Nell.

'And you won't tell anyone until I'm gone?'

'Why do you have to put that burden on me? It's not fair!'

'But we've always been so close, Nell. Who else can I turn to? You will promise?'

'Now then,' said Edward's voice, cheerfully. He had come up behind them. 'What's he been saying about me? You mustn't believe a word of it, whatever it is!'

'Horrible things,' said Charlie with a quick grin, 'and every one true. You really must have a guilty conscience, Edward. Note that,

Nell. A man with an uneasy mind!' He slapped Edward on the back and laughed.

'I promise you he hasn't,' said Nell, taking Edward's arm again. 'He's only teasing. Charlie always is.'

As she turned to go with Edward, she caught Charlie's eyes and gave a nod. What else could she do, she thought. She loved him dearly for all his faults and could not trip him up at this last moment. It would be depriving a happy child. Yet it was typical of him to the last. Now she would have to deal with Louise. She knew he would always take the easiest way, convincing himself at the same time that it hurt others least. She supposed it was a good idea, for what else would Charlie do but drift?

Louise approached and took Edward and Nell by the hands.

'I know I have said this to you both before,' she said, 'but I am so pleased for you.' She looked round, saw that they were not overheard. 'Edward, I want to say to you that you have been very kind to me, when I needed someone to care. I haven't forgotten that, and I don't want it to be an embarrassment between any of us.'

Edward blushed vigorously. He had not forgotten either but did not want to be reminded.

'I suppose I am only saying this because we are amongst other people, and I would be too embarrassed to say it if we were alone. I think we all understand.'

She hoped that would be sufficient. It seemed so far from Kent and country dances and now everything was changed. It should all be buried and forgotten.

Fifteen

The room in the London Tavern was so packed that suffocation seemed imminent. Half an hour before the appointed time of one o'clock, an estimated seven hundred proprietors had forced their way into the hall, the gallery and the very stairs, jamming it all solid. The temperature rose with the mass of bodies, and tempers became frayed. Fat men were unpopular as never before, and thin men were hated for pushing their way through.

Henry was crammed in at the back. He had fought to stay there, as he intended to slip away before the meeting ended but the pressure from behind had tended to push him forwards. He had not intended to come at all, but as the day and time had come, he found that he had to know what the next act of the play had to offer. He was not interested in the shares of the Eastern Counties, despite his substantial holding. With the help of Jane he had been able to meet the call on them, but he saw it all as money thrown away in the bigger issue. He had a personal interest in Hudson that he could not deny, despite his protests that he was finished with railways.

He supposed it was the manner of the man's end that fascinated him. Having been instrumental in bringing it about, he felt it was cowardly not to see the consequence. The man who pulls a trigger should be brave enough to see the wound and mutilation. He had explained it to Jane, and she had seemed to understand. He expected no joy from being in at the kill and felt no exultation. Rather he had steeled himself to do his duty and watch.

Shouting from the front drew everyone's attention. Men were emerging from a door at the far end of the room where the directors would sit. A storm of booing broke out, cries of 'Where's Hudson?' followed by 'Off, off, off!'

Waddington, the deputy-chairman, had taken the chair with his co-directors. The uproar was bestial and terrifying. Henry felt sorry for the men who had to face this mob, but where *was* Hudson? He found that he himself was shouting the same question, and was ashamed. Waddington, after much raising of hands and calling to order, finally managed to make himself heard.

'Gentlemen, I attend before you today as a matter of duty. I hope, gentlemen, that you will support me in the discharge of that duty. If I had not thought proper to appear today, you might then have said I had not attended to it. As your deputy-chairman in the absence of your chairman, I claim from you that right you should accord to every man – to be heard!'

Waddington was shaking. Although a member of Parliament and accustomed to certain rigours, this was clearly worse than anything he had confronted before. The catcalls and jeering continued while he spoke.

'Gentlemen, I was extremely anxious, and so were my honourable colleagues, that Mr Hudson should attend here this day, and the first intimation I received that he would not be present was on Monday morning last.'

'He's ashamed to show himself!' bellowed one man. 'Ashamed, ashamed!' came the chant.

'Gentlemen, do hear me patiently,' shouted Waddington. 'I received a letter from Mr Hudson on Monday morning last and immediately convened a meeting of the directors resident in London. We read the letter and we dictated a letter to be sent in reply, which requested him to answer. He has not done so.' He paused for the expected ululation and groans.

'It may be that Mr Hudson is not at home!'

This was greeted with roars of laughter.

'But at all events he has placed me in a very painful position, and in justification of my appearing before you today I shall take the opportunity of reading Mr Hudson's letter, and, gentlemen, I wish to say at the outset, in conducting the proceedings of the day, I and the directors around me have only one desire, which is that you should know as much of this concern as they know themselves!'

Waddington had got a grasp of the situation now. There was a round of applause, drowned out by cheering. Sweet music to the besieged man's ears. Henry was gripping his hands tight in suspense. It was an extraordinary occasion. The business of the day was no one's concern at the moment.

'The letter from Mr Hudson reads as follows,' said Waddington with as much solemnity as if he were about to read a proclamation of martial law.

'"Newby Park, Thirsk.

'"My dear sir,

'"As I feel I cannot go thoroughly along with you in reference to the steam-boat question, I have made up my mind not to attend the meeting on Wednesday next..."'

'What steam-boat question?' demanded voices from all over the hall.

'The question of a link from London to Harwich and the packet,' replied Waddington. The meeting let out a communal gasp. It was a matter of the most trivial importance financially, the merest of excuses feebly clutched at. Waddington held up a hand for silence. He had it.

"'I sincerely wish you well through it. I hope if any attack is made on me you will if you can defend me with reference to your company. I unfortunately hold a large stake and bought at a very great price and lose terribly by the concern; they invited us, they were in a ruined condition both as to stock and credit.'"

The yelling and protest at this point were to be expected, and Waddington himself seemed to take a grim satisfaction in them. He held up his hand again. Again, as if mesmerised, silence fell on the mob. Now listen, his very face and gesture seemed to say.

"'I shall resign whenever it may suit you and the Board. By not attending I shall avoid the Norfolk question, which I could not but throw over.

I am yours very truly,

"'George Hudson'"

'What was the reply, the reply, the reply?' chanted the hall.

'The following is the answer I sent to Mr Hudson,' said Waddington, producing a second piece of paper with a flourish. He held up his hand again.

"'My dear Sir,

Upon receipt of your letter I convened a meeting of our directors residing in London and read your letter to them. It leaves us all in considerable difficulty as to the best course to be pursued; but my impression is that as the steam-boat matter is approved of in the report of the Board, and as no vote on the Norfolk amalgamation will have to be taken at the meeting, it is difficult to explain your absence from the meeting on any ground stated in your letter. Besides which, I read your letter as not wishing your opinion on these two matters to be brought forward, lest they should disturb the action of myself and the Board at the meeting, as entertaining opposite opinions. It appears therefore to us that as you have determined on resigning your seat, it would be better for you to do this previous to the meeting.'"

Waddington could not contain them any longer with his upraised hand. There was thunderous applause and cheering again. He raised both hands. There is more, the gesture said.

"'Should you concur in this and send me the resignation, to be at the Board prior to the meeting, you can give such reasons for the step as you wish and I will make them known. The feeling of all is one of regret that we shall lose the valuable services your experience and knowledge enable you to give to every company with which you are associated.'"

Waddington paused for the jeering laughter.

'"I will not fail to notice the point named in your letter if you are attacked.

'"I am, my dear Sir, yours very truly,

David Waddington."'

'What was the reply, the reply, the reply?' thundered the hall.

'We have endeavoured to communicate with York to see if the letter has been received. We sent one letter to Newby Park and one to York to make matters more certain. Our Secretary however could not get an answer, being told that the wires are out of order!'

Henry had heard enough. He started to push his way out through the thicket of men that surrounded him. They hardly noticed as he barged his way through. Sweat was running down their faces as they roared and bayed. This was the kill, and they loved it. There would be more to come when they heard the company results.

Somewhere in the hall was William Cash the Quaker with his polite 'thees' and 'thous', well briefed by Prance and Love respectfully to insist on a further committee of inquiry. The Midland Railway itself would be next and Wylie and Brancker would get their way this time. On the flank, the Prance Committee was even now sharpening its swords and quills and waiting for Hudson to appear before it lunged into the attack.

'Hudson shall not escape us!' a red-faced fellow was bellowing as Henry squeezed out of the door, his ears ringing. He was glad to be out in the street. The air was cold but seemed fresh and pure, although it was only stale London stuff.

'Going, Mr Kelleway?' asked a familiar voice. Henry turned, surprised, to find Braxton at his elbow. He was smiling kindly and with pleasure, nursing his stove-pipe hat under one arm.

'Mr Braxton!' Henry exclaimed, lost for words. He felt a great warmth at seeing such kindliness.

'It's not pretty work, is it, this butchery? Up like a rocket they say, down like the stick. I expect you're glad to see an end to it?'

'Yes. I've seen all I want to see.' He remembered how at first he had loathed the man, misjudging him completely through his own arrogance. He had a sudden sense of loss.

'We won't lose touch, will we, Mr Braxton? I should appreciate it if we did not.'

'I would like to think we've become friends,' said the forthright Braxton, putting it into words, but avoiding Henry's eyes. He was suddenly shy.

'Then promise to visit me.'

'I will do that.'

'But these things are too easily said,' persisted Henry. 'We are all so busy we don't fulfill them. Visit me in a week, tell me all that happens.'

'I shall. I look forward to it.'

Braxton extended a meaty hand, and shook Henry's vigorously.

'You're going back in?' asked Henry, extending the moment of friendship.

'Yes. It may not be edifying, but it's my business. Everything has to be pulled out in one piece when it's all over.'

Henry nodded and Braxton turned away, pushing past the red-faced fellow. He also turned and walked briskly along the pavement, unbuttoning his coat to let the air blow about him. Cleanse him. He could still hear the pack baying although he was half-way down the street. People stopped and stared towards the hall. What in this civilised day and age could cause such excitement?

He turned the corner with a skip, feeling quite light-headed. No way, he reminded himself, for a judge to behave. The carriage was waiting, the horse munching peacefully in its nosebag, the driver swaddled in a greatcoat and blanket. The man was ruminatively smoking a clay pipe and when he saw Henry he made an effort to extinguish it and unravel himself at the same time.

'You'll set yourself on fire!' said Henry. 'I can get in by myself.'

Jane was sitting inside, reading.

'What are you doing, flapping through the streets with your coat flying?'

'I needed fresh air. Cool fresh air.'

'How was it?'

'It was awe-inspiring. An object lesson in the laws of commerce. Inevitable, fascinating and horrible. I'll stick to my realm of the law, all dust and precedent. Still, I'm glad I came. I had to see it out.'

'What about Hudson? What happened?'

Henry put an arm around her, sat back in the seat.

'I'm afraid *he* didn't see it out. He didn't even come.'

He banged on the roof with his fist and they jolted homewards.